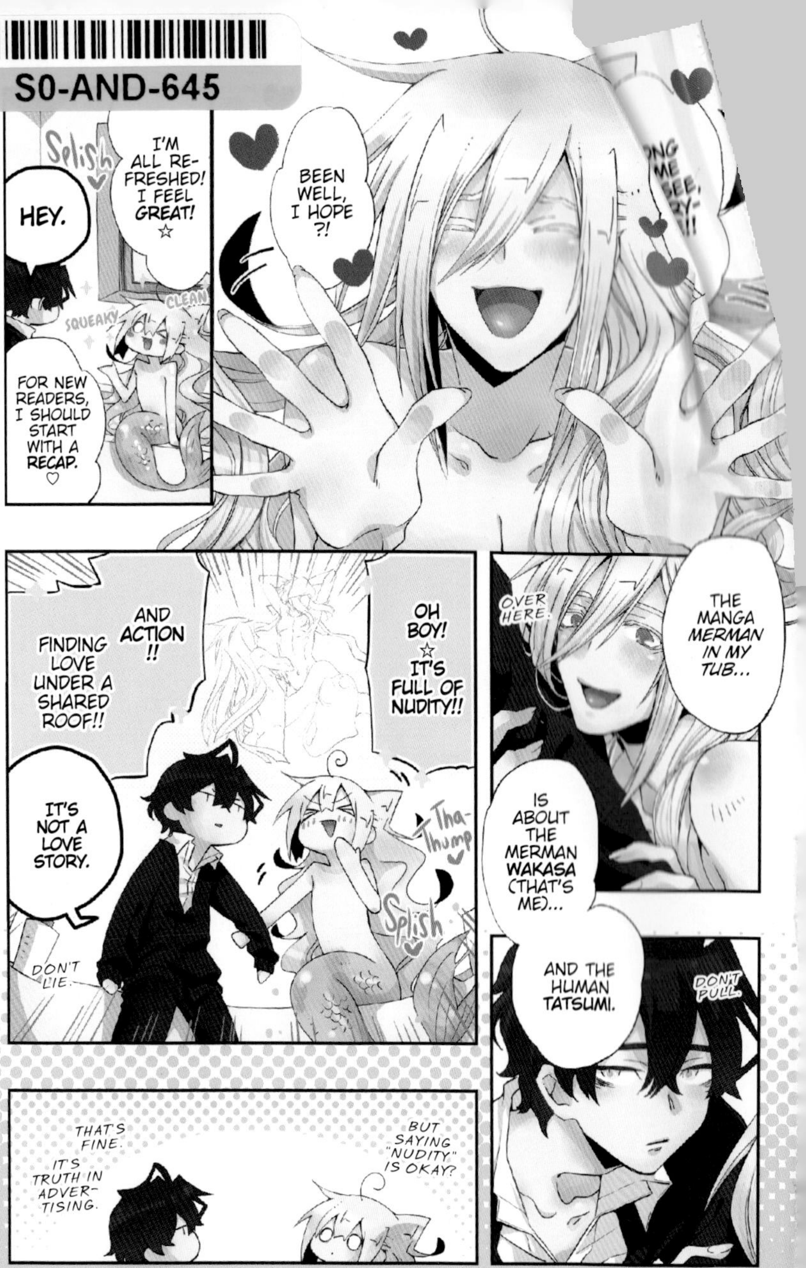
BEEN WELL, I HOPE?!
I'M ALL RE-FRESHED! I FEEL GREAT! ☆
HEY.
Splish
SQUEAKY CLEAN
FOR NEW READERS, I SHOULD START WITH A RECAP. ♡
OVER HERE.
THE MANGA MERMAN IN MY TUB...
IS ABOUT THE MERMAN WAKASA (THAT'S ME)...
AND THE HUMAN TATSUMI.
DON'T PULL.
OH BOY! ☆ IT'S FULL OF NUDITY!!
AND ACTION!!
FINDING LOVE UNDER A SHARED ROOF!!
Tha-thump
IT'S NOT A LOVE STORY.
Splish
DON'T LIE.
BUT SAYING "NUDITY" IS OKAY?
THAT'S FINE.
IT'S TRUTH IN ADVERTISING.

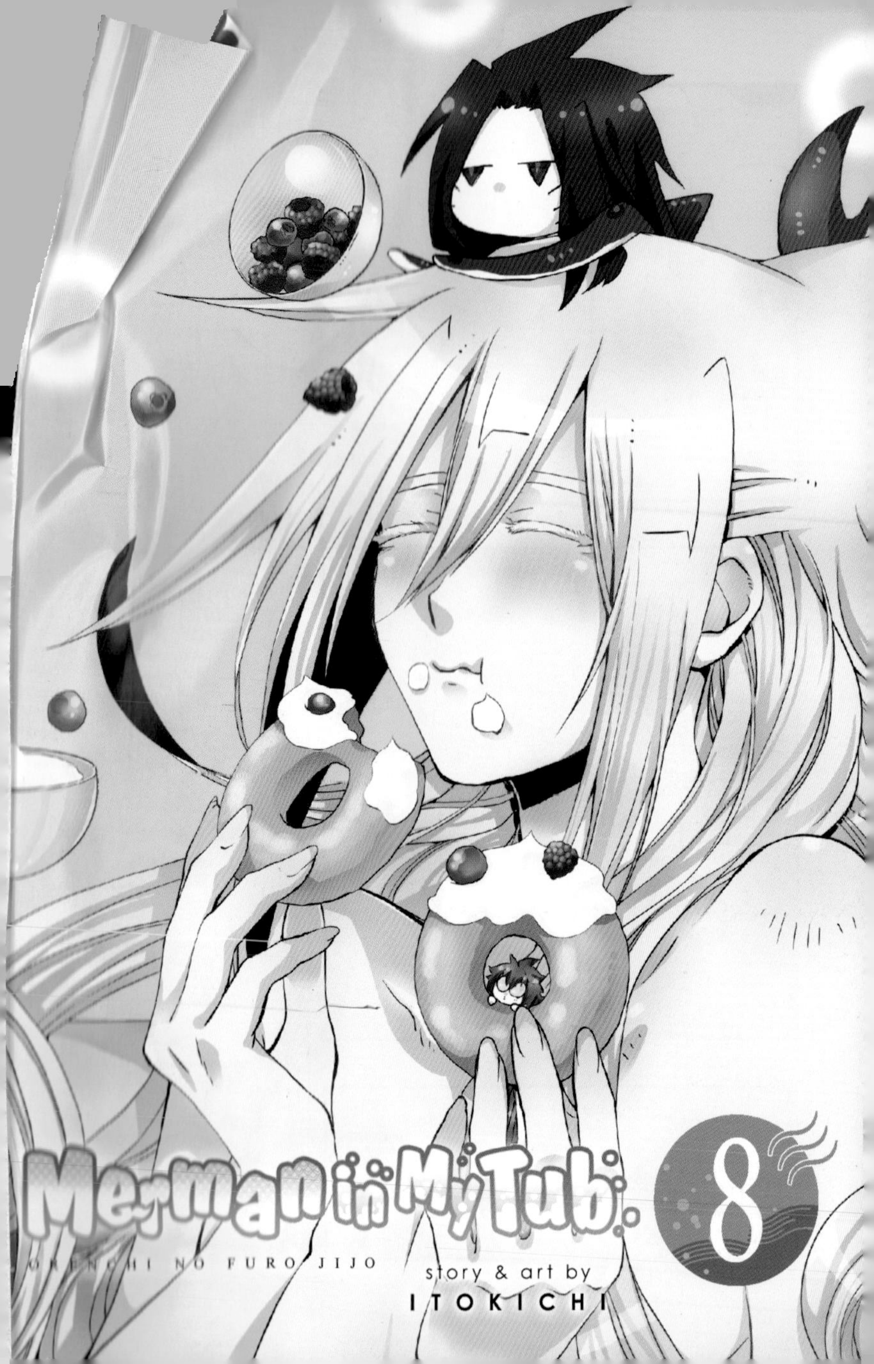
Merman in My Tub
8
ORENCHI NO FURO JIJO
story & art by
ITOKICHI

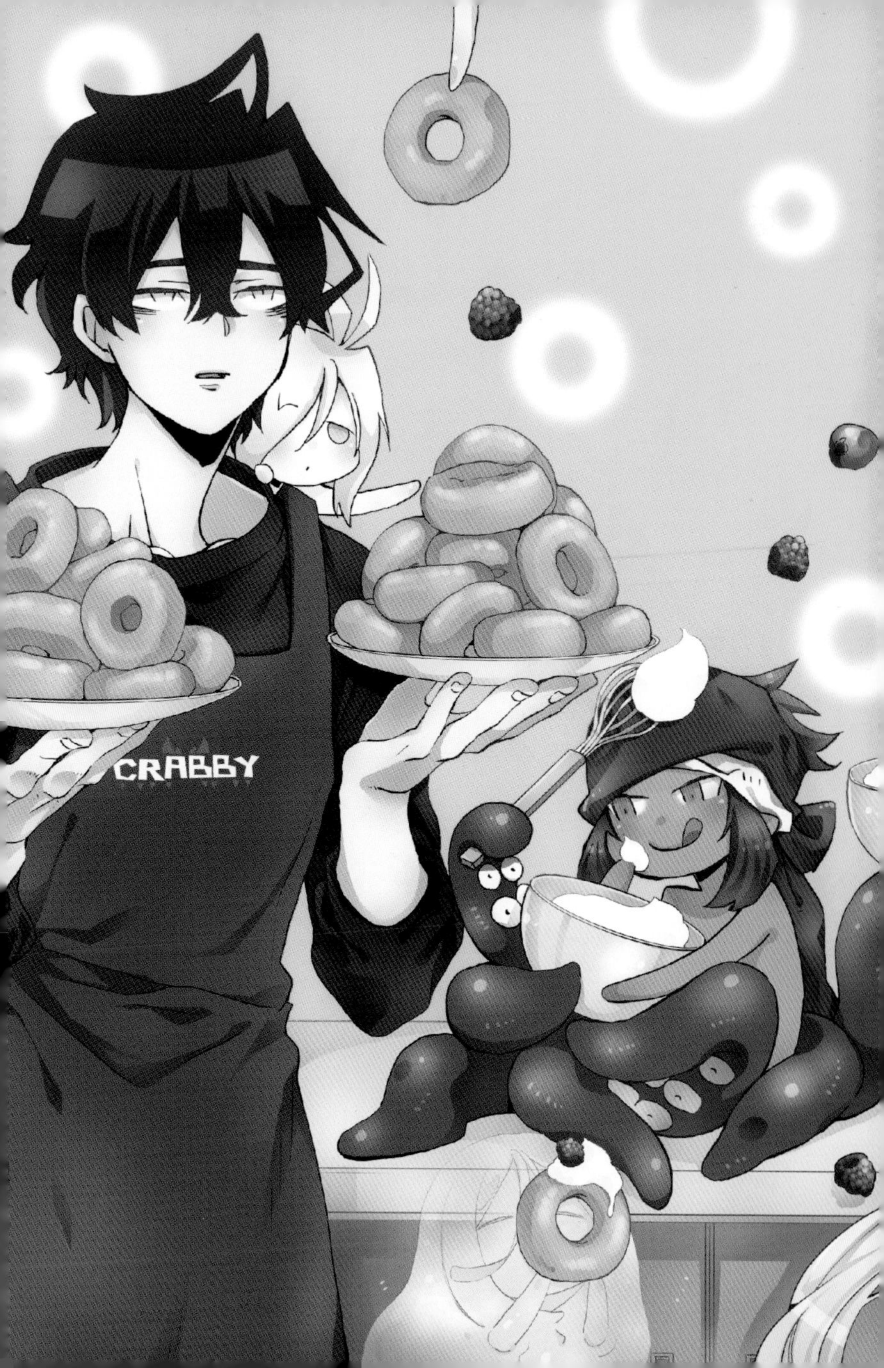
CRABBY

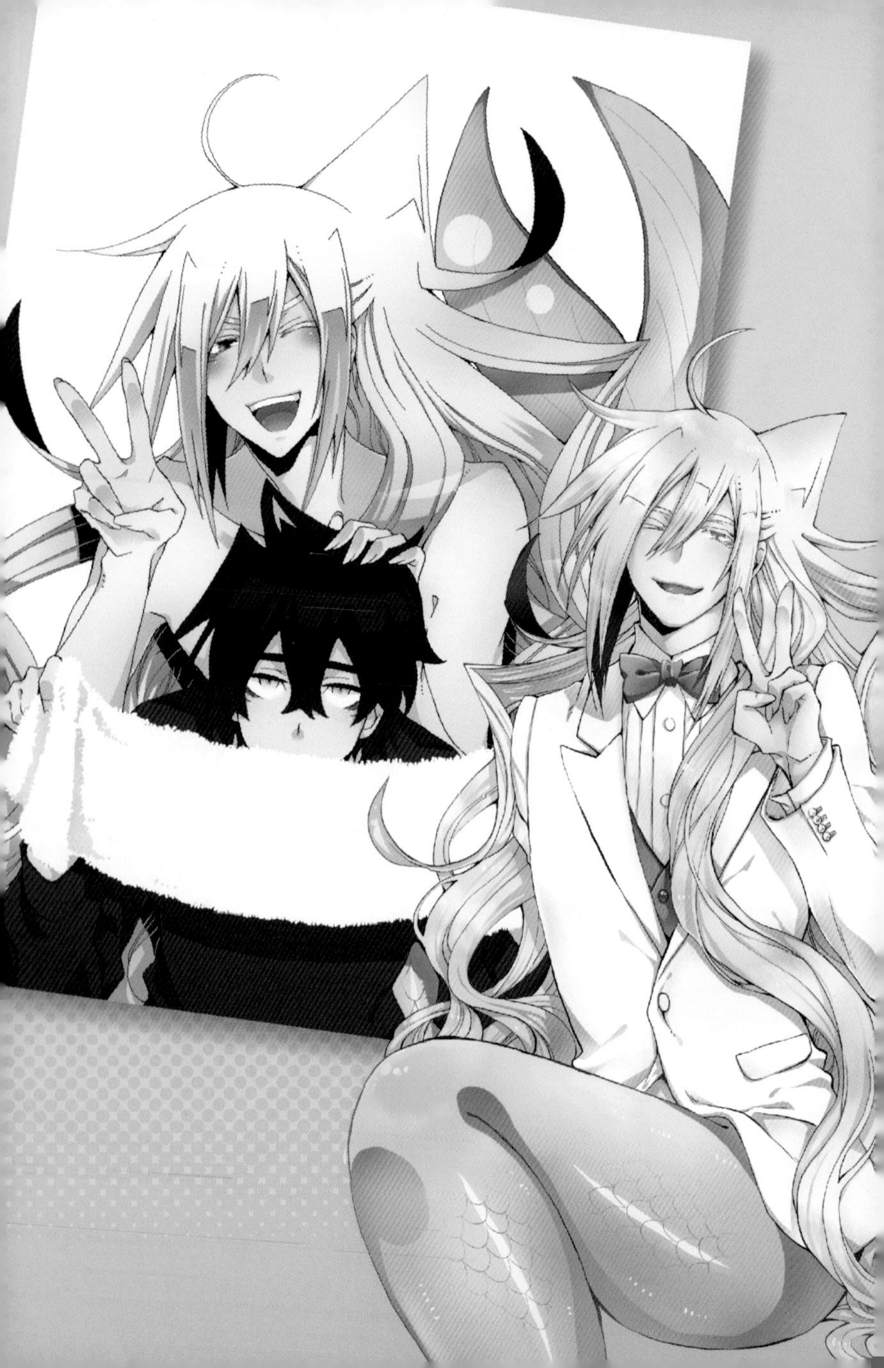

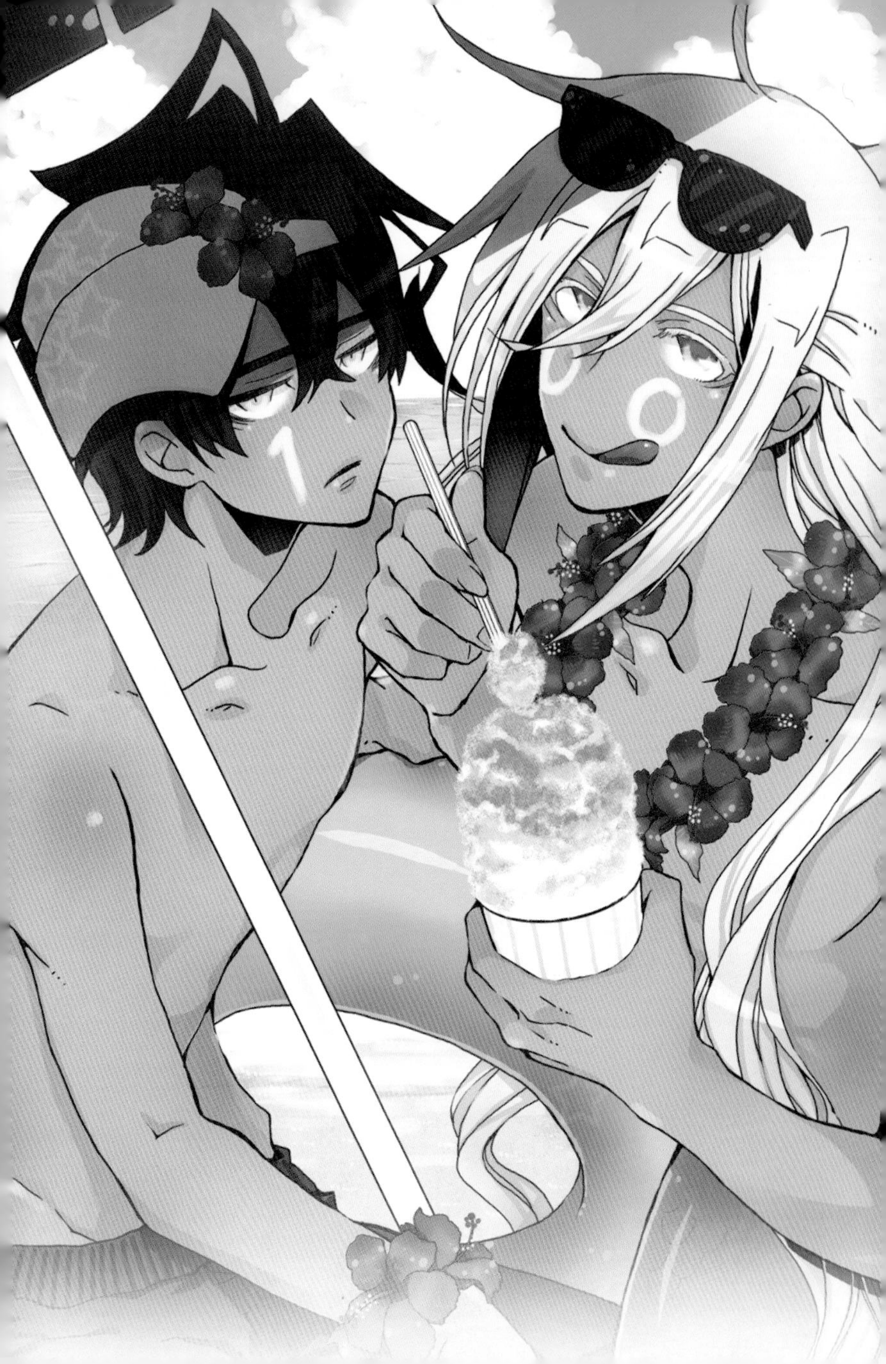

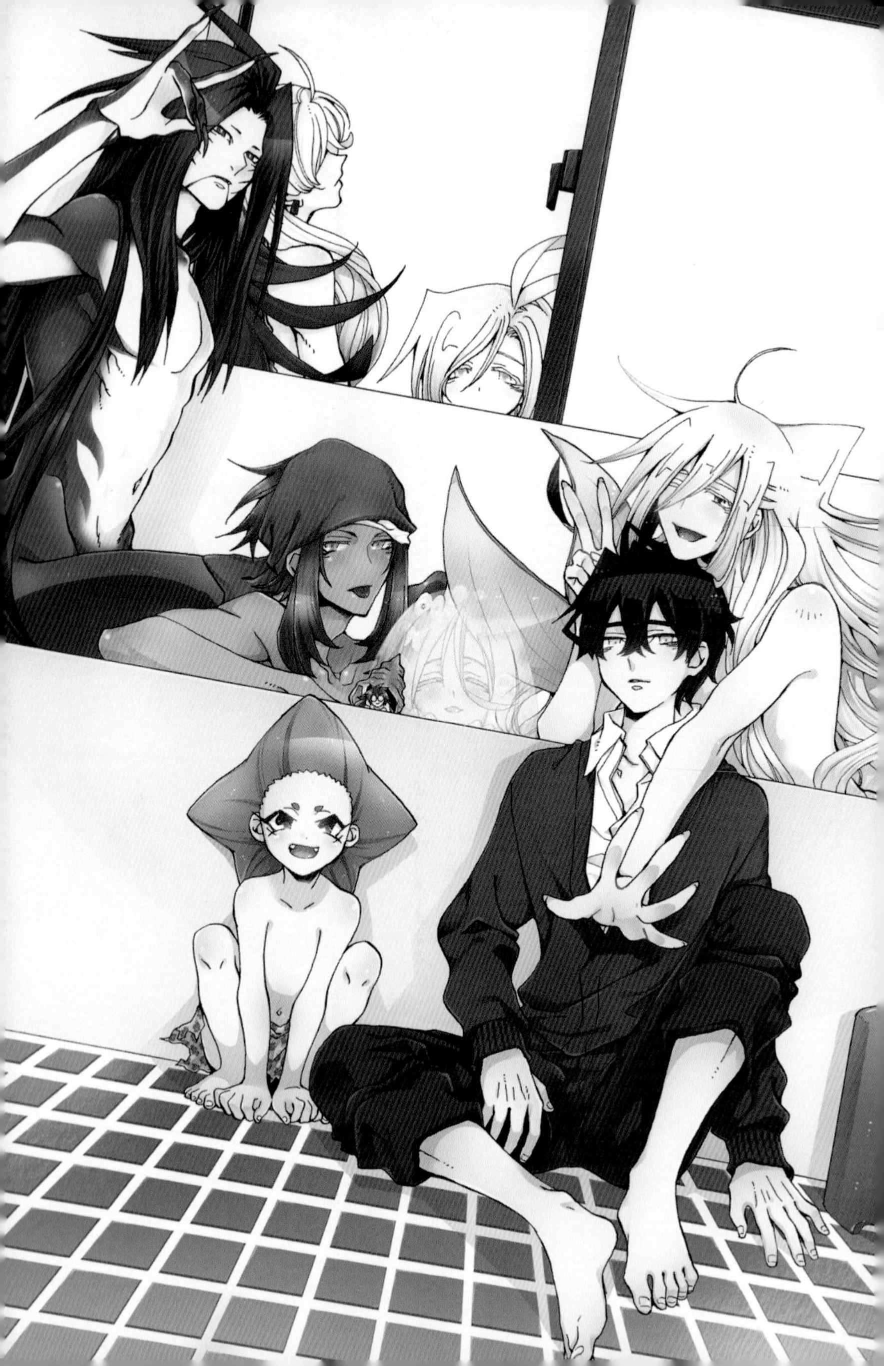

PICTURE BOOK OF LIVING CREATURES
(...OR APPEARING CHARACTERS)

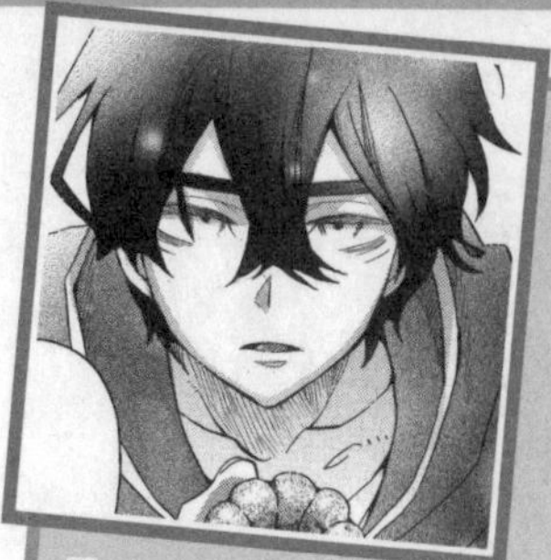

TATSUMI

The owner of the house. High school boy. He's good at cooking and household chores.

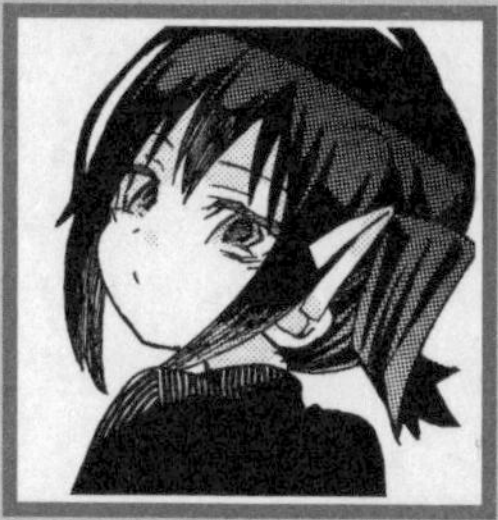

KASUMI

Tatsumi's little sister. Loves her big brother very much. Sees Wakasa as her rival.

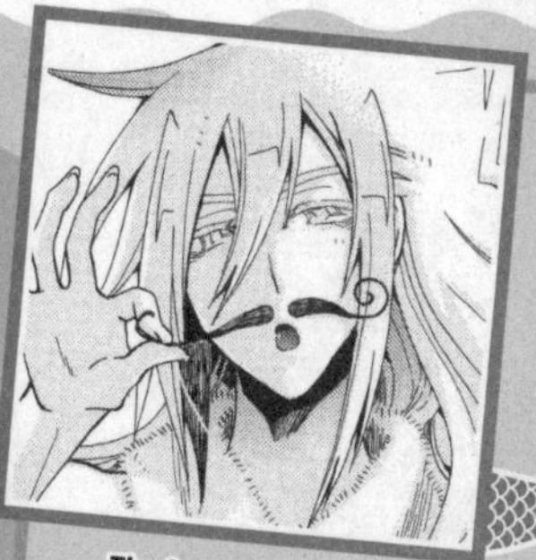

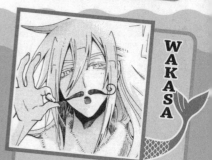

WAKASA

The freeloading fish in Tatsumi's house. His age...don't ask.

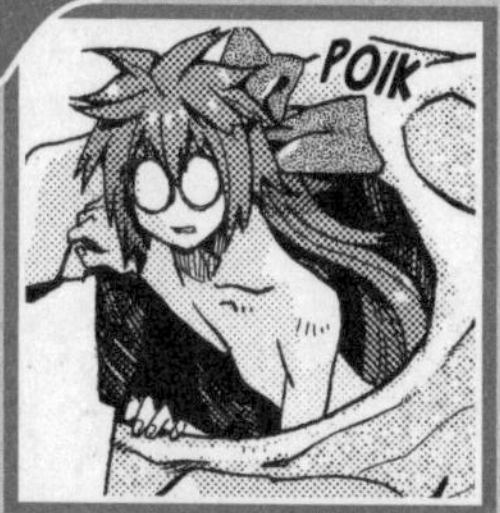
POIK

MAKI

This super-nearsighted snail is always beating up on himself.

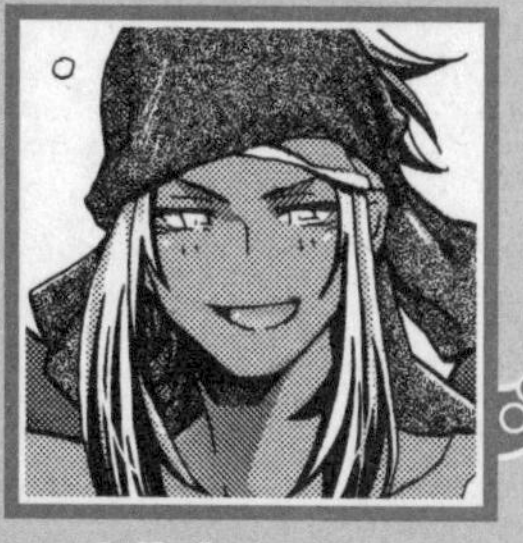

TAKASU

A gifted masseuse, this octopus is Wakasa's longtime friend.

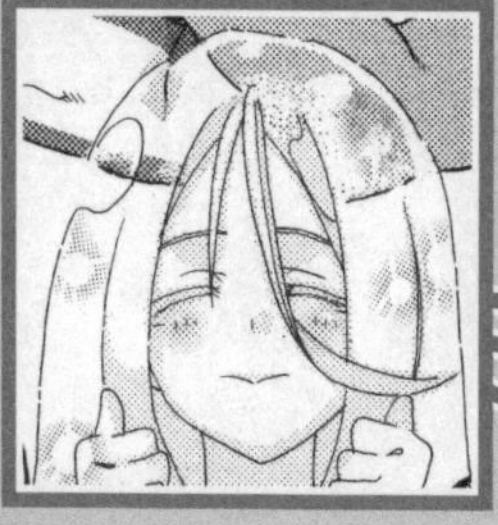

MIKUNI

This jellyfish's body is ninety-nine percent water. He loves A*uarius.

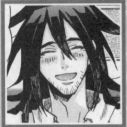

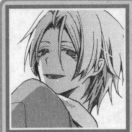

SOUSUKE

Tatsumi's friend.
He has two older sisters.

UNCLE HISATORA

Tatsumi's uncle, who makes Tatsumi test his sketchy medications.

GOROMARU

YUM!

Skilled at clinging, this starfish often goes unnoticed.

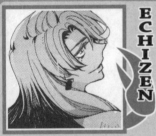

ECHIZEN

A super-sadistic crab trying to take Wakasa back to the sea.

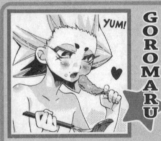

AGARI

This shark seems to be Wakasa's senpai.

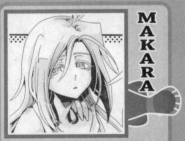

MAKARA

A young clownfish boy who turns into a girl when close to human men.

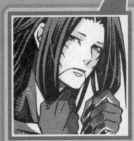

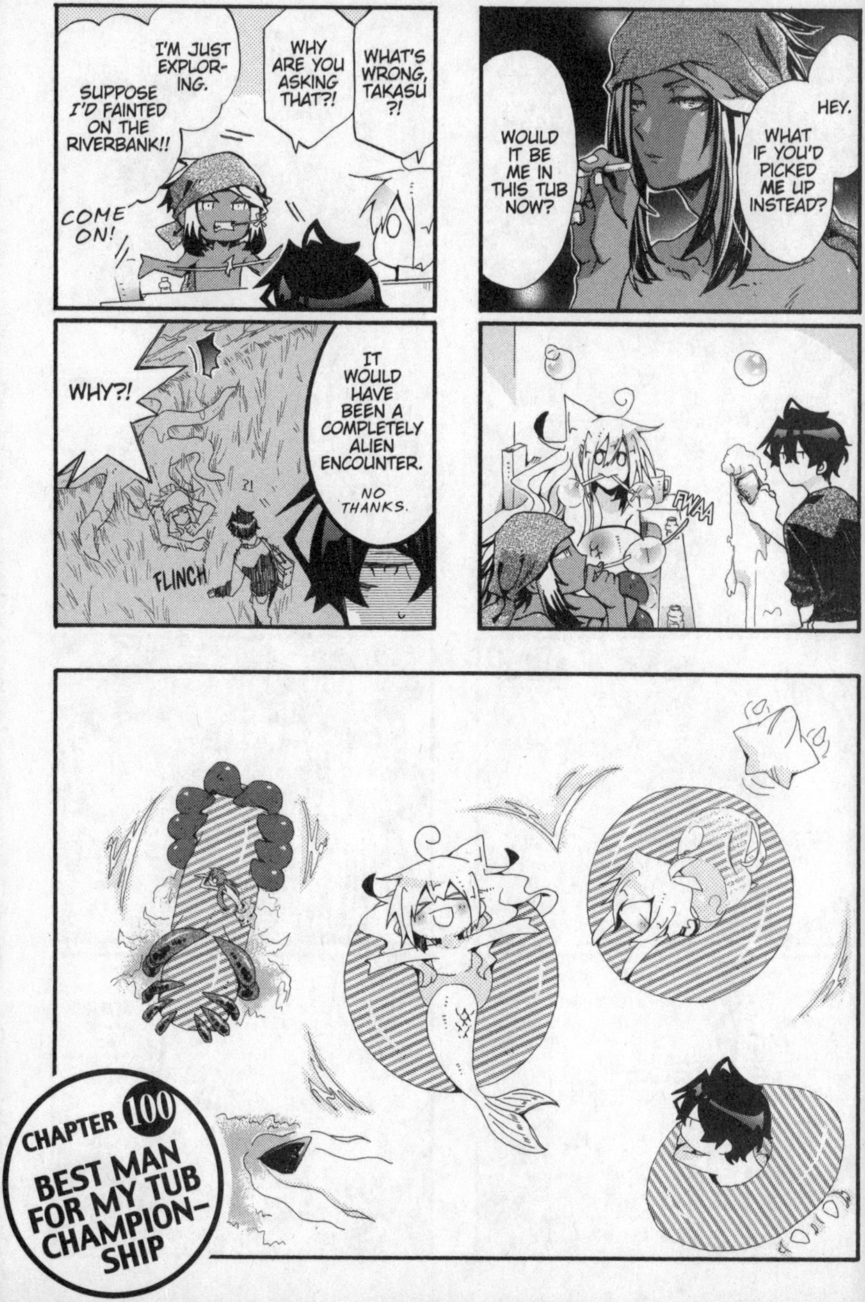
HEY.
WHAT IF YOU'D PICKED ME UP INSTEAD?
WOULD IT BE ME IN THIS TUB NOW?
WHAT'S WRONG, TAKASU?!
WHY ARE YOU ASKING THAT?!
I'M JUST EXPLORING.
SUPPOSE I'D FAINTED ON THE RIVERBANK!!
COME ON!
FWAA
IT WOULD HAVE BEEN A COMPLETELY ALIEN ENCOUNTER.
NO THANKS.
WHY?!
?!
FLINCH
CHAPTER 100
BEST MAN FOR MY TUB CHAMPIONSHIP

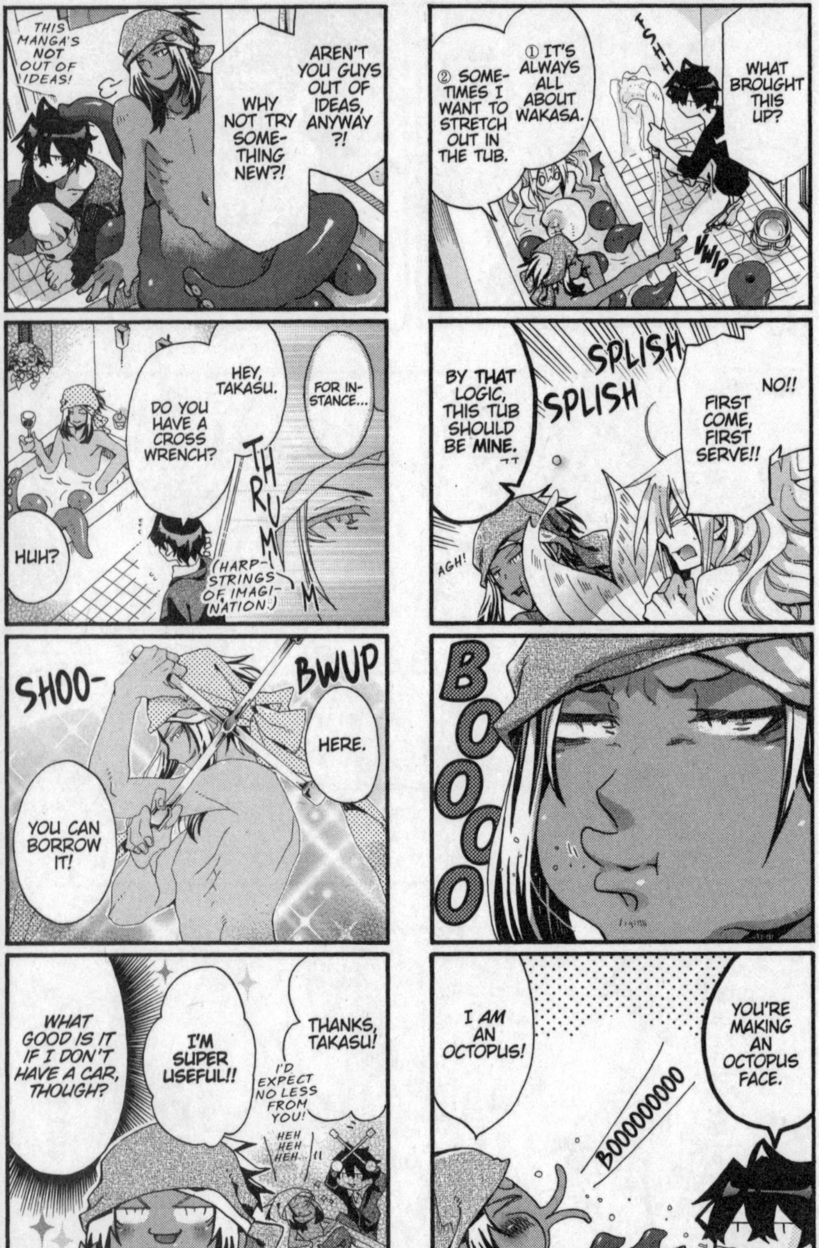
WHAT BROUGHT THIS UP?
FSHH
① IT'S ALWAYS ALL ABOUT WAKASA.
② SOMETIMES I WANT TO STRETCH OUT IN THE TUB.
VWIP
NO!! FIRST COME, FIRST SERVE!!
SPLISH
SPLISH
BY THAT LOGIC, THIS TUB SHOULD BE MINE.
AGH!
BOOOOO
YOU'RE MAKING AN OCTOPUS FACE.
BOOOOOOOOO
I AM AN OCTOPUS!
AREN'T YOU GUYS OUT OF IDEAS, ANYWAY?!
WHY NOT TRY SOMETHING NEW?!
THIS MANGA'S NOT OUT OF IDEAS!
FOR INSTANCE...
HEY, TAKASU.
DO YOU HAVE A CROSS WRENCH?
THRUMM
(HARP-STRINGS OF IMAGINATION.)
HUH?
BWUP
HERE.
SHOO-
YOU CAN BORROW IT!
THANKS, TAKASU!
I'D EXPECT NO LESS FROM YOU!
HEH HEH HEH...
I'M SUPER USEFUL!!
WHAT GOOD IS IT IF I DON'T HAVE A CAR, THOUGH?

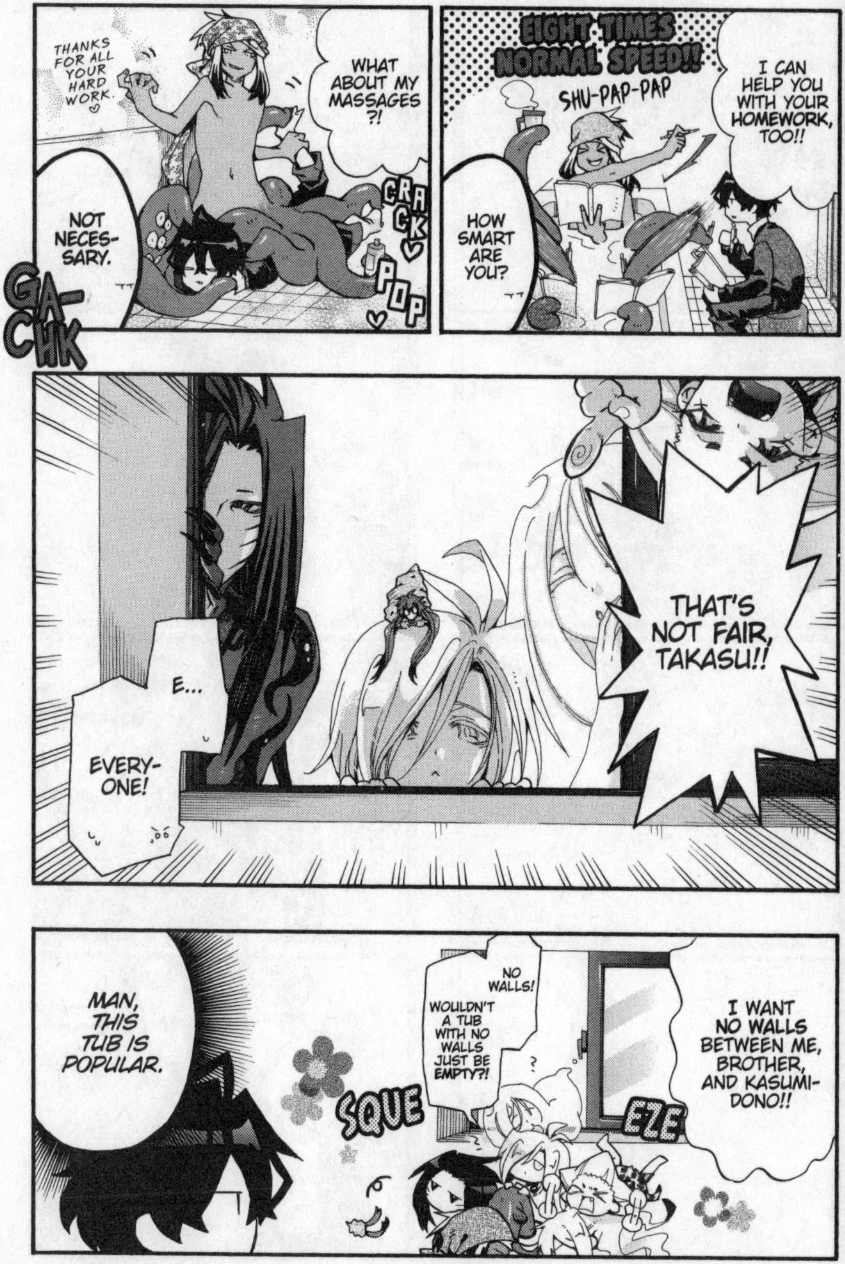
EIGHT TIMES NORMAL SPEED!!
SHU-PAP-PAP
I CAN HELP YOU WITH YOUR HOMEWORK, TOO!!
HOW SMART ARE YOU?
WHAT ABOUT MY MASSAGES?!
THANKS FOR ALL YOUR HARD WORK.
CRACK
POP
NOT NECES-SARY.
GA-CHK
THAT'S NOT FAIR, TAKASU!!
E...
EVERY-ONE!
I WANT NO WALLS BETWEEN ME, BROTHER, AND KASUMI-DONO!!
NO WALLS!
WOULDN'T A TUB WITH NO WALLS JUST BE EMPTY?!
?
SQUE EZE
MAN, THIS TUB IS POPULAR.

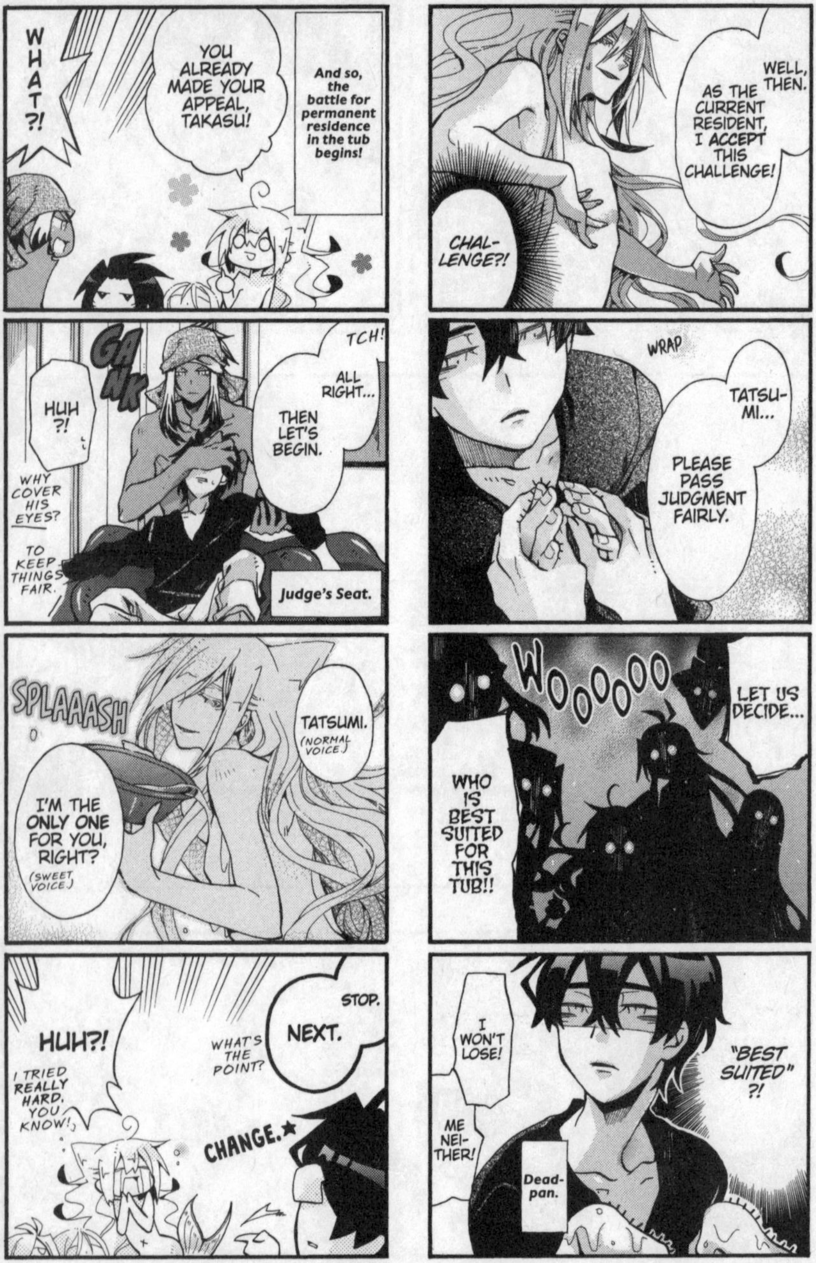
WELL, THEN.
AS THE CURRENT RESIDENT, I ACCEPT THIS CHALLENGE!
CHAL-LENGE?!
And so, the battle for permanent residence in the tub begins!
YOU ALREADY MADE YOUR APPEAL, TAKASU!
WHAT?!
WRAP
TATSUMI...
PLEASE PASS JUDGMENT FAIRLY.
TCH!
ALL RIGHT...
THEN LET'S BEGIN.
GANK
HUH?!
WHY COVER HIS EYES?
TO KEEP THINGS FAIR.
Judge's Seat.
WOOOOOO
LET US DECIDE...
WHO IS BEST SUITED FOR THIS TUB!!
TATSUMI.
(NORMAL VOICE.)
SPLAAASH
I'M THE ONLY ONE FOR YOU, RIGHT?
(SWEET VOICE.)
"BEST SUITED"?!
I WON'T LOSE!
ME NEITHER!
Dead-pan.
STOP.
NEXT.
WHAT'S THE POINT?
HUH?!
I TRIED REALLY HARD, YOU KNOW!
CHANGE.★

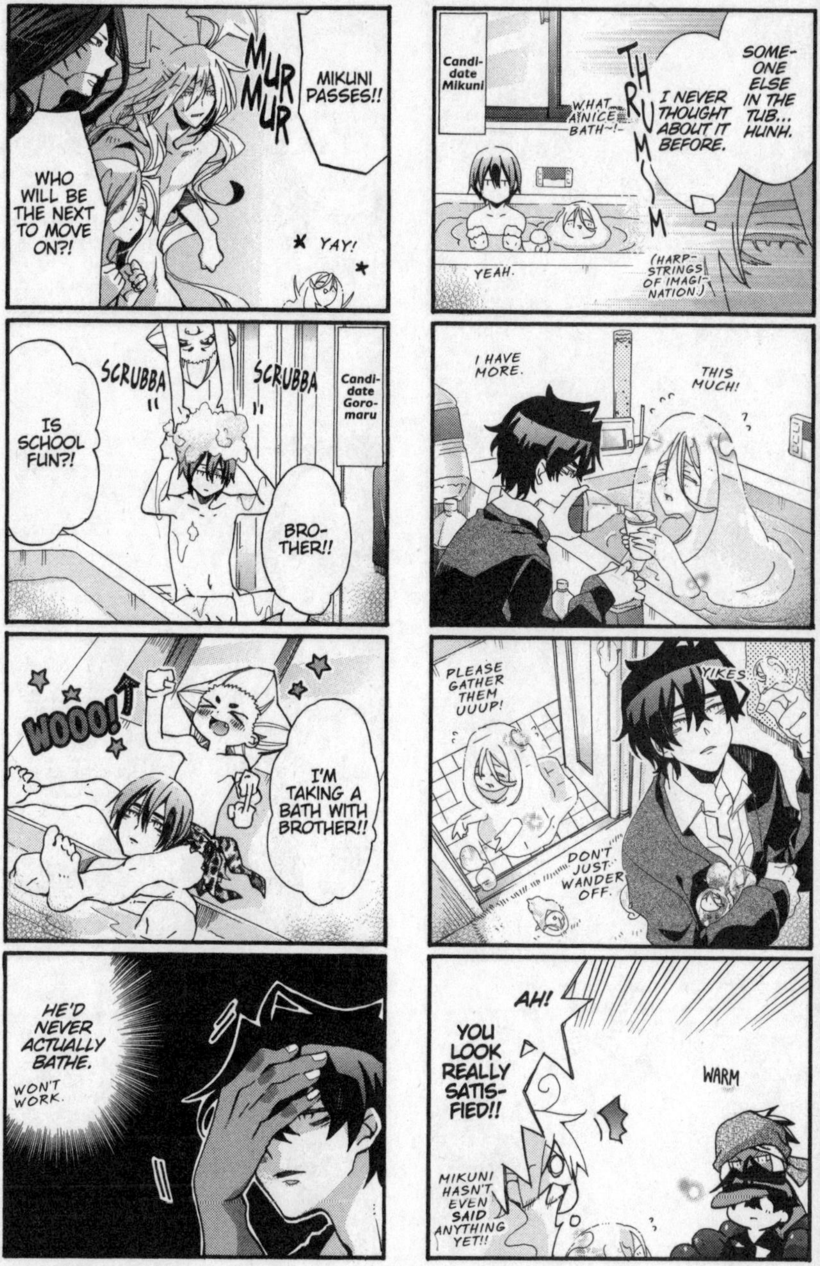
Candidate Mikuni
SOME-ONE ELSE IN THE TUB... HUNH.
I NEVER THOUGHT ABOUT IT BEFORE.
THRUM~M
WHAT A NICE BATH~!
YEAH.
(HARP-STRINGS OF IMAGINATION.)
THIS MUCH!
I HAVE MORE.
YIKES.
PLEASE GATHER THEM UUUP!
DON'T JUST WANDER OFF.
AH!
WARM
YOU LOOK REALLY SATIS-FIED!!
MIKUNI HASN'T EVEN SAID ANYTHING YET!!
MIKUNI PASSES!!
MUR MUR
WHO WILL BE THE NEXT TO MOVE ON?!
YAY!
Candi-date Goro-maru
SCRUBBA
SCRUBBA
IS SCHOOL FUN?!
BRO-THER!!
I'M TAKING A BATH WITH BROTHER!!
WOOO!
HE'D NEVER ACTUALLY BATHE.
WON'T WORK.

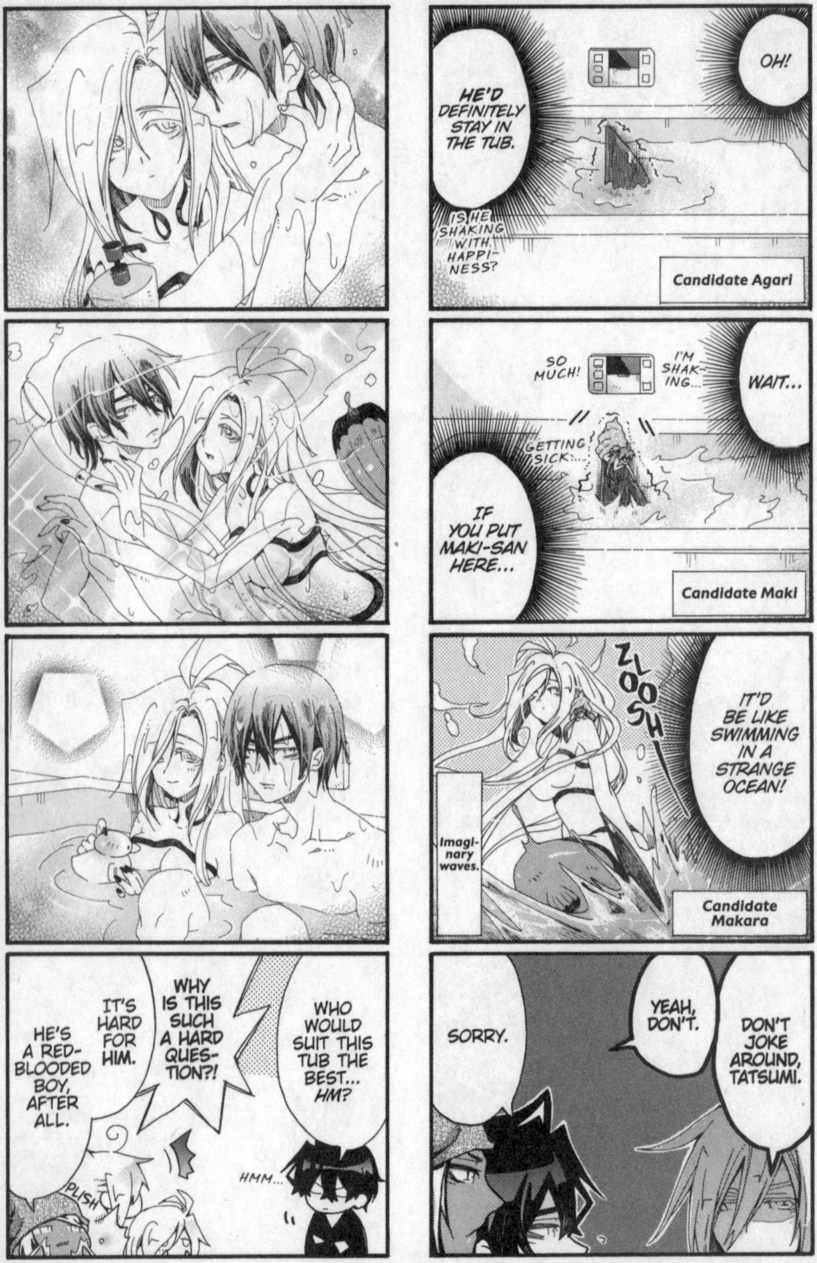
OH!
HE'D DEFINITELY STAY IN THE TUB.
IS HE SHAKING WITH HAPPINESS?
Candidate Agari
WAIT...
I'M SHAKING...
SO MUCH!
IF YOU PUT MAKI-SAN HERE...
GETTING SICK...
Candidate Maki
ZLOOSH
IT'D BE LIKE SWIMMING IN A STRANGE OCEAN!
Imaginary waves.
Candidate Makara
DON'T JOKE AROUND, TATSUMI.
YEAH, DON'T.
SORRY.
WHO WOULD SUIT THIS TUB THE BEST... HM?
WHY IS THIS SUCH A HARD QUESTION?!
IT'S HARD FOR HIM.
HE'S A RED-BLOODED BOY, AFTER ALL.
HMM...
PLISH

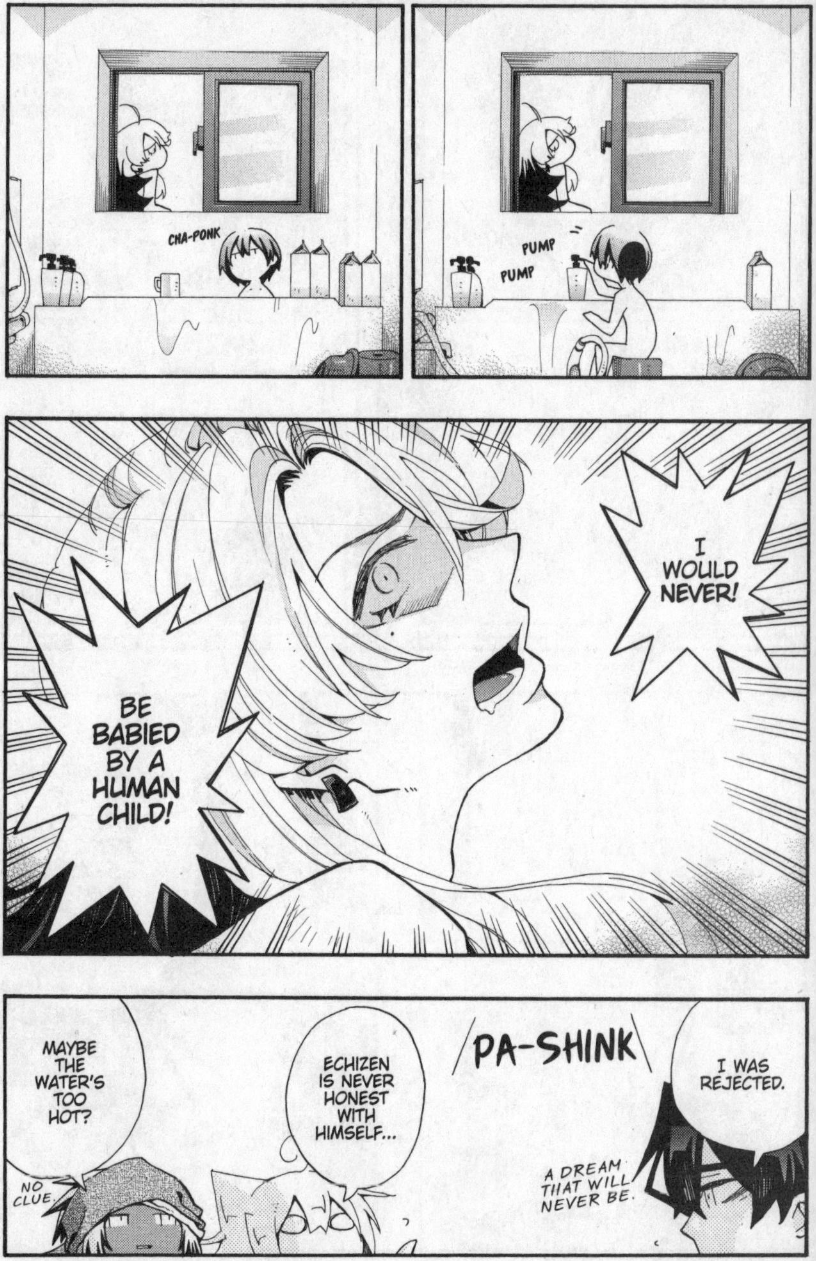
PUMP
PUMP
CHA-PONK
I WOULD NEVER!
BE BABIED BY A HUMAN CHILD!
I WAS REJECTED.
A DREAM THAT WILL NEVER BE.
PA-SHINK
ECHIZEN IS NEVER HONEST WITH HIMSELF...
MAYBE THE WATER'S TOO HOT?
NO CLUE.

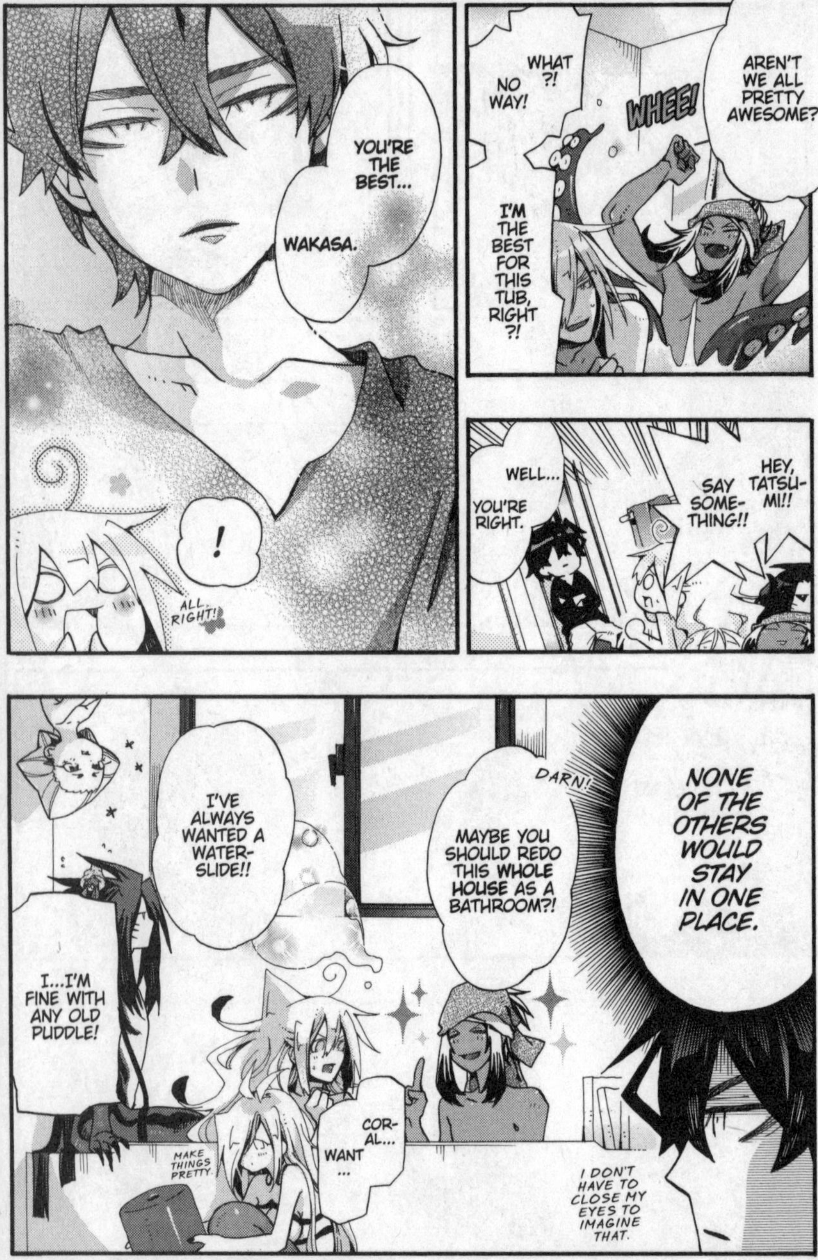
AREN'T WE ALL PRETTY AWESOME?
WHEE!
WHAT?!
NO WAY!
I'M THE BEST FOR THIS TUB, RIGHT?!
HEY, TATSUMI!!
SAY SOMETHING!!
WELL...
YOU'RE RIGHT.
YOU'RE THE BEST...
WAKASA.
!
ALL RIGHT!
NONE OF THE OTHERS WOULD STAY IN ONE PLACE.
DARN!
MAYBE YOU SHOULD REDO THIS WHOLE HOUSE AS A BATHROOM?!
I'VE ALWAYS WANTED A WATER-SLIDE!!
I DON'T HAVE TO CLOSE MY EYES TO IMAGINE THAT.
CORAL... WANT...
MAKE THINGS PRETTY.
I...I'M FINE WITH ANY OLD PUDDLE!

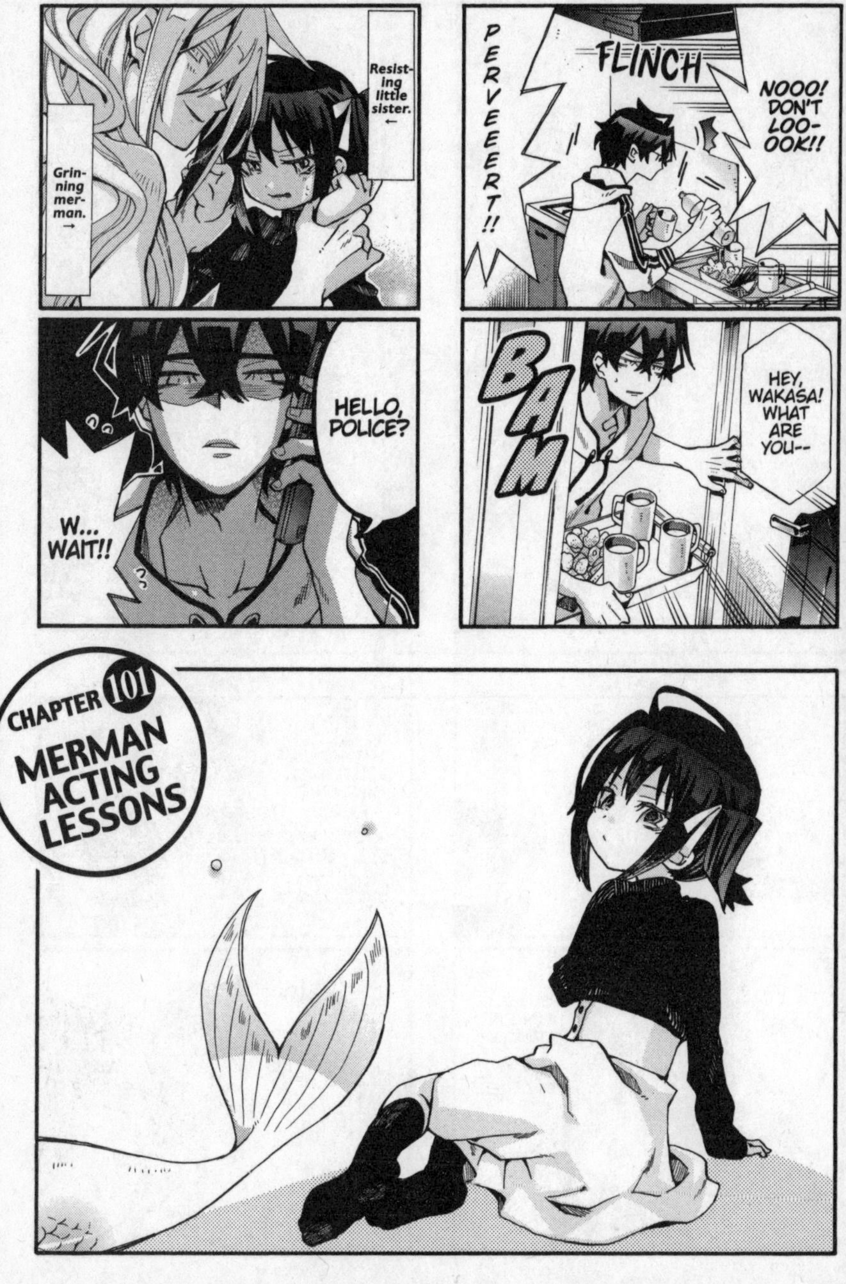
NOOO! DON'T LOO-OOK!!
FLINCH
PERVEEERT!!
Resisting little sister. ←
Grinning merman. →
HEY, WAKASA! WHAT ARE YOU--
BAM
HELLO, POLICE?
W... WAIT!!
CHAPTER 101
MERMAN ACTING LESSONS

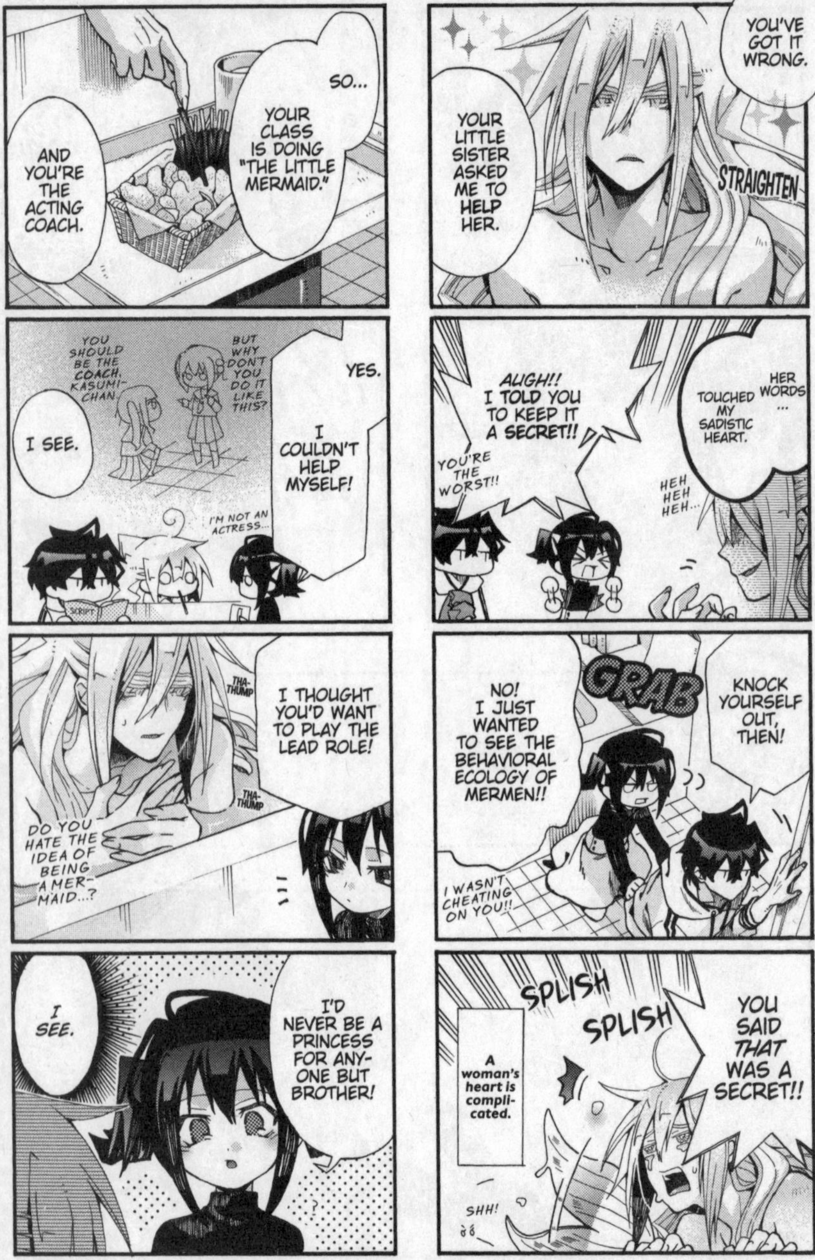
YOU'VE GOT IT WRONG.
YOUR LITTLE SISTER ASKED ME TO HELP HER.
STRAIGHTEN
HER WORDS... TOUCHED MY SADISTIC HEART.
HEH HEH HEH...
AUGH!! I TOLD YOU TO KEEP IT A SECRET!!
YOU'RE THE WORST!!
KNOCK YOURSELF OUT, THEN!
GRAB
NO! I JUST WANTED TO SEE THE BEHAVIORAL ECOLOGY OF MERMEN!!
I WASN'T CHEATING ON YOU!!
YOU SAID THAT WAS A SECRET!!
SPLISH
SPLISH
A woman's heart is complicated.
SHH!
SO... YOUR CLASS IS DOING "THE LITTLE MERMAID."
AND YOU'RE THE ACTING COACH.
YES. I COULDN'T HELP MYSELF!
BUT WHY DON'T YOU DO IT LIKE THIS?
YOU SHOULD BE THE COACH, KASUMI-CHAN.
I SEE.
I'M NOT AN ACTRESS...
SCRIPT
I THOUGHT YOU'D WANT TO PLAY THE LEAD ROLE!
THA-THUMP
THA-THUMP
DO YOU HATE THE IDEA OF BEING A MERMAID...?
I'D NEVER BE A PRINCESS FOR ANYONE BUT BROTHER!
I SEE.

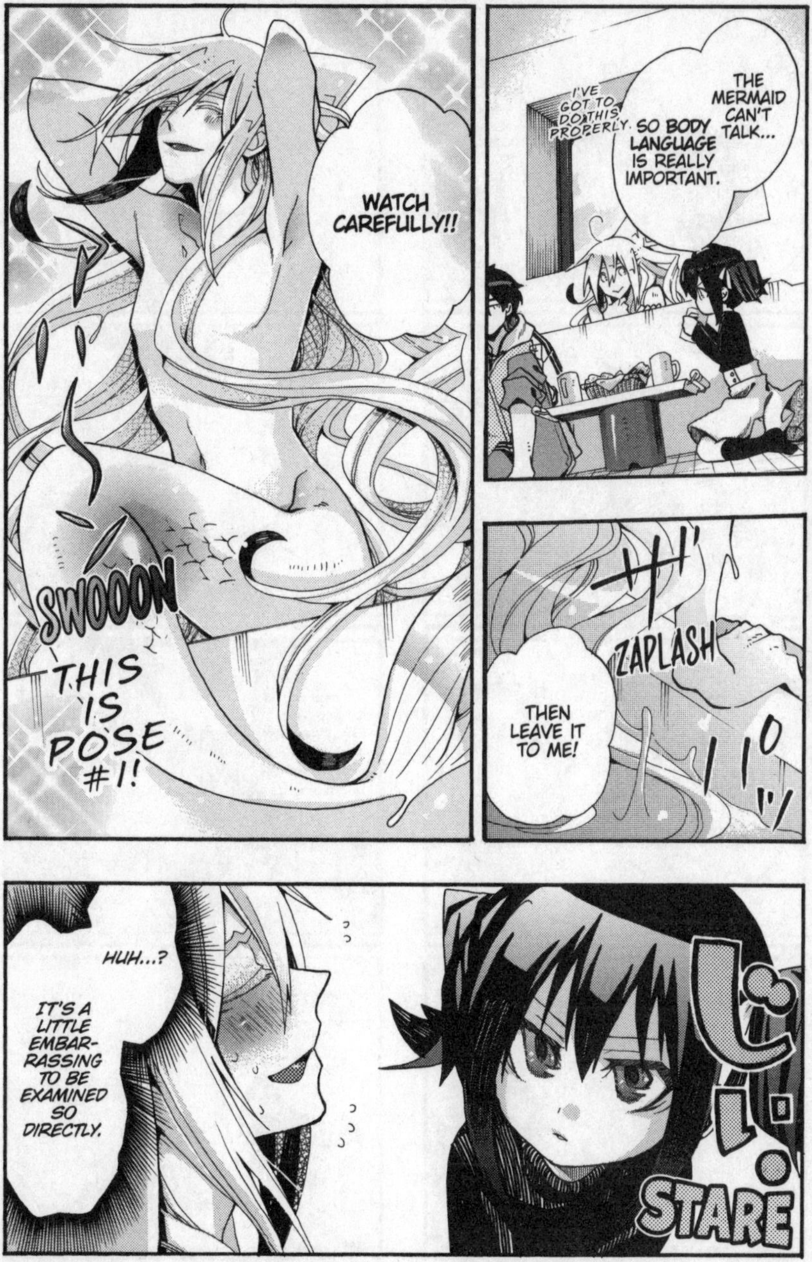
THE MERMAID CAN'T TALK...
SO BODY LANGUAGE IS REALLY IMPORTANT.
I'VE GOT TO DO THIS PROPERLY.
ZAPLASH
THEN LEAVE IT TO ME!
WATCH CAREFULLY!!
SWOOON
THIS IS POSE #1!
STARE
HUH...?
IT'S A LITTLE EMBARRASSING TO BE EXAMINED SO DIRECTLY.

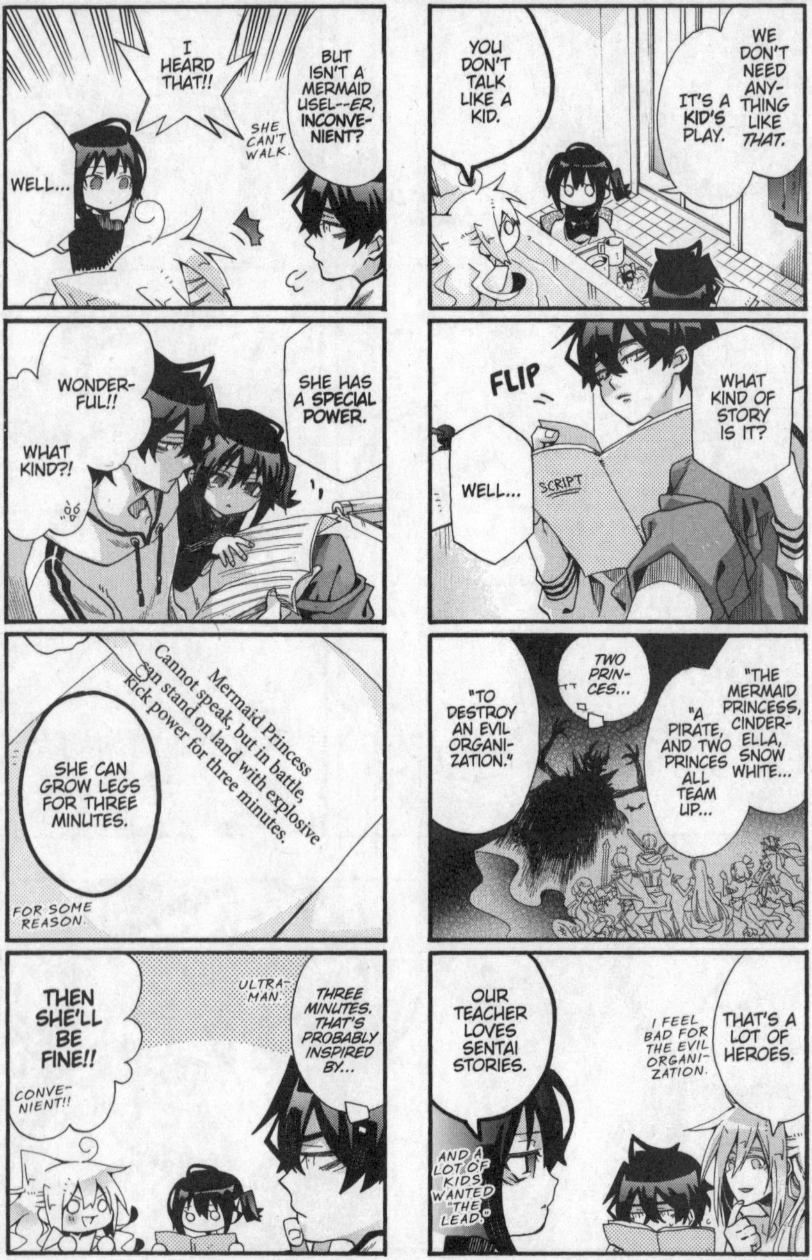
YOU DON'T TALK LIKE A KID.
WE DON'T NEED ANYTHING LIKE THAT.
IT'S A KID'S PLAY.
WHAT KIND OF STORY IS IT?
FLIP
WELL...
SCRIPT
"THE MERMAID PRINCESS, CINDERELLA, SNOW WHITE...
"A PIRATE, AND TWO PRINCES ALL TEAM UP...
"TO DESTROY AN EVIL ORGANIZATION."
TWO PRINCES...
THAT'S A LOT OF HEROES.
I FEEL BAD FOR THE EVIL ORGANIZATION.
OUR TEACHER LOVES SENTAI STORIES.
AND A LOT OF KIDS WANTED "THE LEAD."
BUT ISN'T A MERMAID USEL--ER, INCONVENIENT?
SHE CAN'T WALK.
I HEARD THAT!!
WELL...
SHE HAS A SPECIAL POWER.
WONDERFUL!!
WHAT KIND?!
Mermaid Princess
Cannot speak, but in battle, can stand on land with explosive kick power for three minutes.
SHE CAN GROW LEGS FOR THREE MINUTES.
FOR SOME REASON.
THREE MINUTES. THAT'S PROBABLY INSPIRED BY...
ULTRAMAN.
THEN SHE'LL BE FINE!!
CONVENIENT!!

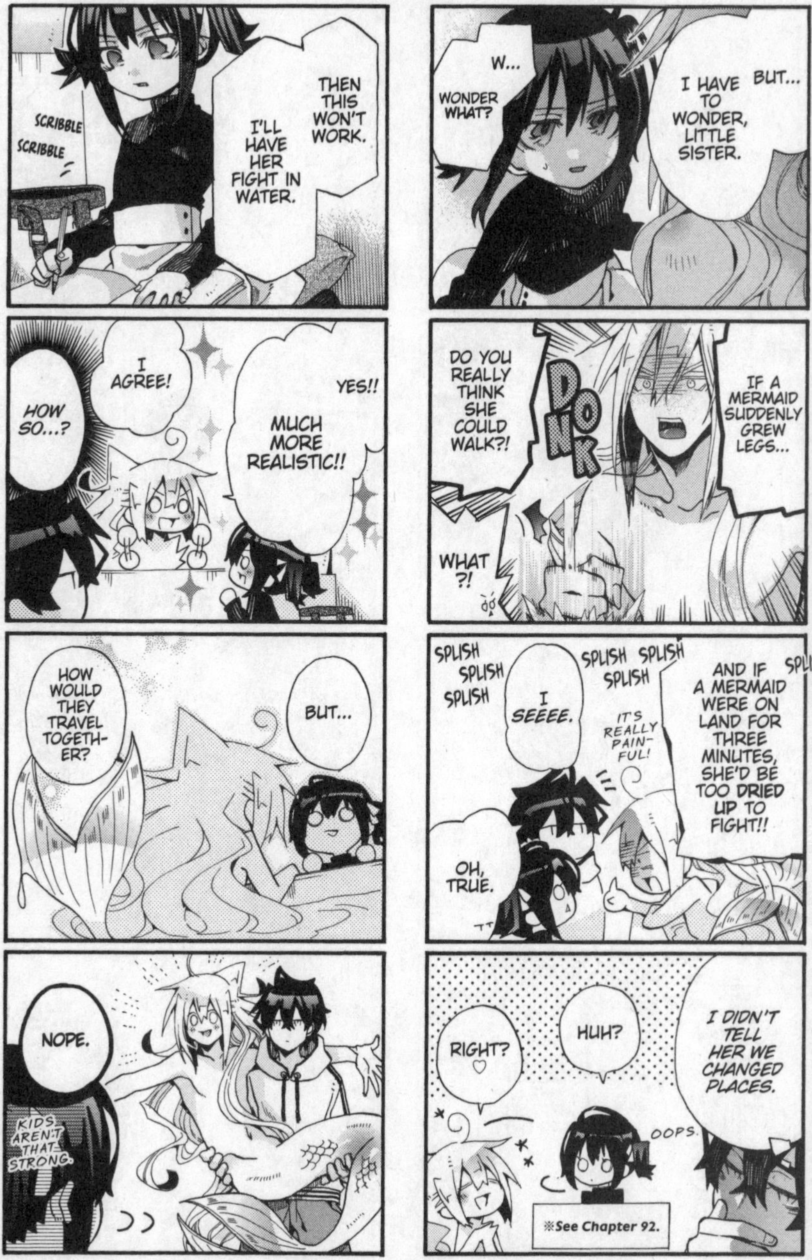
BUT...
I HAVE TO WONDER, LITTLE SISTER.
W... WONDER WHAT?
IF A MERMAID SUDDENLY GREW LEGS...
DO YOU REALLY THINK SHE COULD WALK?!
DONK
WHAT?!
SPLISH
AND IF A MERMAID WERE ON LAND FOR THREE MINUTES, SHE'D BE TOO DRIED UP TO FIGHT!!
SPLISH SPLISH SPLISH
IT'S REALLY PAINFUL!
I SEEEE.
SPLISH SPLISH SPLISH
OH, TRUE.
I DIDN'T TELL HER WE CHANGED PLACES.
HUH?
OOPS.
RIGHT? ♡
※See Chapter 92.
THEN THIS WON'T WORK.
I'LL HAVE HER FIGHT IN WATER.
SCRIBBLE
SCRIBBLE
YES!!
MUCH MORE REALISTIC!!
I AGREE!
HOW SO...?
BUT...
HOW WOULD THEY TRAVEL TOGETHER?
NOPE.
KIDS AREN'T THAT STRONG.

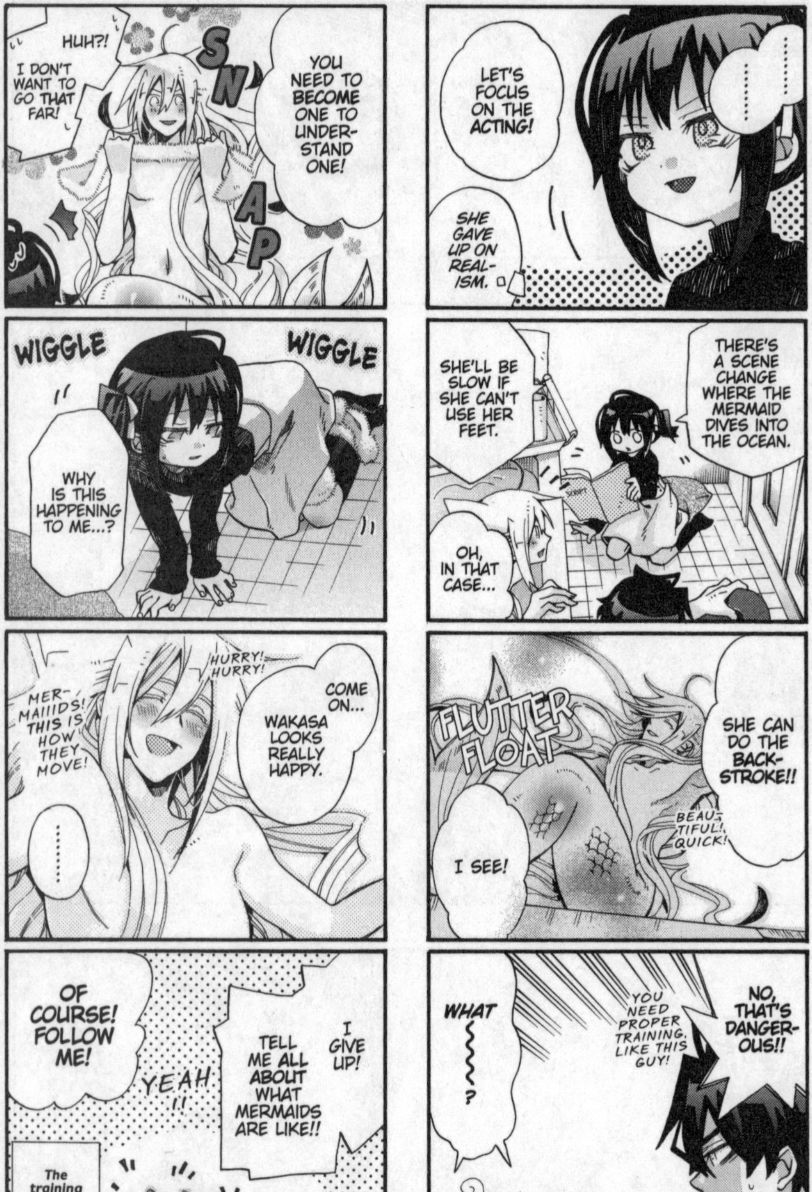
......
LET'S FOCUS ON THE ACTING!
SHE GAVE UP ON REALISM.
THERE'S A SCENE CHANGE WHERE THE MERMAID DIVES INTO THE OCEAN.
SHE'LL BE SLOW IF SHE CAN'T USE HER FEET.
SCRIPT
OH, IN THAT CASE...
SHE CAN DO THE BACKSTROKE!!
FLUTTER FLOAT
BEAUTIFUL! QUICK!
I SEE!
NO, THAT'S DANGEROUS!!
YOU NEED PROPER TRAINING, LIKE THIS GUY!
WHAT~~~?
YOU NEED TO BECOME ONE TO UNDERSTAND ONE!
SNAP
HUH?!
I DON'T WANT TO GO THAT FAR!
WIGGLE WIGGLE
WHY IS THIS HAPPENING TO ME...?
COME ON... WAKASA LOOKS REALLY HAPPY.
HURRY! HURRY!
MER-MAIIIDS! THIS IS HOW THEY MOVE!
......
I GIVE UP!
TELL ME ALL ABOUT WHAT MERMAIDS ARE LIKE!!
OF COURSE! FOLLOW ME!
YEAH!!
The training went on for hours.

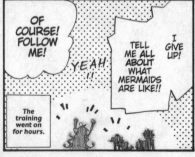

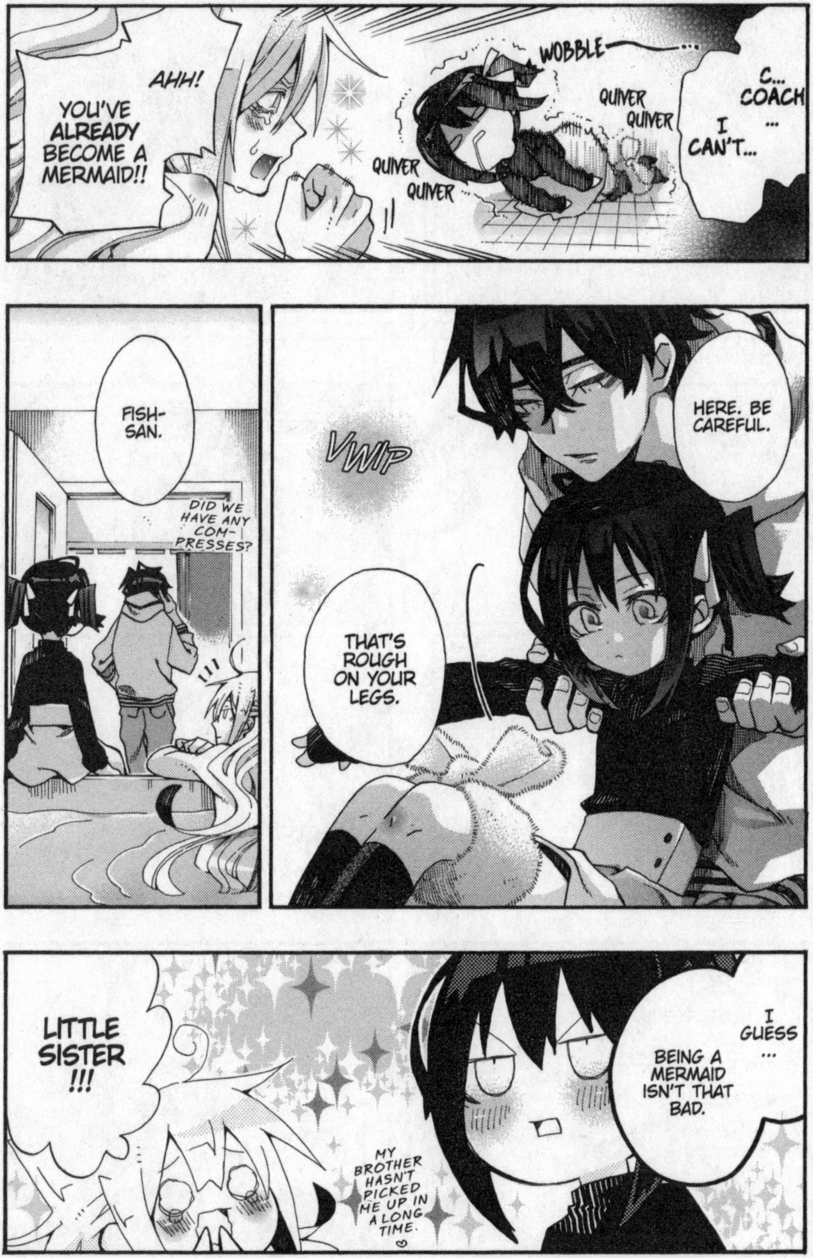
C... COACH ... I CAN'T...
WOBBLE...
QUIVER QUIVER
QUIVER QUIVER
AHH!
YOU'VE ALREADY BECOME A MERMAID!!
HERE. BE CAREFUL.
VWIP
THAT'S ROUGH ON YOUR LEGS.
FISH-SAN.
DID WE HAVE ANY COM-PRESSES?
I GUESS... BEING A MERMAID ISN'T THAT BAD.
MY BROTHER HASN'T PICKED ME UP IN A LONG TIME.
LITTLE SISTER!!!

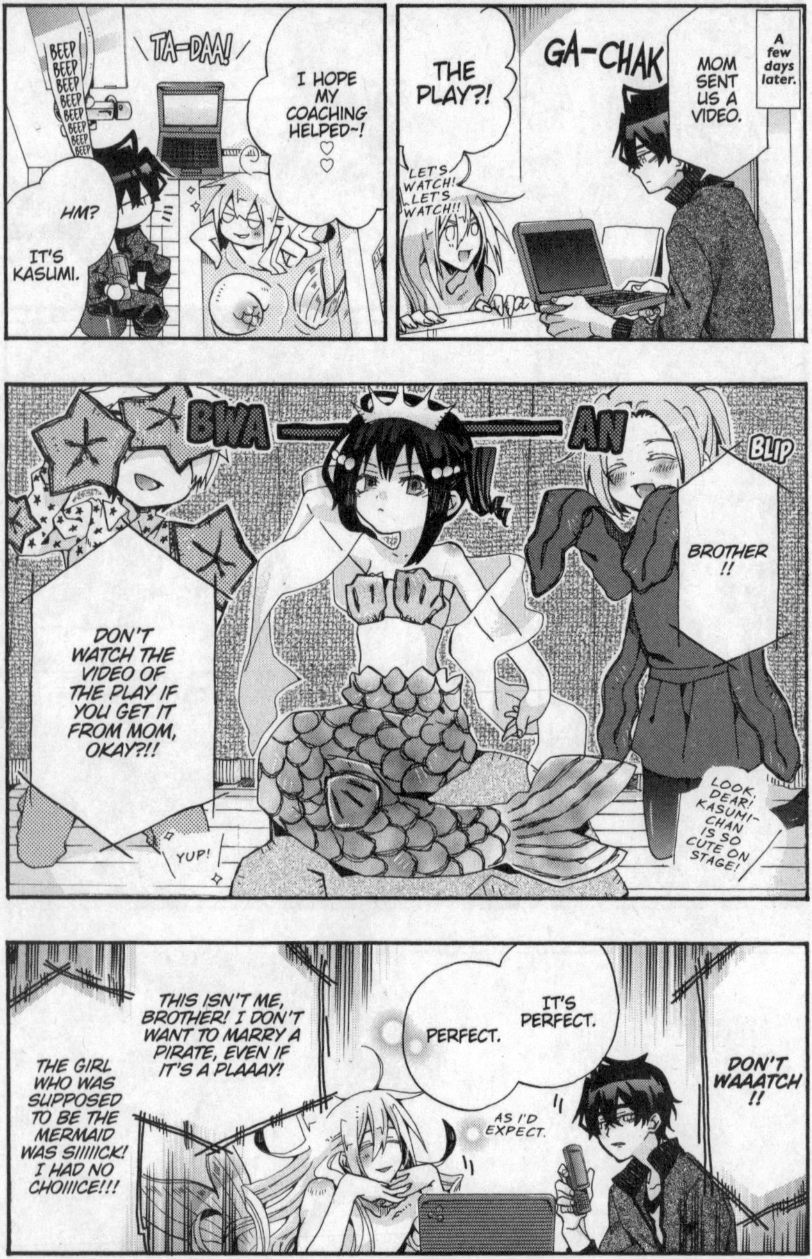
A few days later.
MOM SENT US A VIDEO.
GA-CHAK
THE PLAY?!
LET'S WATCH! LET'S WATCH!!
I HOPE MY COACHING HELPED~! ♡ ♡
TA-DAA!
BEEP BEEP BEEP BEEP BEEP BEEP BEEP BEEP
HM?
IT'S KASUMI.
BWA—AN
BLIP
BROTHER !!
LOOK, DEAR! KASUMI-CHAN IS SO CUTE ON STAGE!
DON'T WATCH THE VIDEO OF THE PLAY IF YOU GET IT FROM MOM, OKAY?!!
YUP!
DON'T WAAATCH !!
IT'S PERFECT.
PERFECT.
AS I'D EXPECT.
THIS ISN'T ME, BROTHER! I DON'T WANT TO MARRY A PIRATE, EVEN IF IT'S A PLAAAY!
THE GIRL WHO WAS SUPPOSED TO BE THE MERMAID WAS SIIIICK! I HAD NO CHOIIICE!!!

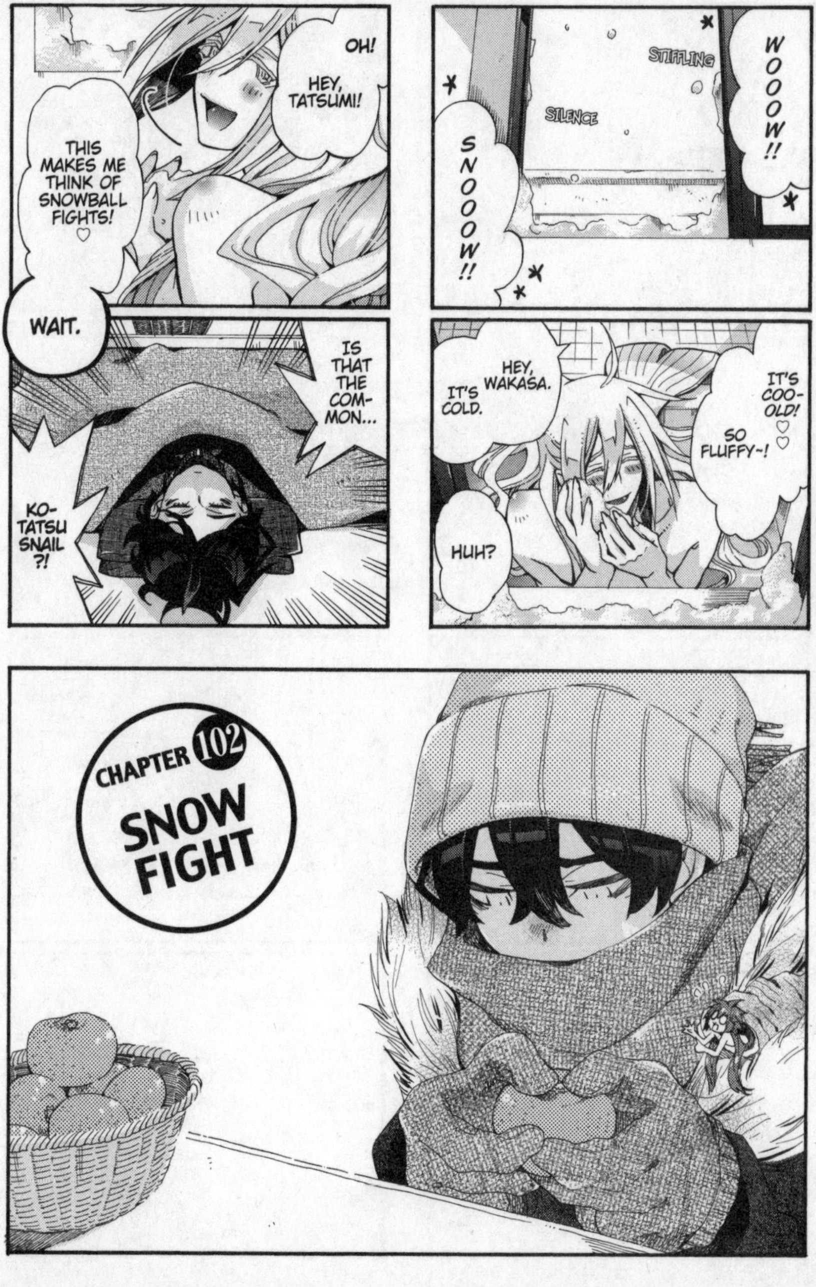
WOOOOW!!
SNOOOOW!!
STIFFLING
SILENCE
OH!
HEY, TATSUMI!
THIS MAKES ME THINK OF SNOWBALL FIGHTS! ♡
IT'S COOO-OLD! ♡
SO FLUFFY~! ♡
HEY, WAKASA.
IT'S COLD.
HUH?
WAIT.
IS THAT THE COM-MON...
KO-TATSU SNAIL?!
CHAPTER 102
SNOW FIGHT

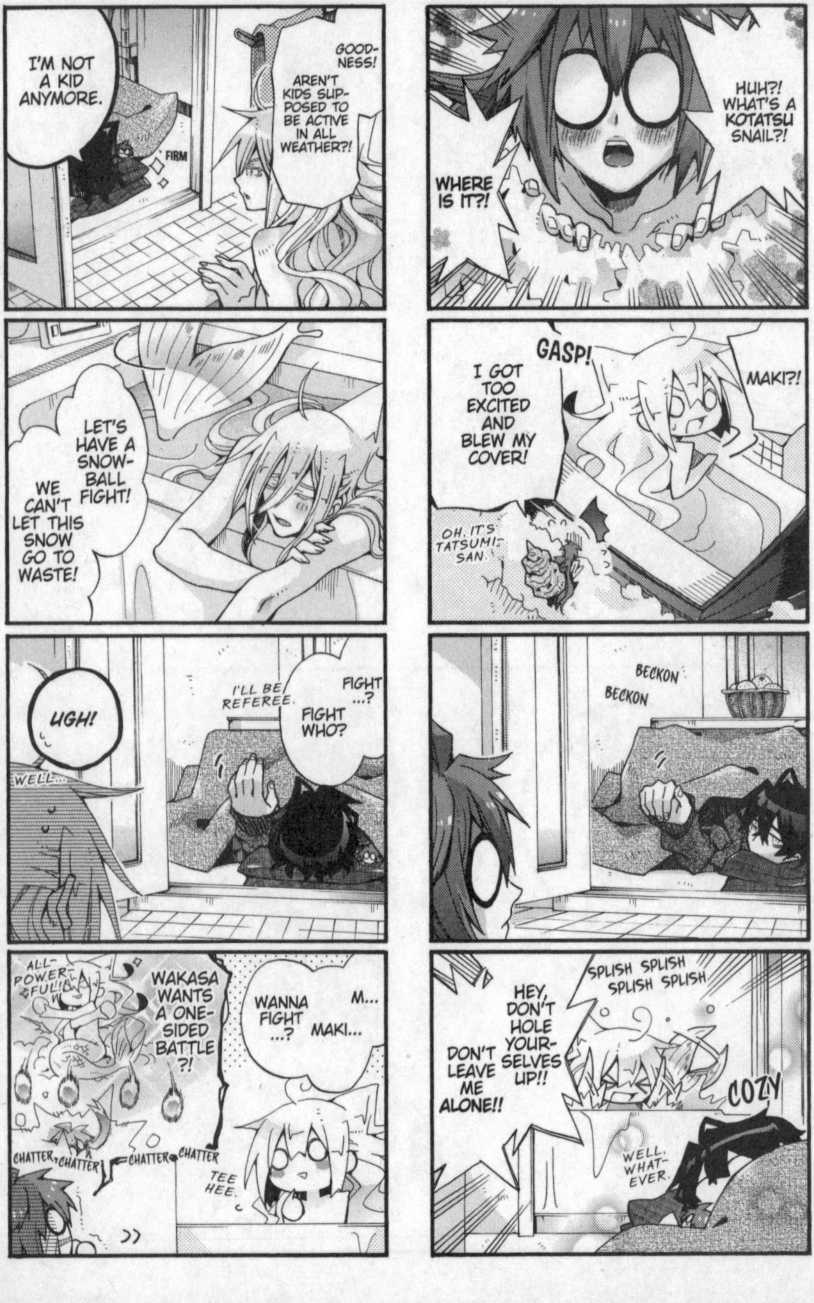
HUH?! WHAT'S A KOTATSU SNAIL?!
WHERE IS IT?!
GOOD-NESS!
AREN'T KIDS SUP-POSED TO BE ACTIVE IN ALL WEATHER?!
I'M NOT A KID ANYMORE.
FIRM
MAKI?!
GASP!
I GOT TOO EXCITED AND BLEW MY COVER!
OH, IT'S TATSUMI-SAN.
LET'S HAVE A SNOW-BALL FIGHT!
WE CAN'T LET THIS SNOW GO TO WASTE!
BECKON
BECKON
FIGHT ...?
FIGHT WHO?
I'LL BE REFEREE.
UGH!
WELL...
SPLISH SPLISH SPLISH SPLISH
HEY, DON'T HOLE YOUR-SELVES UP!!
DON'T LEAVE ME ALONE!!
COZY
WELL, WHAT-EVER.
M... MAKI...
WANNA FIGHT ...?
WAKASA WANTS A ONE-SIDED BATTLE?!
ALL-POWER-FUL!
CHATTER CHATTER CHATTER CHATTER
TEE HEE.

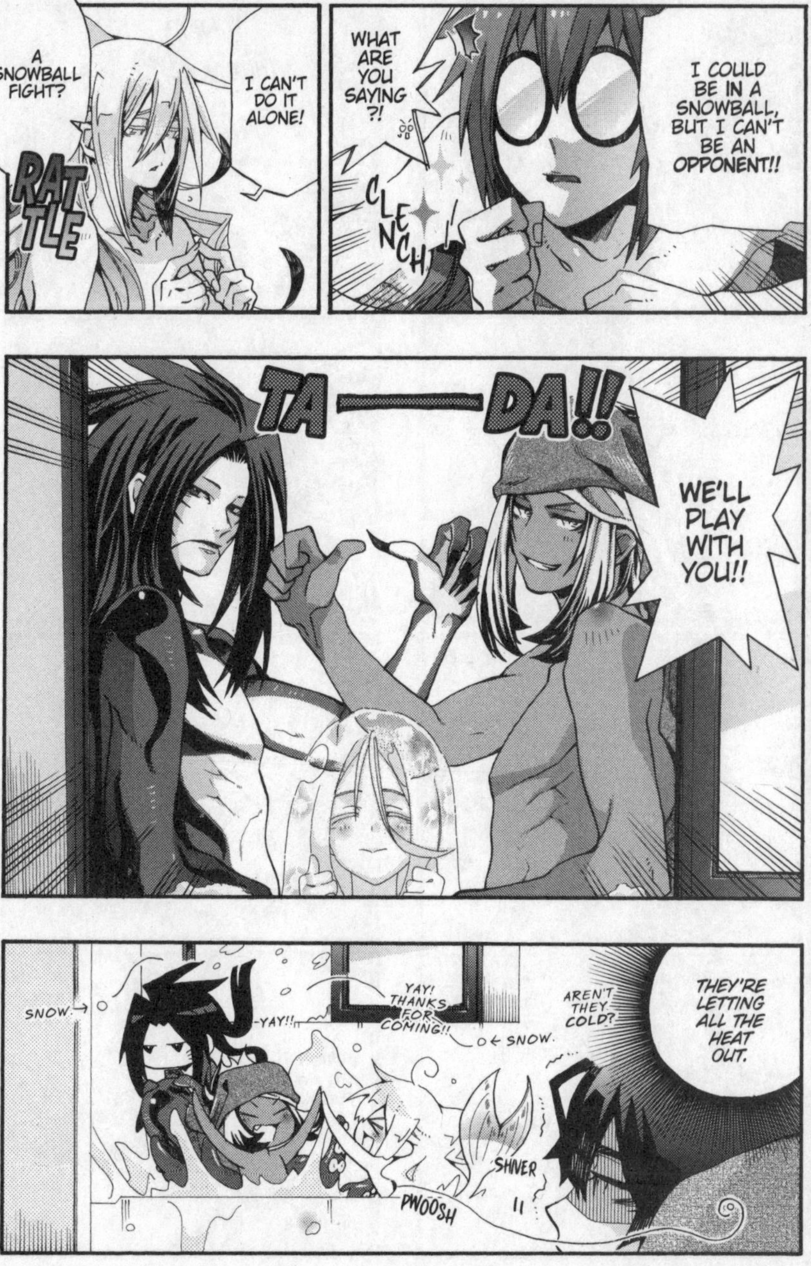
I COULD BE IN A SNOWBALL, BUT I CAN'T BE AN OPPONENT!!
WHAT ARE YOU SAYING?!
CLENCH
I CAN'T DO IT ALONE!
A SNOWBALL FIGHT?
RATTLE
WE'LL PLAY WITH YOU!!
TA——DA!!
THEY'RE LETTING ALL THE HEAT OUT.
AREN'T THEY COLD?
SHIVER
YAY! THANKS FOR COMING!!
← SNOW.
-YAY!!
SNOW →
PWOOSH

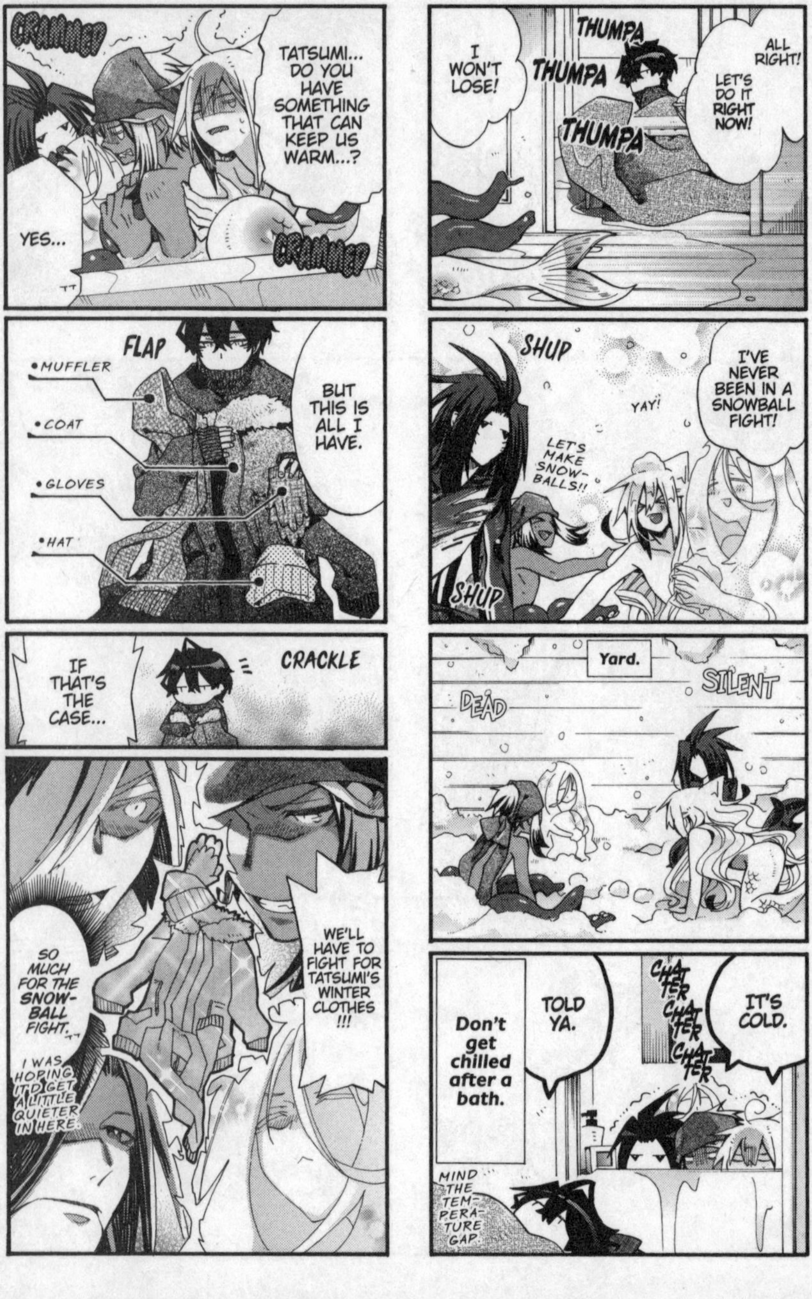
ALL RIGHT!
LET'S DO IT RIGHT NOW!
THUMPA
THUMPA
THUMPA
I WON'T LOSE!
I'VE NEVER BEEN IN A SNOWBALL FIGHT!
YAY!
SHUP
LET'S MAKE SNOW-BALLS!!
SHUP
Yard.
SILENT
DEAD
IT'S COLD.
CHATTER CHATTER CHATTER
TOLD YA.
Don't get chilled after a bath.
MIND THE TEM-PERA-TURE GAP.
TATSUMI... DO YOU HAVE SOMETHING THAT CAN KEEP US WARM...?
CRAMMED
CRAMMED
YES...
BUT THIS IS ALL I HAVE.
FLAP
•MUFFLER
•COAT
•GLOVES
•HAT
CRACKLE
IF THAT'S THE CASE...
WE'LL HAVE TO FIGHT FOR TATSUMI'S WINTER CLOTHES!!!
SO MUCH FOR THE SNOW-BALL FIGHT.
I WAS HOPING IT'D GET A LITTLE QUIETER IN HERE.

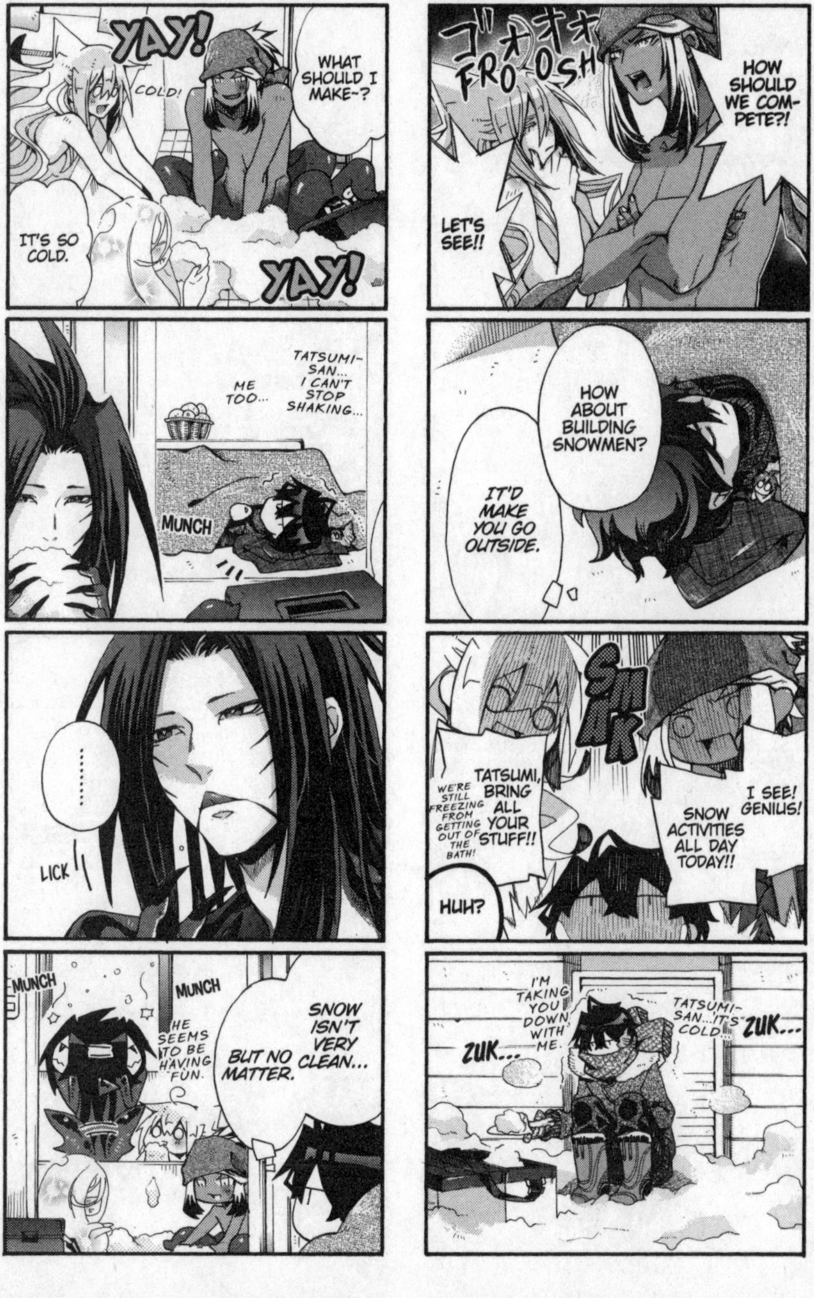
HOW SHOULD WE COMPETE?!
FRO-OSH
LET'S SEE!!
HOW ABOUT BUILDING SNOWMEN?
IT'D MAKE YOU GO OUTSIDE.
I SEE! GENIUS!
SNOW ACTIVITIES ALL DAY TODAY!!
SHAK
TATSUMI, BRING ALL YOUR STUFF!!
WE'RE STILL FREEZING FROM GETTING OUT OF THE BATH!
HUH?
ZUK...
TATSUMI-SAN...IT'S COLD...
I'M TAKING YOU DOWN WITH ME.
ZUK...
WHAT SHOULD I MAKE~?
YAY!
COLD!
YAY!
IT'S SO COLD.
TATSUMI-SAN... I CAN'T STOP SHAKING...
ME TOO...
MUNCH
......
LICK
SNOW ISN'T VERY CLEAN...
BUT NO MATTER.
MUNCH
HE SEEMS TO BE HAVING FUN.
MUNCH

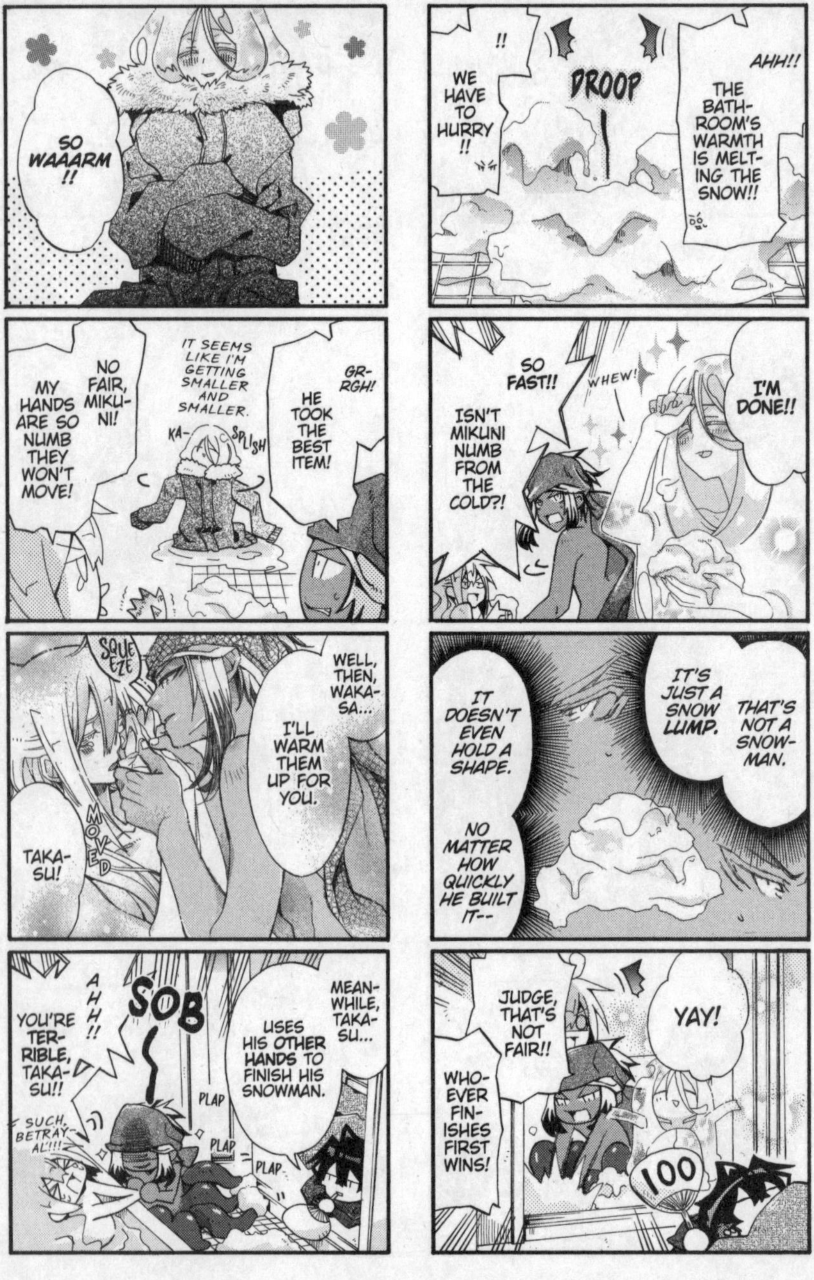
!!
DROOP
AHH!! THE BATHROOM'S WARMTH IS MELTING THE SNOW!!
WE HAVE TO HURRY!!
I'M DONE!!
WHEW!
SO FAST!!
ISN'T MIKUNI NUMB FROM THE COLD?!
IT'S JUST A SNOW LUMP.
THAT'S NOT A SNOWMAN.
IT DOESN'T EVEN HOLD A SHAPE.
NO MATTER HOW QUICKLY HE BUILT IT--
YAY!
JUDGE, THAT'S NOT FAIR!!
WHOEVER FINISHES FIRST WINS!
100
SO WAAARM!!
GR-RGH!
HE TOOK THE BEST ITEM!
IT SEEMS LIKE I'M GETTING SMALLER AND SMALLER.
KA-SPLISH
NO FAIR, MIKUNI!
MY HANDS ARE SO NUMB THEY WON'T MOVE!
WELL, THEN, WAKASA...
I'LL WARM THEM UP FOR YOU.
SQUEEZE
MOVED
TAKASU!
MEANWHILE, TAKASU...
USES HIS OTHER HANDS TO FINISH HIS SNOWMAN.
PLAP
PLAP
PLAP
SOB
AHH!!
YOU'RE TERRIBLE, TAKASU!!
SUCH BETRAYAL!!!

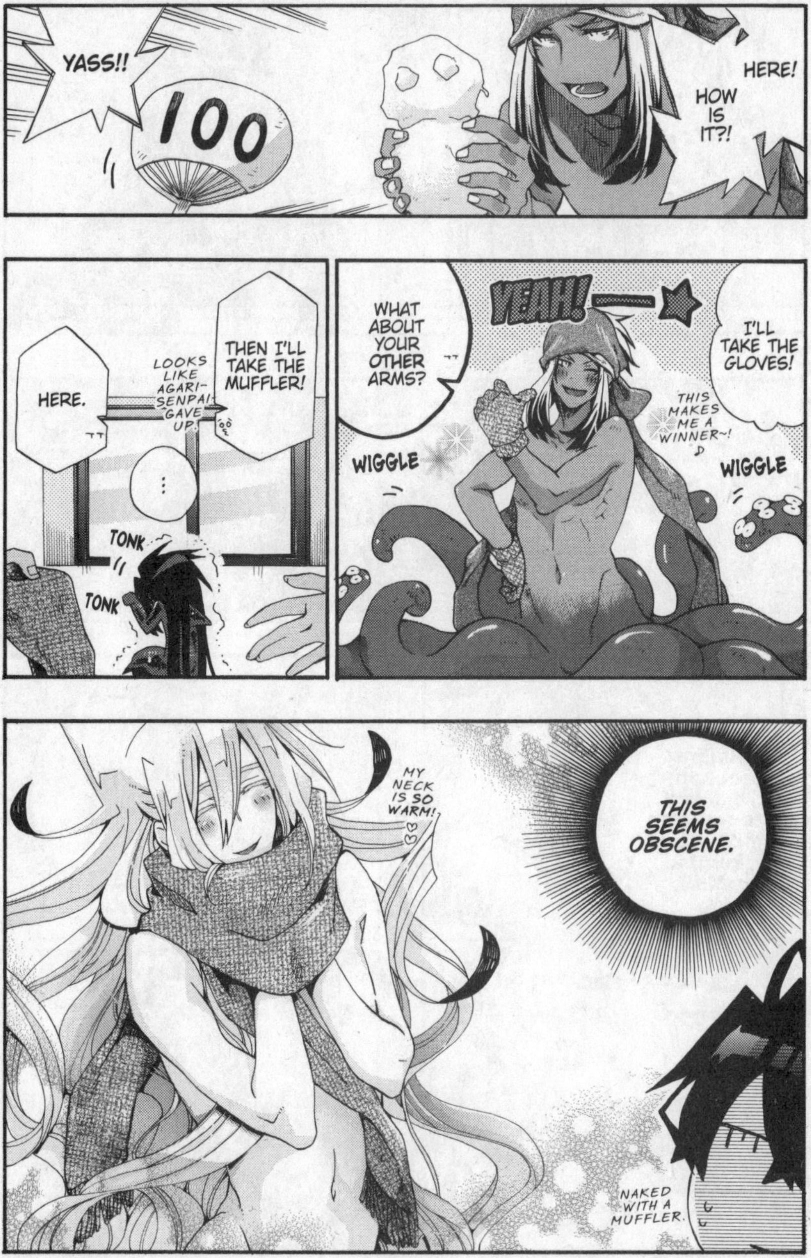
HERE!
HOW IS IT?!
YASS!!
100
I'LL TAKE THE GLOVES!
THIS MAKES ME A WINNER~! ♪
YEAH!—★
WHAT ABOUT YOUR OTHER ARMS?
WIGGLE
WIGGLE
THEN I'LL TAKE THE MUFFLER!
LOOKS LIKE AGARI-SENPAI GAVE UP.
HERE.
...
TONK
TONK
THIS SEEMS OBSCENE.
MY NECK IS SO WARM!
NAKED WITH A MUFFLER.

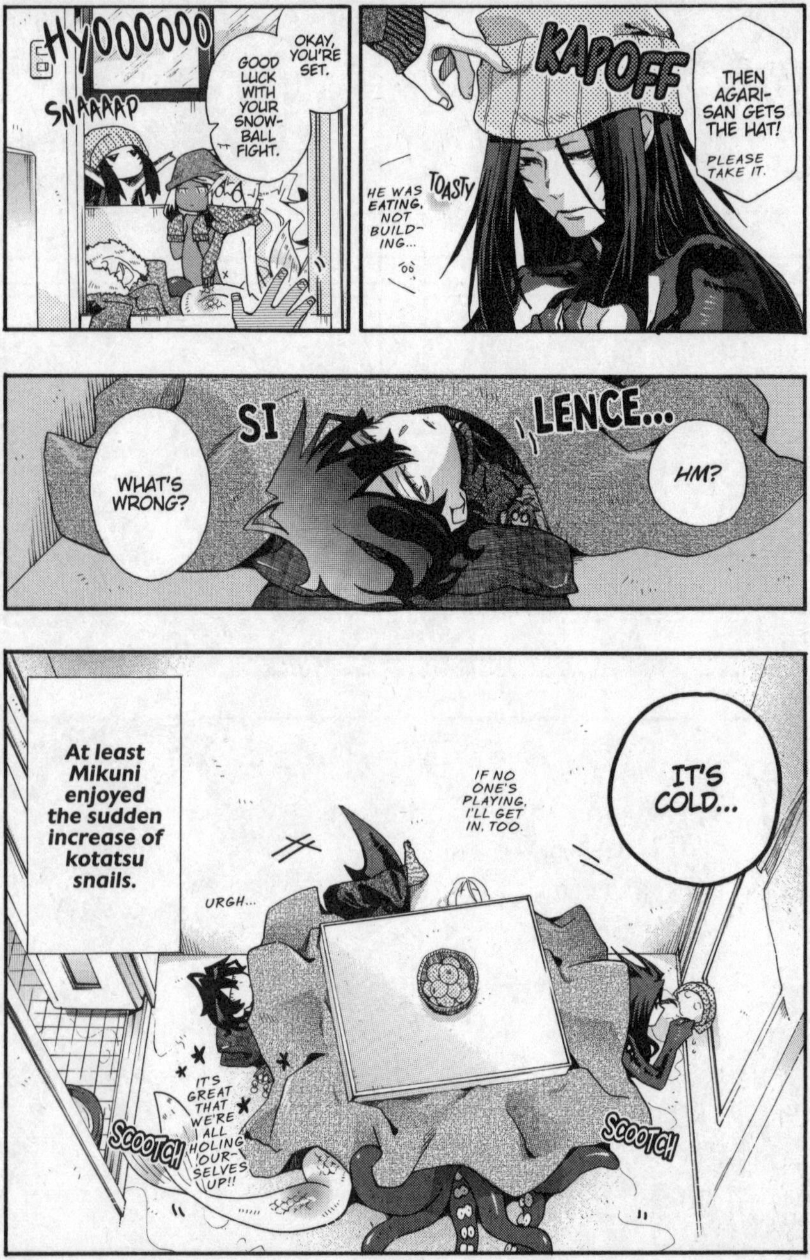
KAPOFF
THEN AGARI-SAN GETS THE HAT!
PLEASE TAKE IT.
TOASTY
HE WAS EATING, NOT BUILDING...
HYOOOOOO
OKAY, YOU'RE SET.
GOOD LUCK WITH YOUR SNOW-BALL FIGHT.
SNAAAAP
SI
LENCE...
HM?
WHAT'S WRONG?
IT'S COLD...
IF NO ONE'S PLAYING, I'LL GET IN, TOO.
At least Mikuni enjoyed the sudden increase of kotatsu snails.
URGH...
SCOOTCH
IT'S GREAT THAT WE'RE ALL HOLING OUR-SELVES UP!!
SCOOTCH

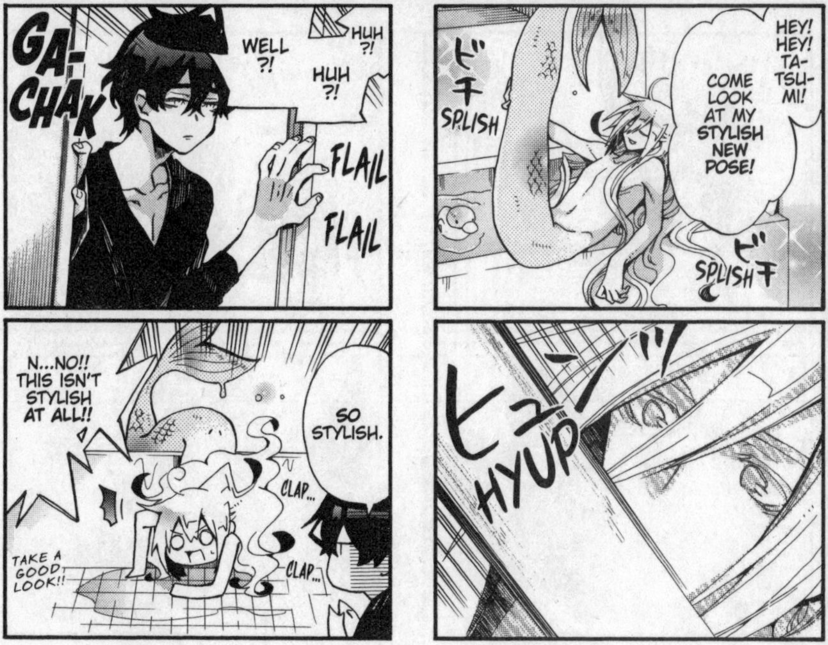
HEY! HEY! TA-TSU-MI!
COME LOOK AT MY STYLISH NEW POSE!
ビチ SPLISH
ビチ SPLISH
GA-CHAK
WELL ?!
HUH ?!
HUH ?!
FLAIL
FLAIL
ヒューッ HYUP
SO STYLISH.
CLAP...
CLAP...
N...NO!! THIS ISN'T STYLISH AT ALL!!
TAKE A GOOD LOOK!!

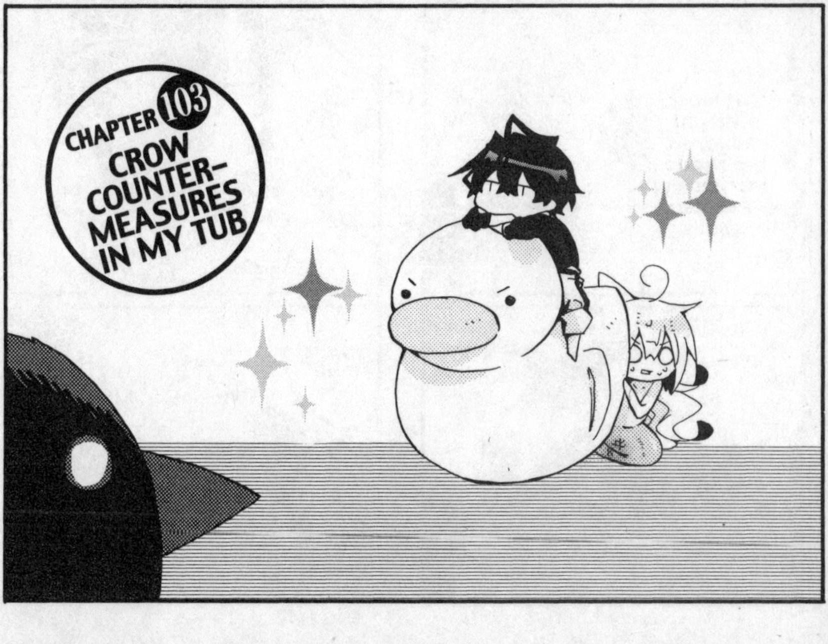
CHAPTER 103
CROW COUNTER-MEASURES IN MY TUB

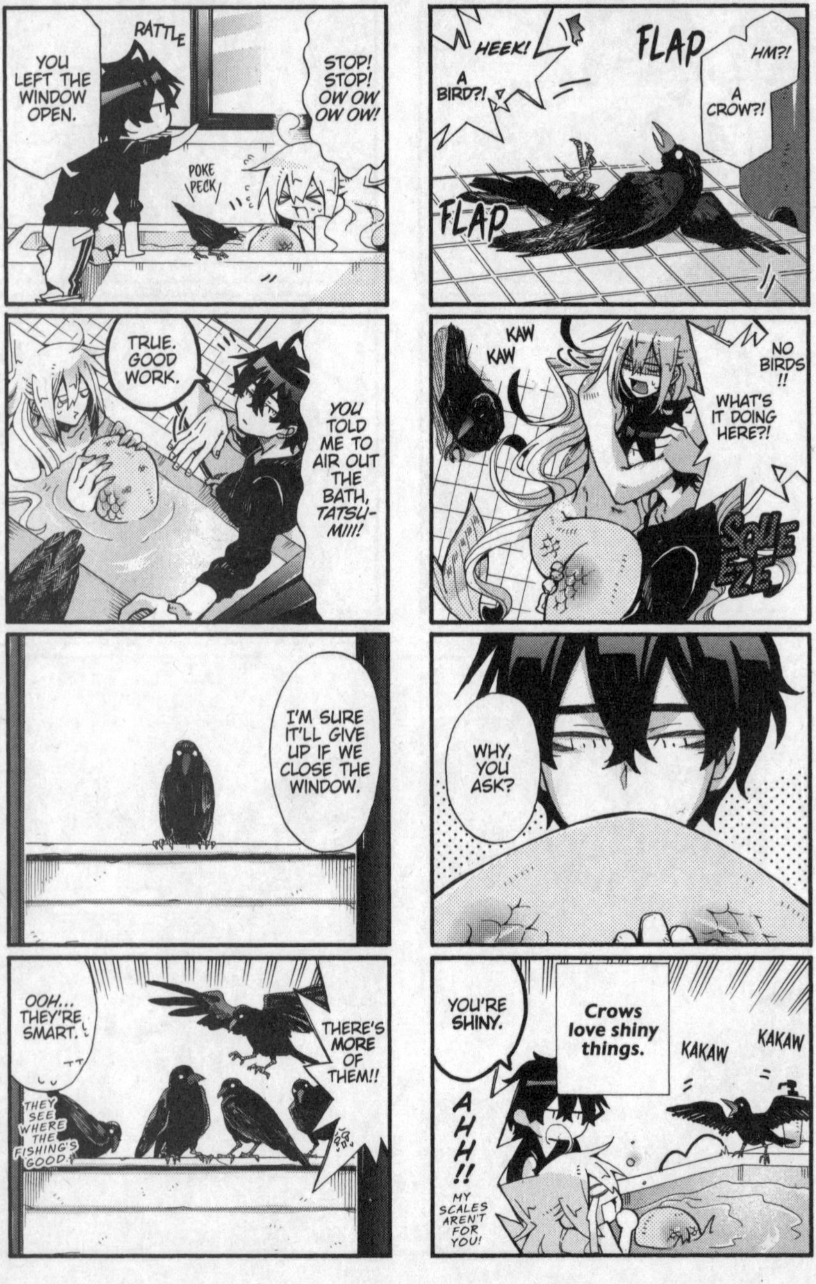
HM?! A CROW?!
FLAP
HEEK! A BIRD?!
FLAP
STOP! STOP! OW OW OW OW!
RATTLE
YOU LEFT THE WINDOW OPEN.
POKE PECK
NO BIRDS!! WHAT'S IT DOING HERE?!
KAW KAW
SQUEEZE
YOU TOLD ME TO AIR OUT THE BATH, TATSUMI!!!
TRUE. GOOD WORK.
WHY, YOU ASK?
I'M SURE IT'LL GIVE UP IF WE CLOSE THE WINDOW.
KAKAW
Crows love shiny things.
KAKAW
YOU'RE SHINY.
AHH!! MY SCALES AREN'T FOR YOU!
THERE'S MORE OF THEM!!
OOH... THEY'RE SMART.
THEY SEE WHERE THE FISHING'S GOOD.

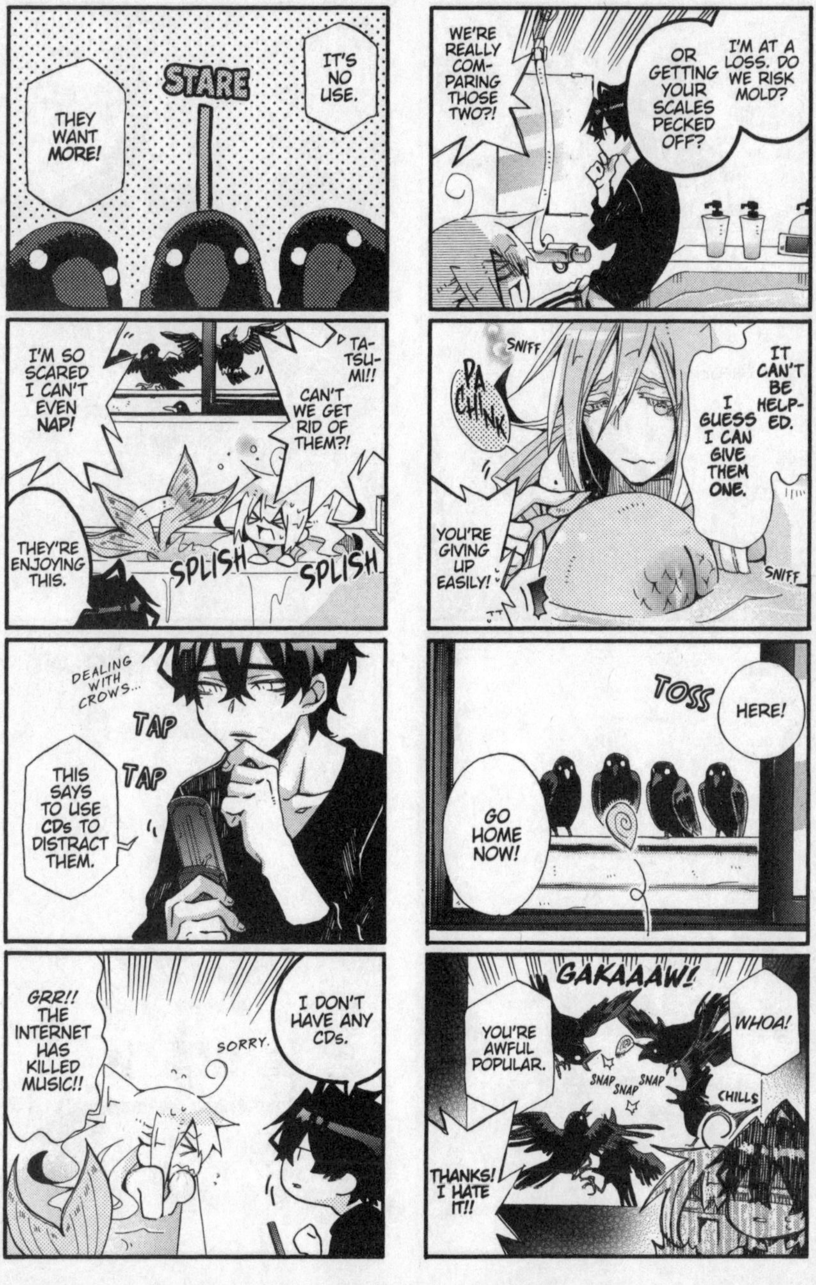
I'M AT A LOSS. DO WE RISK MOLD?
OR GETTING YOUR SCALES PECKED OFF?
WE'RE REALLY COM-PARING THOSE TWO?!
SNIFF
PA CHINK
IT CAN'T BE HELP-ED.
I GUESS I CAN GIVE THEM ONE.
YOU'RE GIVING UP EASILY!
SNIFF
TOSS
HERE!
GO HOME NOW!
GAKAAAW!
WHOA!
YOU'RE AWFUL POPULAR.
SNAP SNAP SNAP
CHILLS
THANKS! I HATE IT!!
STARE
IT'S NO USE.
THEY WANT MORE!
TA-TSU-MI!!
CAN'T WE GET RID OF THEM?!
I'M SO SCARED I CAN'T EVEN NAP!
THEY'RE ENJOYING THIS.
SPLISH
SPLISH
DEALING WITH CROWS...
TAP
TAP
THIS SAYS TO USE CDs TO DISTRACT THEM.
I DON'T HAVE ANY CDs.
SORRY.
GRR!! THE INTERNET HAS KILLED MUSIC!!

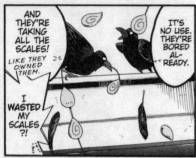

SOME-THING SHINY LIKE CDs... HUNH.
STARE
?
WE HAVE SHINY THINGS.
TONS.
HUH?
DINGA LING LING LING LING
HEY.
KEEP IT UP.
GAKAAAW?!
WE... WE DID IT?
IT'S NO USE. THEY'RE BORED AL-READY.
AND THEY'RE TAKING ALL THE SCALES!
LIKE THEY OWNED THEM.
I WASTED MY SCALES ?!
WE CAN ALSO TRY BLOCKING THEM WITH WIRES...
SRUPRUPRUP
TWANG
TWANG
......
A! SUPER! WIN!!!
SILENCE...
WE DID IT!!

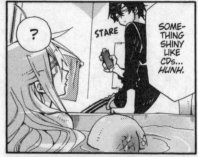

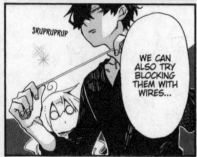

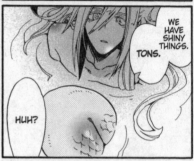

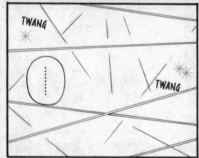

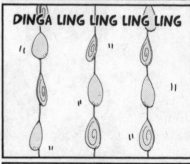

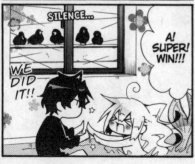

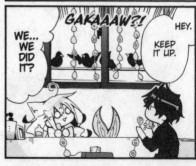

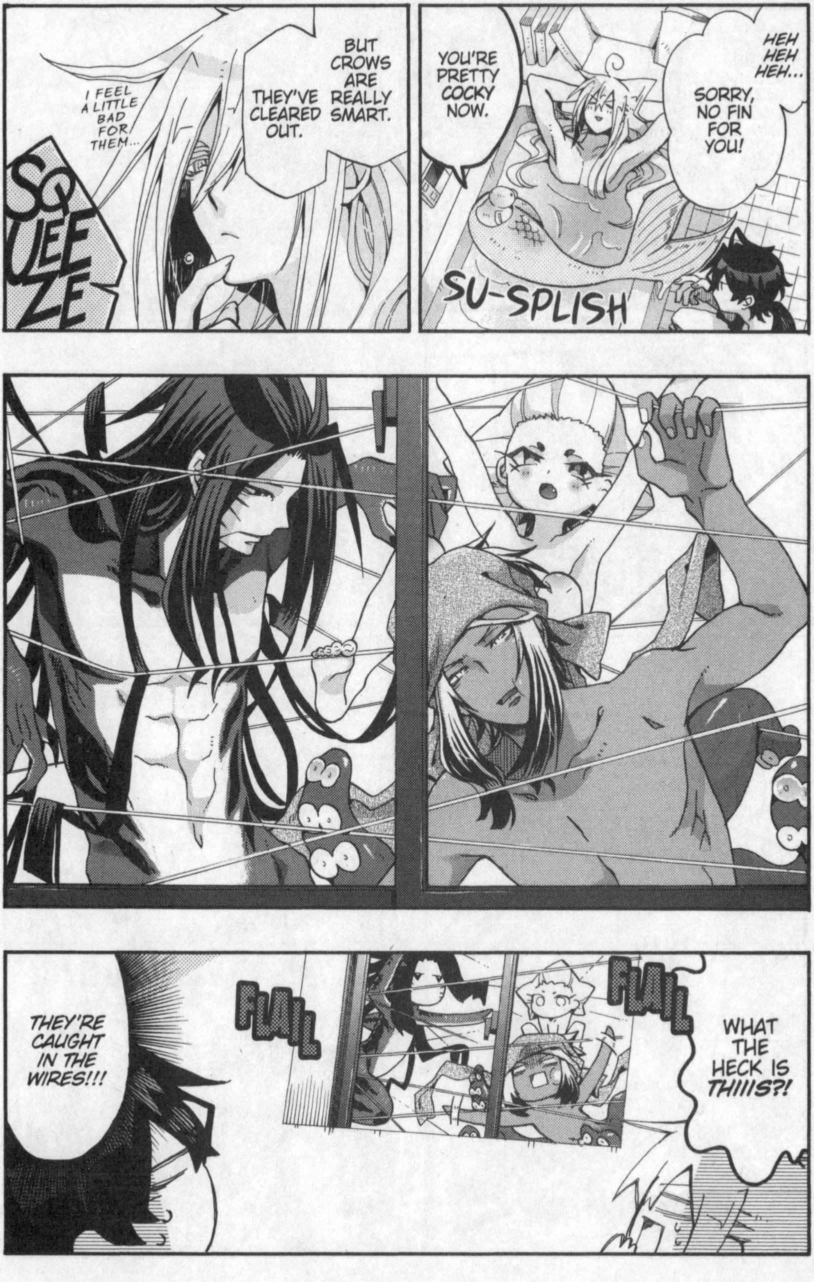
HEH HEH HEH...
SORRY, NO FIN FOR YOU!
YOU'RE PRETTY COCKY NOW.
SU-SPLISH
BUT CROWS ARE REALLY SMART.
THEY'VE CLEARED OUT.
I FEEL A LITTLE BAD FOR THEM...
SQUEEZE
WHAT THE HECK IS THIIIS?!
FLAIL
FLAIL
THEY'RE CAUGHT IN THE WIRES!!!

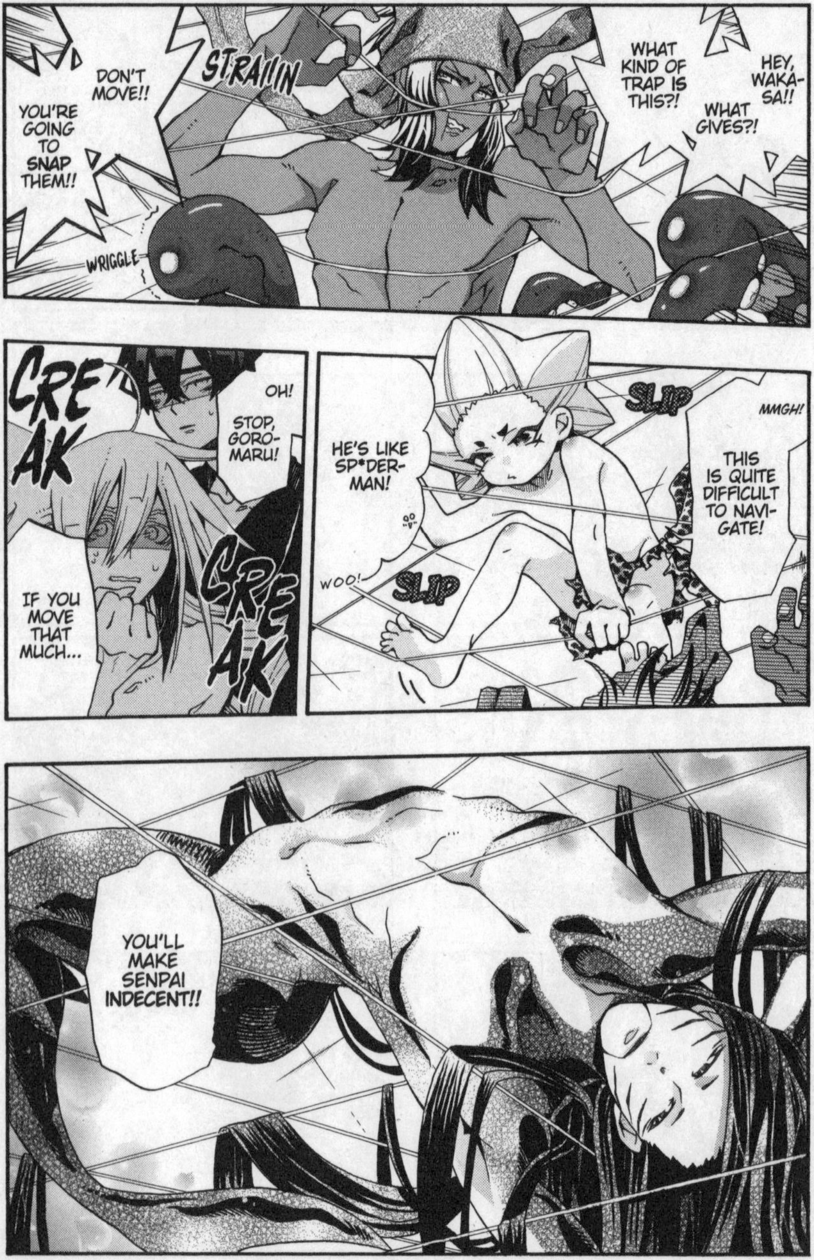
HEY, WAKA-SA!!
WHAT GIVES?!
WHAT KIND OF TRAP IS THIS?!
STRAIIIN
DON'T MOVE!!
YOU'RE GOING TO SNAP THEM!!
WRIGGLE
MMGH!
THIS IS QUITE DIFFICULT TO NAVI-GATE!
SLIP
HE'S LIKE SP*DER-MAN!
WOO!
SLIP
OH!
STOP, GORO-MARU!
CREAK
CREAK
IF YOU MOVE THAT MUCH...
YOU'LL MAKE SENPAI INDECENT!!

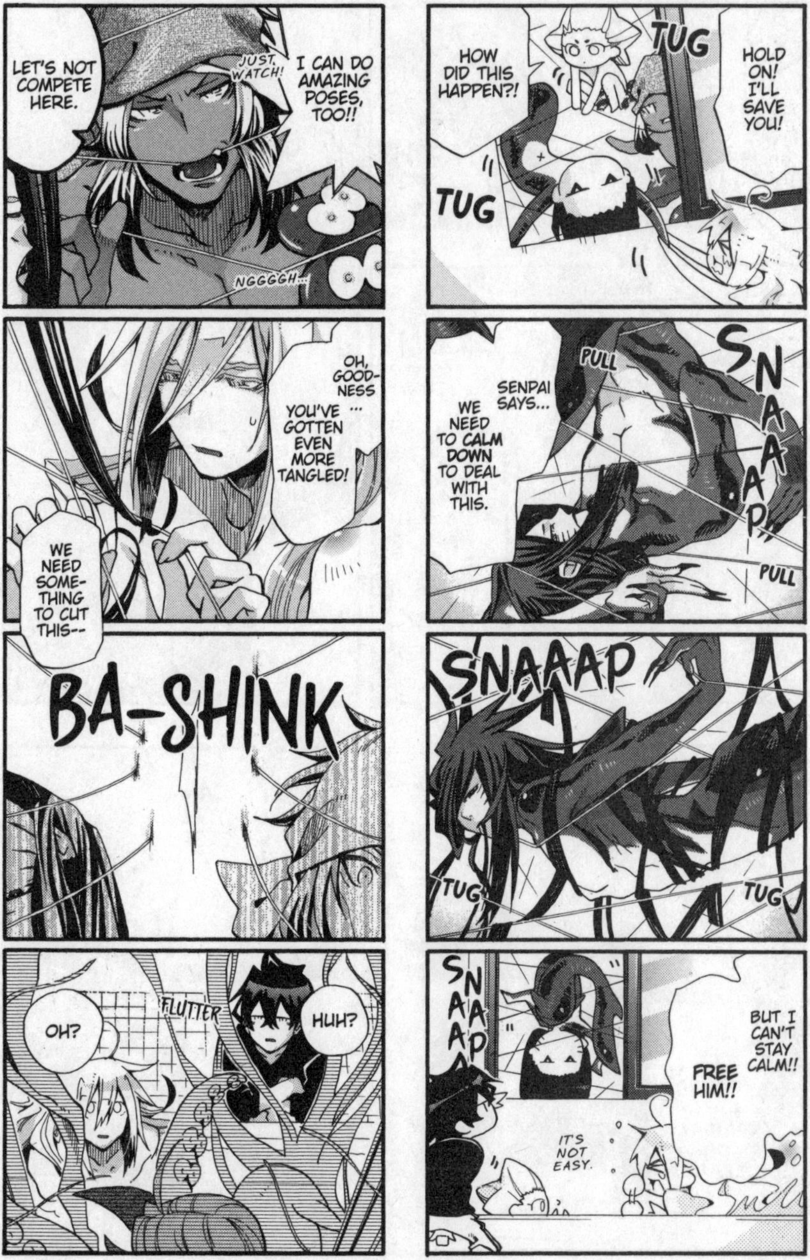
TUG
HOLD ON! I'LL SAVE YOU!
HOW DID THIS HAPPEN?!
TUG
SNAAAP
PULL
SENPAI SAYS...
WE NEED TO CALM DOWN TO DEAL WITH THIS.
PULL
SNAAAP
TUG
TUG
BUT I CAN'T STAY CALM!!
FREE HIM!!
IT'S NOT EASY.
SNAAAP
I CAN DO AMAZING POSES, TOO!!
JUST WATCH!
LET'S NOT COMPETE HERE.
NGGGGH...
OH, GOODNESS...
YOU'VE GOTTEN EVEN MORE TANGLED!
WE NEED SOMETHING TO CUT THIS--
BA-SHINK
HUH?
FLUTTER
OH?

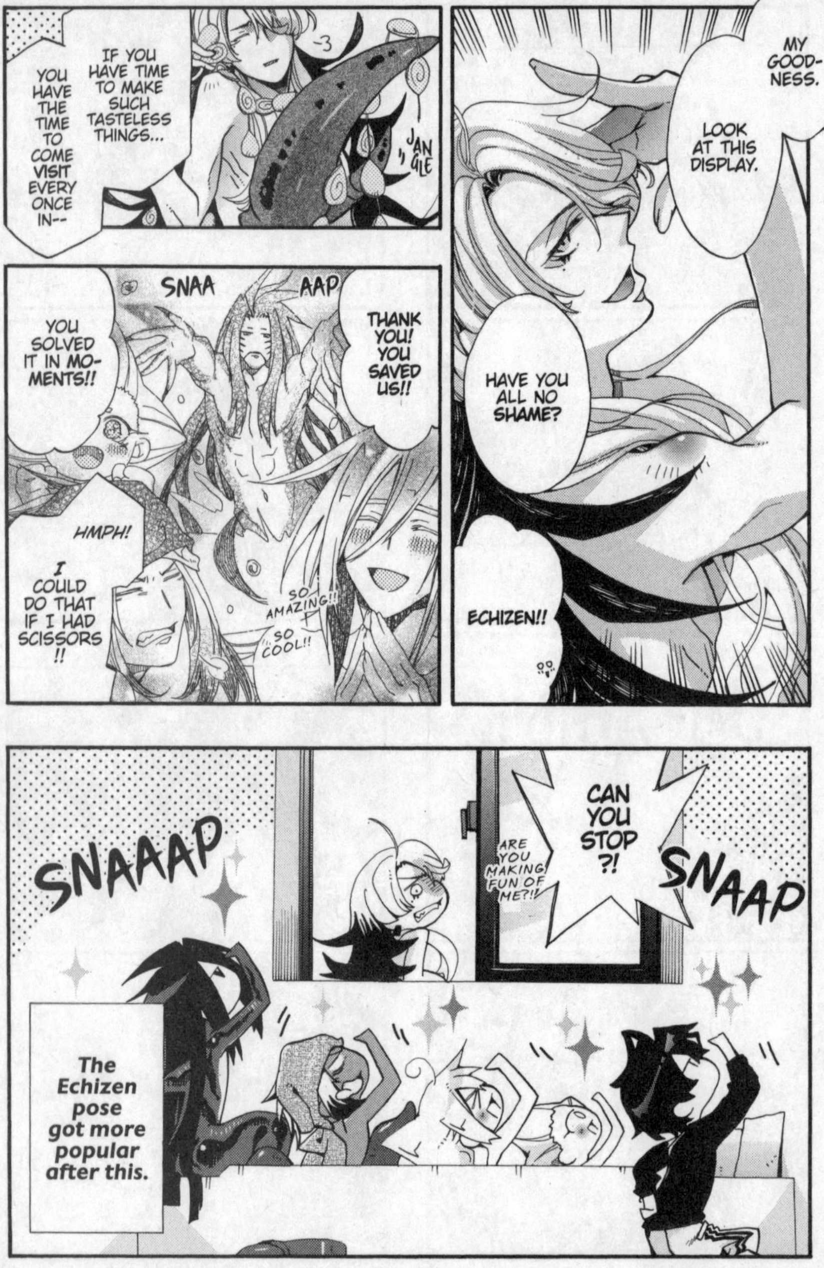
MY GOODNESS.
LOOK AT THIS DISPLAY.
HAVE YOU ALL NO SHAME?
ECHIZEN!!
JANGLE
IF YOU HAVE TIME TO MAKE SUCH TASTELESS THINGS...
YOU HAVE THE TIME TO COME VISIT EVERY ONCE IN--
SNAA AAP
THANK YOU! YOU SAVED US!!
YOU SOLVED IT IN MO-MENTS!!
SO AMAZING!!
SO COOL!!
HMPH!
I COULD DO THAT IF I HAD SCISSORS!!
SNAAP
CAN YOU STOP?!
ARE YOU MAKING FUN OF ME?!
SNAAAP
The Echizen pose got more popular after this.

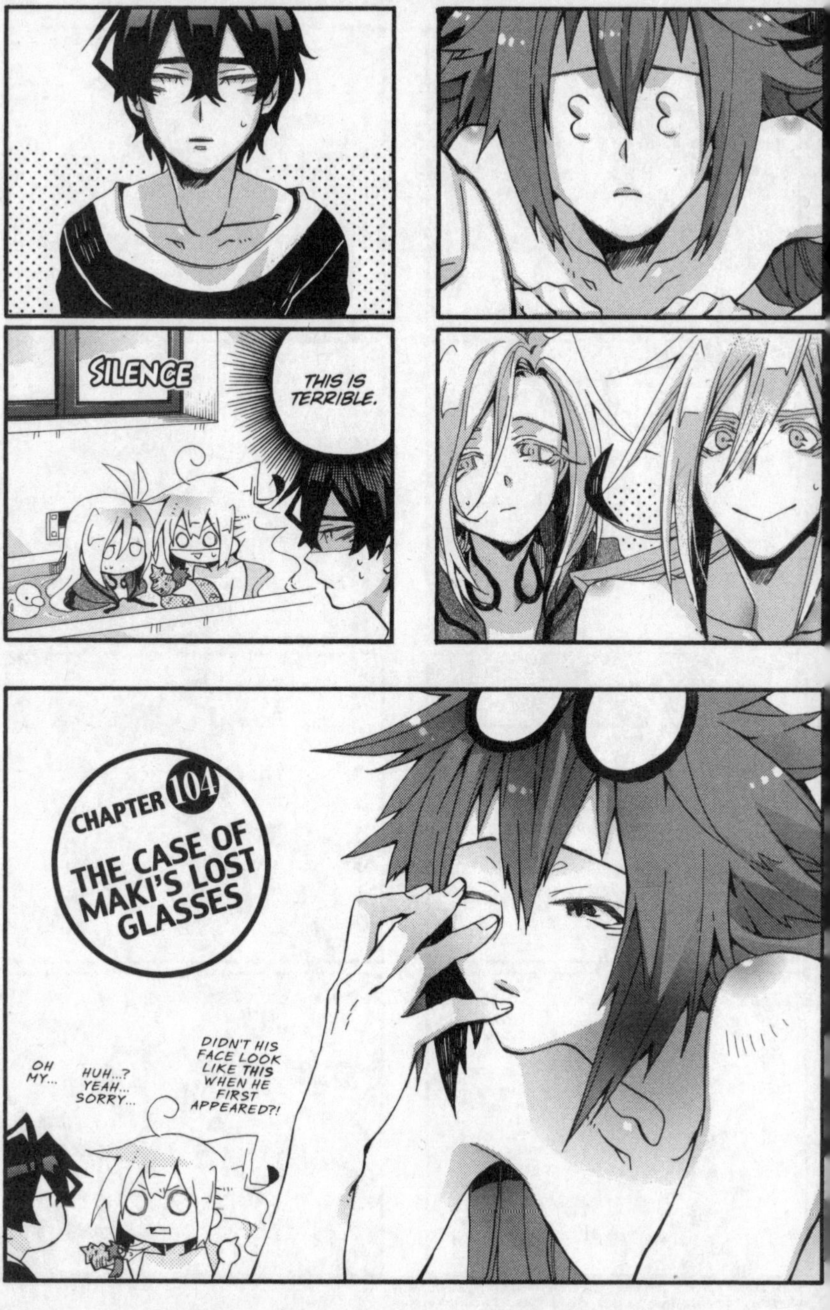
THIS IS TERRIBLE.
SILENCE
CHAPTER 104
THE CASE OF MAKI'S LOST GLASSES
DIDN'T HIS FACE LOOK LIKE THIS WHEN HE FIRST APPEARED?!
HUH...? YEAH... SORRY...
OH MY...

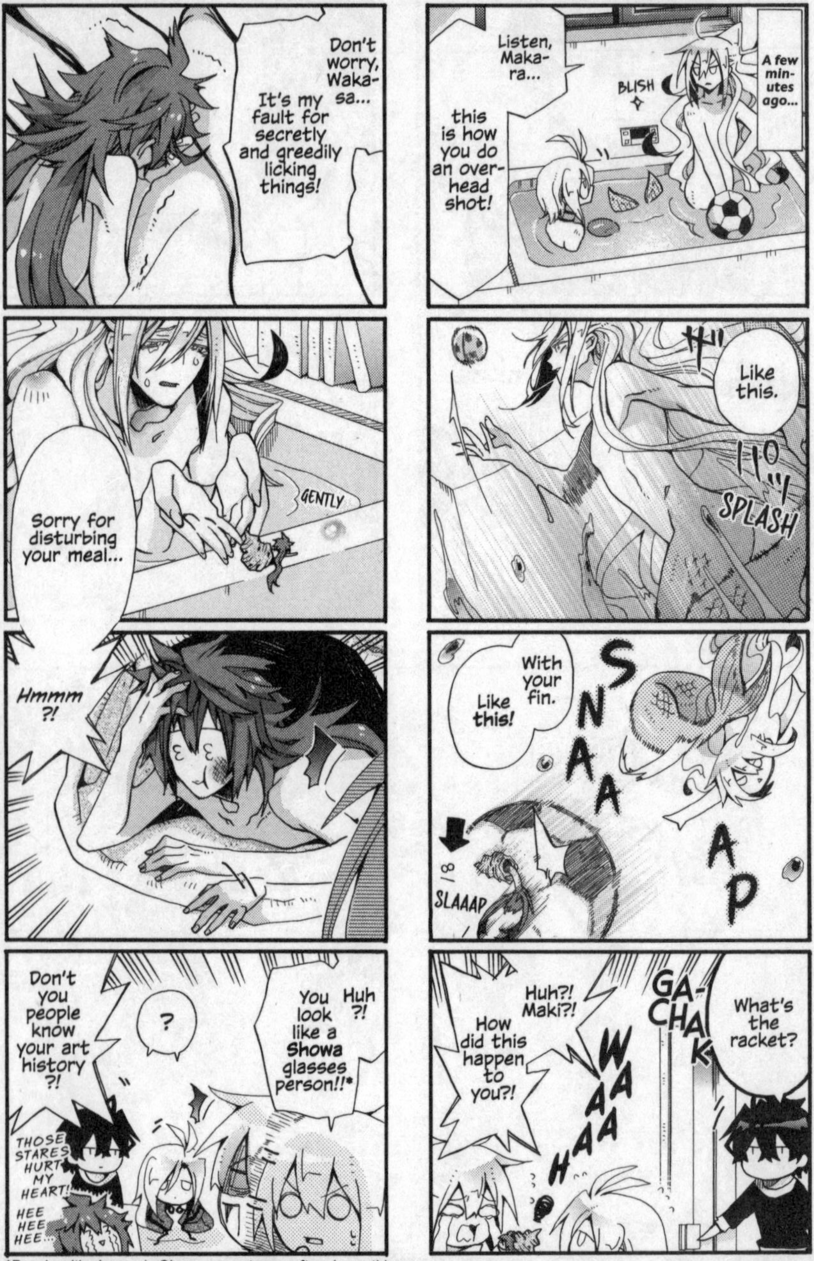
A few minutes ago...
Listen, Makara...
this is how you do an overhead shot!
BLISH
Don't worry, Waka-sa...
It's my fault for secretly and greedily licking things!
Like this.
SPLASH
GENTLY
Sorry for disturbing your meal...
With your fin.
Like this!
SNAAAAP
SLAAAP
Hmmm?!
What's the racket?
GA-CHAK
Huh?! Maki?!
How did this happen to you?!
WAAAAH
Huh?!
You look like a Showa glasses person!!*
?
Don't you people know your art history?!
THOSE STARES HURT MY HEART!
HEE HEE HEE...

*People with glasses in Showa-era art were often drawn this way when they removed their glasses. We're now in the Reiwa era.

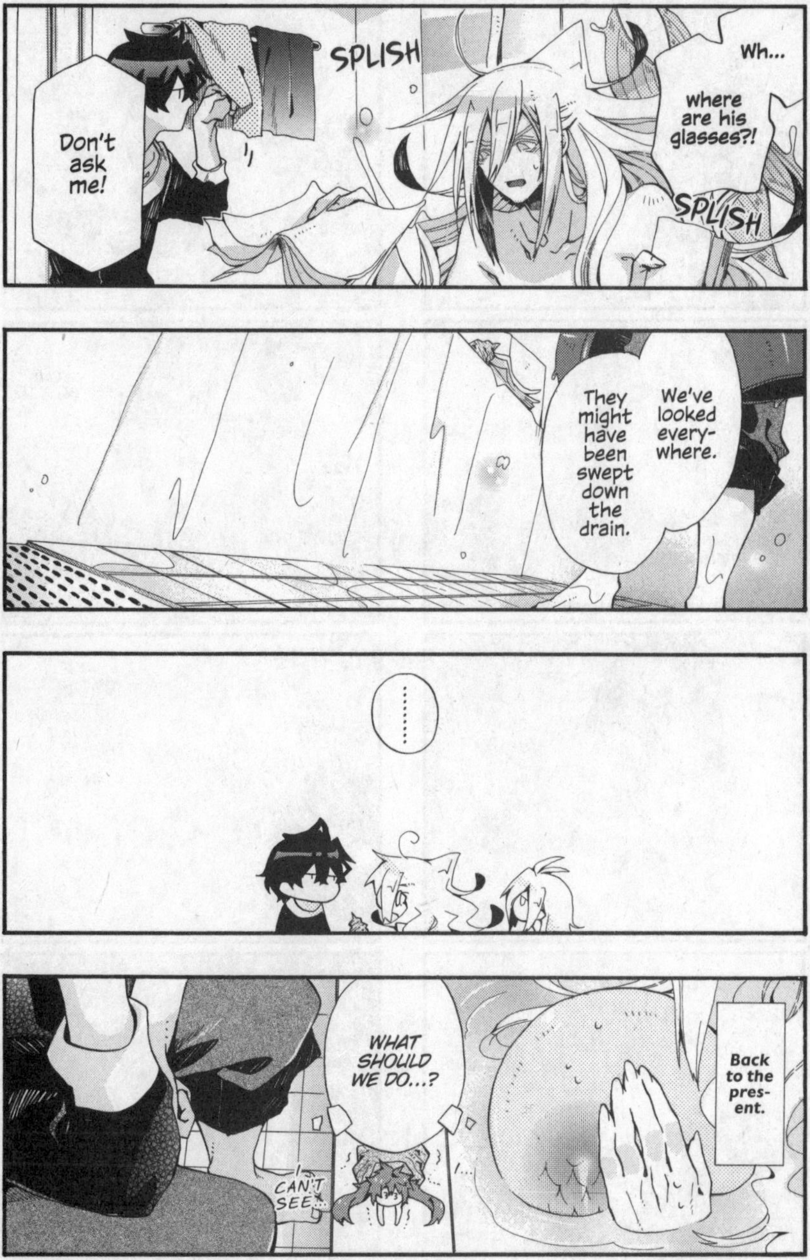
Wh...
where are his glasses?!
SPLISH
SPLISH
Don't ask me!
We've looked every-where.
They might have been swept down the drain.
......
Back to the pres-ent.
WHAT SHOULD WE DO...?
I... CAN'T SEE...

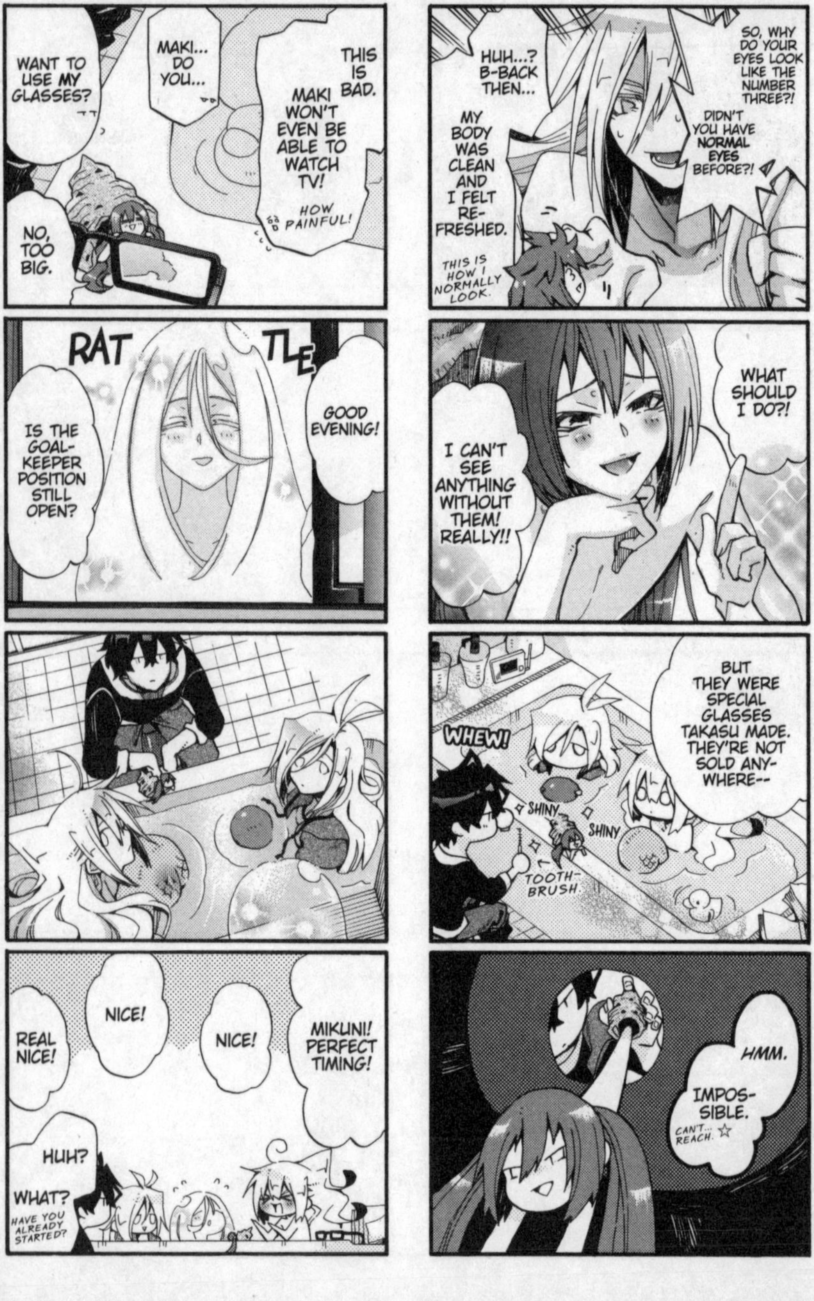
SO, WHY DO YOUR EYES LOOK LIKE THE NUMBER THREE?!
DIDN'T YOU HAVE NORMAL EYES BEFORE?!
HUH...? B-BACK THEN...
MY BODY WAS CLEAN AND I FELT RE-FRESHED.
THIS IS HOW I NORMALLY LOOK.
WHAT SHOULD I DO?!
I CAN'T SEE ANYTHING WITHOUT THEM! REALLY!!
BUT THEY WERE SPECIAL GLASSES TAKASU MADE. THEY'RE NOT SOLD ANY-WHERE--
WHEW!
SHINY
SHINY
TOOTH-BRUSH
HMM.
IMPOS-SIBLE.
CAN'T... REACH. ☆
THIS IS BAD.
MAKI WON'T EVEN BE ABLE TO WATCH TV!
HOW PAINFUL!
MAKI... DO YOU...
WANT TO USE MY GLASSES?
NO, TOO BIG.
RATTLE
GOOD EVENING!
IS THE GOAL-KEEPER POSITION STILL OPEN?
MIKUNI! PERFECT TIMING!
NICE!
NICE!
REAL NICE!
HUH?
WHAT?
HAVE YOU ALREADY STARTED?

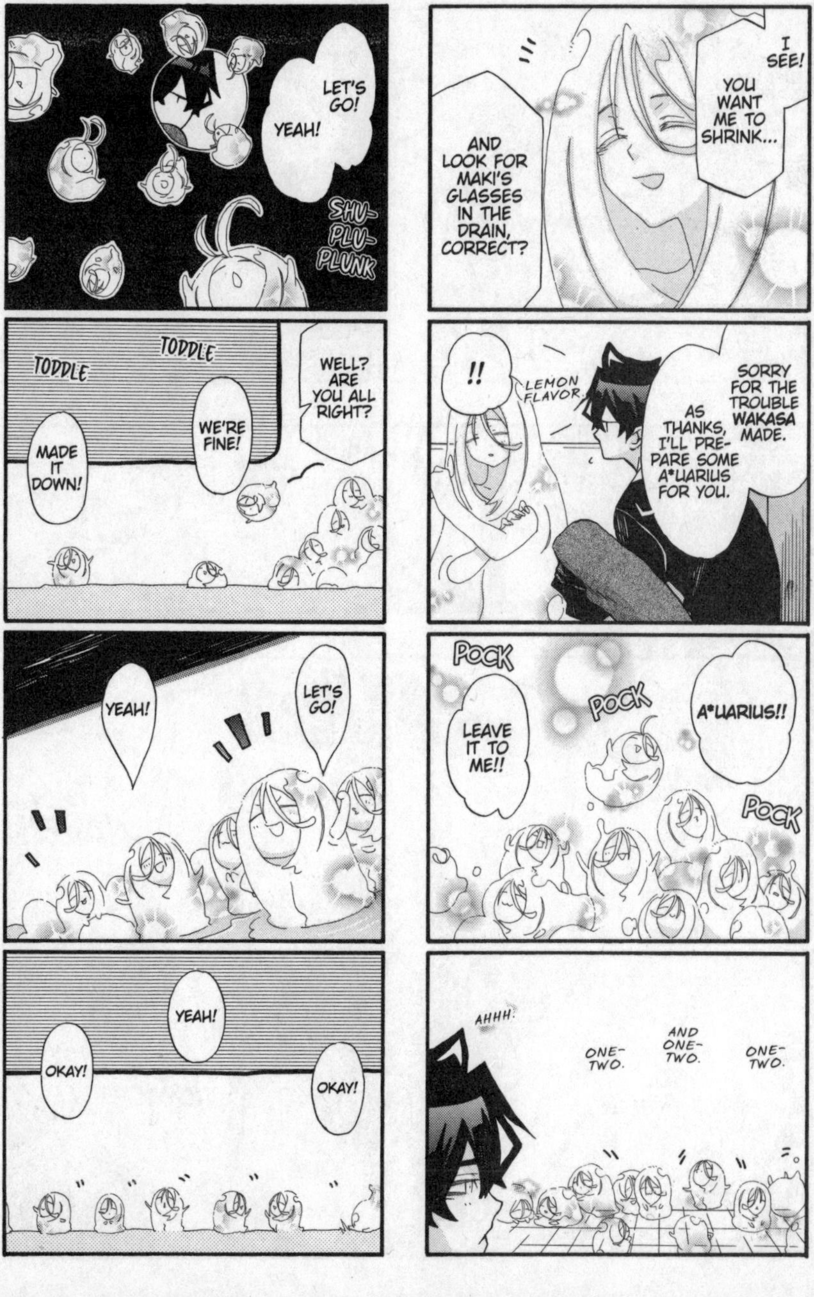
I SEE!
YOU WANT ME TO SHRINK...
AND LOOK FOR MAKI'S GLASSES IN THE DRAIN, CORRECT?
LET'S GO!
YEAH!
SHU-PLU-PLUNK
SORRY FOR THE TROUBLE WAKASA MADE.
AS THANKS, I'LL PREPARE SOME A*UARIUS FOR YOU.
LEMON FLAVOR.
!!
WELL? ARE YOU ALL RIGHT?
TODDLE
WE'RE FINE!
TODDLE
MADE IT DOWN!
A*UARIUS!!
POCK
POCK
LEAVE IT TO ME!!
POCK
LET'S GO!
YEAH!
ONE-TWO.
AND ONE-TWO.
ONE-TWO.
AHHH.
OKAY!
YEAH!
OKAY!

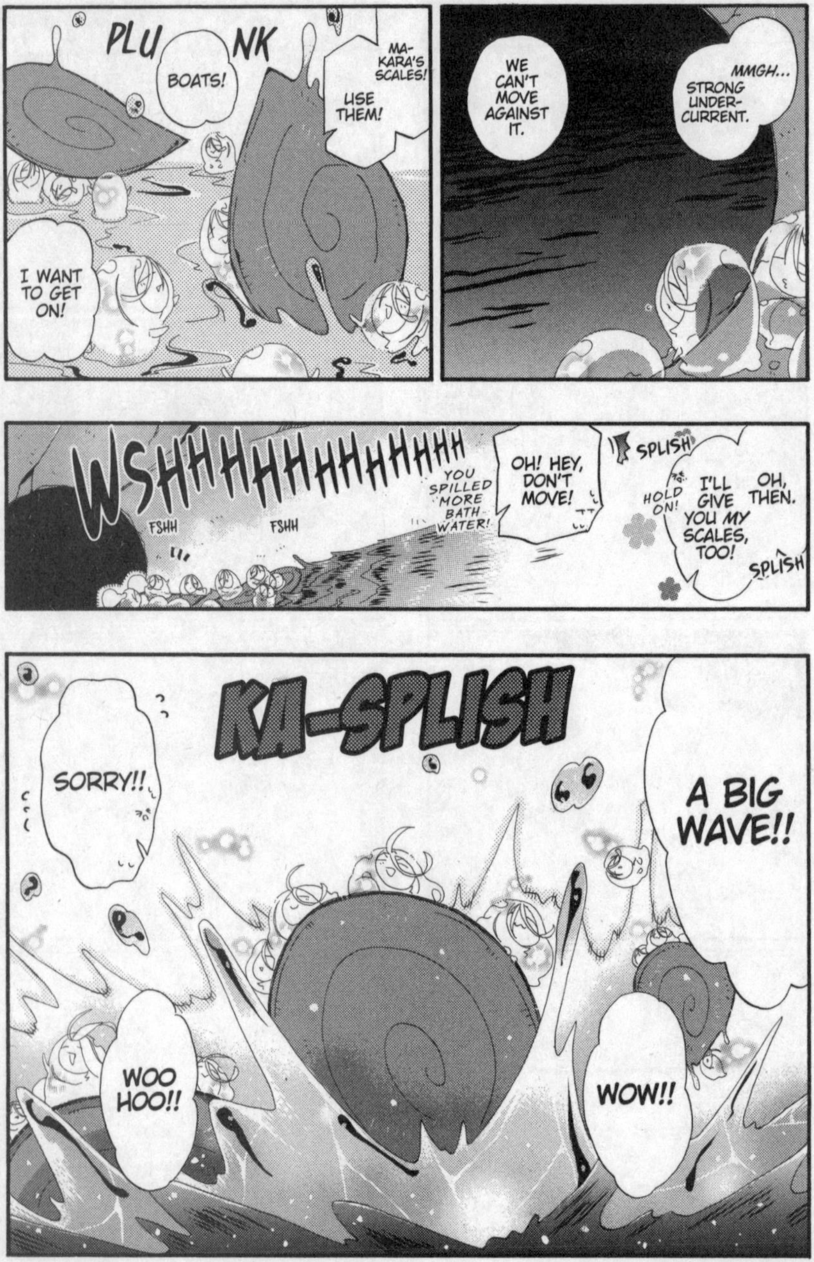
MMGH... STRONG UNDER-CURRENT.
WE CAN'T MOVE AGAINST IT.
MA-KARA'S SCALES!
USE THEM!
PLU NK
BOATS!
I WANT TO GET ON!
SPLISH
OH, THEN. I'LL GIVE YOU MY SCALES, TOO!
SPLISH
HOLD ON!
OH! HEY, DON'T MOVE!
YOU SPILLED MORE BATH WATER!
WSHHHHHHHHHHHHH
FSHH
FSHH
A BIG WAVE!!
KA-SPLISH
SORRY!!
WOW!!
WOO HOO!!

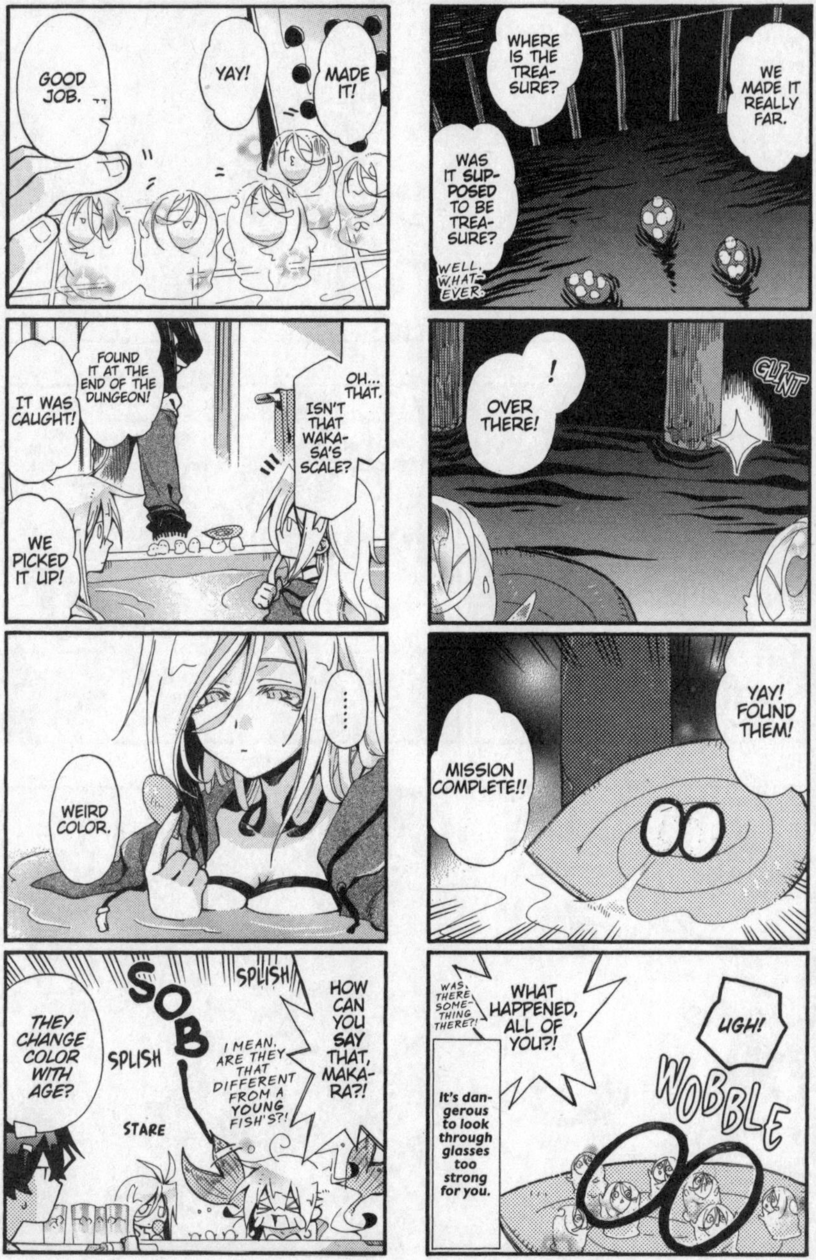
WE MADE IT REALLY FAR.
WHERE IS THE TREASURE?
WAS IT SUPPOSED TO BE TREASURE?
WELL, WHATEVER.
GLINT
!
OVER THERE!
YAY! FOUND THEM!
MISSION COMPLETE!!
UGH!
WOBBLE
WHAT HAPPENED, ALL OF YOU?!
WAS THERE SOMETHING THERE?!
It's dangerous to look through glasses too strong for you.
MADE IT!
YAY!
GOOD JOB.
OH... THAT. ISN'T THAT WAKASA'S SCALE?
FOUND IT AT THE END OF THE DUNGEON!
IT WAS CAUGHT!
WE PICKED IT UP!
......
WEIRD COLOR.
HOW CAN YOU SAY THAT, MAKARA?!
SPLISH
SOB
I MEAN, ARE THEY THAT DIFFERENT FROM A YOUNG FISH'S?!
SPLISH
THEY CHANGE COLOR WITH AGE?
STARE

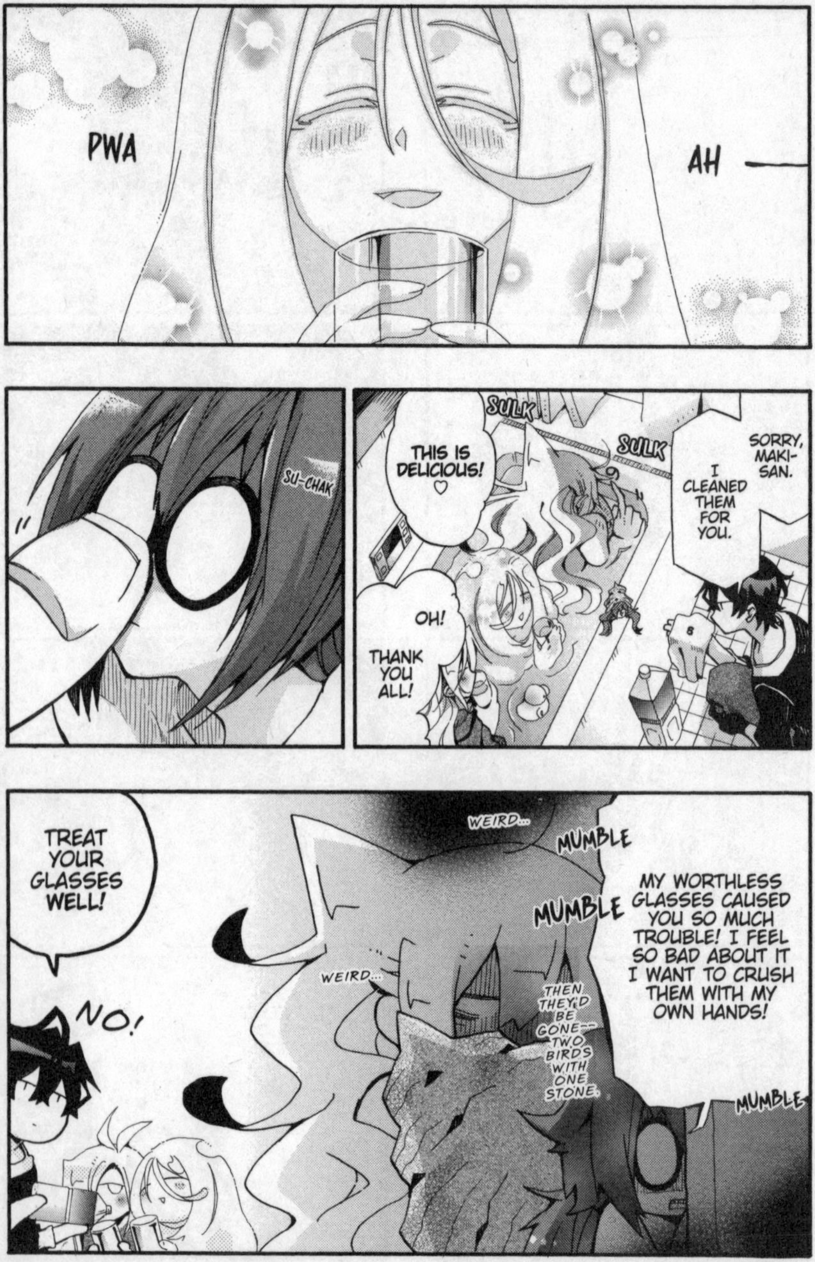
AH —
PWA
SORRY, MAKI-SAN.
I CLEANED THEM FOR YOU.
SULK
SULK
THIS IS DELICIOUS! ♡
OH!
THANK YOU ALL!
SU-CHAK
WEIRD...
MUMBLE
MY WORTHLESS GLASSES CAUSED YOU SO MUCH TROUBLE! I FEEL SO BAD ABOUT IT I WANT TO CRUSH THEM WITH MY OWN HANDS!
MUMBLE
THEN THEY'D BE GONE-- TWO BIRDS WITH ONE STONE.
MUMBLE
WEIRD...
TREAT YOUR GLASSES WELL!
NO!

Merman
in My Tub

オレん家のフロ事情

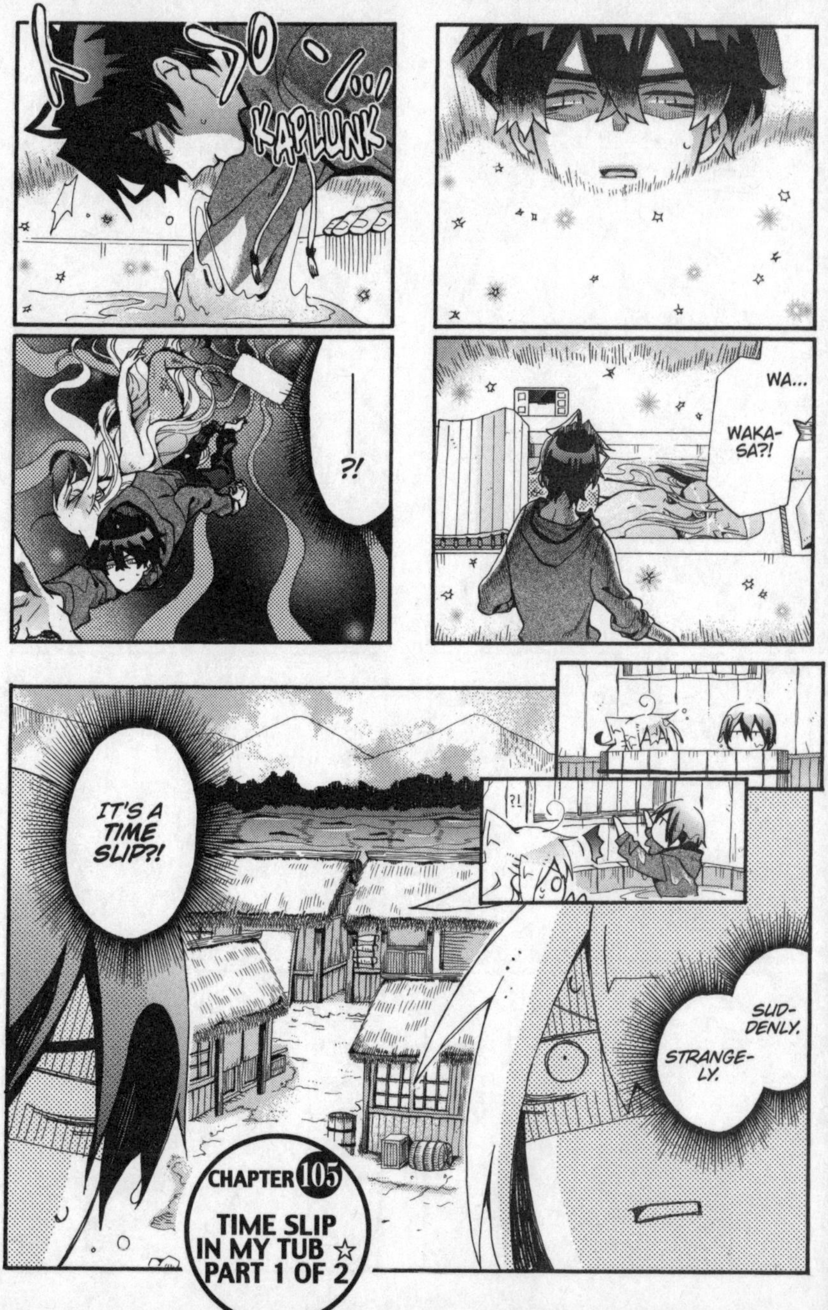
KAPLUNK
WA...
WAKA-SA?!
——
?!
?!
SUD-DENLY.
STRANGE-LY.
IT'S A TIME SLIP?!
CHAPTER 105
TIME SLIP IN MY TUB ☆ PART 1 OF 2

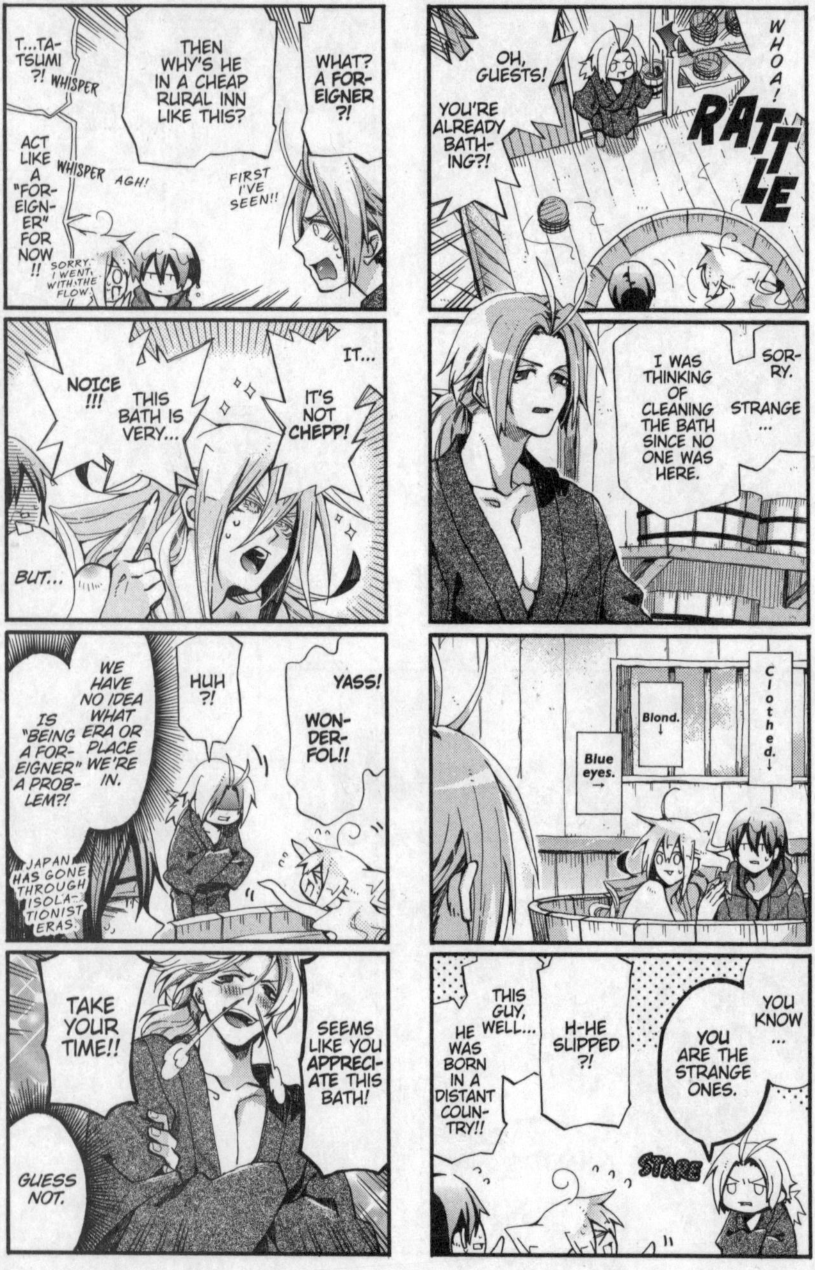
WHOA!
RATTLE
OH, GUESTS!
YOU'RE ALREADY BATHING?!
SORRY. STRANGE...
I WAS THINKING OF CLEANING THE BATH SINCE NO ONE WAS HERE.
Clothed.↓
Blond.↓
Blue eyes.→
YOU KNOW... YOU ARE THE STRANGE ONES.
H-HE SLIPPED?!
THIS GUY, WELL... HE WAS BORN IN A DISTANT COUNTRY!!
STARE
WHAT? A FOREIGNER?!
FIRST I'VE SEEN!!
THEN WHY'S HE IN A CHEAP RURAL INN LIKE THIS?
T...TATSUMI?! WHISPER
ACT LIKE A "FOREIGNER" FOR NOW!! WHISPER
AGH!
SORRY. I WENT WITH THE FLOW.
IT... IT'S NOT CHEPP!
THIS BATH IS VERY...
NOICE!!!
BUT...
YASS! WONDERFOL!!
HUH?!
WE HAVE NO IDEA WHAT ERA OR PLACE WE'RE IN.
IS "BEING A FOREIGNER" A PROBLEM?!
JAPAN HAS GONE THROUGH ISOLATIONIST ERAS.
SEEMS LIKE YOU APPRECIATE THIS BATH!
TAKE YOUR TIME!!
GUESS NOT.

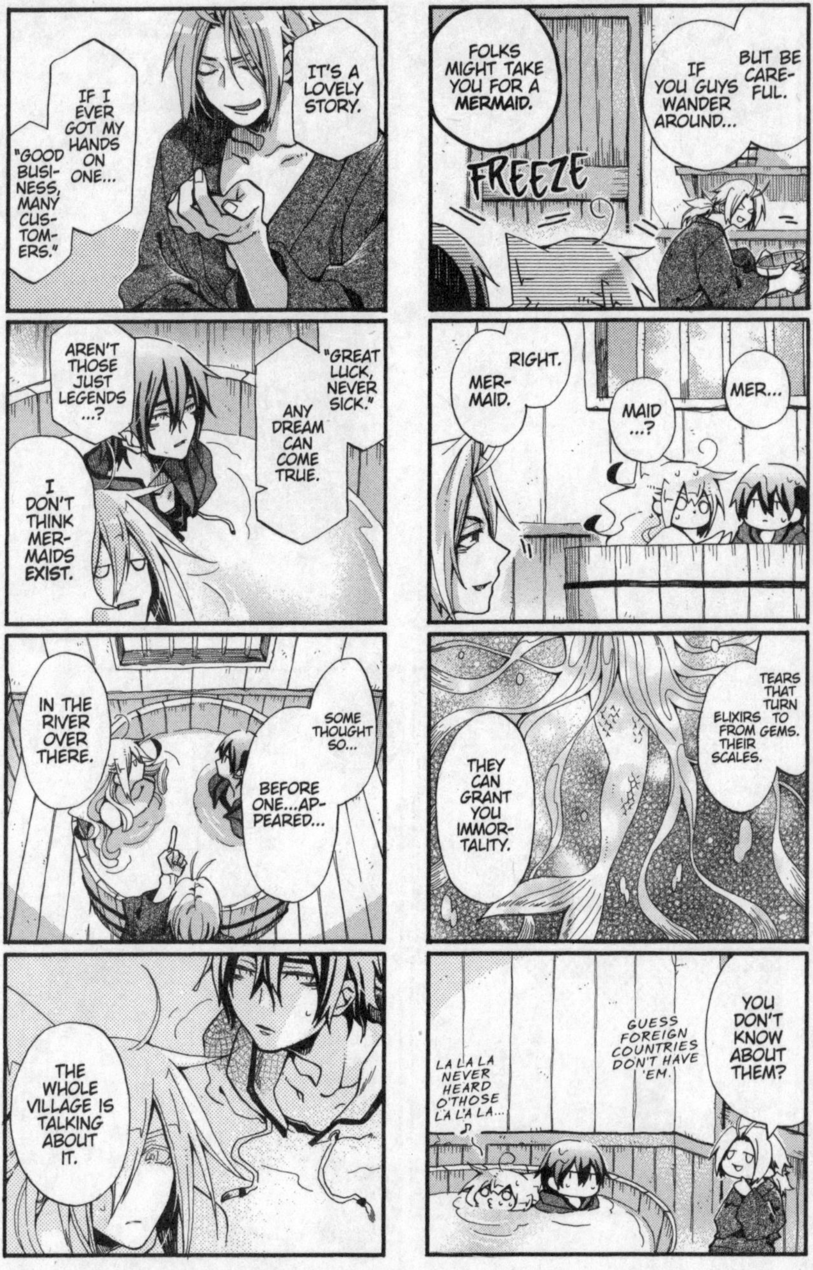
BUT BE CAREFUL.
IF YOU GUYS WANDER AROUND...
FOLKS MIGHT TAKE YOU FOR A MERMAID.
FREEZE
MER...
MAID ...?
RIGHT.
MERMAID.
TEARS THAT TURN TO GEMS.
ELIXIRS FROM THEIR SCALES.
THEY CAN GRANT YOU IMMORTALITY.
YOU DON'T KNOW ABOUT THEM?
GUESS FOREIGN COUNTRIES DON'T HAVE 'EM.
LA LA LA NEVER HEARD O'THOSE LA LA LA... ♪
IT'S A LOVELY STORY.
IF I EVER GOT MY HANDS ON ONE...
"GOOD BUSINESS, MANY CUSTOMERS."
"GREAT LUCK, NEVER SICK."
ANY DREAM CAN COME TRUE.
AREN'T THOSE JUST LEGENDS ...?
I DON'T THINK MERMAIDS EXIST.
SOME THOUGHT SO...
BEFORE ONE...APPEARED...
IN THE RIVER OVER THERE.
THE WHOLE VILLAGE IS TALKING ABOUT IT.

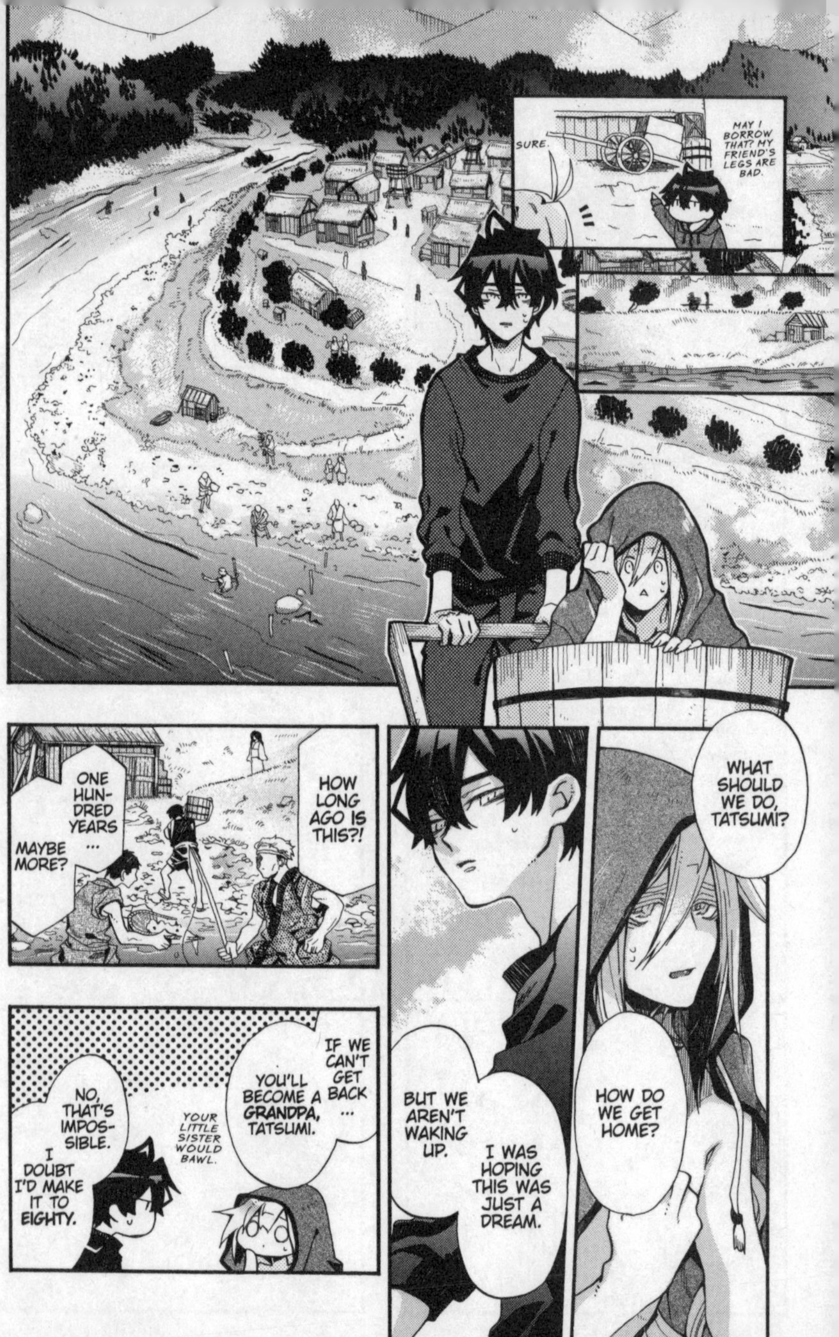
MAY I BORROW THAT? MY FRIEND'S LEGS ARE BAD.
SURE.
WHAT SHOULD WE DO, TATSUMI?
HOW DO WE GET HOME?
I WAS HOPING THIS WAS JUST A DREAM.
BUT WE AREN'T WAKING UP.
HOW LONG AGO IS THIS?!
ONE HUNDRED YEARS...
MAYBE MORE?
IF WE CAN'T GET BACK...
YOU'LL BECOME A GRANDPA, TATSUMI.
YOUR LITTLE SISTER WOULD BAWL.
NO, THAT'S IMPOSSIBLE.
I DOUBT I'D MAKE IT TO EIGHTY.

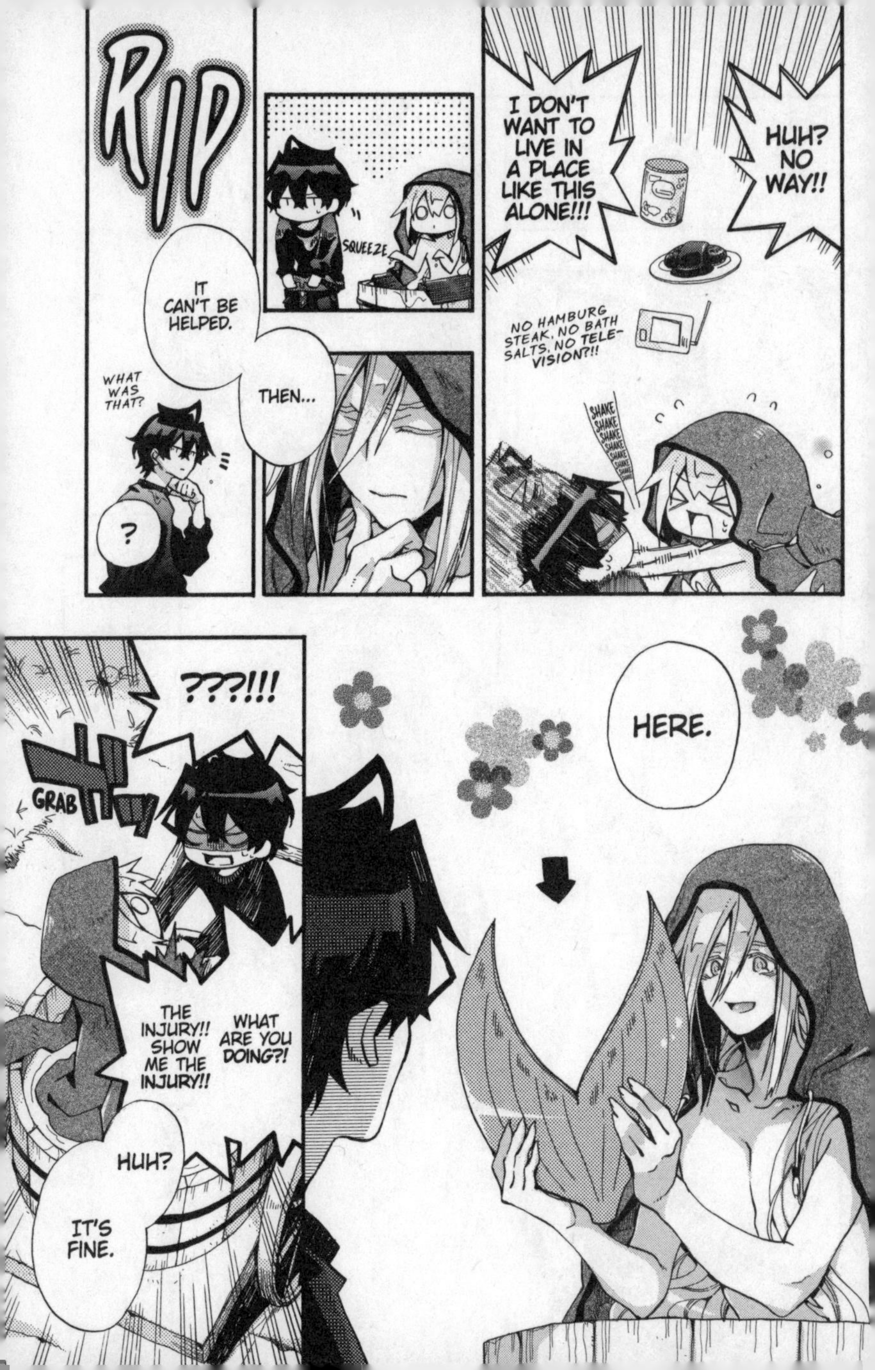
HUH? NO WAY!!
I DON'T WANT TO LIVE IN A PLACE LIKE THIS ALONE!!!
NO HAMBURG STEAK, NO BATH SALTS, NO TELE-VISION?!!
SHAKE SHAKE SHAKE SHAKE SHAKE SHAKE SHAKE
SQUEEZE
IT CAN'T BE HELPED.
THEN...
RIP
WHAT WAS THAT?
?
HERE.
???!!!
GRAB
WHAT ARE YOU DOING?!
THE INJURY!! SHOW ME THE INJURY!!
HUH?
IT'S FINE.

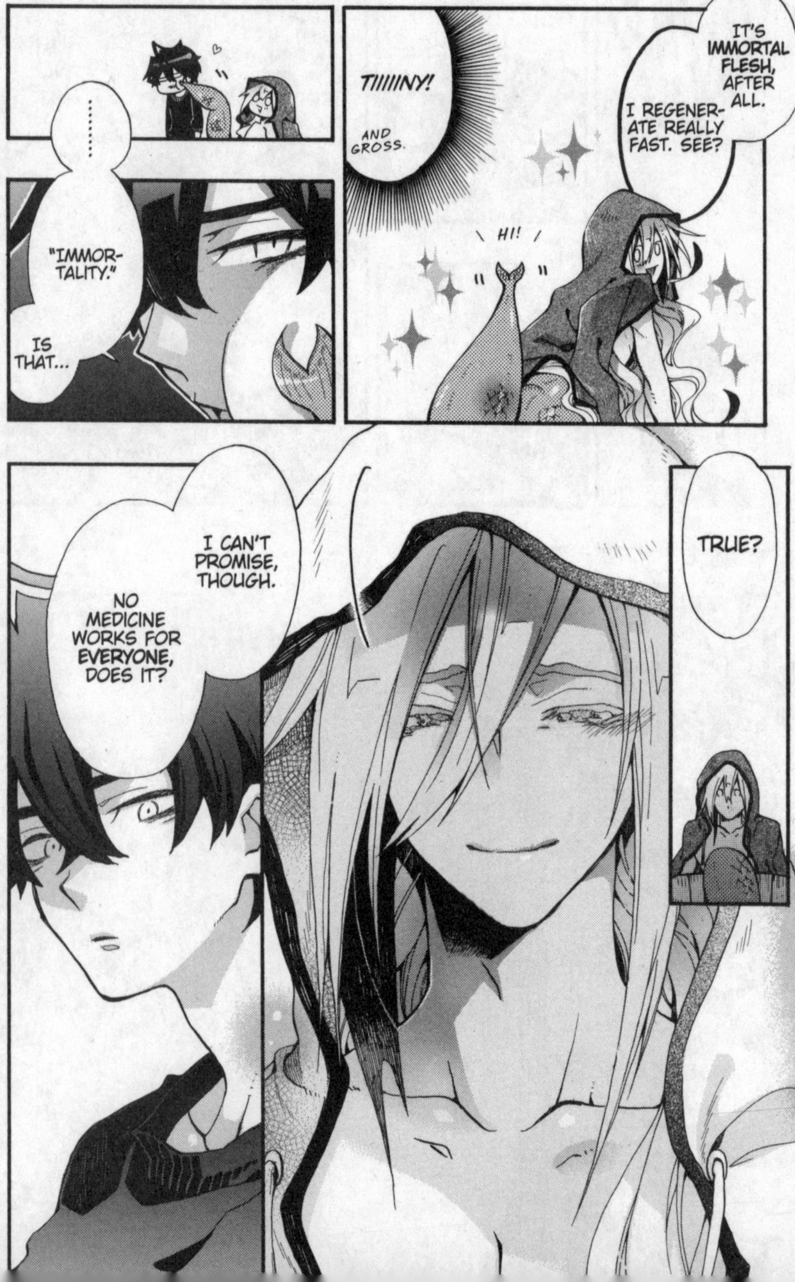
IT'S IMMORTAL FLESH, AFTER ALL.
I REGENERATE REALLY FAST. SEE?
HI!
TIIIIINY!
AND GROSS.
......
"IMMORTALITY."
IS THAT...
TRUE?
I CAN'T PROMISE, THOUGH.
NO MEDICINE WORKS FOR EVERYONE, DOES IT?

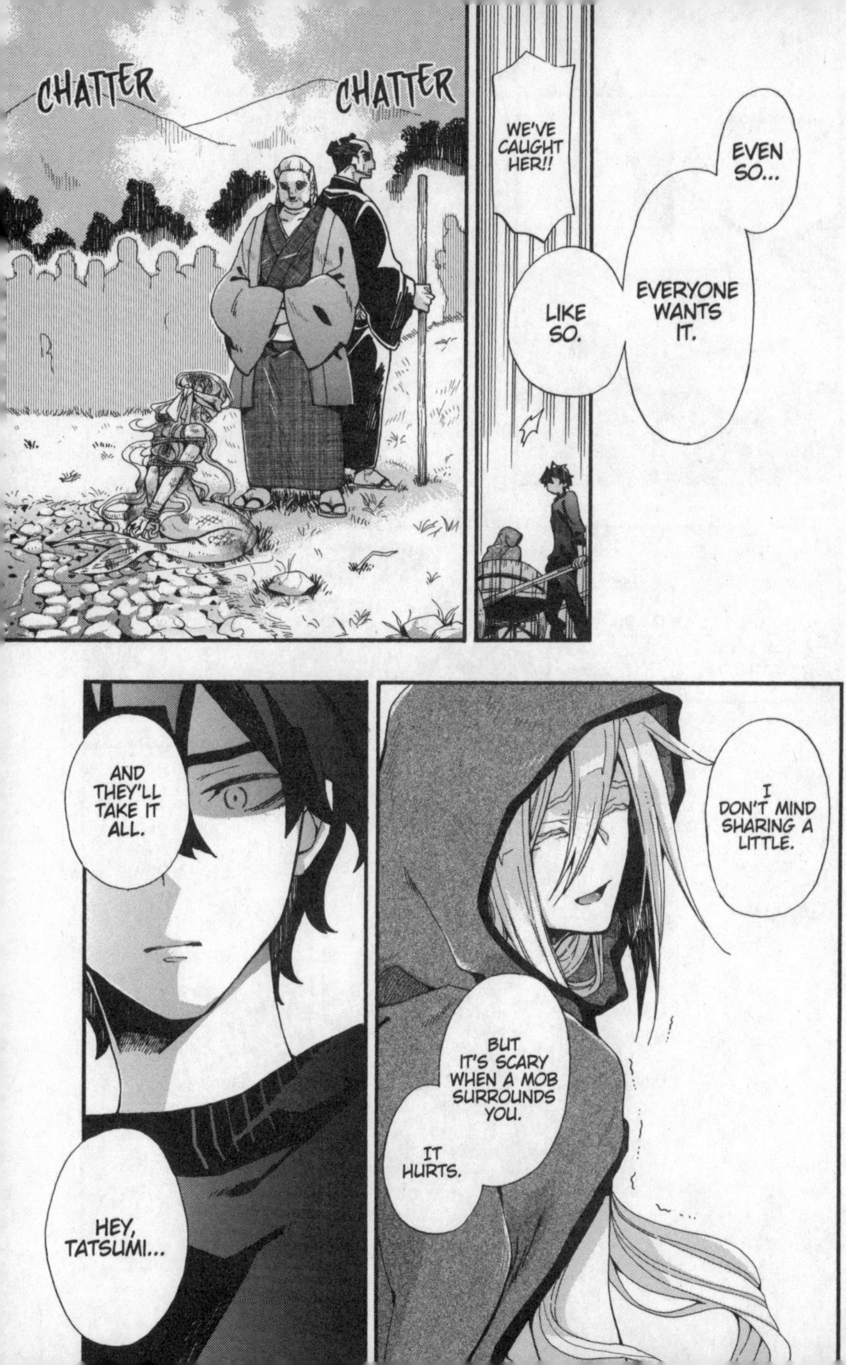
WE'VE CAUGHT HER!!
EVEN SO...
EVERYONE WANTS IT.
LIKE SO.
CHATTER
CHATTER
I DON'T MIND SHARING A LITTLE.
BUT IT'S SCARY WHEN A MOB SURROUNDS YOU.
IT HURTS.
AND THEY'LL TAKE IT ALL.
HEY, TATSUMI...

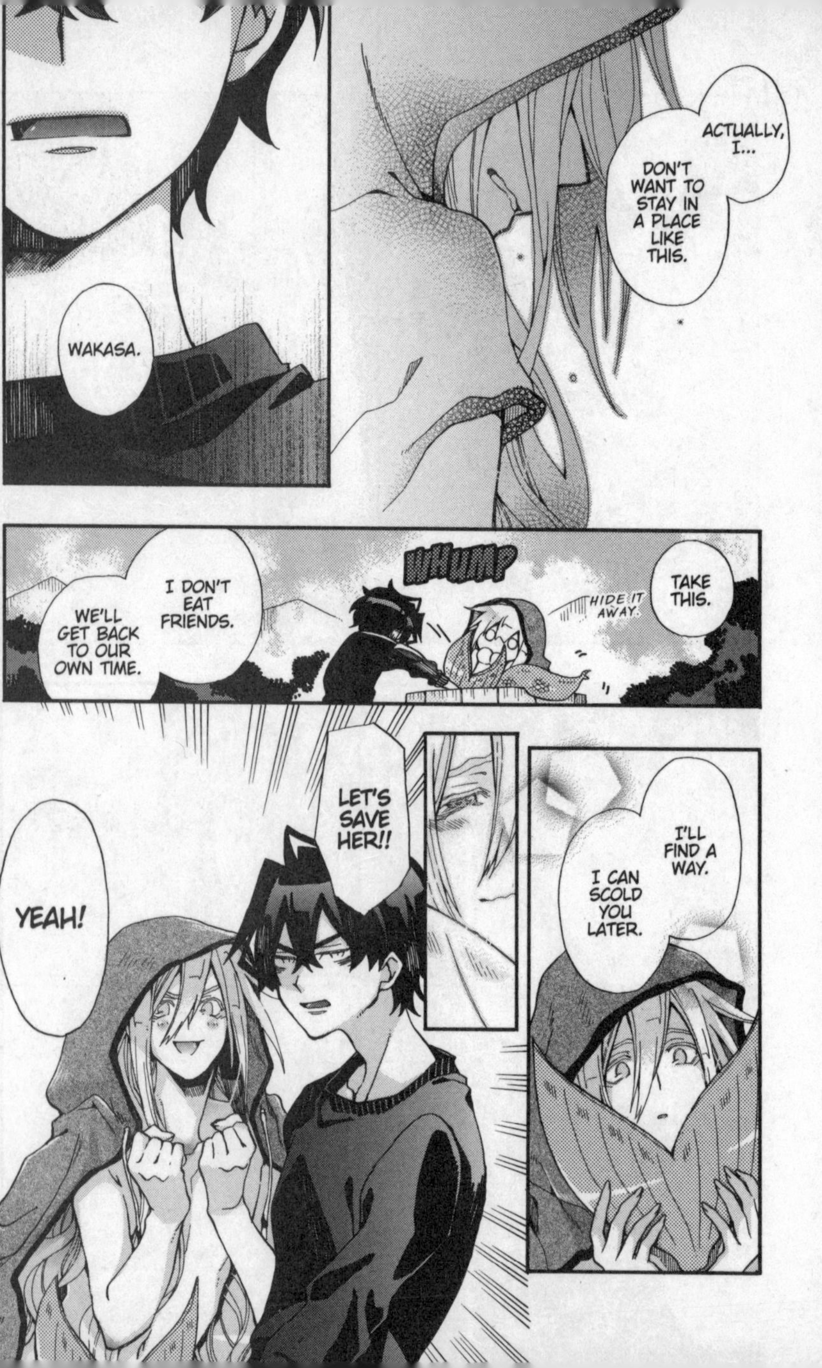
ACTUALLY, I...
DON'T WANT TO STAY IN A PLACE LIKE THIS.
WAKASA.
TAKE THIS.
HIDE IT AWAY.
WHUMP
I DON'T EAT FRIENDS.
WE'LL GET BACK TO OUR OWN TIME.
I'LL FIND A WAY.
I CAN SCOLD YOU LATER.
LET'S SAVE HER!!
YEAH!

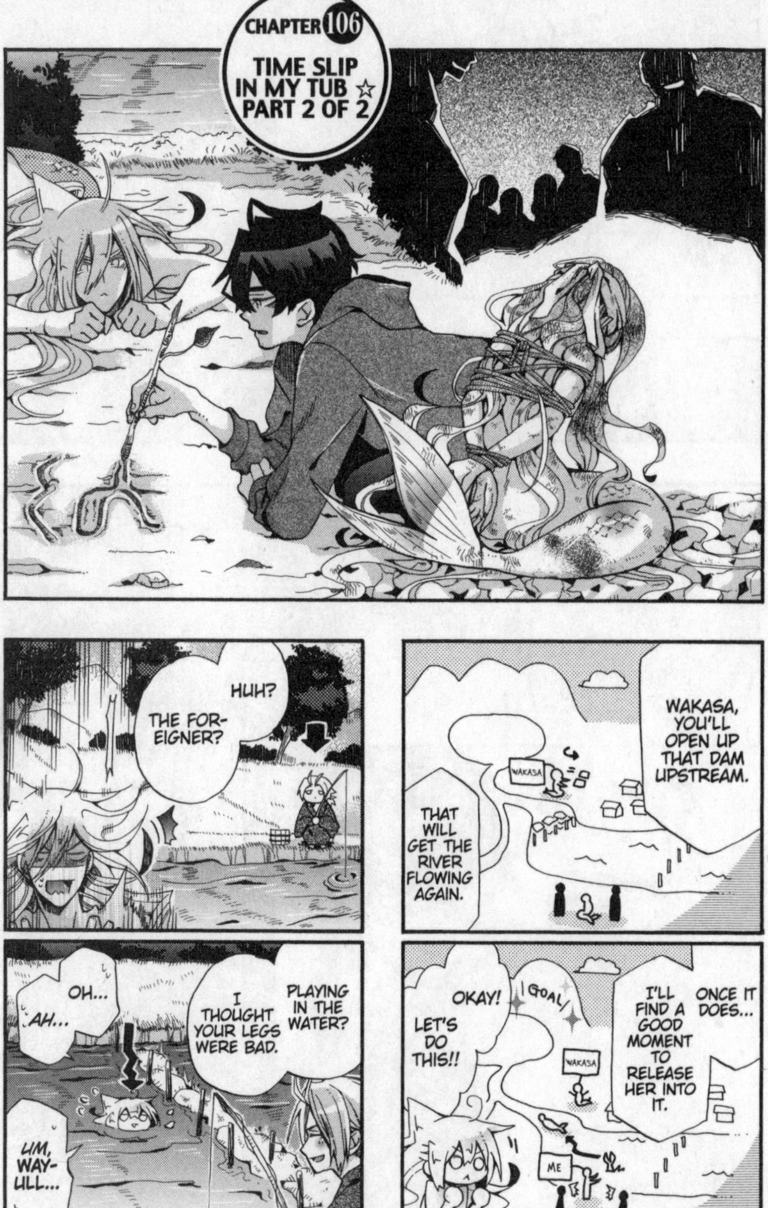
CHAPTER 106
TIME SLIP IN MY TUB ☆ PART 2 OF 2
WAKASA, YOU'LL OPEN UP THAT DAM UPSTREAM.
WAKASA
THAT WILL GET THE RIVER FLOWING AGAIN.
HUH?
THE FOR-EIGNER?
ONCE IT DOES...
I'LL FIND A GOOD MOMENT TO RELEASE HER INTO IT.
GOAL
WAKASA
ME
OKAY!
LET'S DO THIS!!
PLAYING IN THE WATER?
I THOUGHT YOUR LEGS WERE BAD.
OH...
AH...
UM, WAY-ULL...

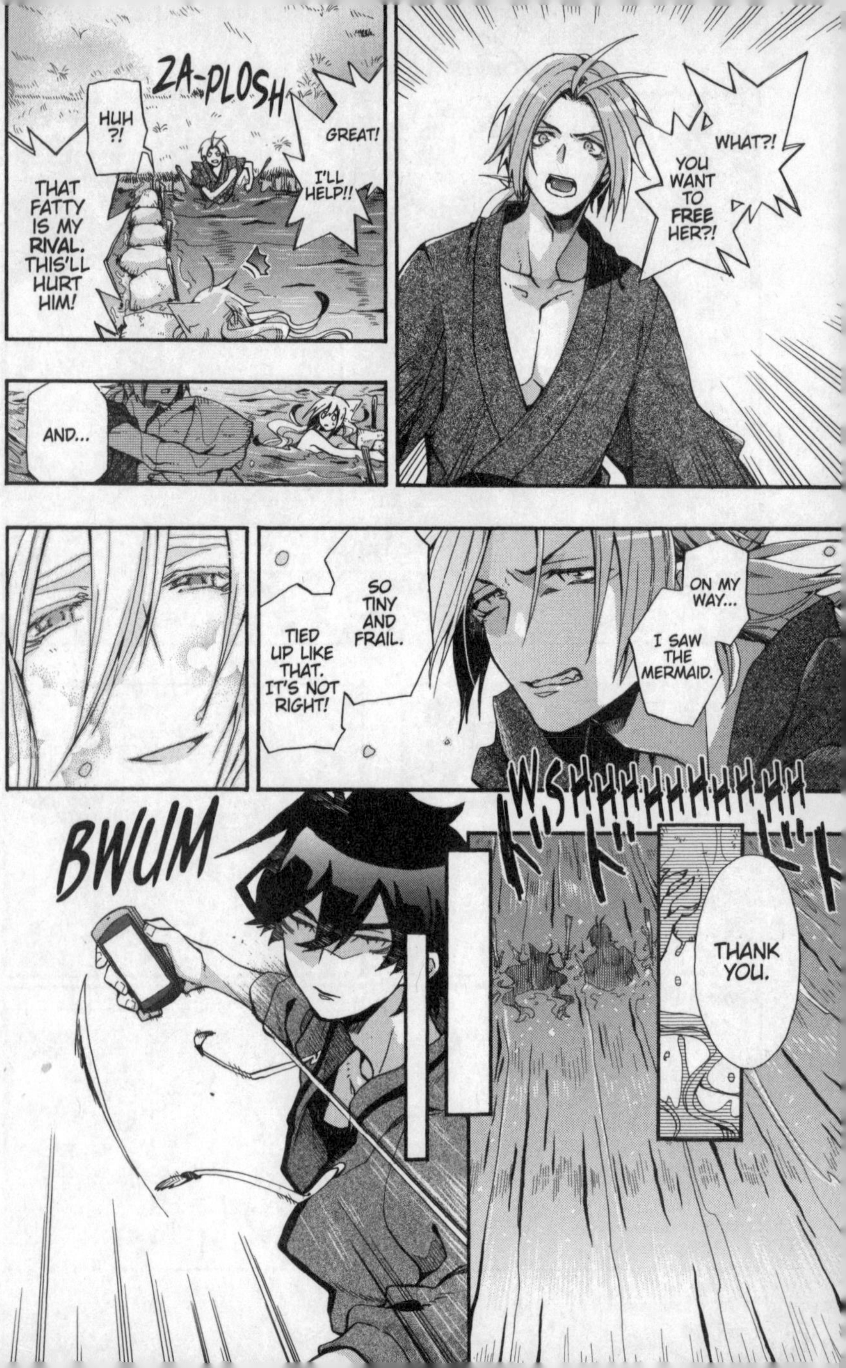
WHAT?!
YOU WANT TO FREE HER?!
ZA-PLOSH
GREAT!
I'LL HELP!!
HUH?!
THAT FATTY IS MY RIVAL. THIS'LL HURT HIM!
AND...
ON MY WAY...
I SAW THE MERMAID.
SO TINY AND FRAIL.
TIED UP LIKE THAT. IT'S NOT RIGHT!
WSHHHHHHHHHHH
THANK YOU.
BWUM

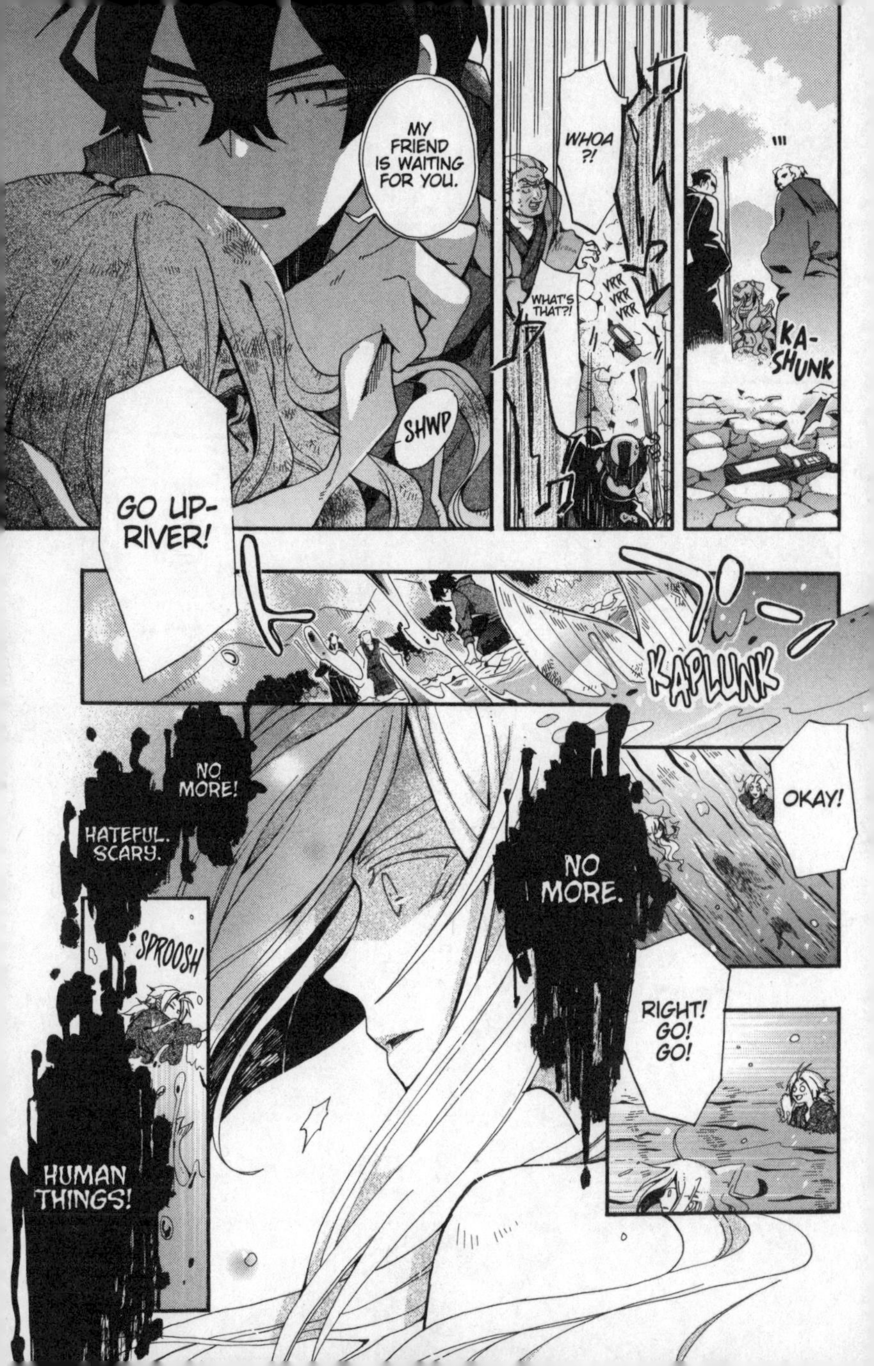
...
KA-SHUNK
WHOA?!
VRR VRR VRR
WHAT'S THAT?!
MY FRIEND IS WAITING FOR YOU.
SHWP
GO UP-RIVER!
KAPLUNK
OKAY!
RIGHT! GO! GO!
NO MORE.
NO MORE!
HATEFUL. SCARY.
HUMAN THINGS!
SPROOSH

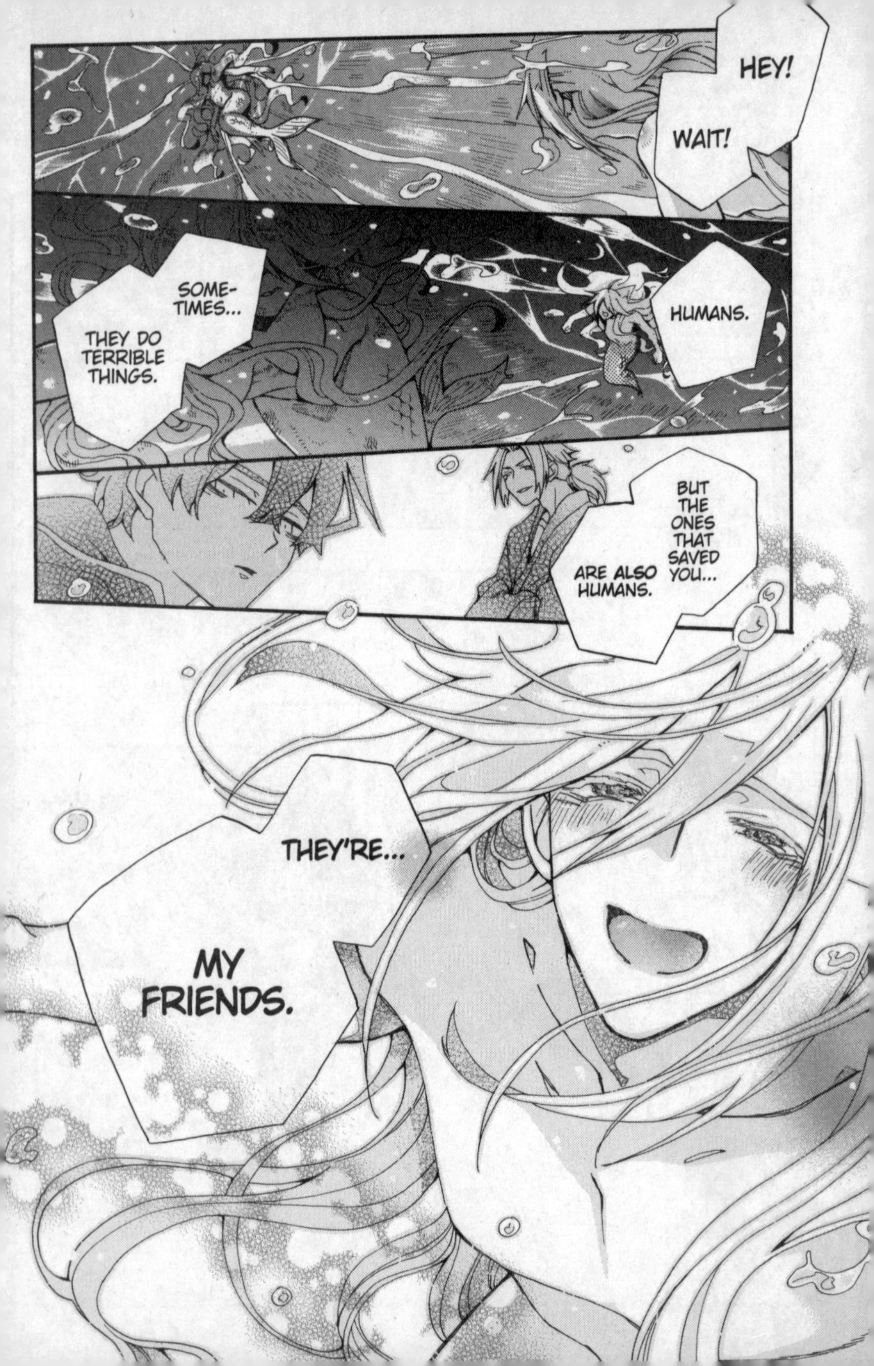
HEY!
WAIT!
HUMANS.
SOME-TIMES...
THEY DO TERRIBLE THINGS.
BUT THE ONES THAT SAVED YOU...
ARE ALSO HUMANS.
THEY'RE...
MY FRIENDS.

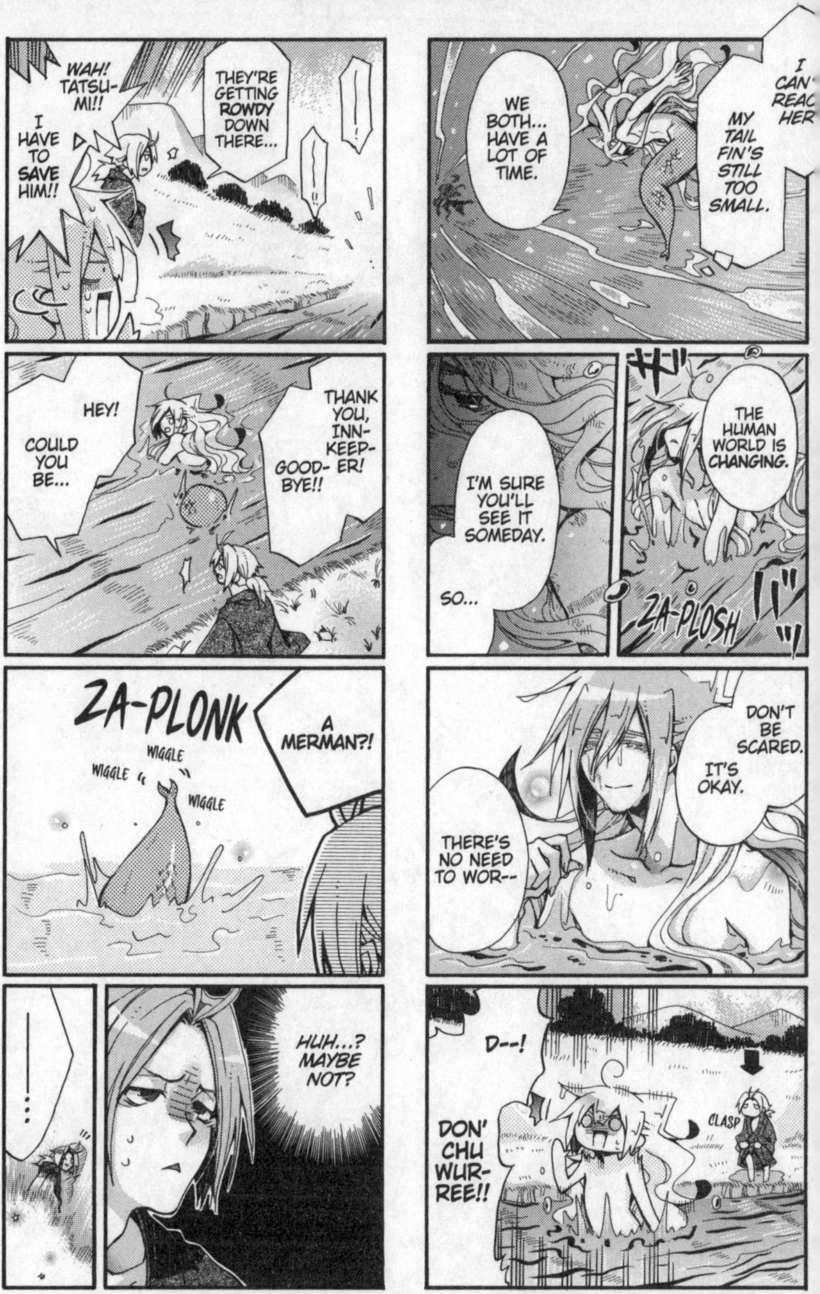
I CAN' REAC HER
MY TAIL FIN'S STILL TOO SMALL.
WE BOTH... HAVE A LOT OF TIME.
THEY'RE GETTING ROWDY DOWN THERE...
!
!!
WAH! TATSUMI!!
I HAVE TO SAVE HIM!!
THE HUMAN WORLD IS CHANGING.
ZA-PLOSH
I'M SURE YOU'LL SEE IT SOMEDAY.
SO...
THANK YOU, INNKEEPER! GOODBYE!!
HEY!
COULD YOU BE...
DON'T BE SCARED.
IT'S OKAY.
THERE'S NO NEED TO WOR--
A MERMAN?!
ZA-PLONK
WIGGLE WIGGLE WIGGLE
D--!
CLASP
DON' CHU WURREE!!
HUH...? MAYBE NOT?
......

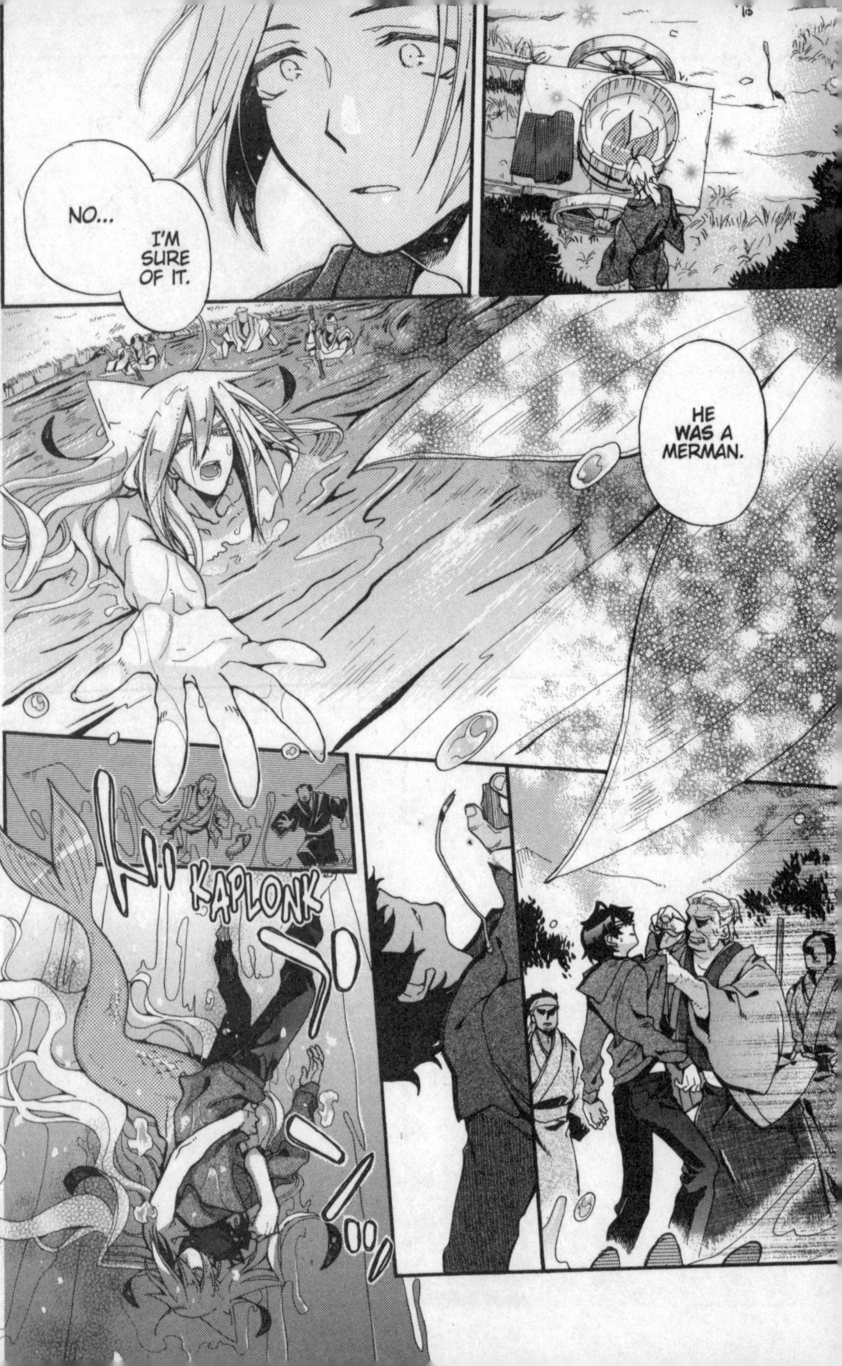
NO...
I'M SURE OF IT.
HE WAS A MERMAN.
KAPLONK

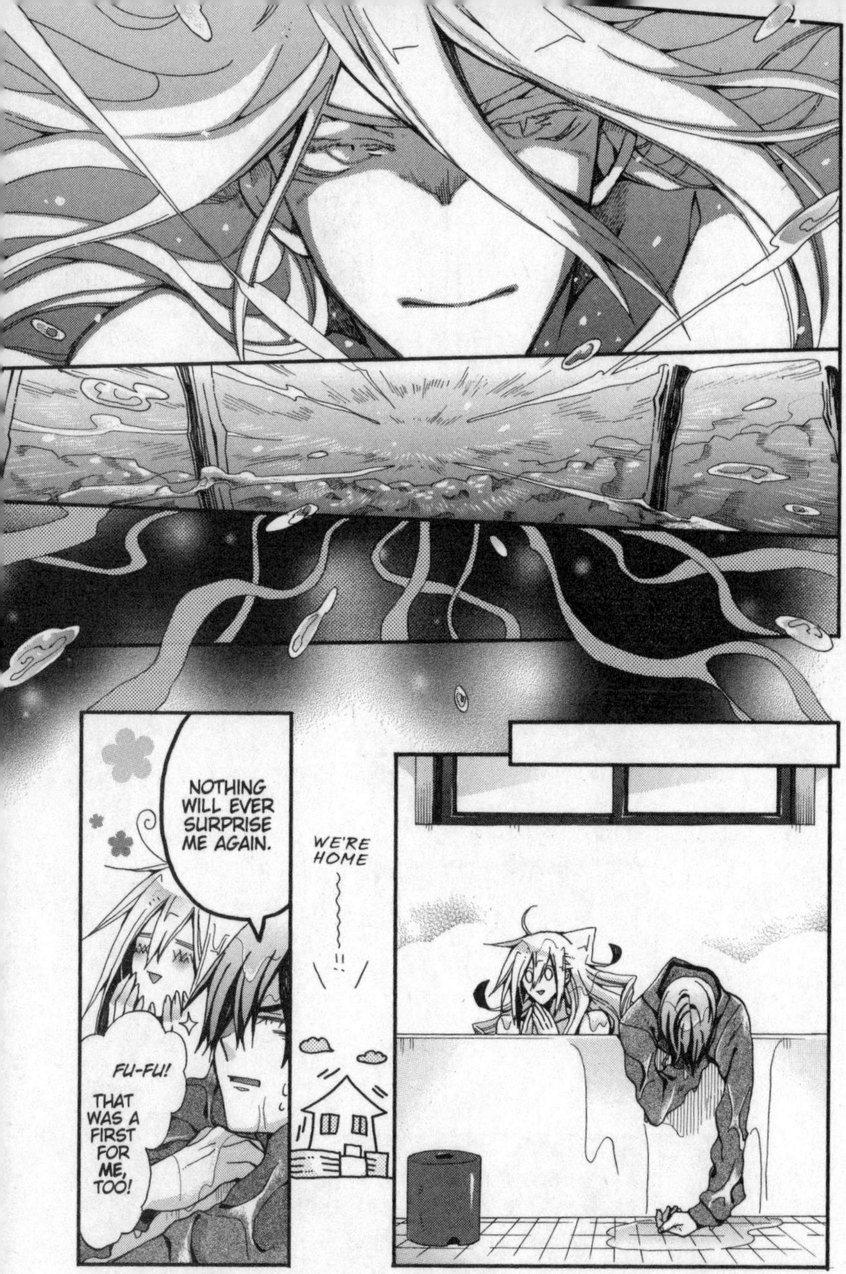
WE'RE HOME ~~~~~!!
NOTHING WILL EVER SURPRISE ME AGAIN.
FU-FU!
THAT WAS A FIRST FOR ME, TOO!

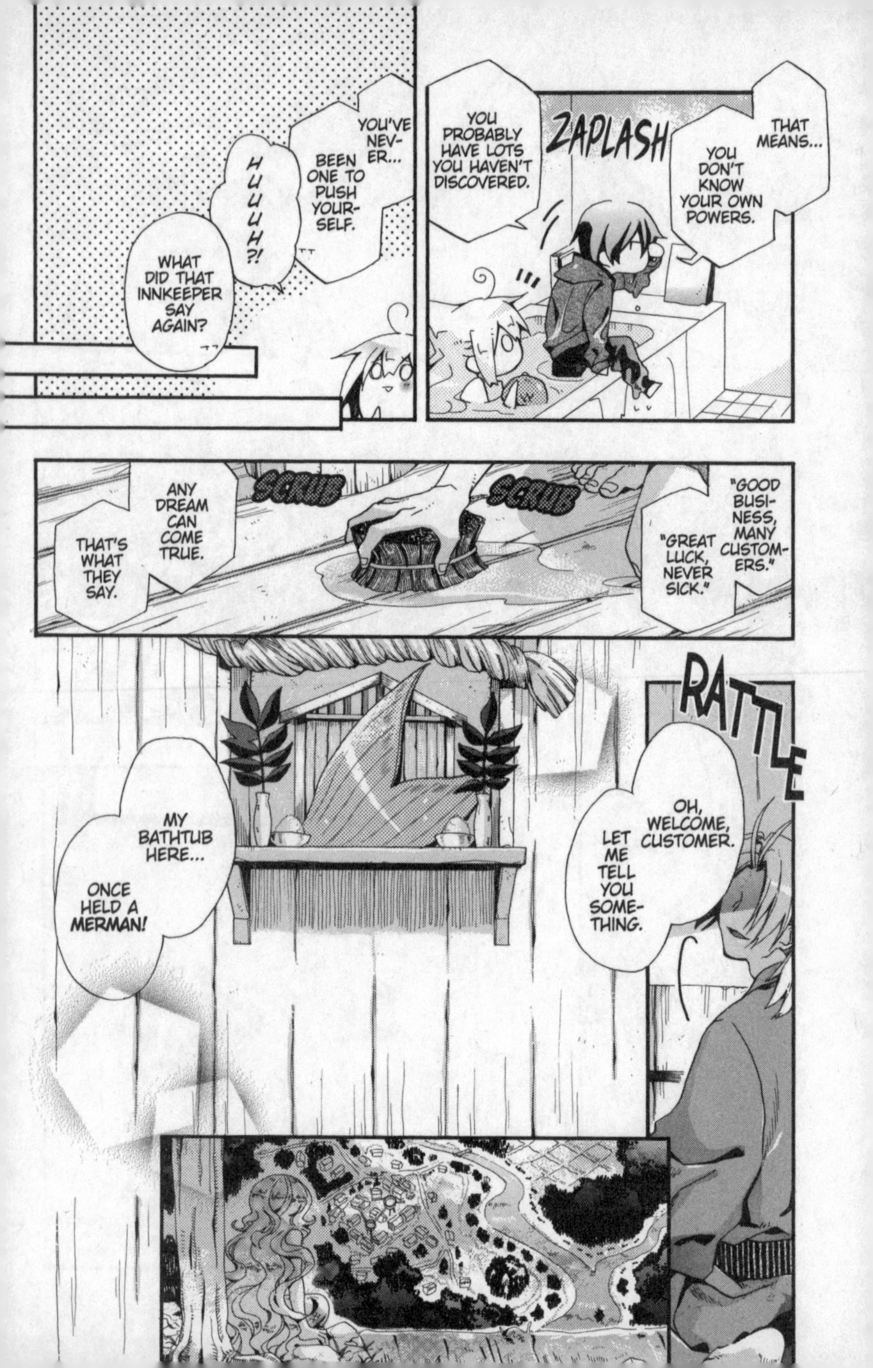
THAT MEANS...
YOU DON'T KNOW YOUR OWN POWERS.
ZAPLASH
YOU PROBABLY HAVE LOTS YOU HAVEN'T DISCOVERED.
YOU'VE NEVER...
BEEN ONE TO PUSH YOURSELF.
HUUUH?!
WHAT DID THAT INNKEEPER SAY AGAIN?
"GOOD BUSINESS, MANY CUSTOMERS."
"GREAT LUCK, NEVER SICK."
SCRUB
SCRUB
ANY DREAM CAN COME TRUE.
THAT'S WHAT THEY SAY.
RATTLE
OH, WELCOME, CUSTOMER.
LET ME TELL YOU SOMETHING.
MY BATHTUB HERE...
ONCE HELD A MERMAN!

Merman in My Tub

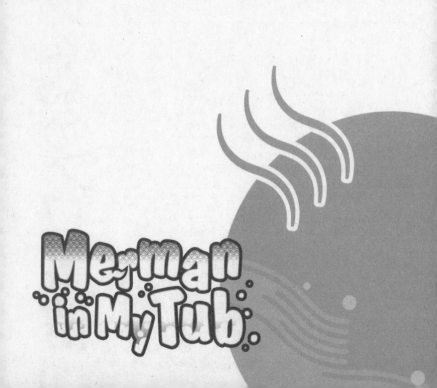

オレん家（ち）のフロ事情

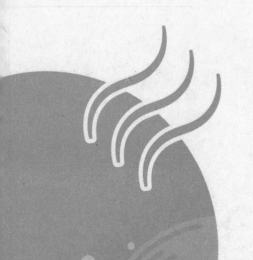

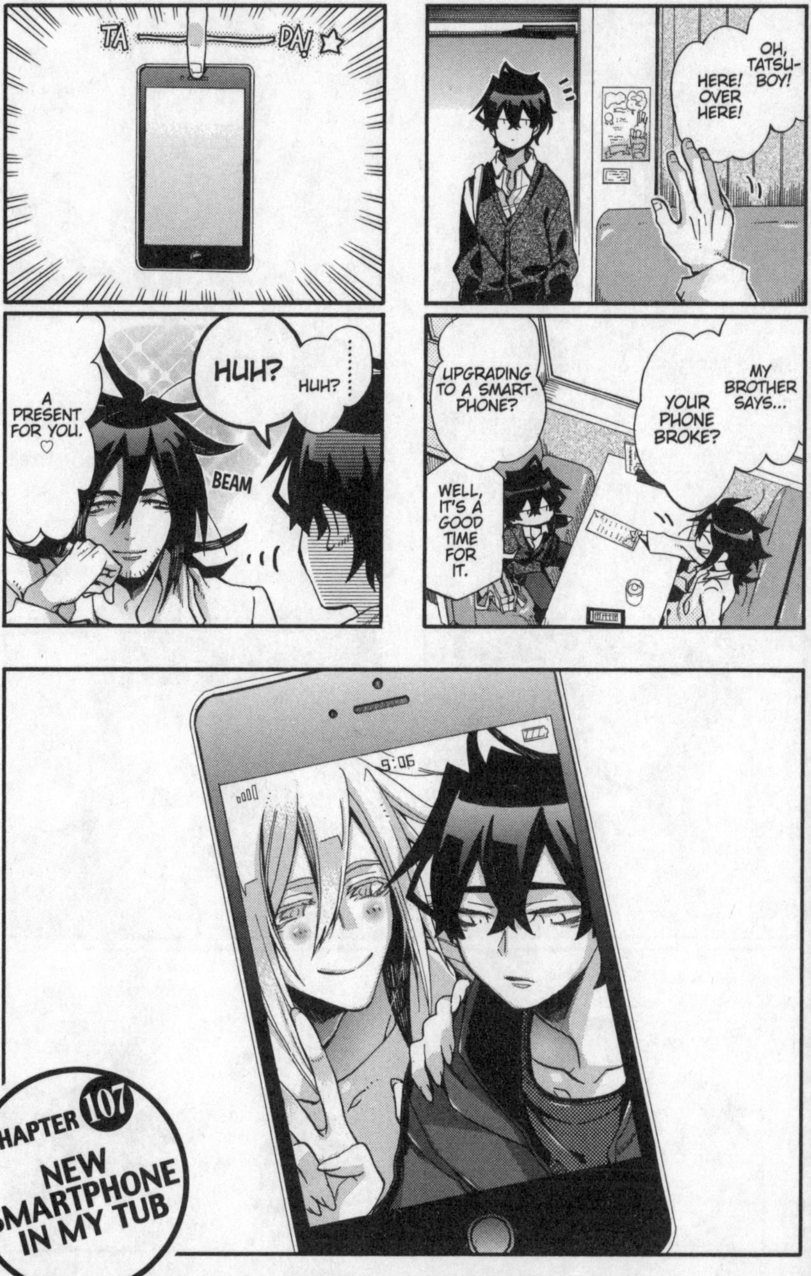
OH, TATSU-BOY!
HERE! OVER HERE!
TA—DA! ☆
MY BROTHER SAYS...
YOUR PHONE BROKE?
UPGRADING TO A SMART-PHONE?
WELL, IT'S A GOOD TIME FOR IT.
HUH?......
HUH?
A PRESENT FOR YOU. ♡
BEAM
9:06
CHAPTER 107
NEW SMARTPHONE IN MY TUB

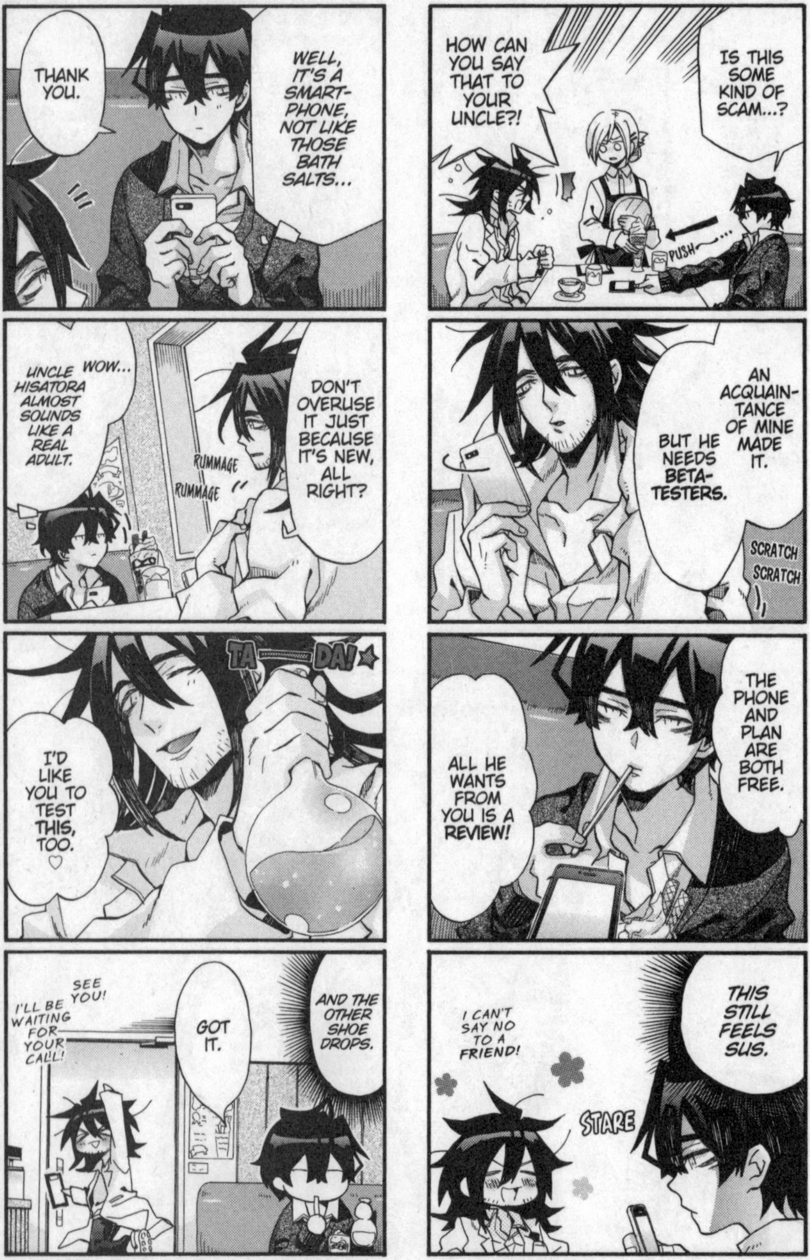
IS THIS SOME KIND OF SCAM...?
HOW CAN YOU SAY THAT TO YOUR UNCLE?!
PUSH
WELL, IT'S A SMARTPHONE, NOT LIKE THOSE BATH SALTS...
THANK YOU.
AN ACQUAINTANCE OF MINE MADE IT.
BUT HE NEEDS BETA-TESTERS.
SCRATCH SCRATCH
DON'T OVERUSE IT JUST BECAUSE IT'S NEW, ALL RIGHT?
RUMMAGE RUMMAGE
WOW... UNCLE HISATORA ALMOST SOUNDS LIKE A REAL ADULT.
THE PHONE AND PLAN ARE BOTH FREE.
ALL HE WANTS FROM YOU IS A REVIEW!
TA-DA!
I'D LIKE YOU TO TEST THIS, TOO. ♡
THIS STILL FEELS SUS.
STARE
I CAN'T SAY NO TO A FRIEND!
AND THE OTHER SHOE DROPS.
GOT IT.
SEE YOU!
I'LL BE WAITING FOR YOUR CALL!

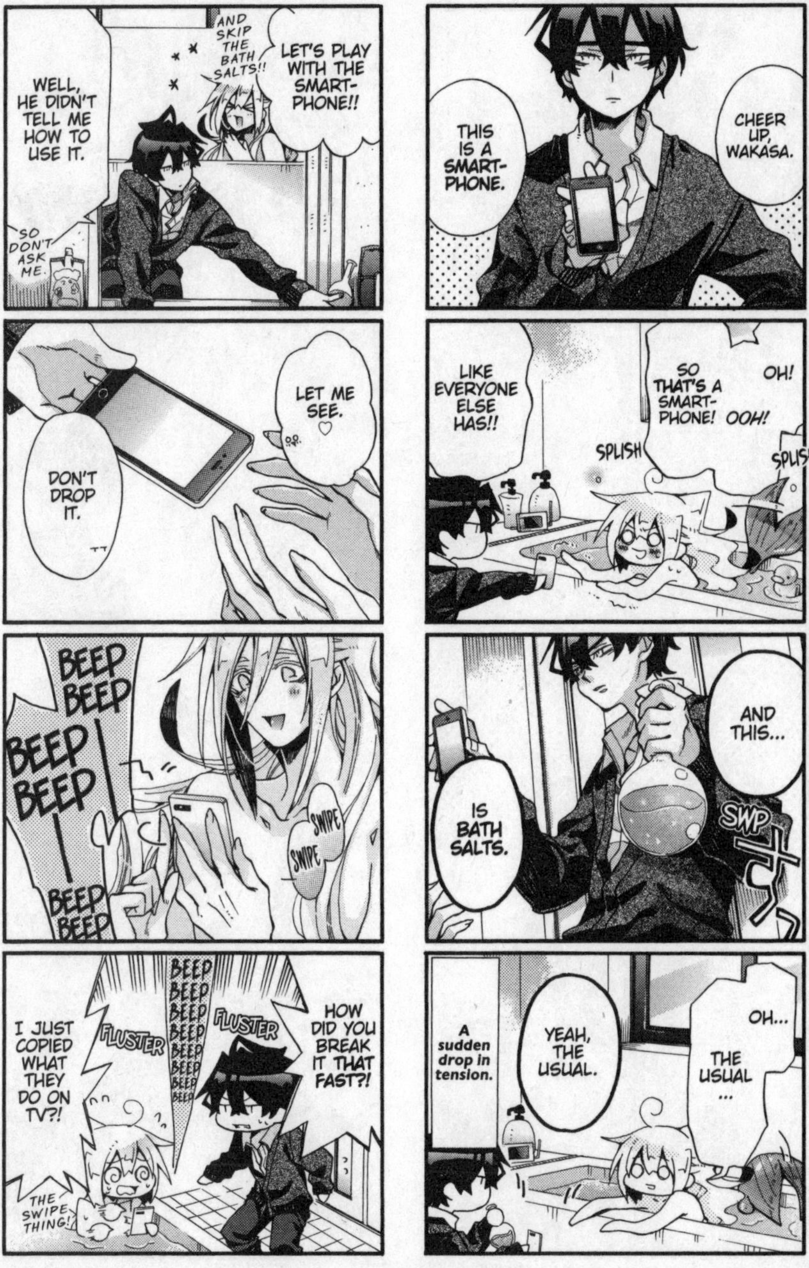
CHEER UP, WAKASA.
THIS IS A SMARTPHONE.
LET'S PLAY WITH THE SMARTPHONE!!
AND SKIP THE BATH SALTS!!
WELL, HE DIDN'T TELL ME HOW TO USE IT.
SO DON'T ASK ME.
OH! OOH!
SO THAT'S A SMARTPHONE!
LIKE EVERYONE ELSE HAS!!
SPLISH
SPLISH
LET ME SEE. ♡
DON'T DROP IT.
AND THIS...
IS BATH SALTS.
SWP
BEEP BEEP
BEEP BEEP
BEEP BEEP
SWIPE
SWIPE
OH...
THE USUAL...
YEAH, THE USUAL.
A sudden drop in tension.
HOW DID YOU BREAK IT THAT FAST?!
FLUSTER
BEEP BEEP BEEP BEEP BEEP BEEP BEEP
FLUSTER
I JUST COPIED WHAT THEY DO ON TV?!
THE SWIPE THING!

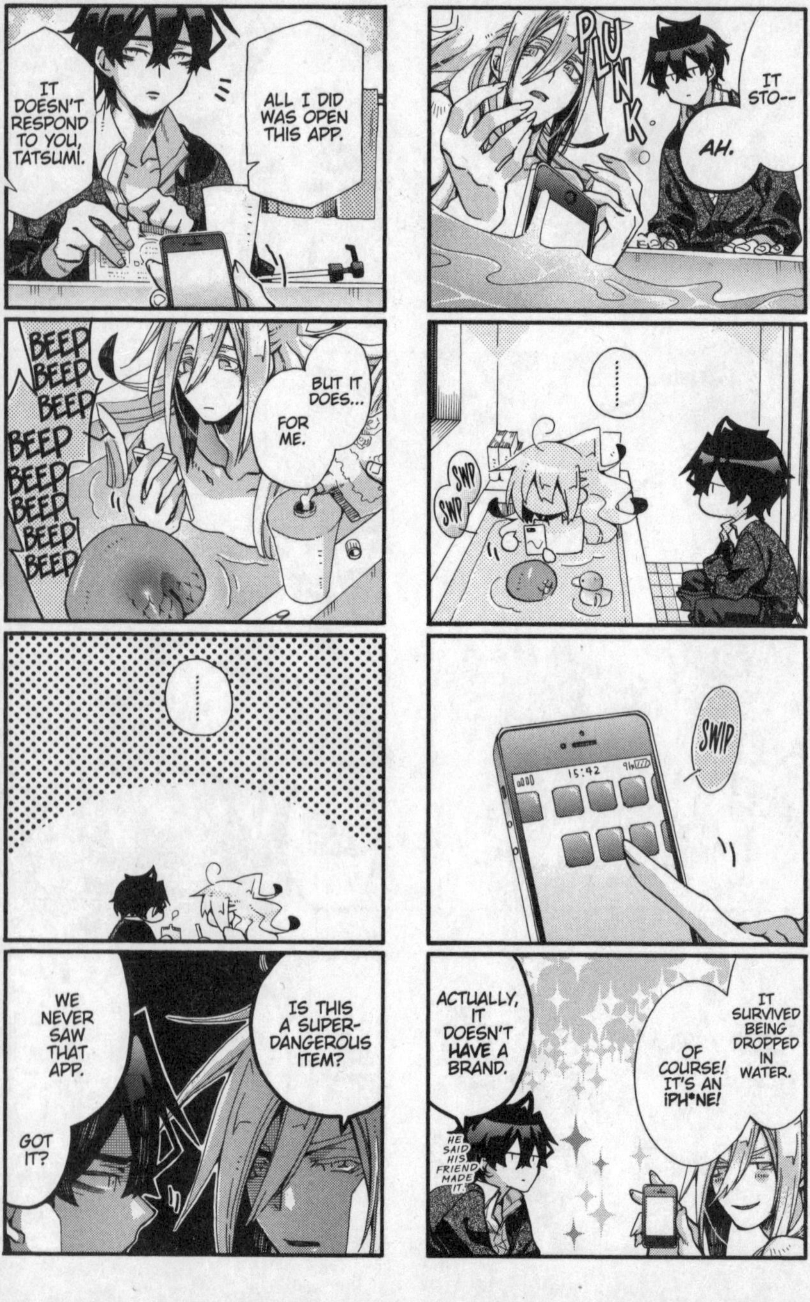
IT STO--
PLUNK
AH.
ALL I DID WAS OPEN THIS APP.
IT DOESN'T RESPOND TO YOU, TATSUMI.
......
SWP SWP
BUT IT DOES... FOR ME.
BEEP BEEP BEEP BEEP BEEP BEEP BEEP BEEP
SWIP
......
IT SURVIVED BEING DROPPED IN WATER.
OF COURSE! IT'S AN iPH*NE!
ACTUALLY, IT DOESN'T HAVE A BRAND.
HE SAID HIS FRIEND MADE IT.
IS THIS A SUPER-DANGEROUS ITEM?
WE NEVER SAW THAT APP.
GOT IT?

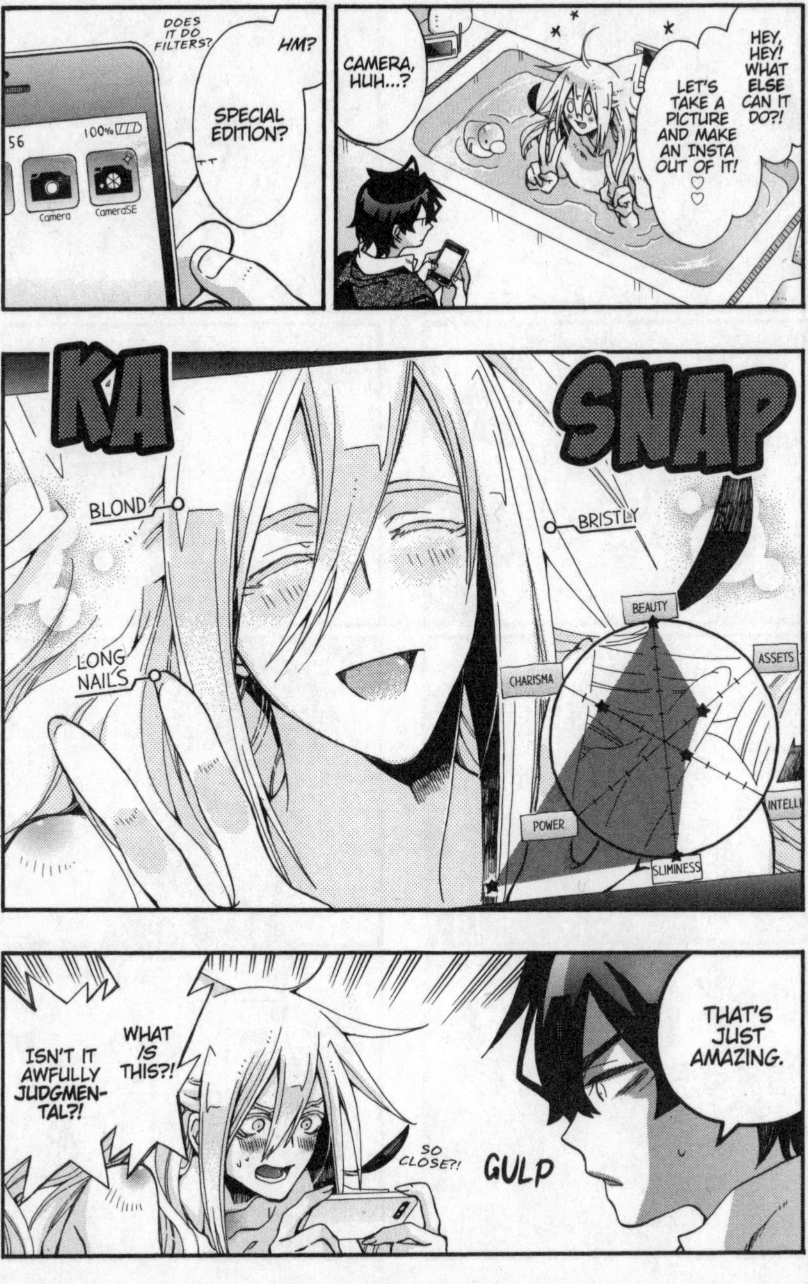
HEY, HEY! WHAT ELSE CAN IT DO?!
LET'S TAKE A PICTURE AND MAKE AN INSTA OUT OF IT! ♡ ♡
CAMERA, HUH...?
HM?
SPECIAL EDITION?
DOES IT DO FILTERS?
100%
56
Camera
CameraSE
KA
SNAP
BRISTLY
BLOND
LONG NAILS
BEAUTY
ASSETS
CHARISMA
INTELL
POWER
SLIMINESS
THAT'S JUST AMAZING.
GULP
SO CLOSE?!
WHAT IS THIS?!
ISN'T IT AWFULLY JUDGMENTAL?!

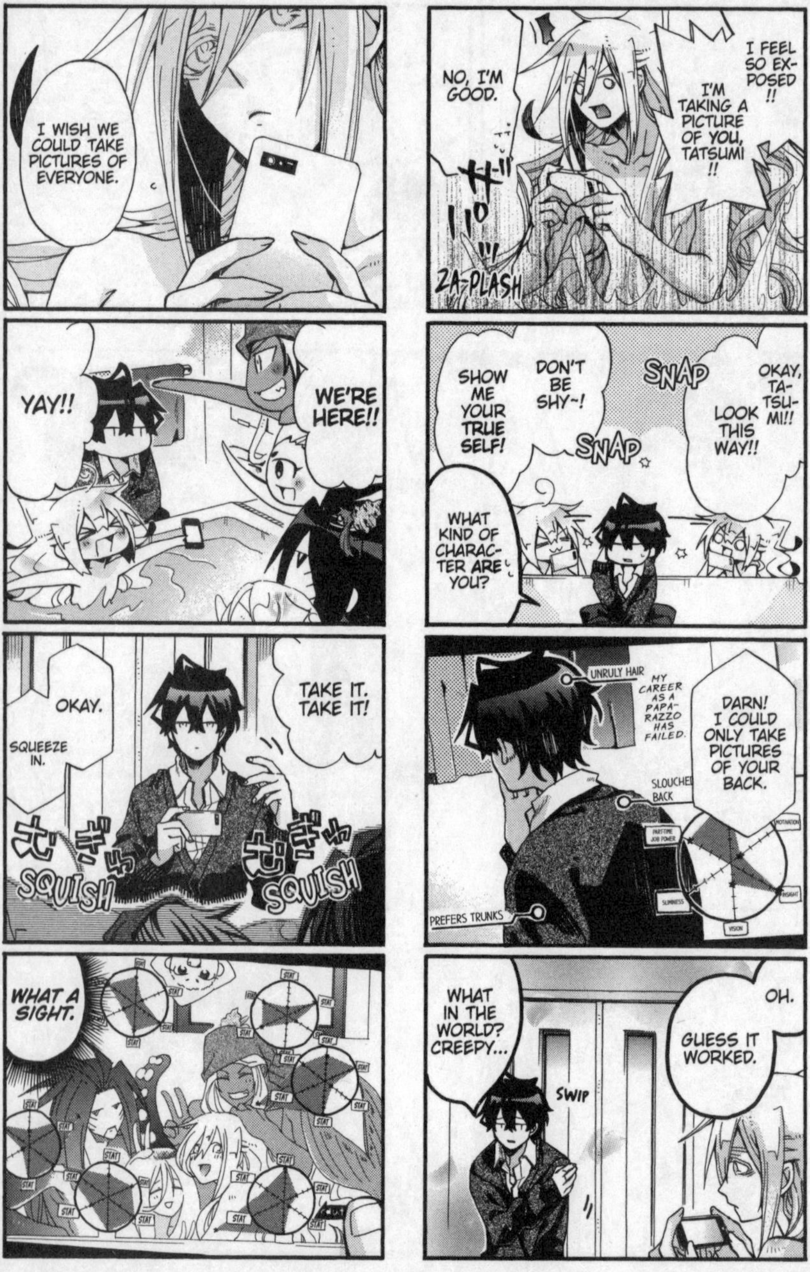
I FEEL SO EX-POSED !!
I'M TAKING A PICTURE OF YOU, TATSUMI !!
NO, I'M GOOD.
ZA-PLASH
I WISH WE COULD TAKE PICTURES OF EVERYONE.
OKAY, TA-TSU-MI!!
LOOK THIS WAY!!
SNAP
DON'T BE SHY~!
SHOW ME YOUR TRUE SELF!
SNAP
WHAT KIND OF CHARAC-TER ARE YOU?
WE'RE HERE!!
YAY!!
DARN! I COULD ONLY TAKE PICTURES OF YOUR BACK.
MY CAREER AS A PAPA-RAZZO HAS FAILED.
UNRULY HAIR
SLOUCHED BACK
MOTIVATION
PARTTIME JOB POWER
INSIGHT
SLIMNESS
VISION
PREFERS TRUNKS
TAKE IT. TAKE IT!
OKAY.
SQUEEZE IN.
むぎゅ
SQUISH
むぎゅ
SQUISH
OH.
GUESS IT WORKED.
WHAT IN THE WORLD? CREEPY...
SWIP
WHAT A SIGHT.

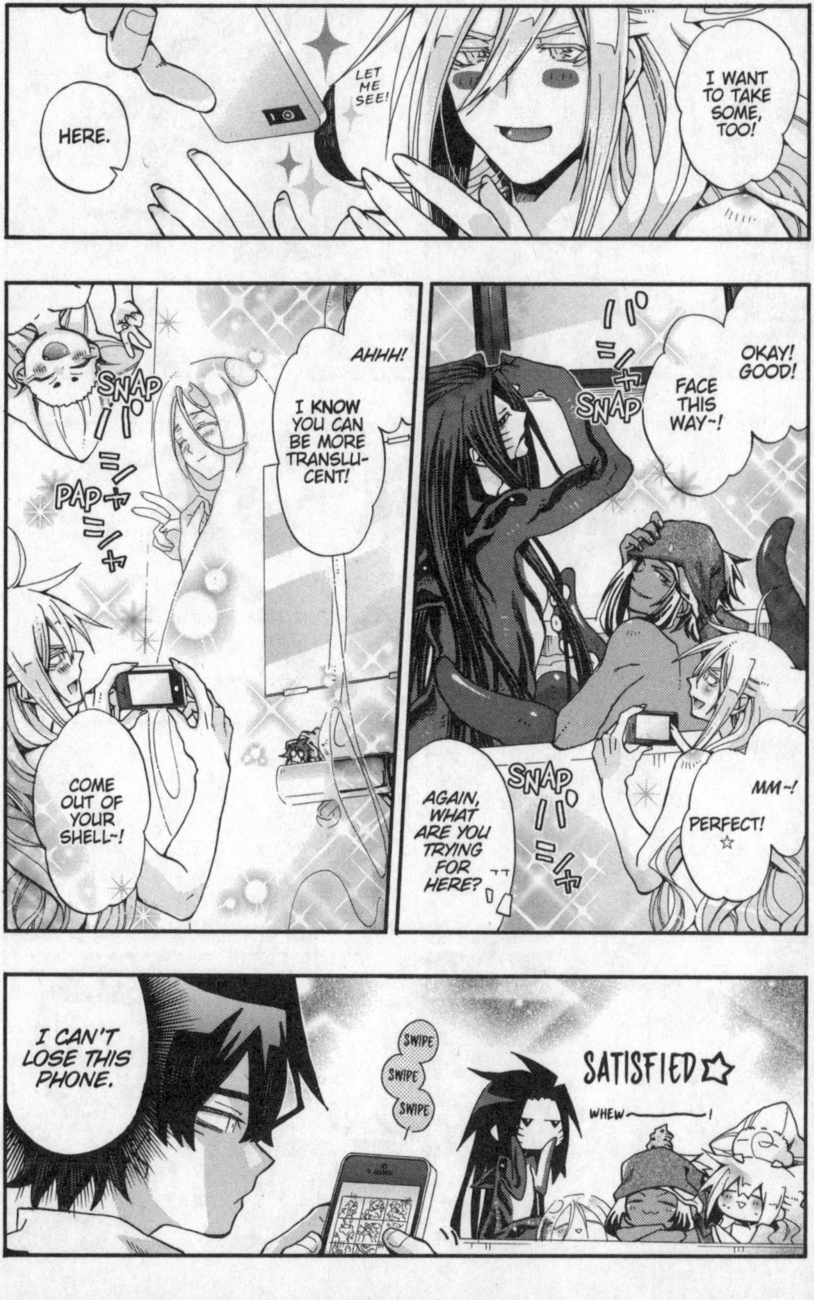
I WANT TO TAKE SOME, TOO!
LET ME SEE!
HERE.
OKAY! GOOD!
FACE THIS WAY~!
SNAP
MM~!
PERFECT! ☆
SNAP
AGAIN, WHAT ARE YOU TRYING FOR HERE?
AHHH!
I KNOW YOU CAN BE MORE TRANSLU-CENT!
SNAP
PAP
COME OUT OF YOUR SHELL~!
SATISFIED ☆
WHEW———!
SWIPE
SWIPE
SWIPE
I CAN'T LOSE THIS PHONE.

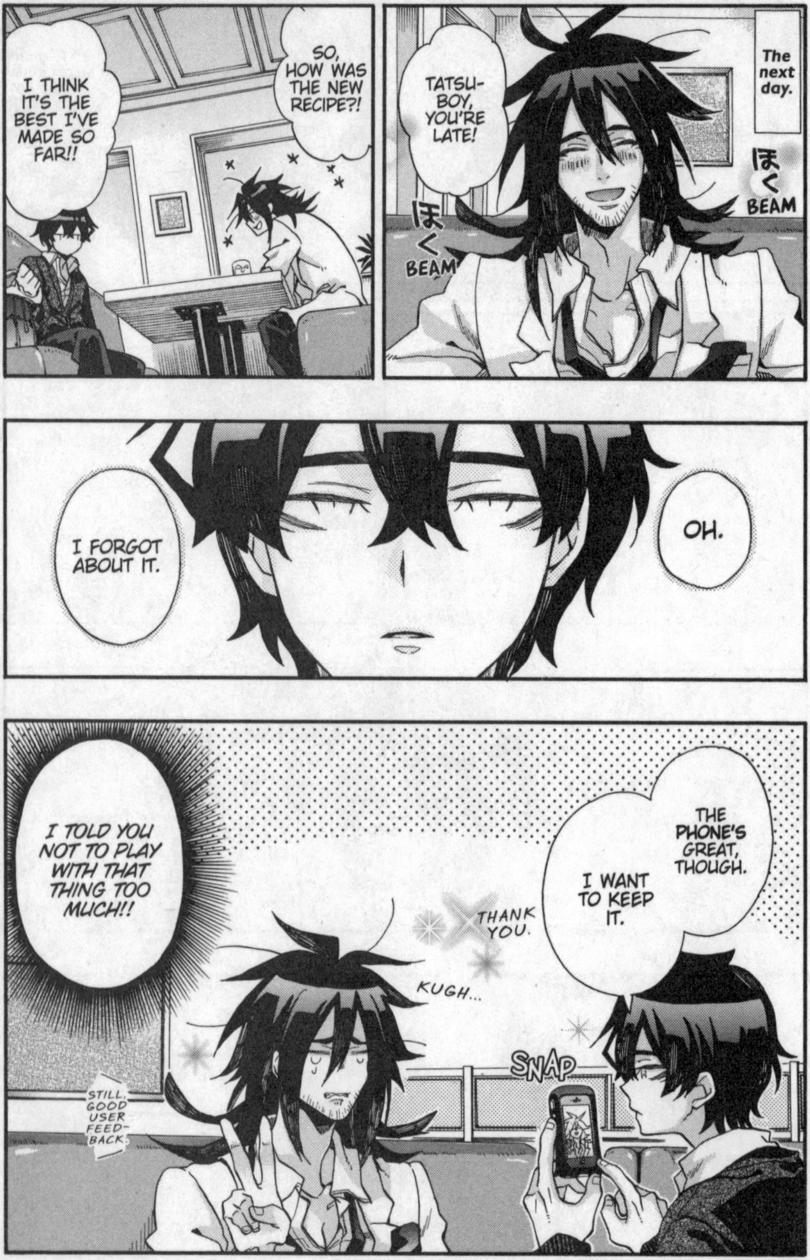
The next day.
TATSU-BOY, YOU'RE LATE!
ほく BEAM
ほく BEAM
SO, HOW WAS THE NEW RECIPE?!
I THINK IT'S THE BEST I'VE MADE SO FAR!!
OH.
I FORGOT ABOUT IT.
THE PHONE'S GREAT, THOUGH.
I WANT TO KEEP IT.
THANK YOU.
KUGH...
SNAP
I TOLD YOU NOT TO PLAY WITH THAT THING TOO MUCH!!
STILL, GOOD USER FEED-BACK.

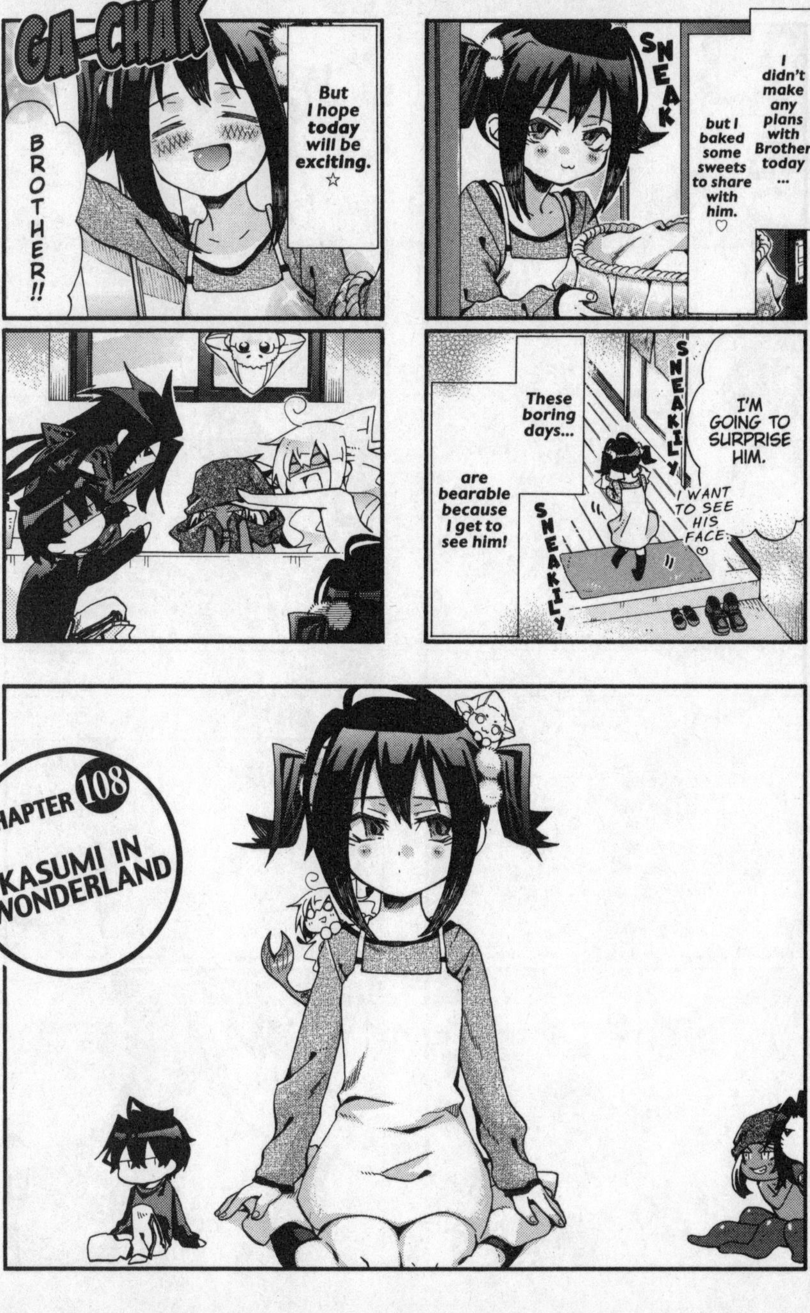

SNEAK
I didn't make any plans with Brother today ...
but I baked some sweets to share with him. ♡
But I hope today will be exciting. ☆
GA-CHAK
BROTHER!!
I'M GOING TO SURPRISE HIM.
I WANT TO SEE HIS FACE. ♡
SNEAKILY
These boring days...
are bearable because I get to see him!
SNEAKILY
CHAPTER 108
KASUMI IN WONDERLAND

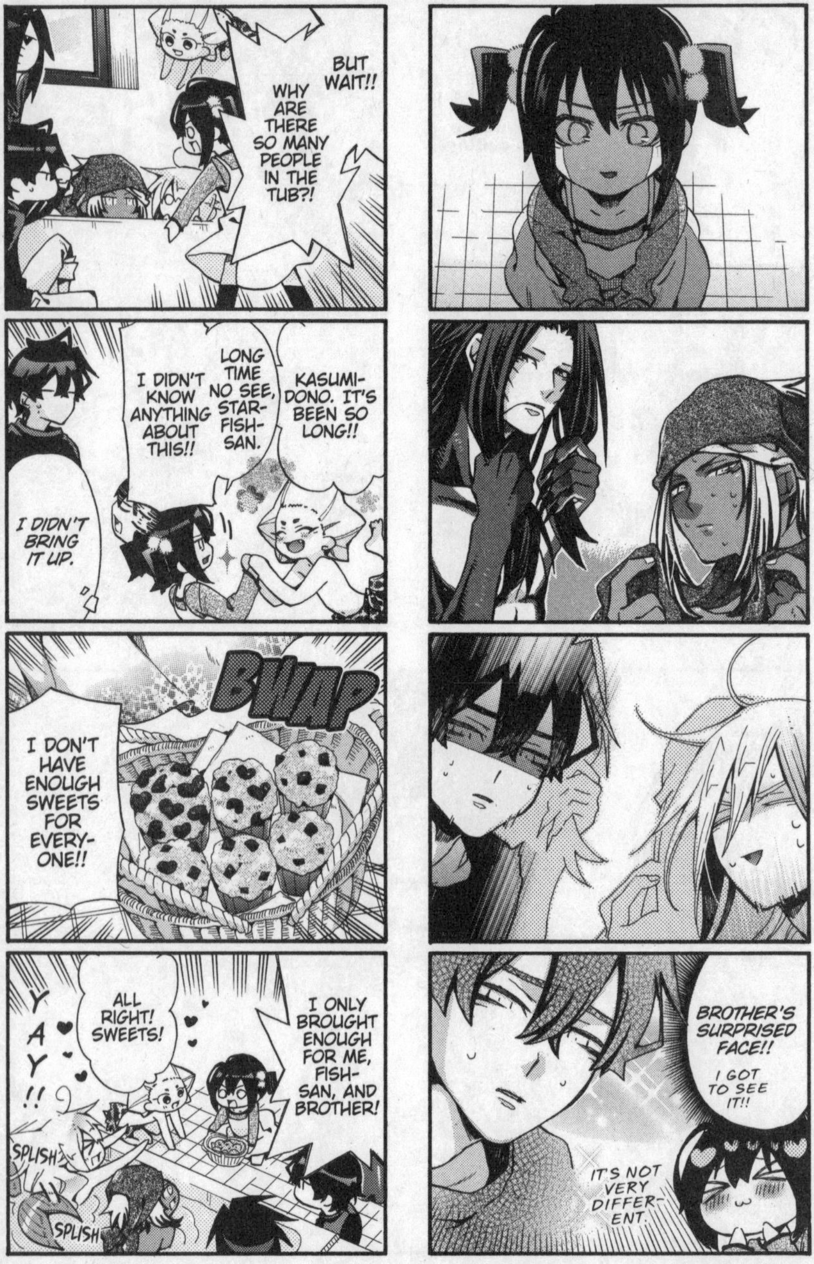
BROTHER'S SURPRISED FACE!!
I GOT TO SEE IT!!
IT'S NOT VERY DIFFERENT.
BUT WAIT!!
WHY ARE THERE SO MANY PEOPLE IN THE TUB?!
KASUMI-DONO. IT'S BEEN SO LONG!!
LONG TIME NO SEE, STAR-FISH-SAN.
I DIDN'T KNOW ANYTHING ABOUT THIS!!
I DIDN'T BRING IT UP.
BWAP
I DON'T HAVE ENOUGH SWEETS FOR EVERY-ONE!!
I ONLY BROUGHT ENOUGH FOR ME, FISH-SAN, AND BROTHER!
ALL RIGHT! SWEETS!
YAY!!
SPLISH
SPLISH

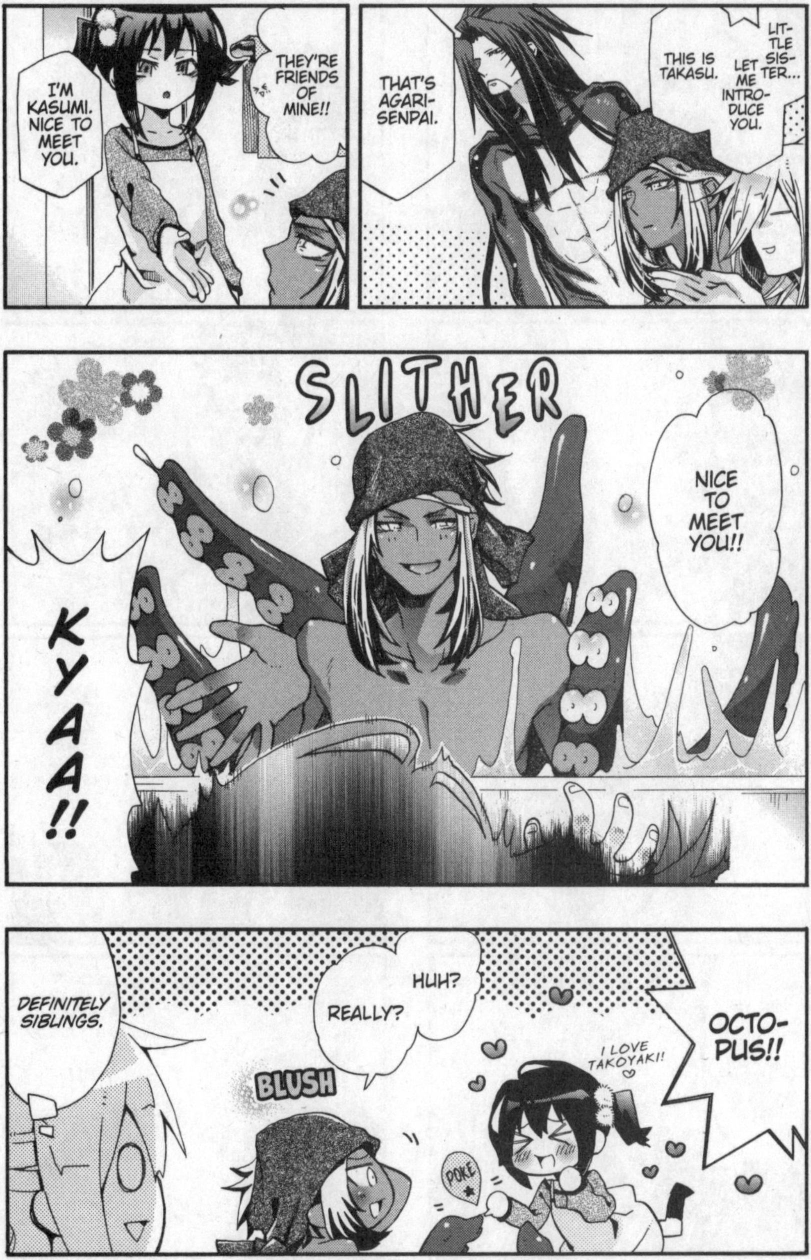
LITTLE SISTER...
LET ME INTRODUCE YOU.
THIS IS TAKASU.
THAT'S AGARI-SENPAI.
THEY'RE FRIENDS OF MINE!!
I'M KASUMI. NICE TO MEET YOU.
SLITHER
NICE TO MEET YOU!!
KYAA!!
OCTO-PUS!!
I LOVE TAKOYAKI!
HUH?
REALLY?
BLUSH
POKE
DEFINITELY SIBLINGS.

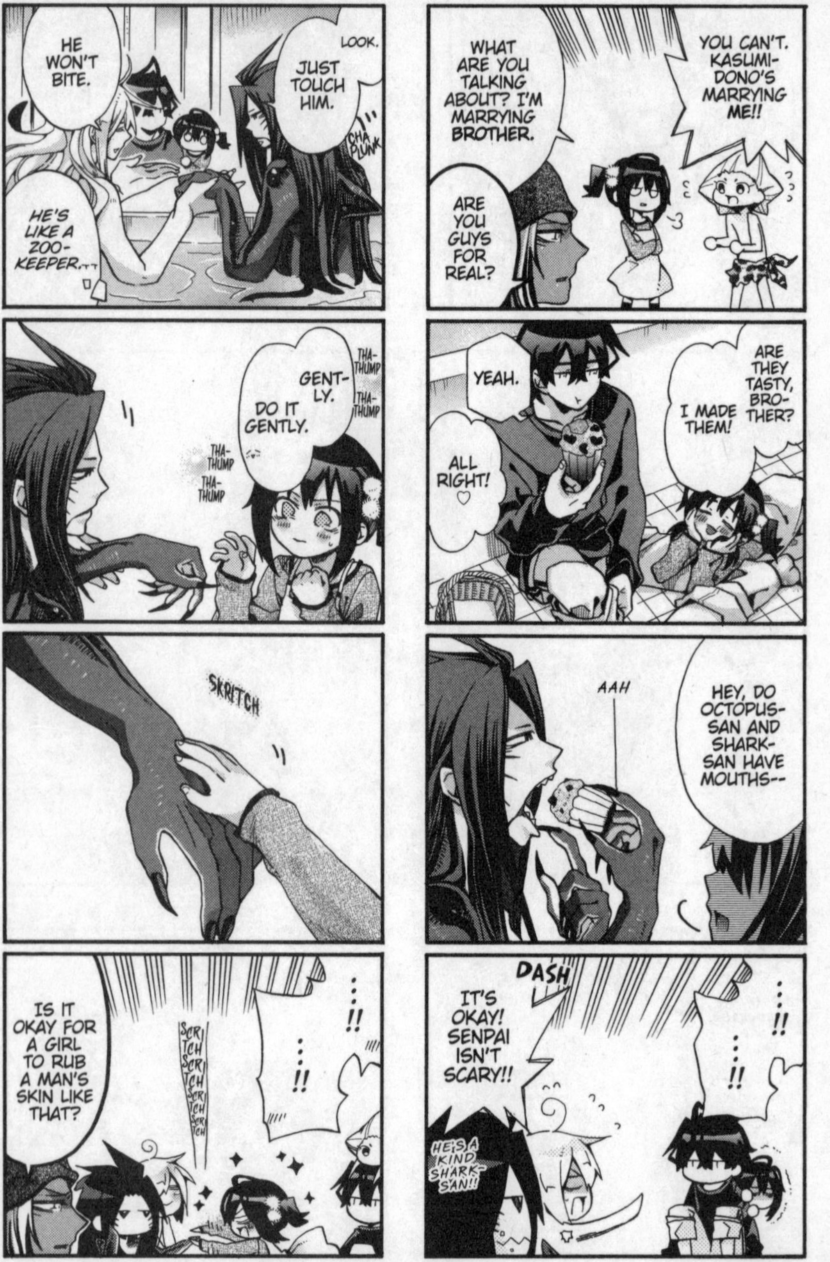
YOU CAN'T. KASUMI-DONO'S MARRYING ME!!
WHAT ARE YOU TALKING ABOUT? I'M MARRYING BROTHER.
ARE YOU GUYS FOR REAL?
ARE THEY TASTY, BROTHER?
I MADE THEM!
YEAH.
ALL RIGHT! ♡
HEY, DO OCTOPUS-SAN AND SHARK-SAN HAVE MOUTHS--
AAH
...!!
...!!
DASH
IT'S OKAY! SENPAI ISN'T SCARY!!
HE'S A KIND SHARK-SAN!!
LOOK.
JUST TOUCH HIM.
CHAPLUNK
HE WON'T BITE.
HE'S LIKE A ZOO-KEEPER...
THA-THUMP THA-THUMP
GENTLY.
DO IT GENTLY.
THA-THUMP THA-THUMP
SKRITCH
...!!
...!!
SCRITCH SCRITCH SCRITCH SCRITCH
IS IT OKAY FOR A GIRL TO RUB A MAN'S SKIN LIKE THAT?

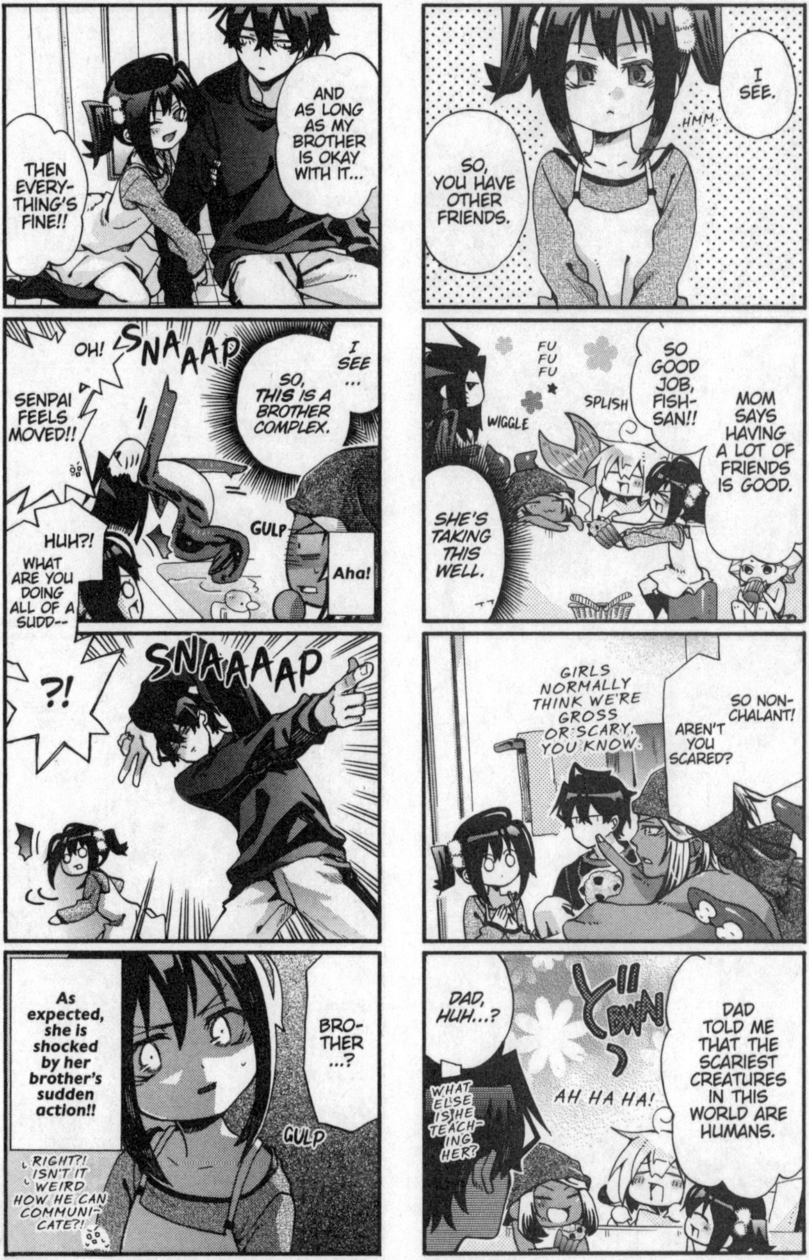
I SEE.
HMM
SO, YOU HAVE OTHER FRIENDS.
MOM SAYS HAVING A LOT OF FRIENDS IS GOOD.
SO GOOD JOB, FISH-SAN!!
FU FU FU
SPLISH
WIGGLE
SHE'S TAKING THIS WELL.
SO NON-CHALANT!
AREN'T YOU SCARED?
GIRLS NORMALLY THINK WE'RE GROSS OR SCARY, YOU KNOW.
DAD TOLD ME THAT THE SCARIEST CREATURES IN THIS WORLD ARE HUMANS.
DAD, HUH...?
AH HA HA!
WHAT ELSE IS HE TEACHING HER?
AND AS LONG AS MY BROTHER IS OKAY WITH IT...
THEN EVERYTHING'S FINE!!
I SEE... SO, THIS IS A BROTHER COMPLEX.
SNAAAP
OH!
SENPAI FEELS MOVED!!
GULP
Aha!
HUH?! WHAT ARE YOU DOING ALL OF A SUDD--
SNAAAAAP
?!
BROTHER...?
As expected, she is shocked by her brother's sudden action!!
GULP
RIGHT?! ISN'T IT WEIRD HOW HE CAN COMMUNICATE?!

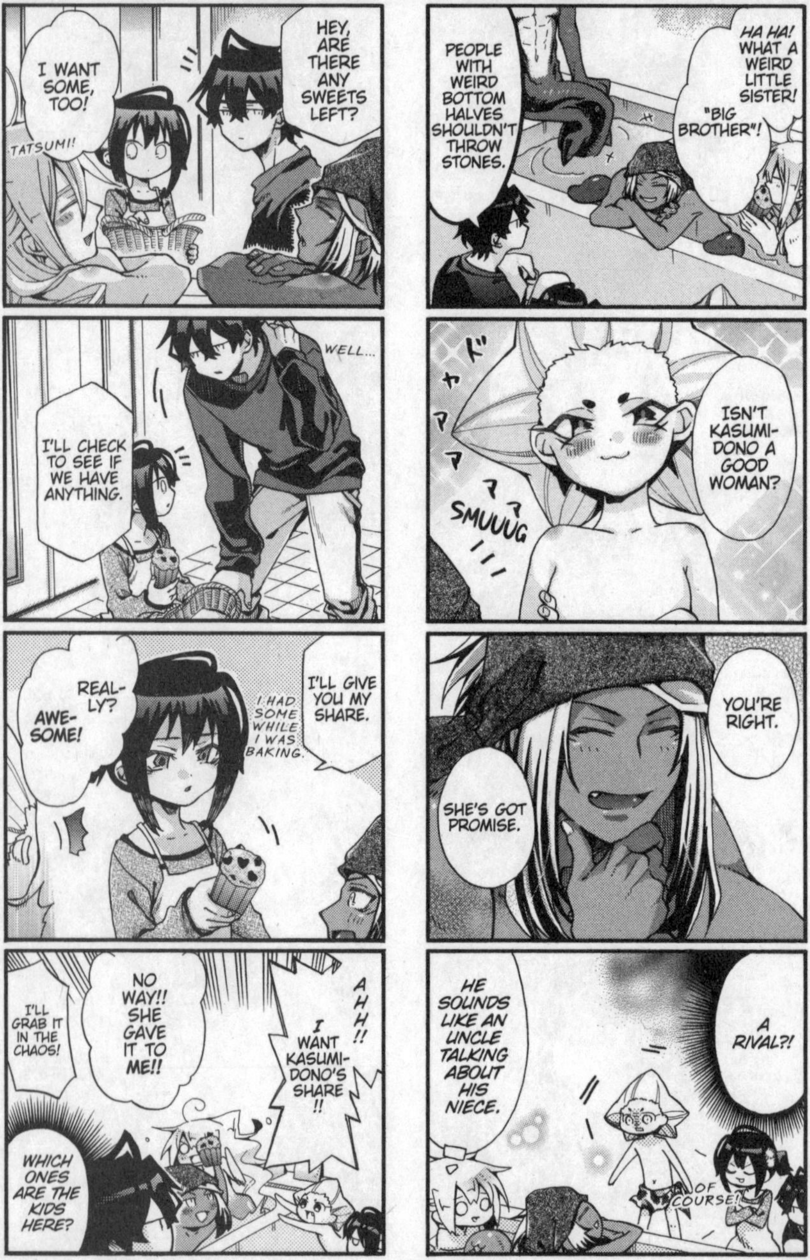
HA HA! WHAT A WEIRD LITTLE SISTER! "BIG BROTHER"!
PEOPLE WITH WEIRD BOTTOM HALVES SHOULDN'T THROW STONES.
ISN'T KASUMI-DONO A GOOD WOMAN?
ドヤァァァ
SMUUUG
YOU'RE RIGHT.
SHE'S GOT PROMISE.
A RIVAL?!
HE SOUNDS LIKE AN UNCLE TALKING ABOUT HIS NIECE.
OF COURSE!
HEY, ARE THERE ANY SWEETS LEFT?
I WANT SOME, TOO!
TATSUMI!
WELL...
I'LL CHECK TO SEE IF WE HAVE ANYTHING.
I'LL GIVE YOU MY SHARE.
I HAD SOME WHILE I WAS BAKING.
REAL-LY?
AWE-SOME!
AHH!! I WANT KASUMI-DONO'S SHARE!!
NO WAY!! SHE GAVE IT TO ME!!
I'LL GRAB IT IN THE CHAOS!
WHICH ONES ARE THE KIDS HERE?

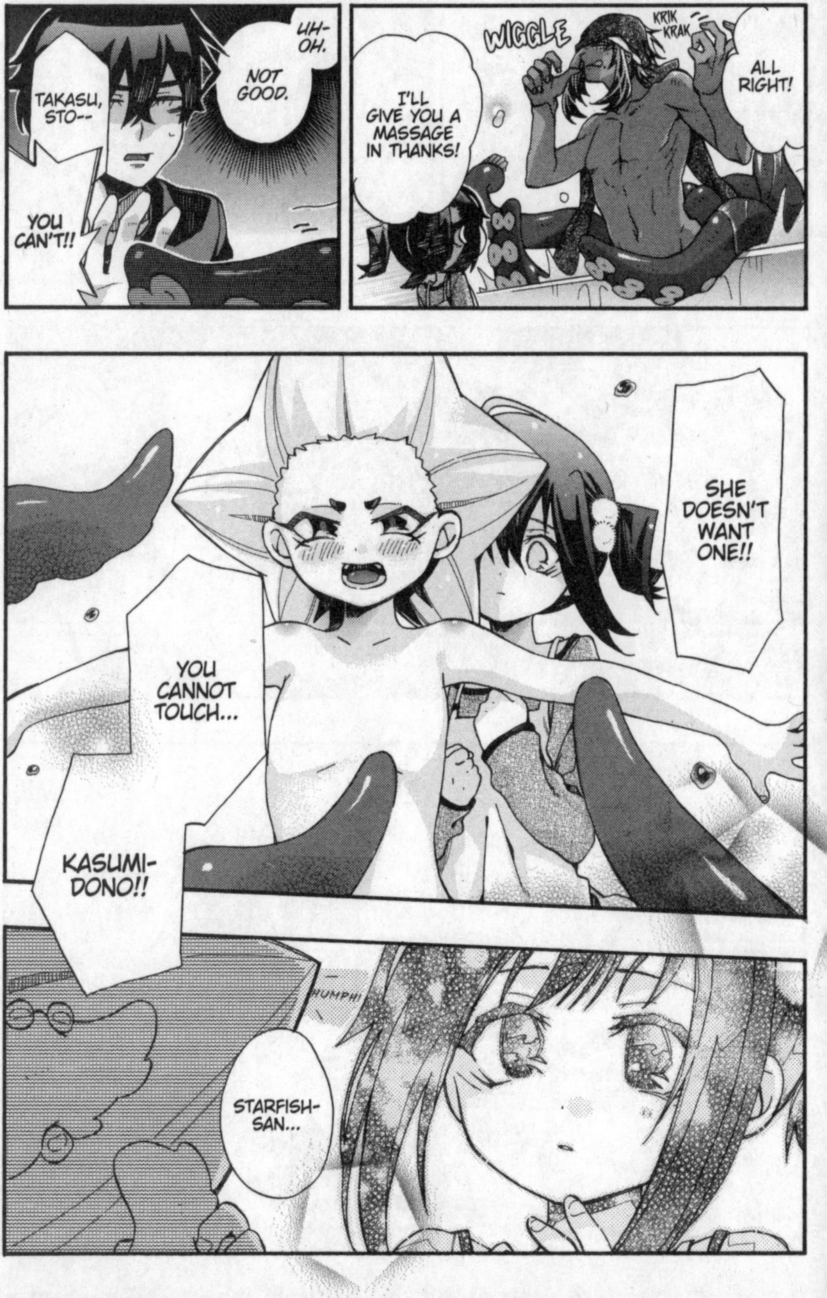
ALL RIGHT!
KRIK KRAK
WIGGLE
I'LL GIVE YOU A MASSAGE IN THANKS!
UH-OH.
NOT GOOD.
TAKASU, STO--
YOU CAN'T!!
SHE DOESN'T WANT ONE!!
YOU CANNOT TOUCH...
KASUMI-DONO!!
HUMPH!
STARFISH-SAN...

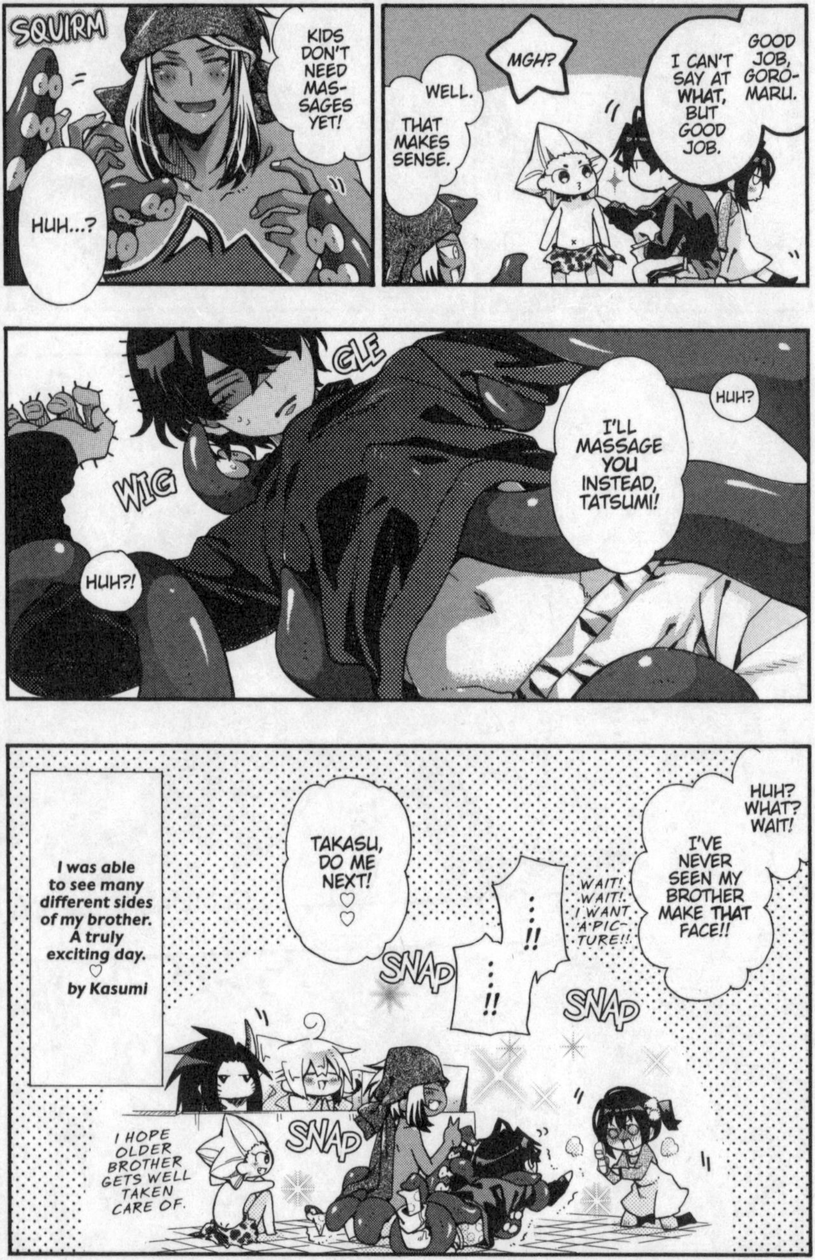
GOOD JOB, GORO-MARU.
I CAN'T SAY AT WHAT, BUT GOOD JOB.
MGH?
WELL.
THAT MAKES SENSE.
SQUIRM
KIDS DON'T NEED MAS-SAGES YET!
HUH...?
HUH?
I'LL MASSAGE YOU INSTEAD, TATSUMI!
GLE
WIG
HUH?!
HUH? WHAT? WAIT!
I'VE NEVER SEEN MY BROTHER MAKE THAT FACE!!
WAIT! WAIT! I WANT A PIC-TURE!!
...!!
...!!
TAKASU, DO ME NEXT! ♡ ♡
SNAP
SNAP
SNAP
I HOPE OLDER BROTHER GETS WELL TAKEN CARE OF.
I was able to see many different sides of my brother. A truly exciting day. ♡ by Kasumi

Merman in My Tub

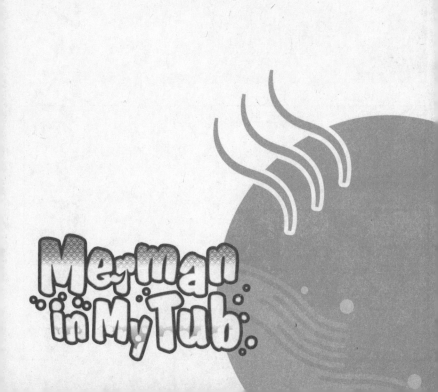

オレんち家のフロ事情

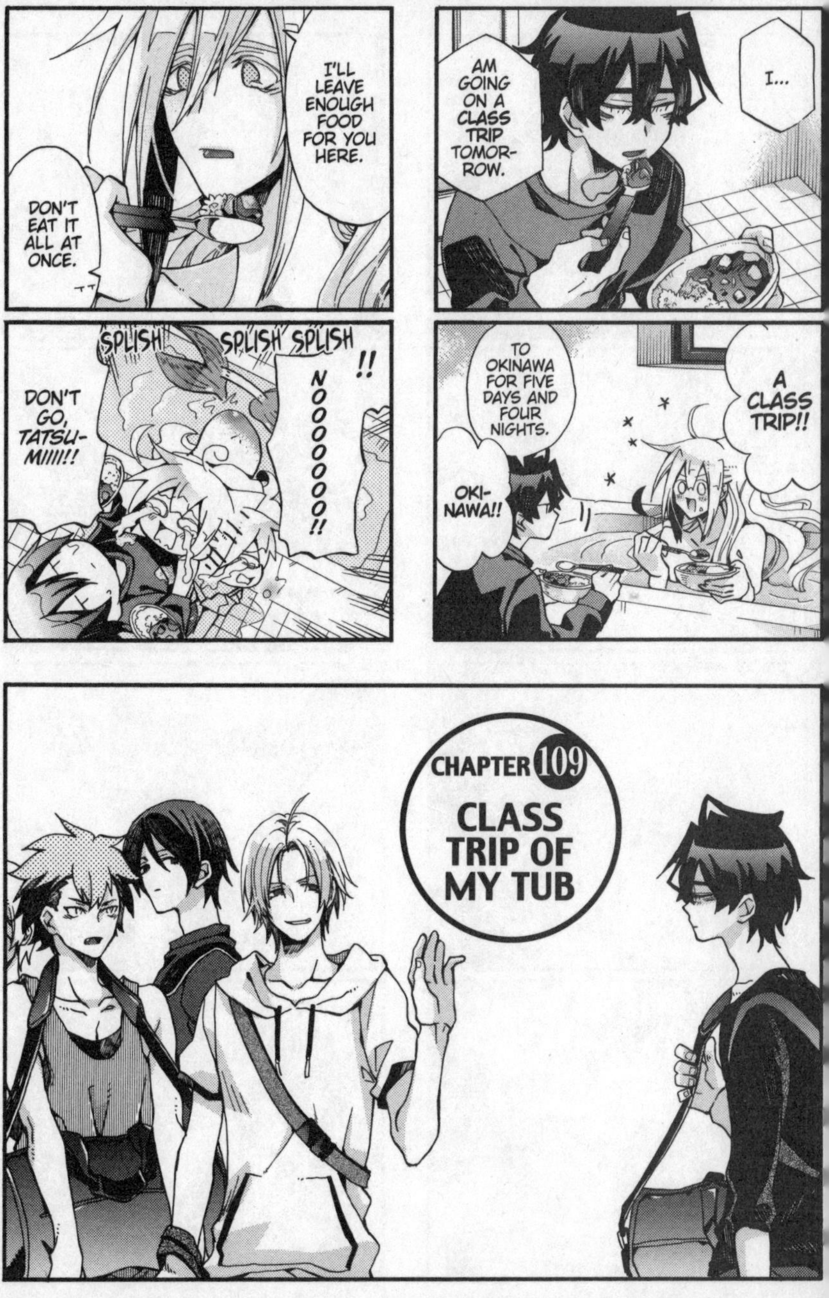
I...
AM GOING ON A CLASS TRIP TOMORROW.
I'LL LEAVE ENOUGH FOOD FOR YOU HERE.
DON'T EAT IT ALL AT ONCE.
A CLASS TRIP!!
TO OKINAWA FOR FIVE DAYS AND FOUR NIGHTS.
OKI-NAWA!!
SPLISH SPLISH SPLISH
!!
NOOOOOOOOO!!
DON'T GO, TATSU-MIIIII!!
CHAPTER 109
CLASS TRIP OF MY TUB

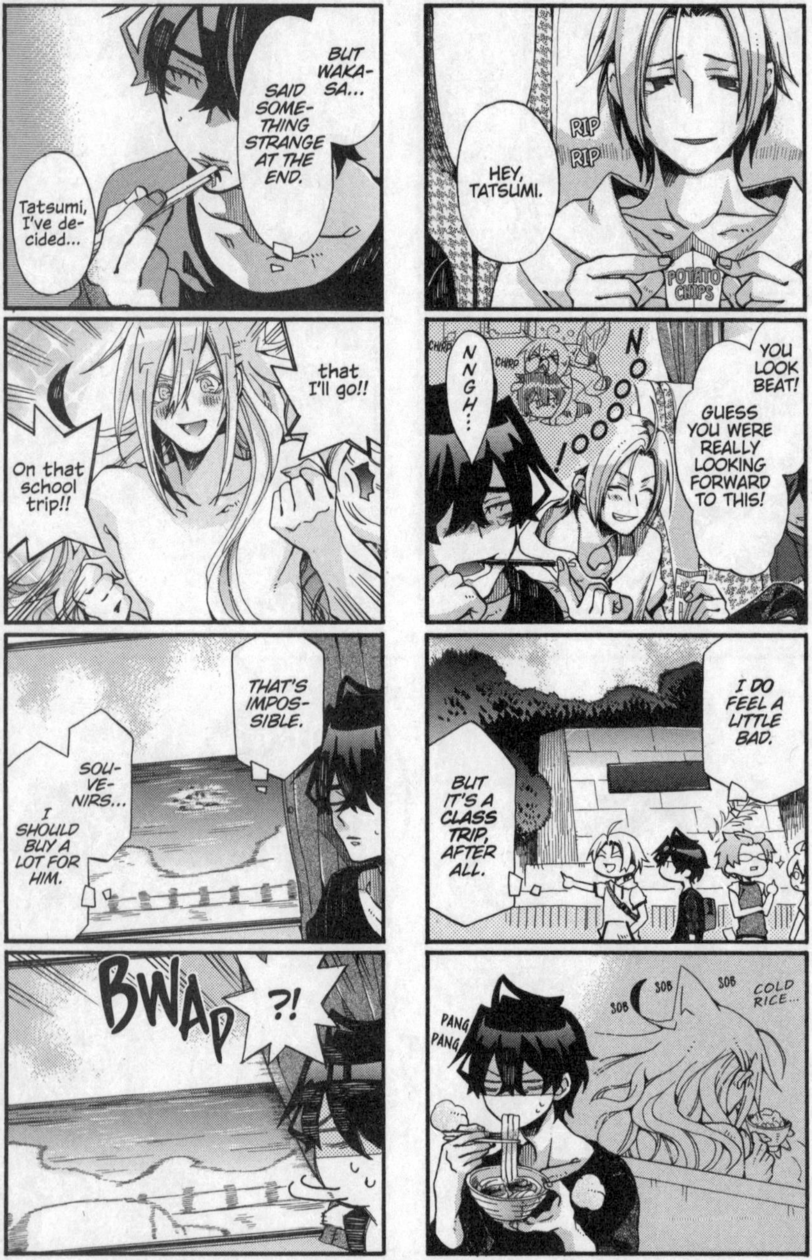
RIP
RIP
HEY, TATSUMI.
POTATO CHIPS
YOU LOOK BEAT! GUESS YOU WERE REALLY LOOKING FORWARD TO THIS!
NOOOOOO!
NNGH...
CHIRP
CHIRP
I DO FEEL A LITTLE BAD.
BUT IT'S A CLASS TRIP, AFTER ALL.
COLD RICE...
SOB
SOB
SOB
PANG
PANG
BUT WAKASA... SAID SOMETHING STRANGE AT THE END.
Tatsumi, I've decided...
that I'll go!!
On that school trip!!
THAT'S IMPOSSIBLE.
SOUVENIRS... I SHOULD BUY A LOT FOR HIM.
?!
BWAP

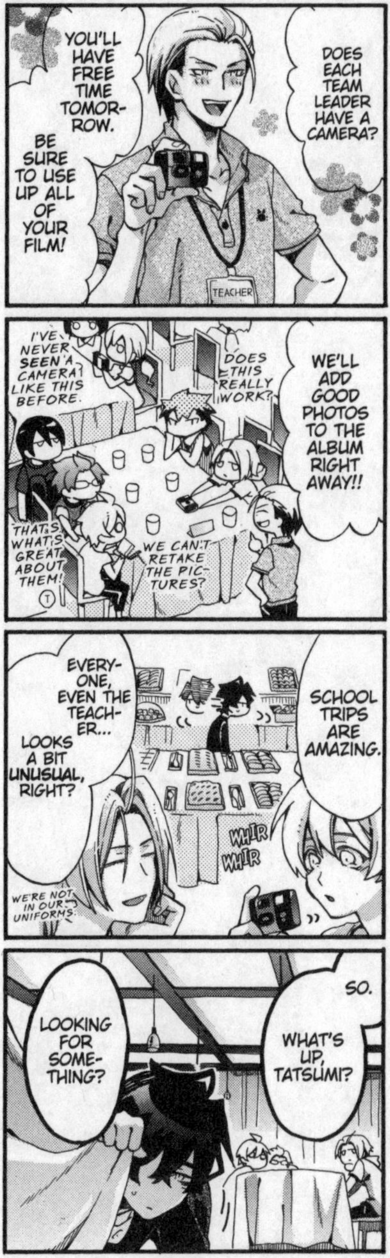
DOES EACH TEAM LEADER HAVE A CAMERA?
YOU'LL HAVE FREE TIME TOMORROW.
BE SURE TO USE UP ALL OF YOUR FILM!
TEACHER
WE'LL ADD GOOD PHOTOS TO THE ALBUM RIGHT AWAY!!
DOES THIS REALLY WORK?
I'VE NEVER SEEN A CAMERA LIKE THIS BEFORE.
WE CAN'T RETAKE THE PICTURES?
THAT'S WHAT'S GREAT ABOUT THEM!
SCHOOL TRIPS ARE AMAZING.
EVERYONE, EVEN THE TEACHER...
LOOKS A BIT UNUSUAL, RIGHT?
WHIR WHIR
WE'RE NOT IN OUR UNIFORMS.
SO.
WHAT'S UP, TATSUMI?
LOOKING FOR SOMETHING?
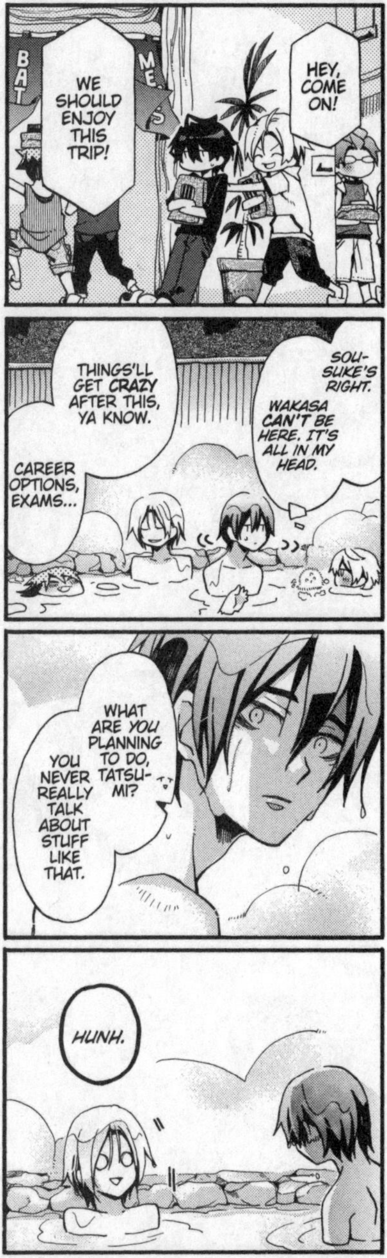
HEY, COME ON!
WE SHOULD ENJOY THIS TRIP!
SOUSUKE'S RIGHT.
WAKASA CAN'T BE HERE. IT'S ALL IN MY HEAD.
THINGS'LL GET CRAZY AFTER THIS, YA KNOW.
CAREER OPTIONS, EXAMS...
WHAT ARE YOU PLANNING TO DO, TATSUMI?
YOU NEVER REALLY TALK ABOUT STUFF LIKE THAT.
HUNH.

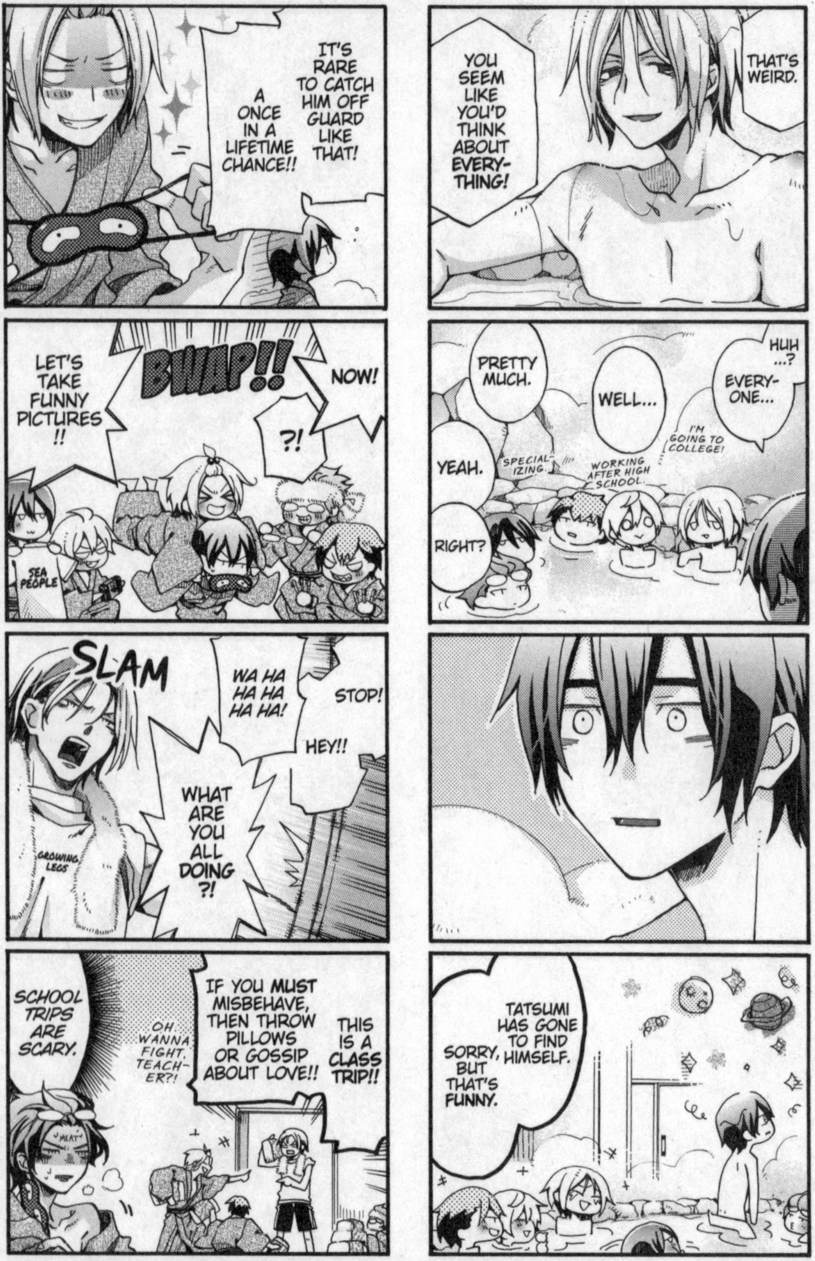
THAT'S WEIRD.
YOU SEEM LIKE YOU'D THINK ABOUT EVERY-THING!
HUH ...? EVERY-ONE...
I'M GOING TO COLLEGE!
WELL...
WORKING AFTER HIGH SCHOOL.
PRETTY MUCH.
SPECIAL-IZING.
YEAH.
RIGHT?
TATSUMI HAS GONE TO FIND HIMSELF.
SORRY, BUT THAT'S FUNNY.
IT'S RARE TO CATCH HIM OFF GUARD LIKE THAT!
A ONCE IN A LIFETIME CHANCE!!
NOW!
BWAP!!
?!
LET'S TAKE FUNNY PICTURES!!
SEA PEOPLE
STOP!
HEY!!
WA HA HA HA HA HA!
SLAM
WHAT ARE YOU ALL DOING?!
GROWING LEGS
THIS IS A CLASS TRIP!!
IF YOU MUST MISBEHAVE, THEN THROW PILLOWS OR GOSSIP ABOUT LOVE!!
OH, WANNA FIGHT, TEACHER?!
MEAT
SCHOOL TRIPS ARE SCARY.

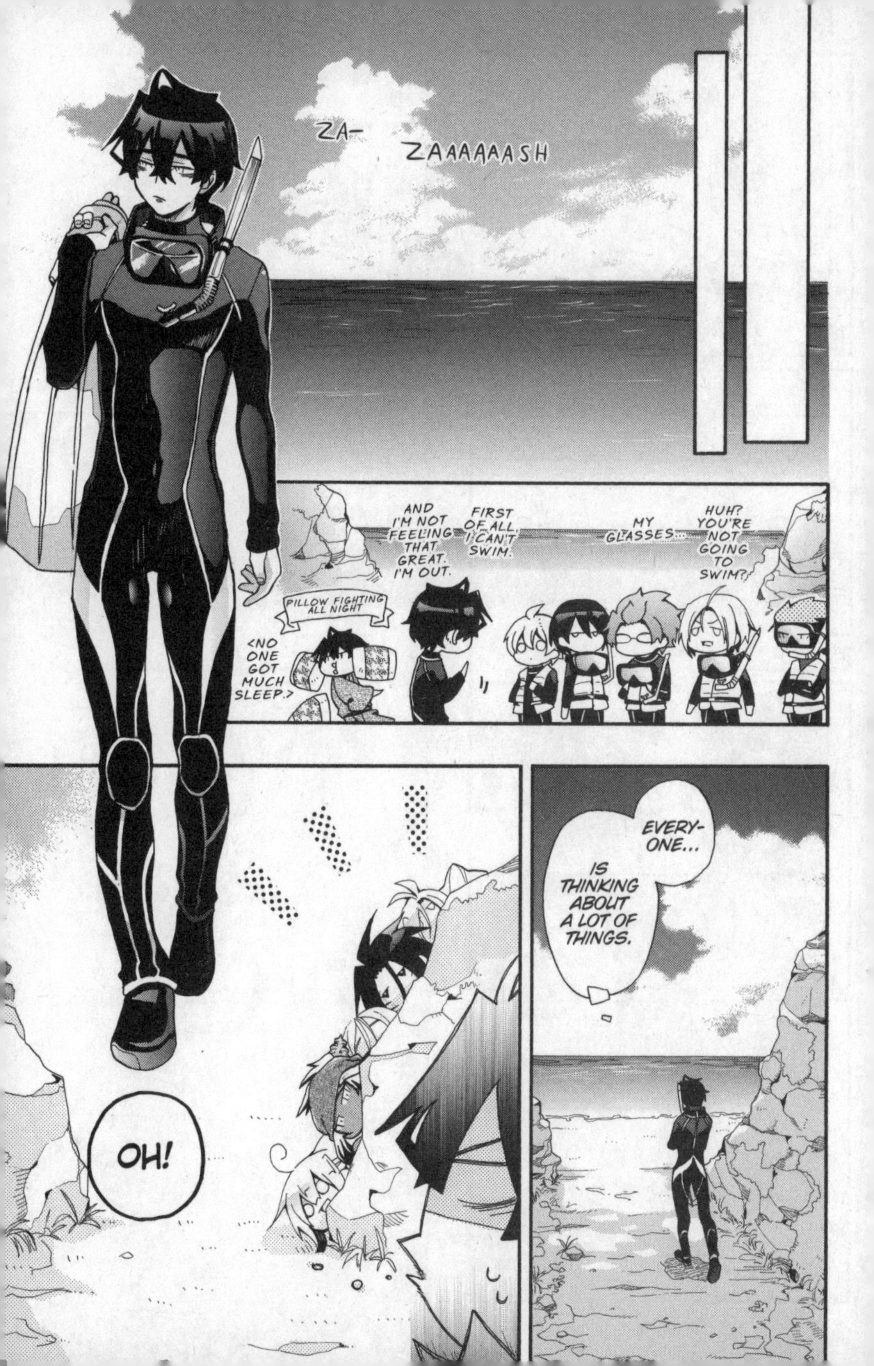
ZA-
ZAAAAAASH
HUH? YOU'RE NOT GOING TO SWIM?
MY GLASSES...
FIRST OF ALL, I CAN'T SWIM.
AND I'M NOT FEELING THAT GREAT. I'M OUT.
PILLOW FIGHTING ALL NIGHT
<NO ONE GOT MUCH SLEEP.>
EVERY-ONE...
IS THINKING ABOUT A LOT OF THINGS.
OH!

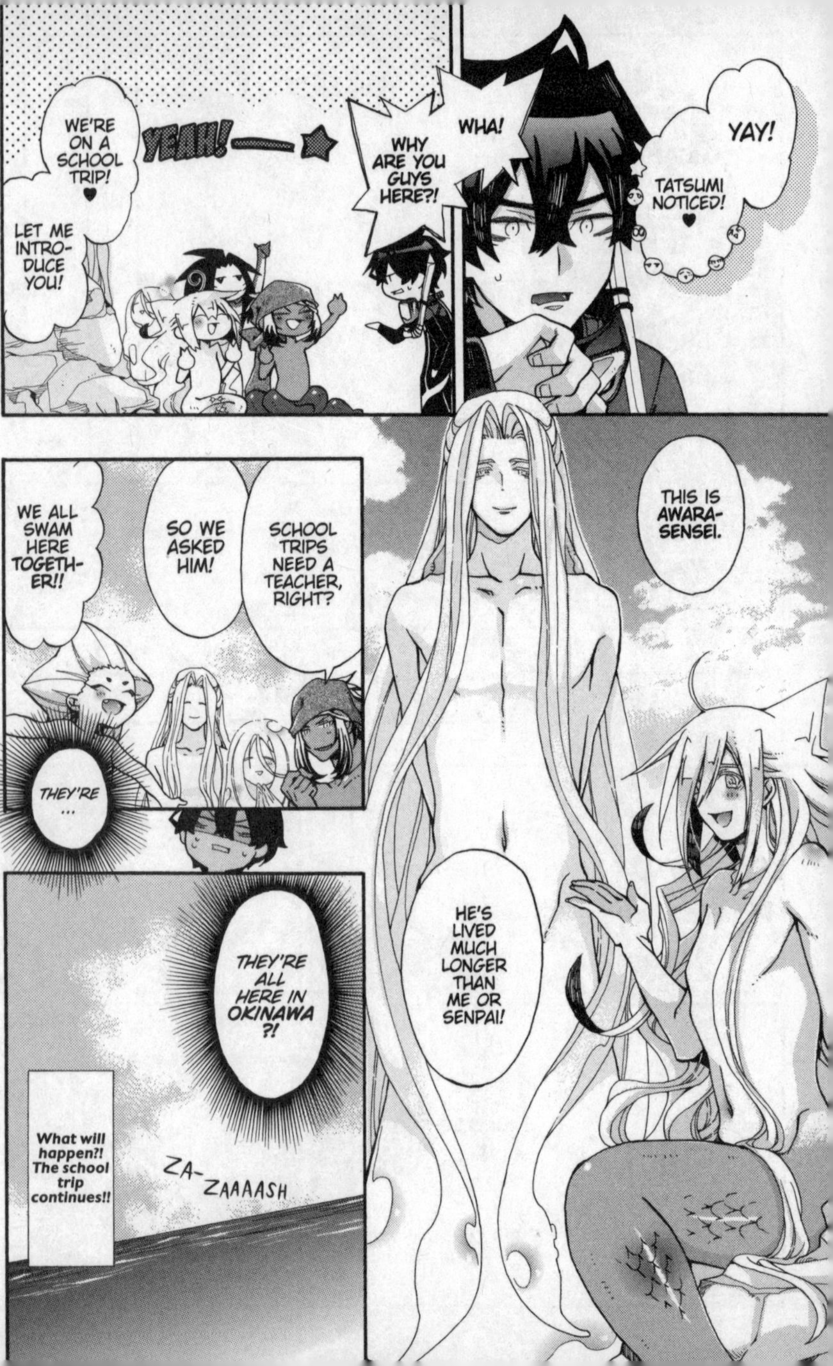
YAY!
TATSUMI NOTICED! ♥
WHA!
WHY ARE YOU GUYS HERE?!
YEAH!
WE'RE ON A SCHOOL TRIP! ♥
LET ME INTRODUCE YOU!
THIS IS AWARA-SENSEI.
HE'S LIVED MUCH LONGER THAN ME OR SENPAI!
SCHOOL TRIPS NEED A TEACHER, RIGHT?
SO WE ASKED HIM!
WE ALL SWAM HERE TOGETHER!!
THEY'RE...
THEY'RE ALL HERE IN OKINAWA?!
ZA-ZAAAASH
What will happen?! The school trip continues!!

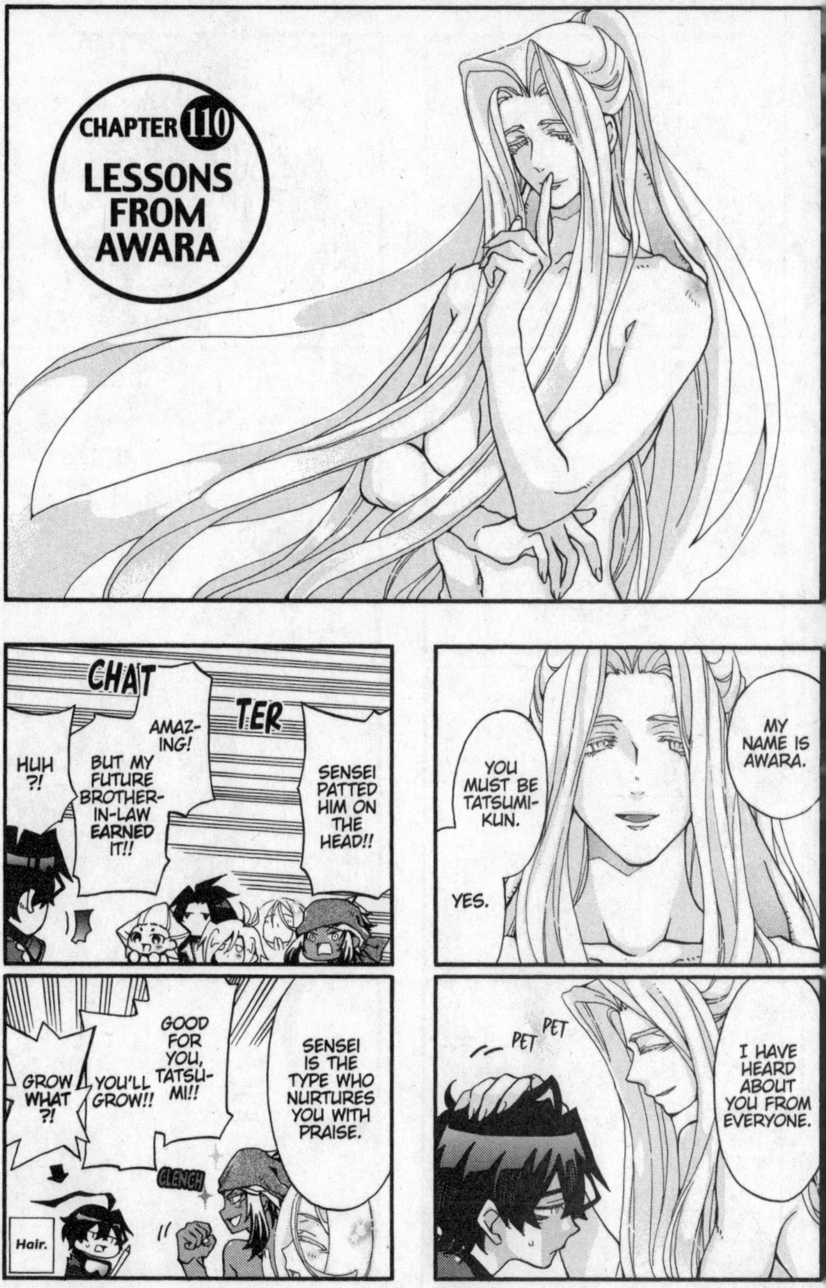
CHAPTER 110
LESSONS FROM AWARA
MY NAME IS AWARA.
YOU MUST BE TATSUMI-KUN.
YES.
CHAT TER
SENSEI PATTED HIM ON THE HEAD!!
AMAZING! BUT MY FUTURE BROTHER-IN-LAW EARNED IT!!
HUH?!
I HAVE HEARD ABOUT YOU FROM EVERYONE.
PET PET
SENSEI IS THE TYPE WHO NURTURES YOU WITH PRAISE.
GOOD FOR YOU, TATSUMI!!
YOU'LL GROW!!
GROW WHAT?!
CLENCH
Hair.

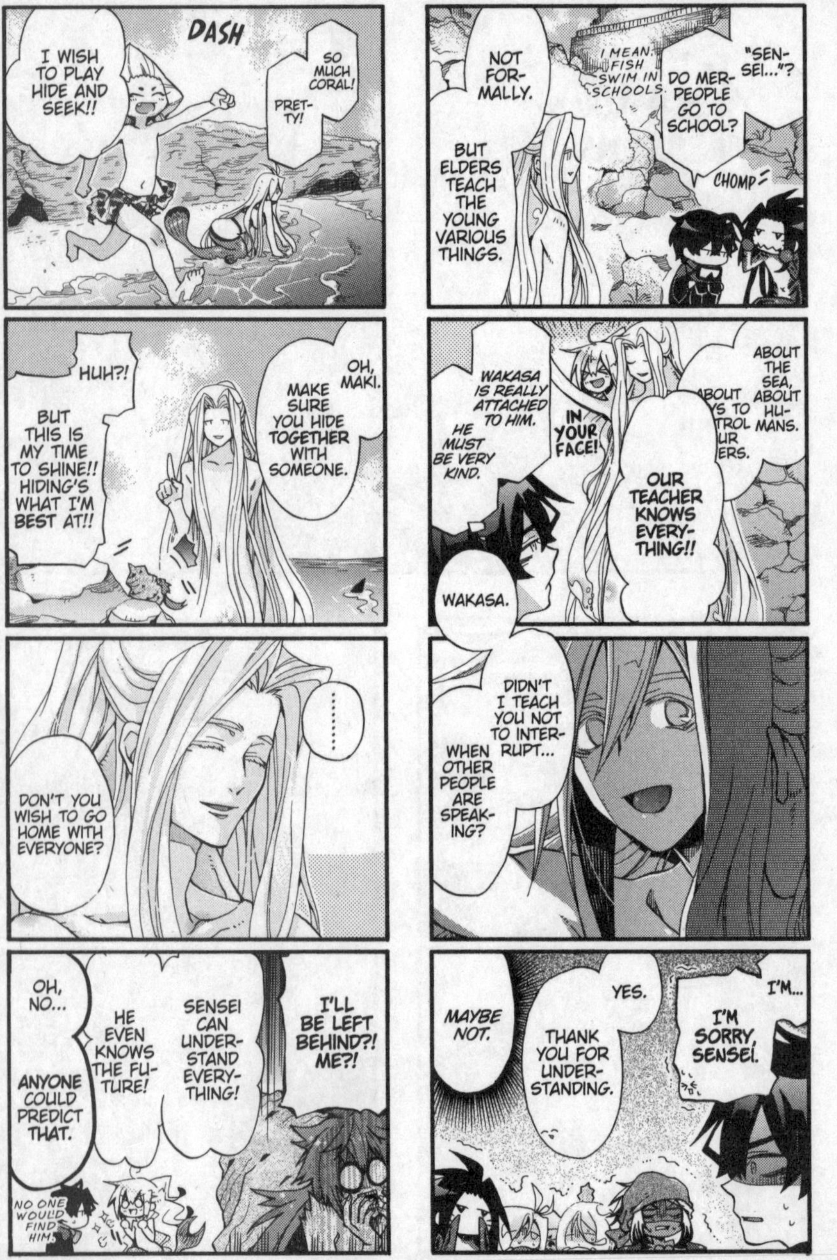
"SEN-SEI..."?
DO MER-PEOPLE GO TO SCHOOL?
I MEAN, FISH SWIM IN SCHOOLS.
NOT FOR-MALLY.
BUT ELDERS TEACH THE YOUNG VARIOUS THINGS.
CHOMP
SO MUCH CORAL!
PRET-TY!
DASH
I WISH TO PLAY HIDE AND SEEK!!
ABOUT THE SEA, ABOUT HU-MANS.
OUR TEACHER KNOWS EVERY-THING!!
IN YOUR FACE!
WAKASA IS REALLY ATTACHED TO HIM.
HE MUST BE VERY KIND.
WAKASA.
OH, MAKI.
MAKE SURE YOU HIDE TOGETHER WITH SOMEONE.
HUH?!
BUT THIS IS MY TIME TO SHINE!! HIDING'S WHAT I'M BEST AT!!
DIDN'T I TEACH YOU NOT TO INTER-RUPT...
WHEN OTHER PEOPLE ARE SPEAK-ING?
......
DON'T YOU WISH TO GO HOME WITH EVERYONE?
I'M...
I'M SORRY, SENSEI.
YES.
THANK YOU FOR UNDER-STANDING.
MAYBE NOT.
I'LL BE LEFT BEHIND?! ME?!
SENSEI CAN UNDER-STAND EVERY-THING!
HE EVEN KNOWS THE FU-TURE!
OH, NO...
ANYONE COULD PREDICT THAT.
NO ONE WOULD FIND HIM.

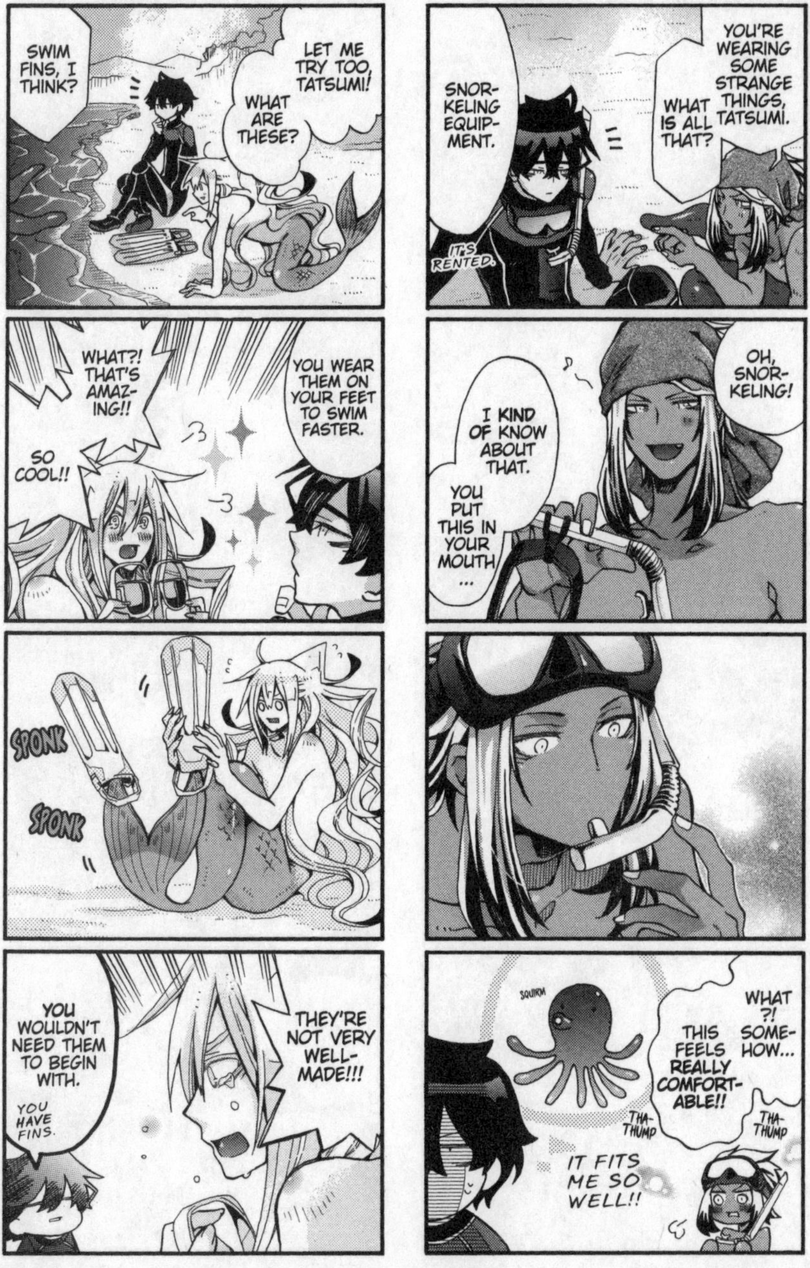
YOU'RE WEARING SOME STRANGE THINGS, TATSUMI.
WHAT IS ALL THAT?
SNOR-KELING EQUIP-MENT.
IT'S RENTED.
OH, SNOR-KELING!
I KIND OF KNOW ABOUT THAT.
YOU PUT THIS IN YOUR MOUTH ...
WHAT ?! SOME-HOW...
THIS FEELS REALLY COMFORT-ABLE!!
THA-THUMP
THA-THUMP
IT FITS ME SO WELL!!
SQUIRM
LET ME TRY TOO, TATSUMI!
WHAT ARE THESE?
SWIM FINS, I THINK?
YOU WEAR THEM ON YOUR FEET TO SWIM FASTER.
WHAT?! THAT'S AMAZ-ING!!
SO COOL!!
SPONK
SPONK
THEY'RE NOT VERY WELL-MADE!!!
YOU WOULDN'T NEED THEM TO BEGIN WITH.
YOU HAVE FINS.

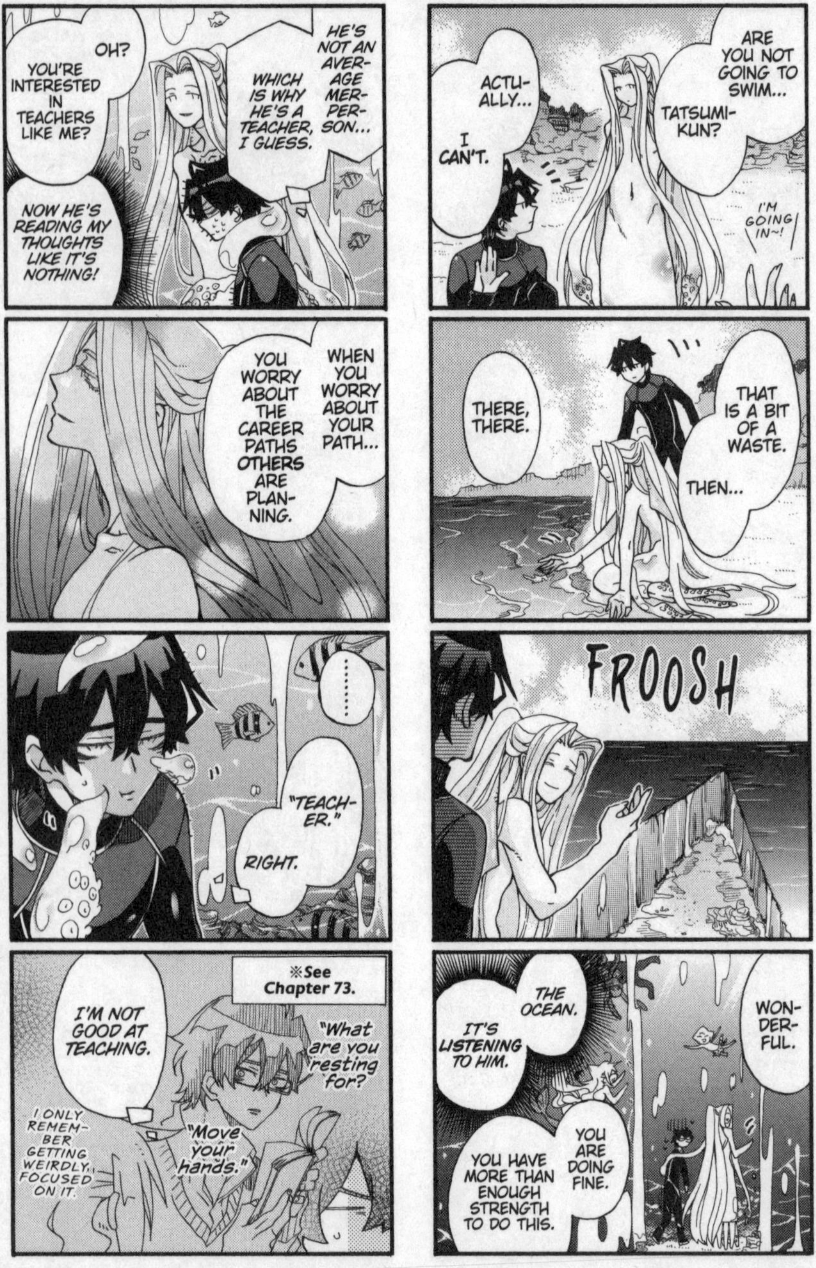
ARE YOU NOT GOING TO SWIM... TATSUMI-KUN?
ACTUALLY... I CAN'T.
I'M GOING IN~!
HE'S NOT AN AVERAGE MERPERSON... WHICH IS WHY HE'S A TEACHER, I GUESS.
OH? YOU'RE INTERESTED IN TEACHERS LIKE ME?
NOW HE'S READING MY THOUGHTS LIKE IT'S NOTHING!
THAT IS A BIT OF A WASTE. THEN...
THERE, THERE.
WHEN YOU WORRY ABOUT YOUR PATH... YOU WORRY ABOUT THE CAREER PATHS OTHERS ARE PLANNING.
FROOSH
......
"TEACHER." RIGHT.
WONDERFUL.
THE OCEAN. IT'S LISTENING TO HIM.
YOU ARE DOING FINE.
YOU HAVE MORE THAN ENOUGH STRENGTH TO DO THIS.
※See Chapter 73.
"What are you resting for?"
I'M NOT GOOD AT TEACHING.
"Move your hands."
I ONLY REMEMBER GETTING WEIRDLY FOCUSED ON IT.

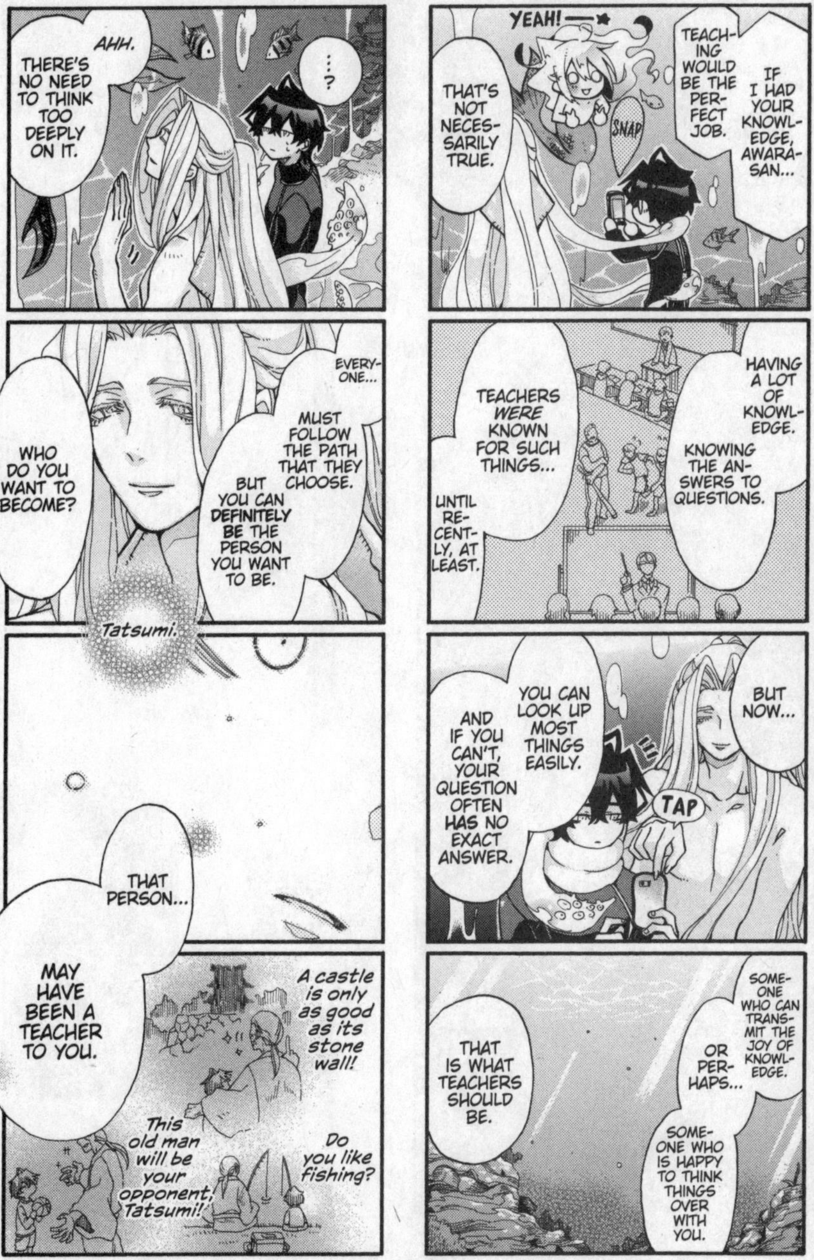
IF I HAD YOUR KNOWLEDGE, AWARA-SAN...
TEACHING WOULD BE THE PERFECT JOB.
YEAH!
THAT'S NOT NECESARILY TRUE.
SNAP
HAVING A LOT OF KNOWLEDGE.
KNOWING THE ANSWERS TO QUESTIONS.
TEACHERS *WERE* KNOWN FOR SUCH THINGS...
UNTIL RECENTLY, AT LEAST.
BUT NOW...
YOU CAN LOOK UP MOST THINGS EASILY.
AND IF YOU CAN'T, YOUR QUESTION OFTEN HAS NO EXACT ANSWER.
TAP
SOMEONE WHO CAN TRANSMIT THE JOY OF KNOWLEDGE.
OR PERHAPS...
SOMEONE WHO IS HAPPY TO THINK THINGS OVER WITH YOU.
THAT IS WHAT TEACHERS SHOULD BE.
...?
AHH. THERE'S NO NEED TO THINK TOO DEEPLY ON IT.
EVERYONE... MUST FOLLOW THE PATH THAT THEY CHOOSE.
BUT YOU CAN **DEFINITELY** BE THE PERSON YOU WANT TO BE.
WHO DO YOU WANT TO BECOME?
Tatsumi.
THAT PERSON...
MAY HAVE BEEN A TEACHER TO YOU.
A castle is only as good as its stone wall!
Do you like fishing?
This old man will be your opponent, Tatsumi!

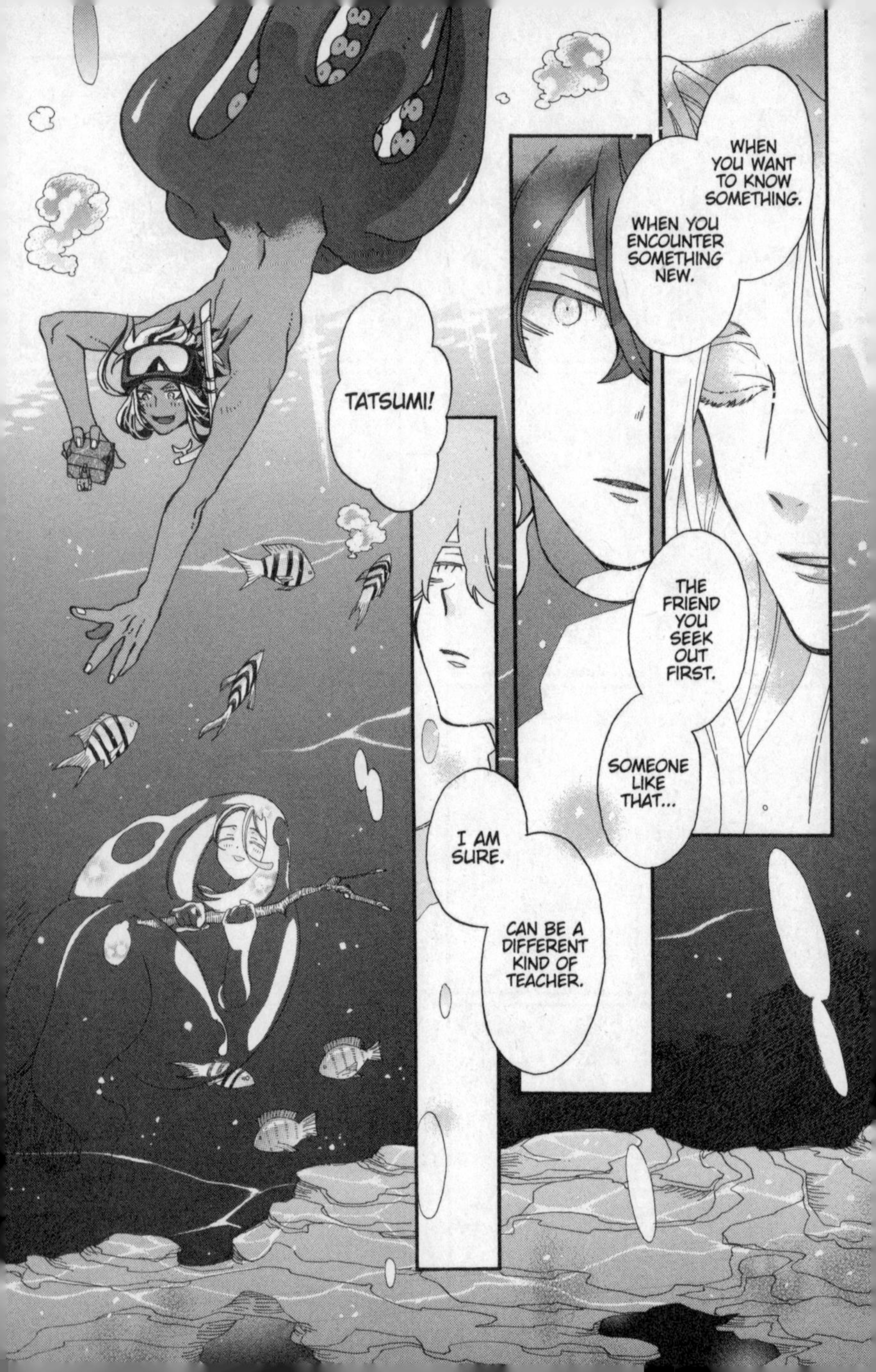
WHEN YOU WANT TO KNOW SOMETHING.
WHEN YOU ENCOUNTER SOMETHING NEW.
THE FRIEND YOU SEEK OUT FIRST.
SOMEONE LIKE THAT...
I AM SURE.
CAN BE A DIFFERENT KIND OF TEACHER.
TATSUMI!

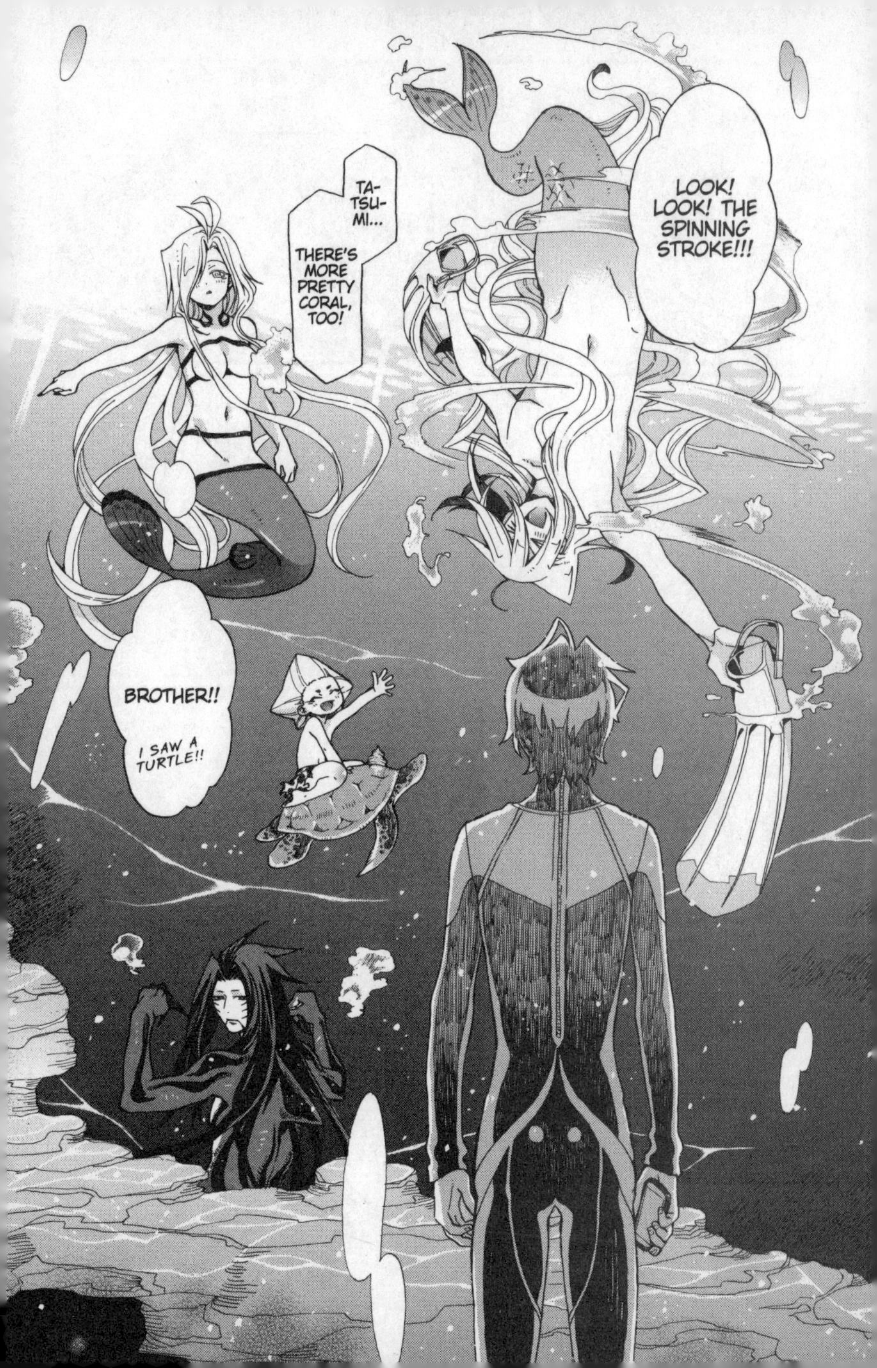
LOOK! LOOK! THE SPINNING STROKE!!!
TA-TSU-MI... THERE'S MORE PRETTY CORAL, TOO!
BROTHER!! I SAW A TURTLE!!

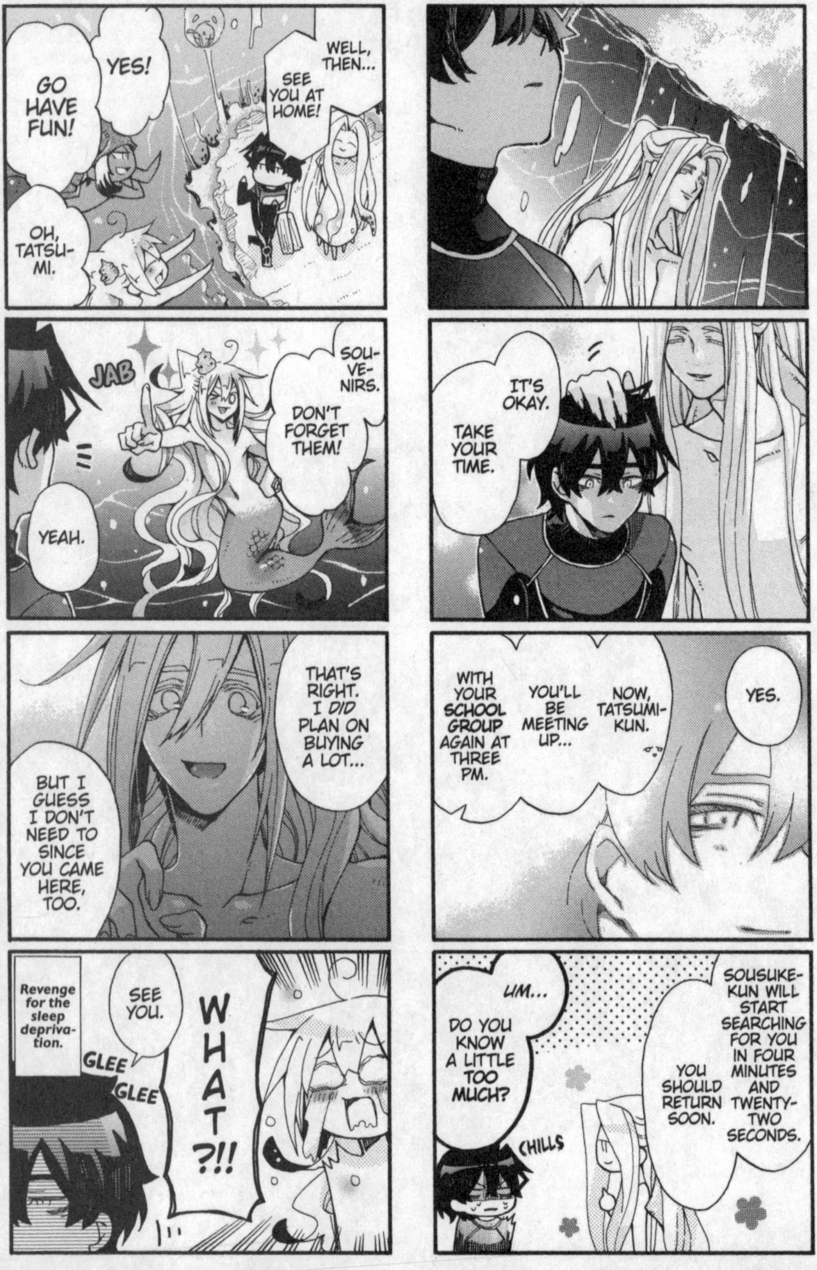
WELL, THEN... SEE YOU AT HOME!
YES!
GO HAVE FUN!
OH, TATSUMI.
IT'S OKAY. TAKE YOUR TIME.
SOUVENIRS. DON'T FORGET THEM!
JAB
YEAH.
YES.
NOW, TATSUMI-KUN. YOU'LL BE MEETING UP... WITH YOUR SCHOOL GROUP AGAIN AT THREE PM.
THAT'S RIGHT. I *DID* PLAN ON BUYING A LOT...
BUT I GUESS I DON'T NEED TO SINCE YOU CAME HERE, TOO.
SOUSUKE-KUN WILL START SEARCHING FOR YOU IN FOUR MINUTES AND TWENTY-TWO SECONDS.
YOU SHOULD RETURN SOON.
UM... DO YOU KNOW A LITTLE TOO MUCH?
CHILLS
WHAT?!!
SEE YOU.
GLEE GLEE
Revenge for the sleep deprivation.

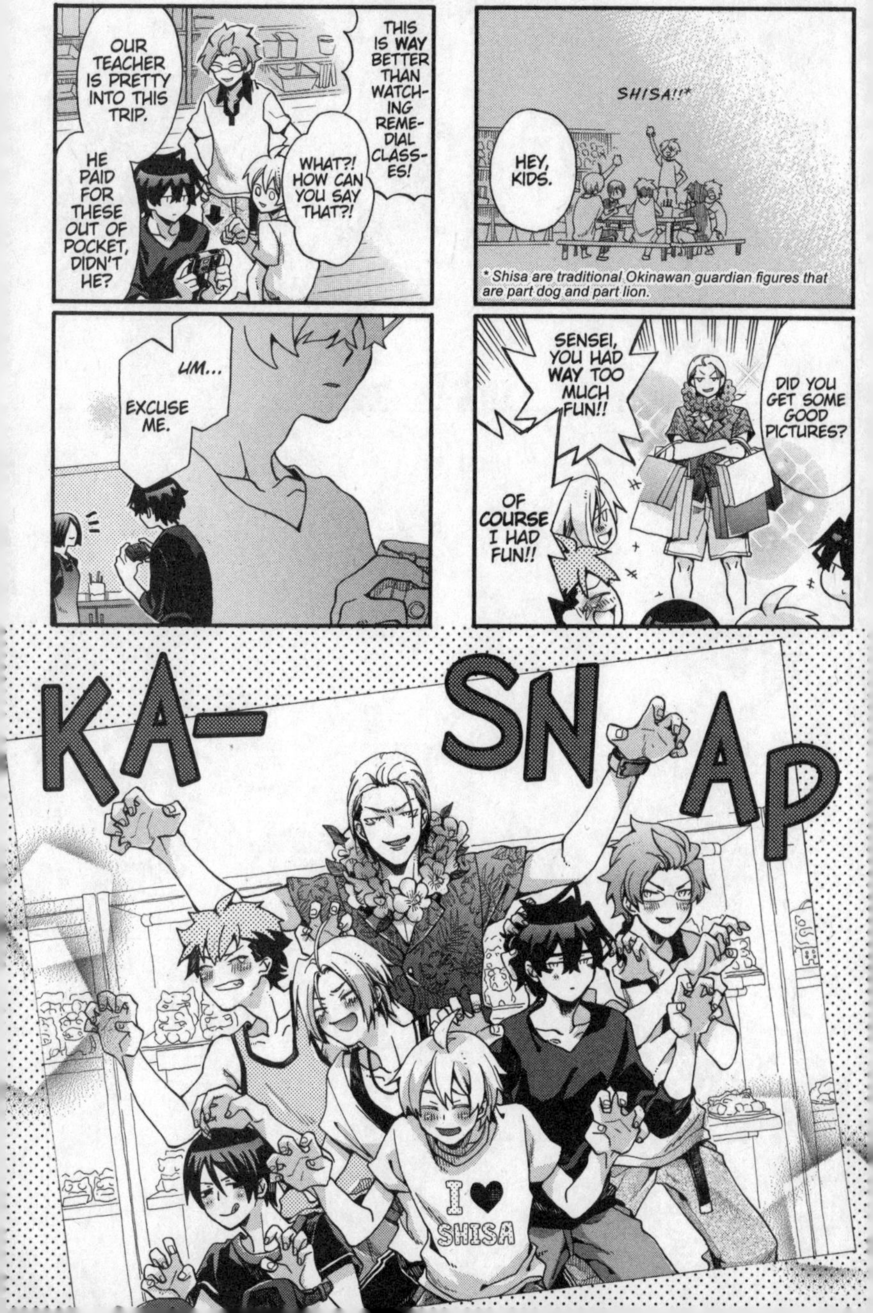
SHISA!!*
HEY, KIDS.
* Shisa are traditional Okinawan guardian figures that are part dog and part lion.
THIS IS WAY BETTER THAN WATCHING REMEDIAL CLASSES!
OUR TEACHER IS PRETTY INTO THIS TRIP.
WHAT?! HOW CAN YOU SAY THAT?!
HE PAID FOR THESE OUT OF POCKET, DIDN'T HE?
DID YOU GET SOME GOOD PICTURES?
SENSEI, YOU HAD WAY TOO MUCH FUN!!
OF COURSE I HAD FUN!!
UM...
EXCUSE ME.
KA-SNAP
I ♥ SHISA

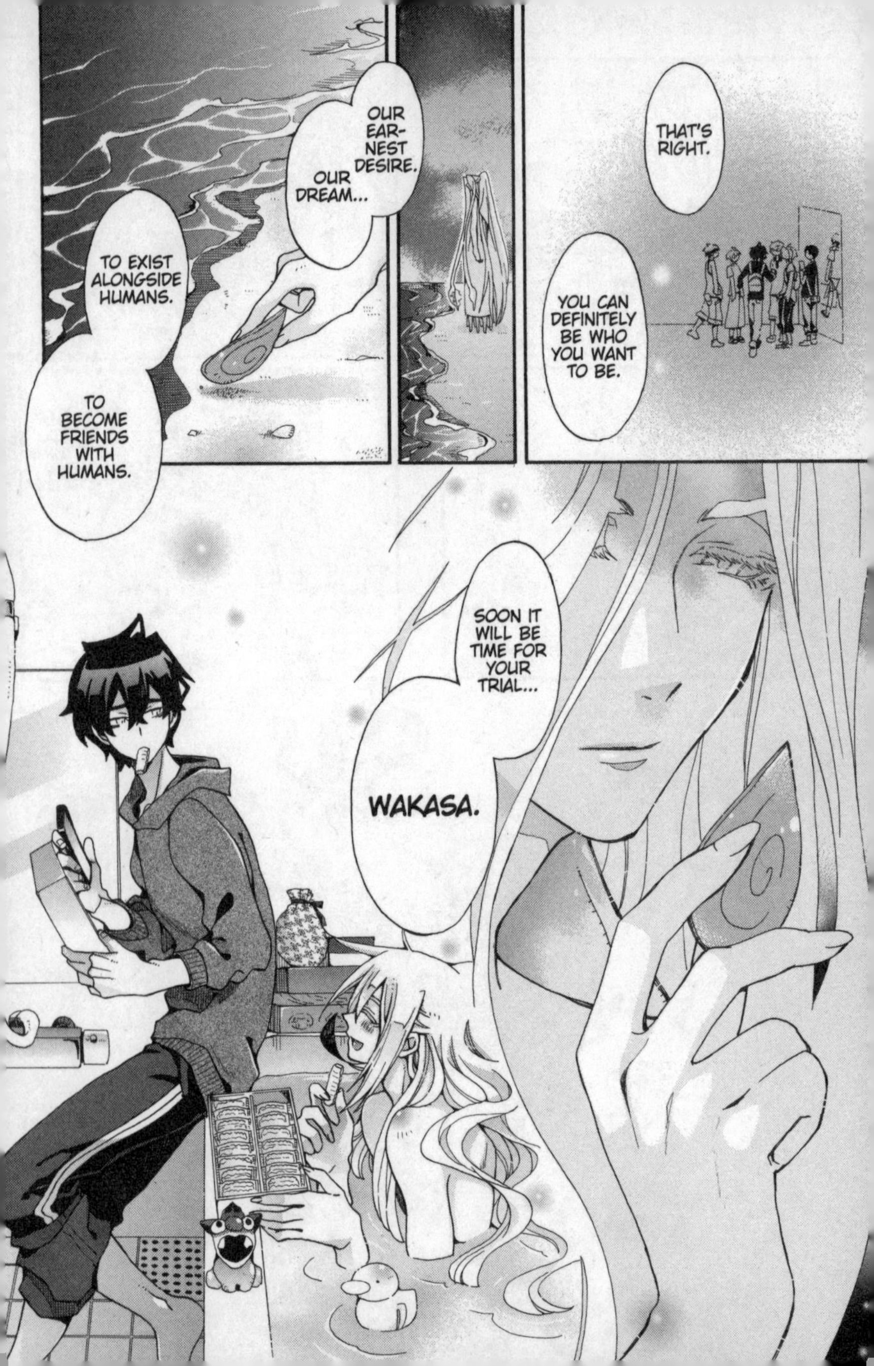
THAT'S RIGHT.
YOU CAN DEFINITELY BE WHO YOU WANT TO BE.
OUR EAR-NEST DESIRE.
OUR DREAM...
TO EXIST ALONGSIDE HUMANS.
TO BECOME FRIENDS WITH HUMANS.
SOON IT WILL BE TIME FOR YOUR TRIAL...
WAKASA.

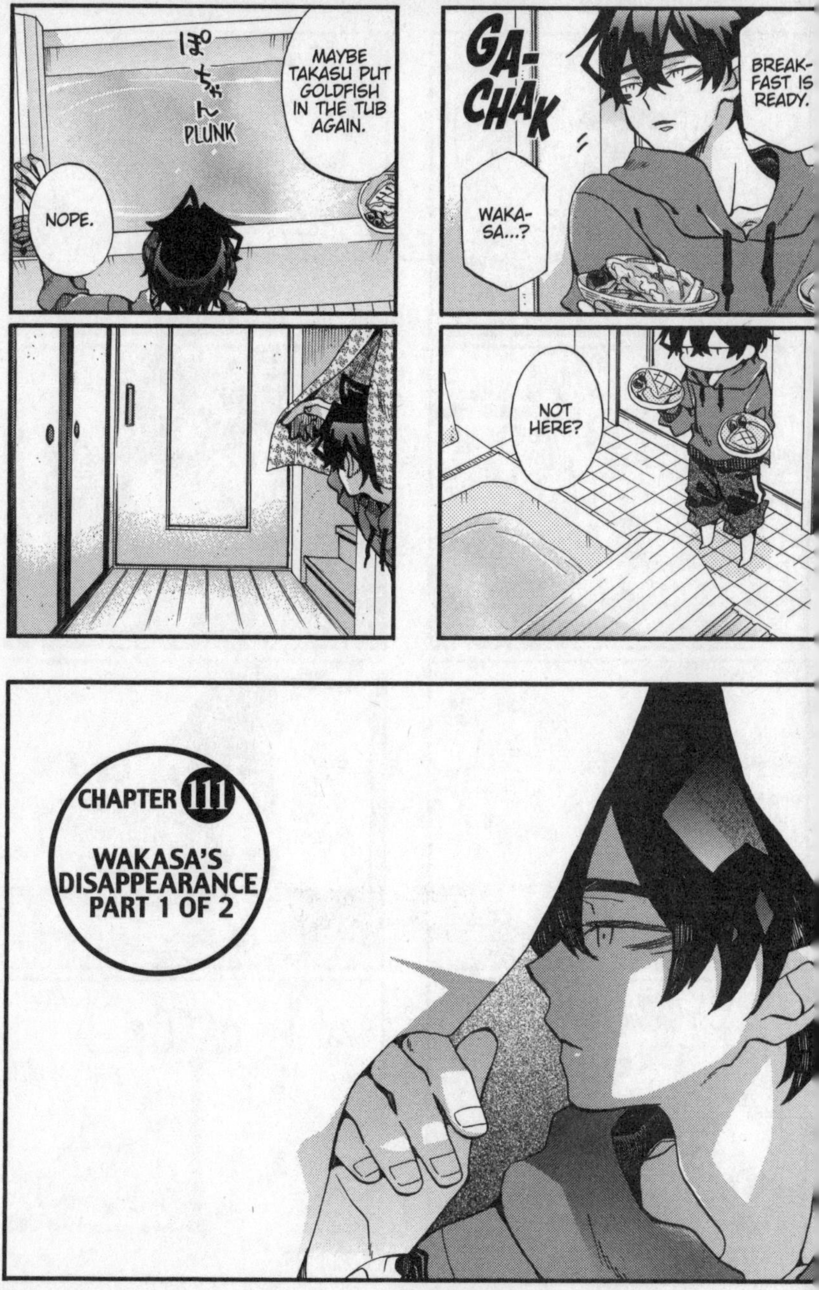
BREAK-FAST IS READY.
GA-CHAK
WAKASA...?
MAYBE TAKASU PUT GOLDFISH IN THE TUB AGAIN.
ぽちゃん
PLUNK
NOPE.
NOT HERE?
CHAPTER 111
WAKASA'S DISAPPEARANCE PART 1 OF 2

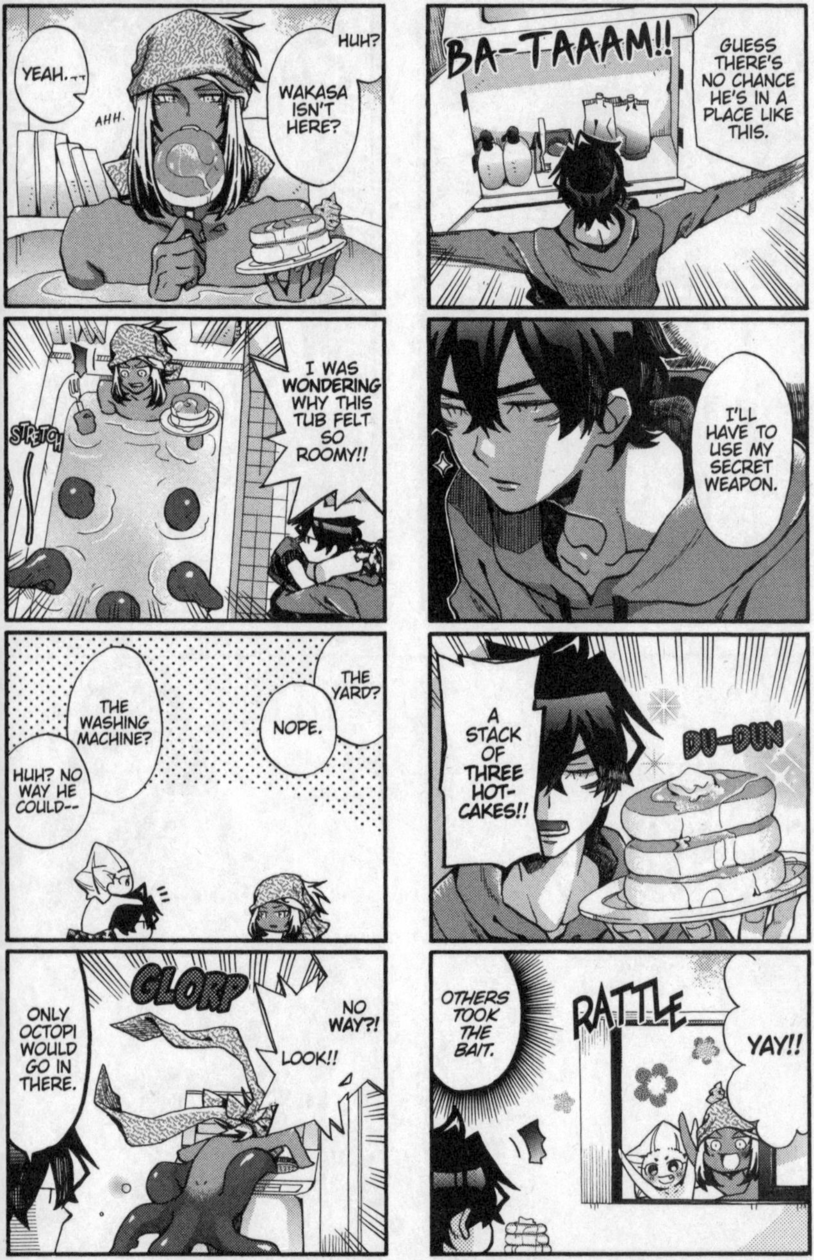
BA-TAAAM!!
GUESS THERE'S NO CHANCE HE'S IN A PLACE LIKE THIS.
I'LL HAVE TO USE MY SECRET WEAPON.
DU-DUN
A STACK OF THREE HOT-CAKES!!
YAY!!
RATTLE
OTHERS TOOK THE BAIT.
HUH?
WAKASA ISN'T HERE?
YEAH...
AHH.
I WAS WONDERING WHY THIS TUB FELT SO ROOMY!!
STRETCH
THE YARD?
NOPE.
THE WASHING MACHINE?
HUH? NO WAY HE COULD--
NO WAY?!
LOOK!!
GLORP
ONLY OCTOPI WOULD GO IN THERE.

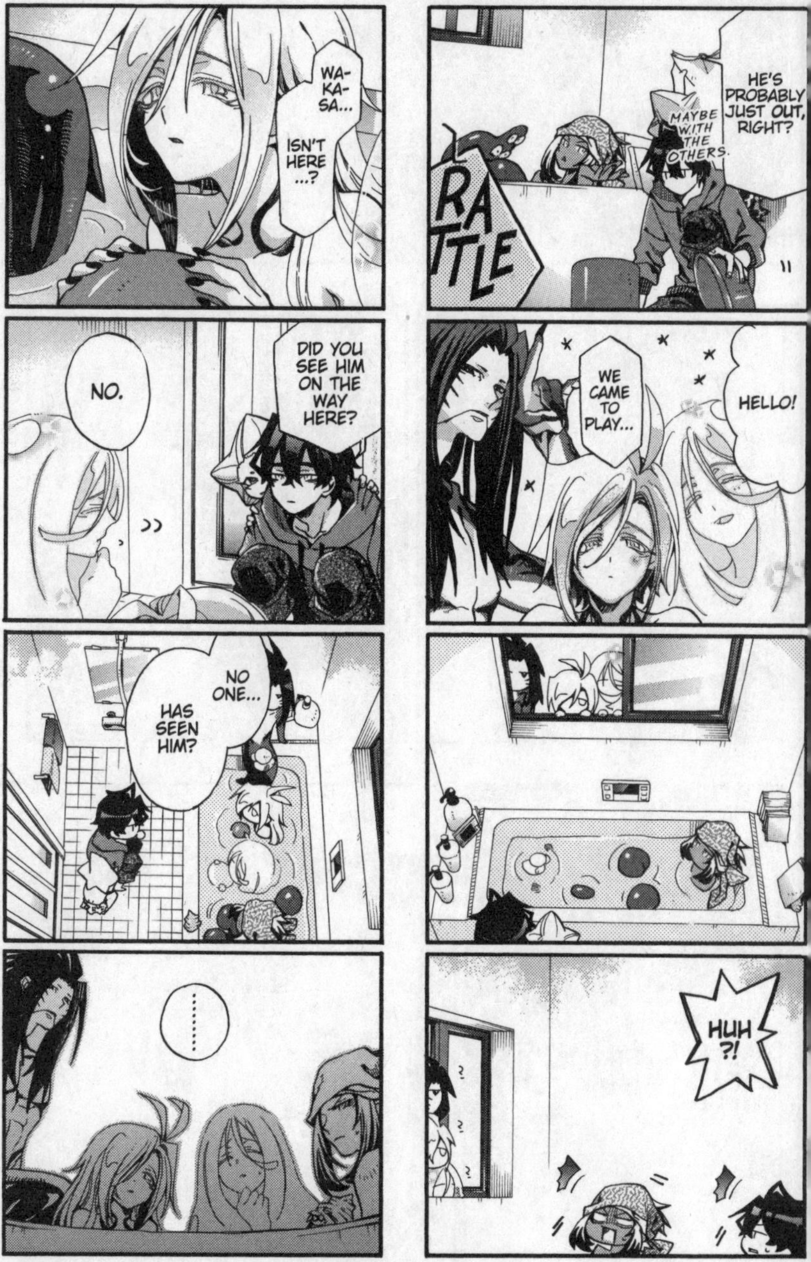
HE'S PROBABLY JUST OUT, RIGHT?
MAYBE WITH THE OTHERS.
WA-KA-SA...
ISN'T HERE ...?
HELLO!
WE CAME TO PLAY...
DID YOU SEE HIM ON THE WAY HERE?
NO.
NO ONE...
HAS SEEN HIM?
HUH ?!
......

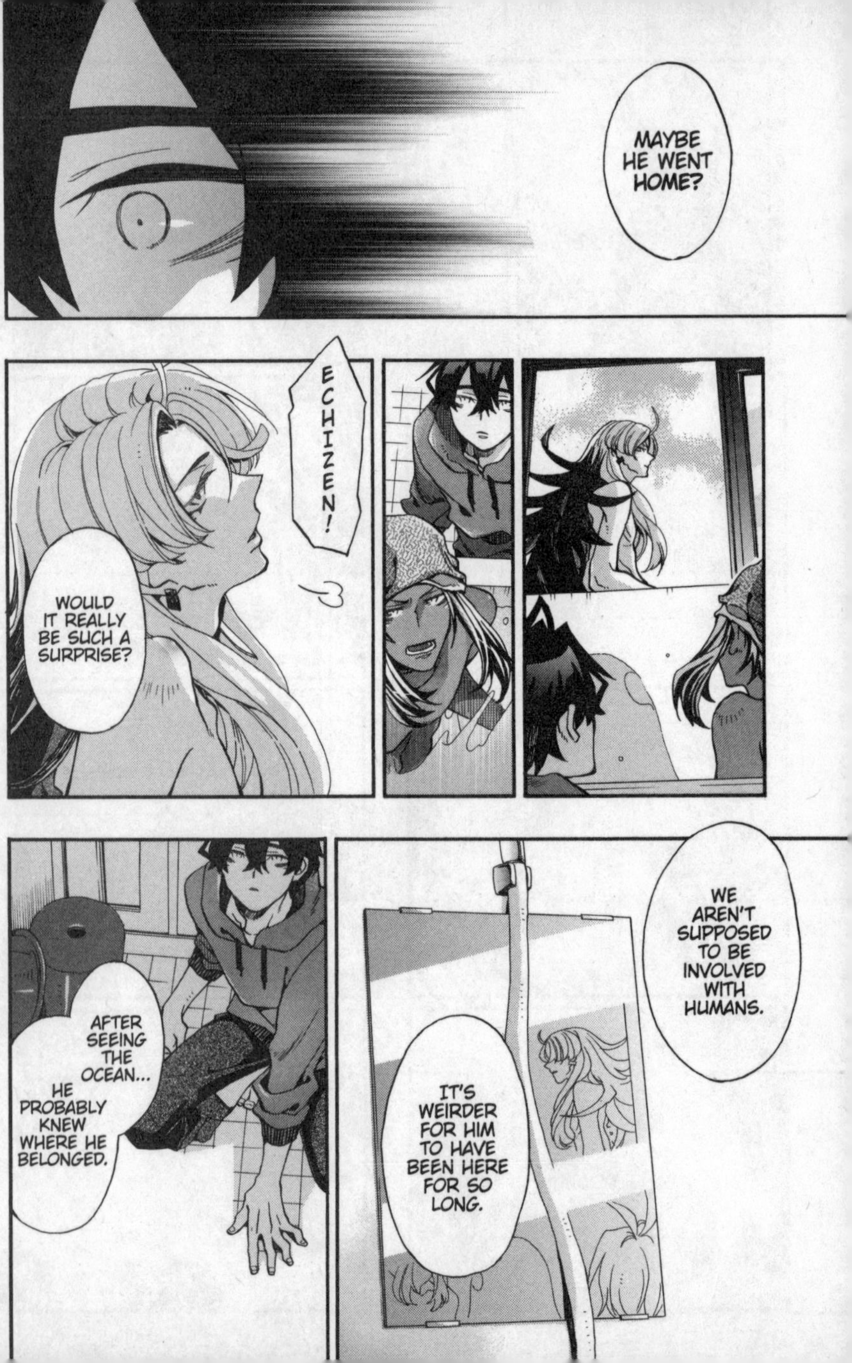
MAYBE HE WENT HOME?
ECHIZEN!
WOULD IT REALLY BE SUCH A SURPRISE?
WE AREN'T SUPPOSED TO BE INVOLVED WITH HUMANS.
IT'S WEIRDER FOR HIM TO HAVE BEEN HERE FOR SO LONG.
AFTER SEEING THE OCEAN...
HE PROBABLY KNEW WHERE HE BELONGED.

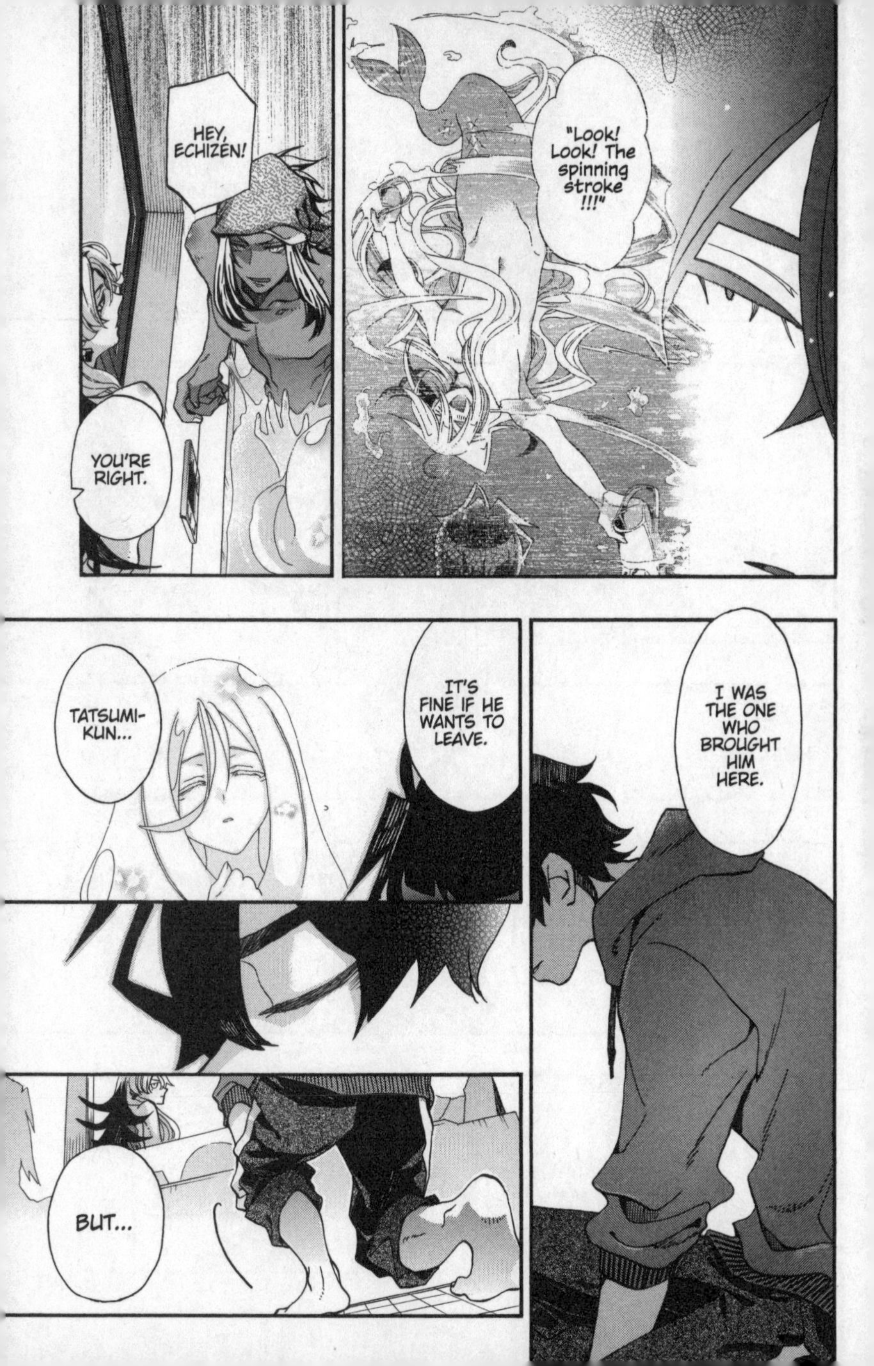
"Look! Look! The spinning stroke!!!"
HEY, ECHIZEN!
YOU'RE RIGHT.
I WAS THE ONE WHO BROUGHT HIM HERE.
IT'S FINE IF HE WANTS TO LEAVE.
TATSUMI-KUN...
BUT...

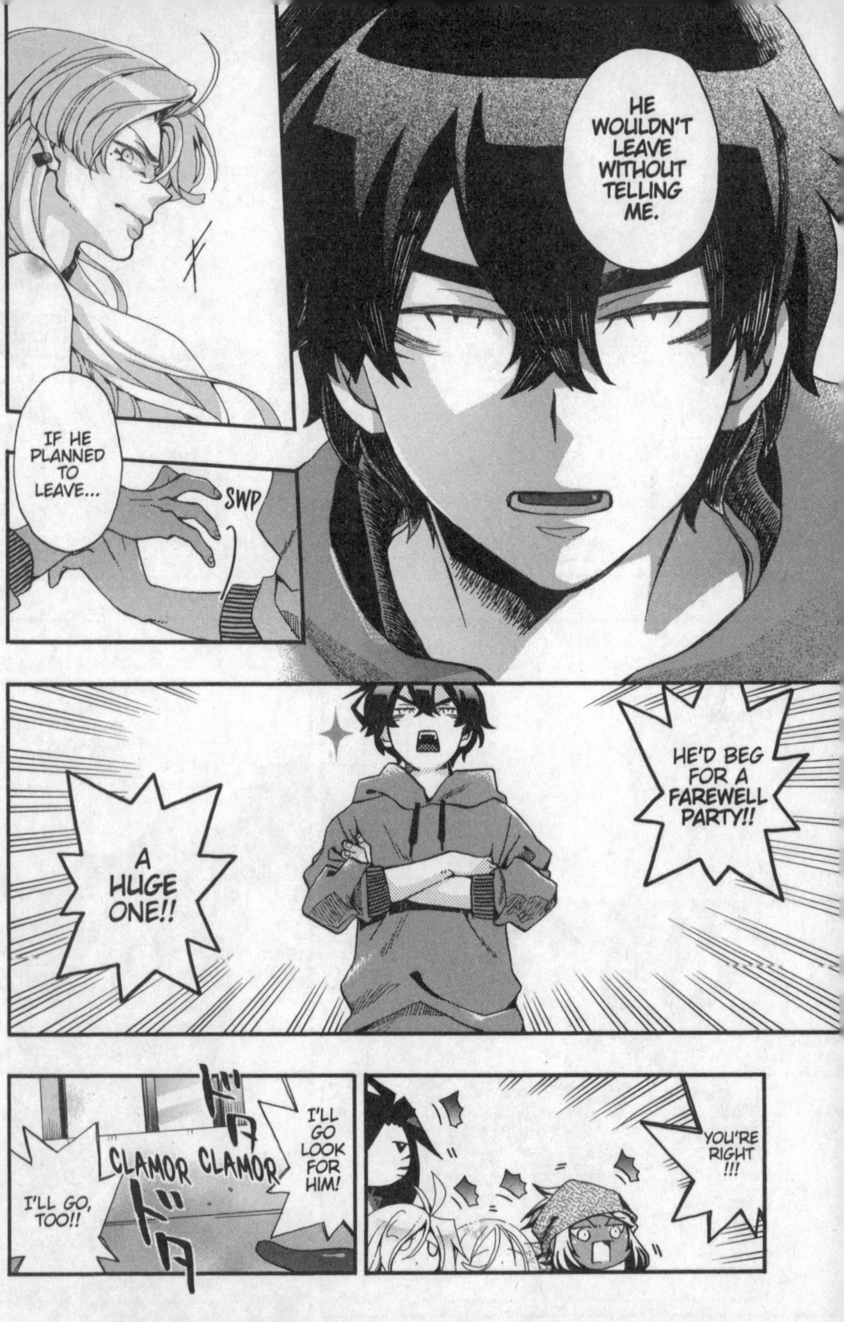
HE WOULDN'T LEAVE WITHOUT TELLING ME.
IF HE PLANNED TO LEAVE...
SWP
HE'D BEG FOR A FAREWELL PARTY!!
A HUGE ONE!!
YOU'RE RIGHT!!!
I'LL GO LOOK FOR HIM!
ドタ
CLAMOR CLAMOR
ドタ
I'LL GO, TOO!!

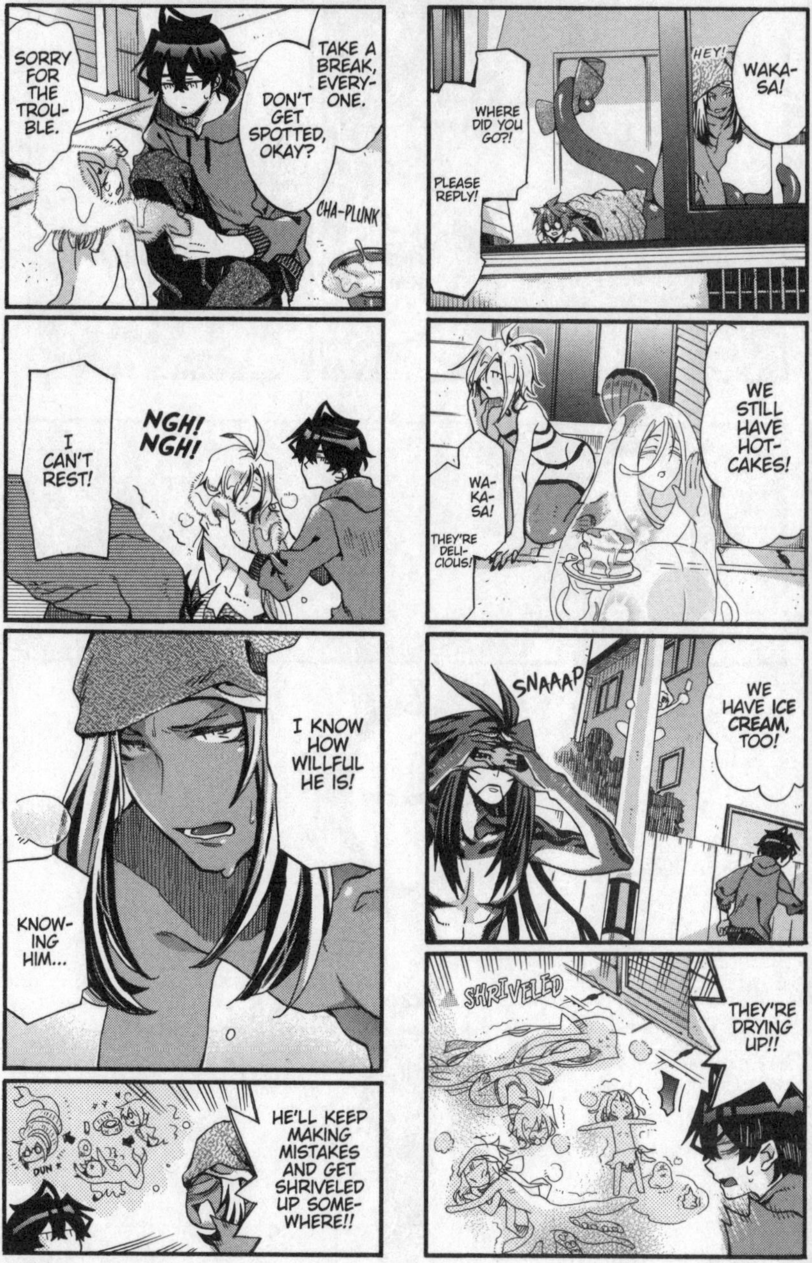
HEY!
WAKA-SA!
WHERE DID YOU GO?!
PLEASE REPLY!
TAKE A BREAK, EVERYONE.
DON'T GET SPOTTED, OKAY?
SORRY FOR THE TROUBLE.
CHA-PLUNK
WE STILL HAVE HOT-CAKES!
WAKA-SA!
THEY'RE DELICIOUS!
NGH! NGH!
I CAN'T REST!
WE HAVE ICE CREAM, TOO!
SNAAAP
I KNOW HOW WILLFUL HE IS!
KNOWING HIM...
THEY'RE DRYING UP!!
SHRIVELED
HE'LL KEEP MAKING MISTAKES AND GET SHRIVELED UP SOME-WHERE!!
DUN

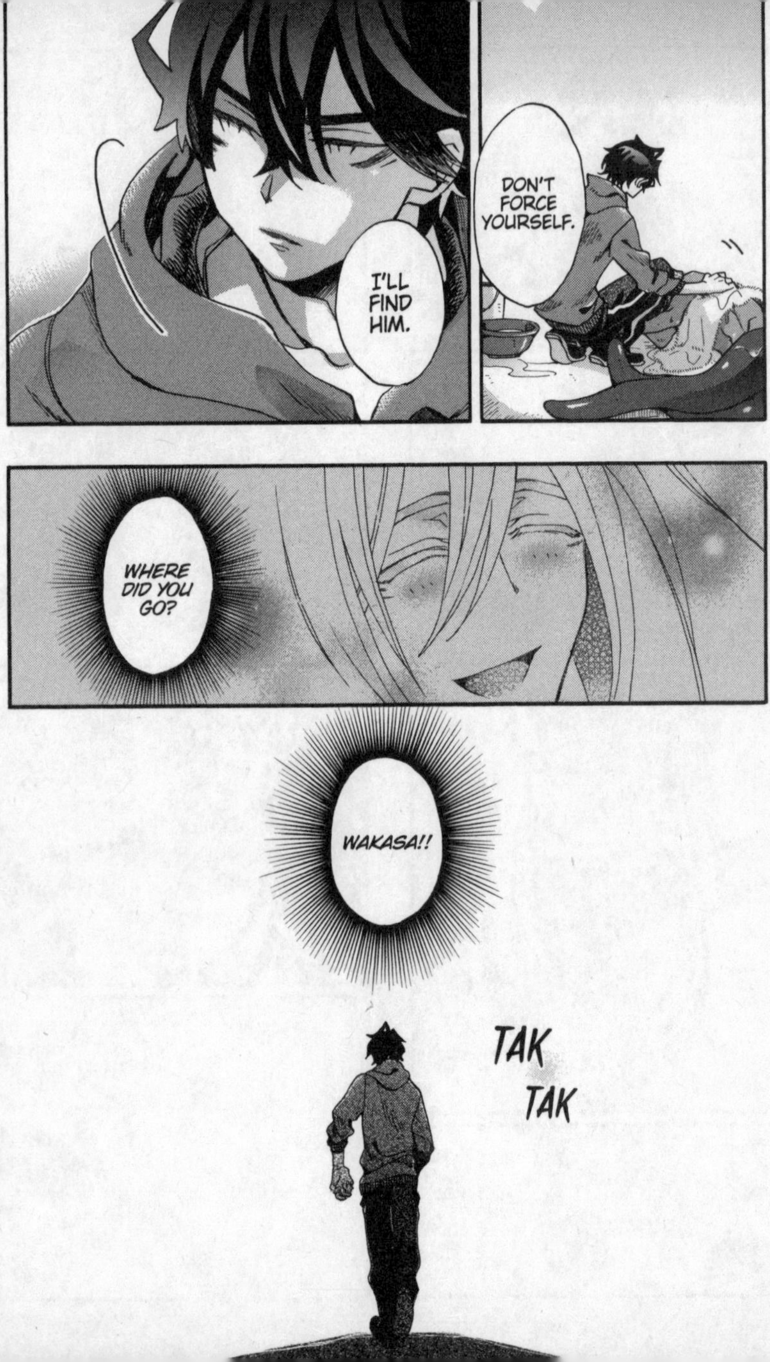
DON'T FORCE YOURSELF.
I'LL FIND HIM.
WHERE DID YOU GO?
WAKASA!!
TAK
TAK

Merman in My Tub

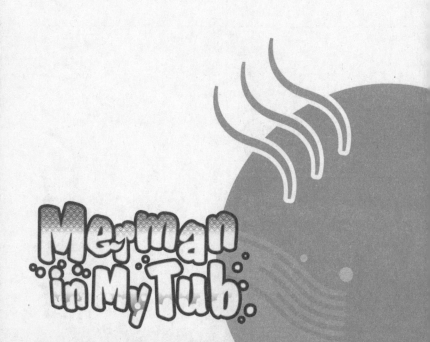

オレん家のフロ事情

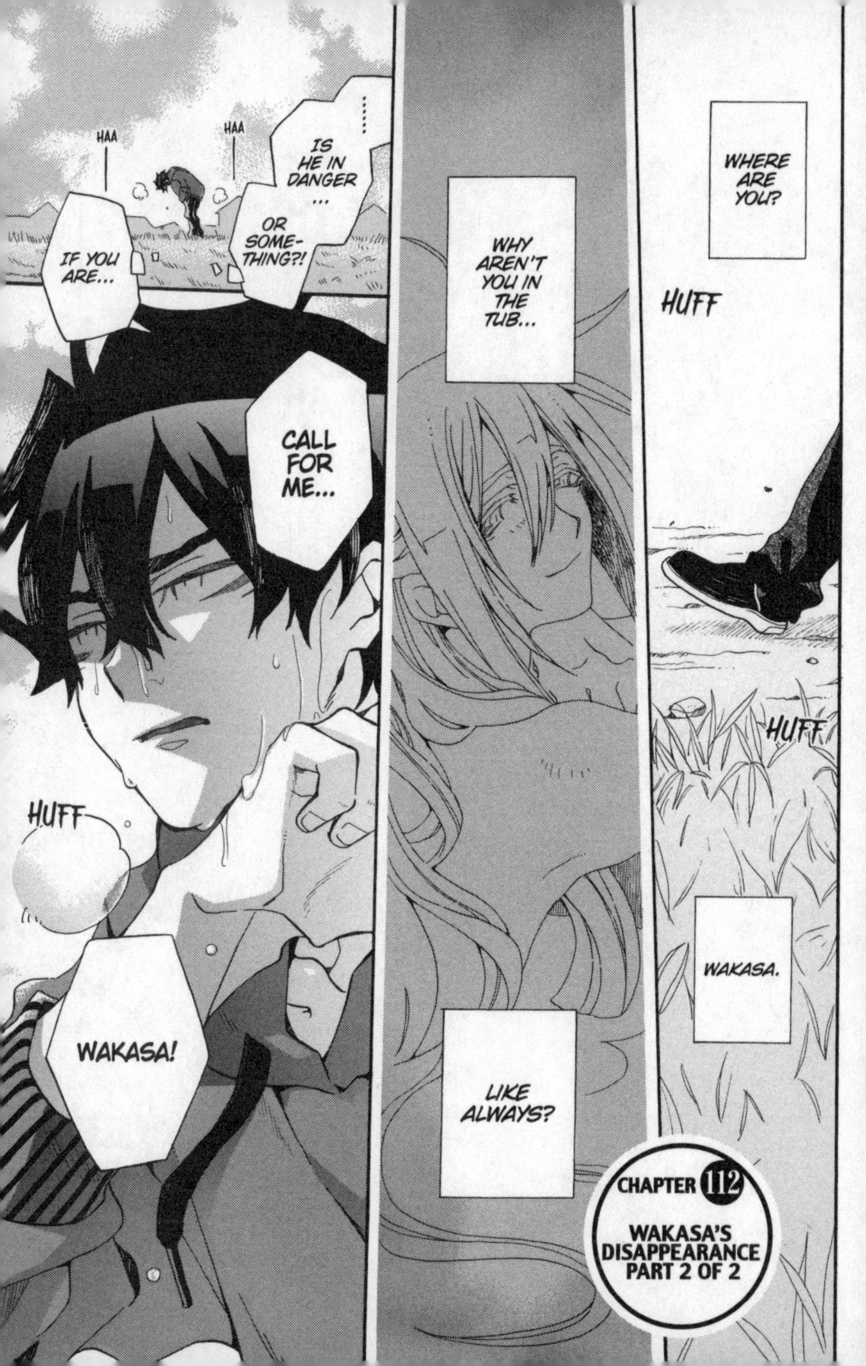
WHERE ARE YOU?
HUFF
HUFF
WAKASA.
CHAPTER 112
WAKASA'S DISAPPEARANCE PART 2 OF 2
WHY AREN'T YOU IN THE TUB...
LIKE ALWAYS?
......
IS HE IN DANGER...
OR SOMETHING?!
HAA
HAA
IF YOU ARE...
CALL FOR ME...
HUFF
WAKASA!

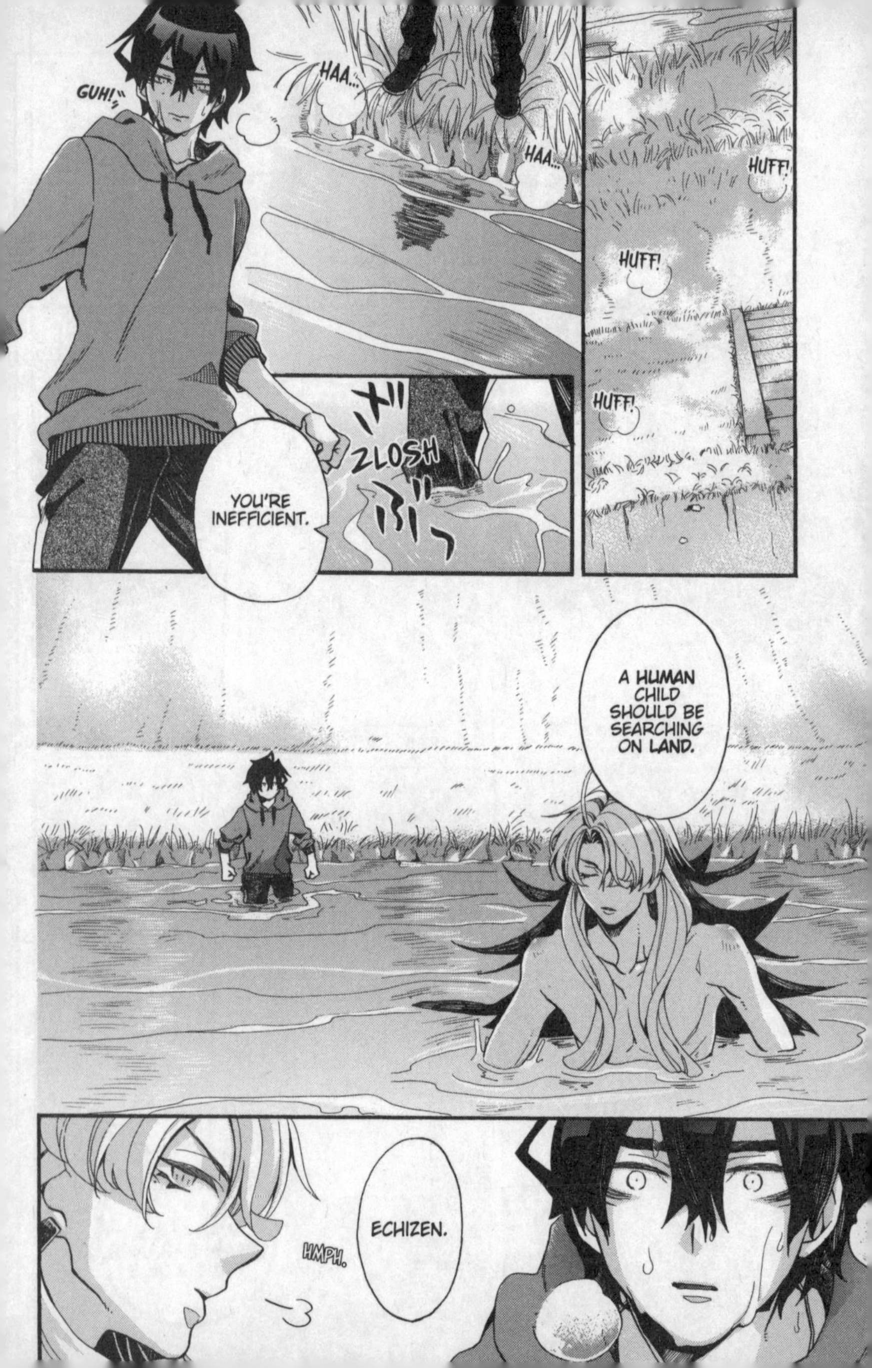
HUFF!
HUFF!
HUFF!
HAA...
HAA...
ZLOSH
GUH!
YOU'RE INEFFICIENT.
A HUMAN CHILD SHOULD BE SEARCHING ON LAND.
ECHIZEN.
HMPH.

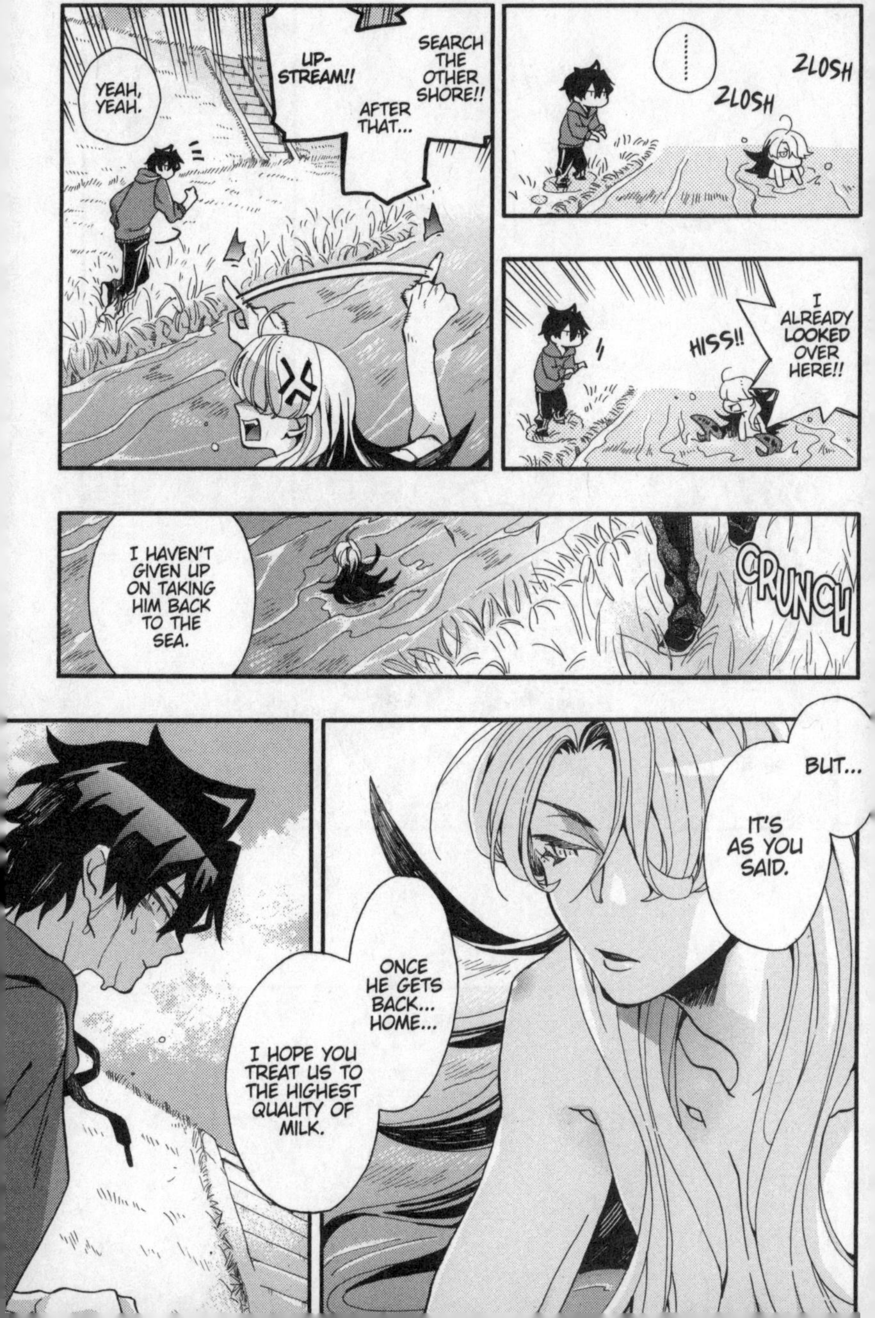
…
ZLOSH
ZLOSH
I ALREADY LOOKED OVER HERE!!
HISS!!
SEARCH THE OTHER SHORE!!
UP-STREAM!!
AFTER THAT…
YEAH, YEAH.
CRUNCH
I HAVEN'T GIVEN UP ON TAKING HIM BACK TO THE SEA.
BUT…
IT'S AS YOU SAID.
ONCE HE GETS BACK… HOME…
I HOPE YOU TREAT US TO THE HIGHEST QUALITY OF MILK.

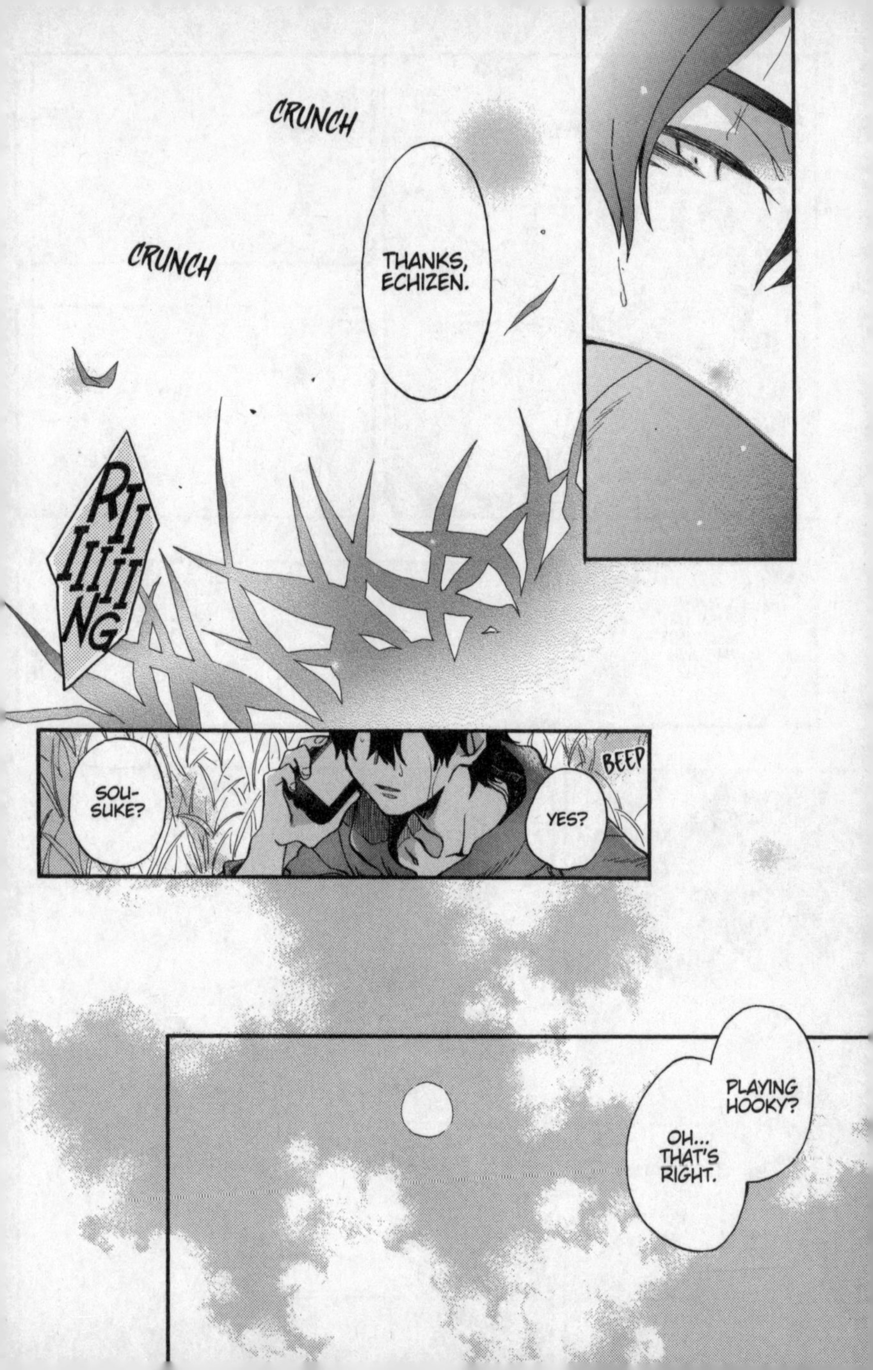
CRUNCH
THANKS, ECHIZEN.
CRUNCH
RIIIIING
BEEP
YES?
SOU-SUKE?
PLAYING HOOKY?
OH... THAT'S RIGHT.

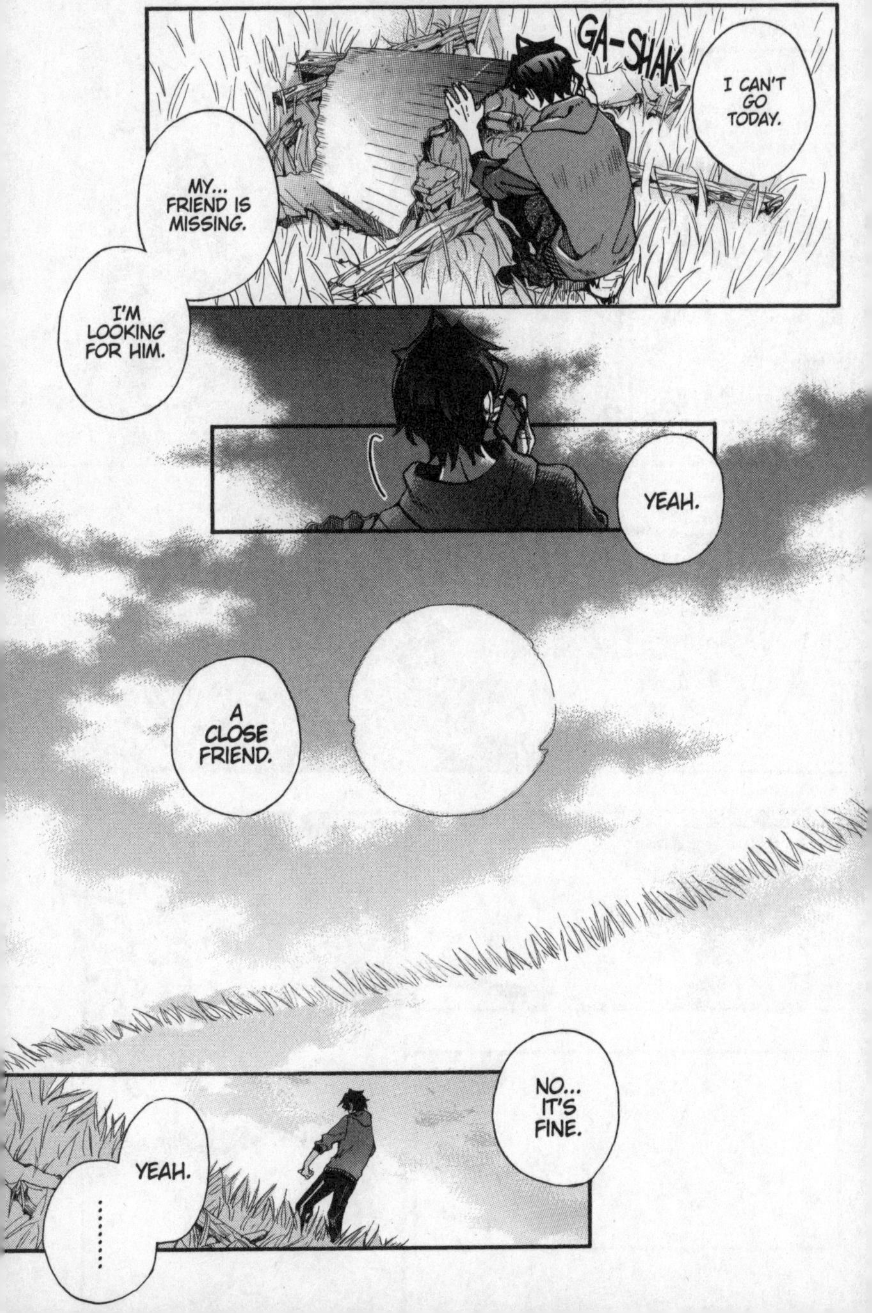
GA-SHAK
I CAN'T GO TODAY.
MY... FRIEND IS MISSING.
I'M LOOKING FOR HIM.
YEAH.
A CLOSE FRIEND.
NO... IT'S FINE.
YEAH.
......

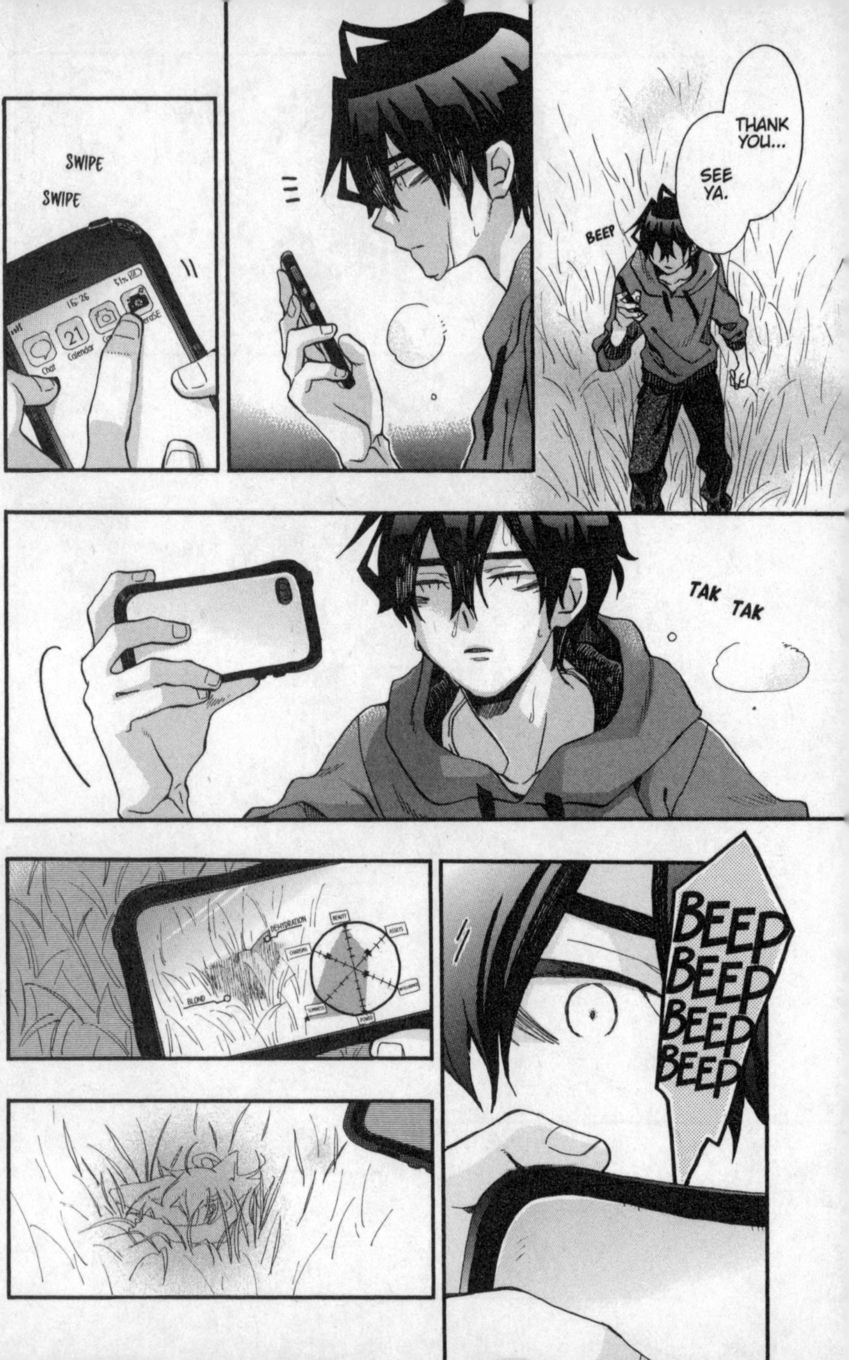
THANK YOU...
SEE YA.
BEEP
SWIPE
SWIPE
15:26
21
Chat
Calendar
TAK TAK
BEEP BEEP BEEP BEEP
DEHYDRATION
BEAUTY
ASSETS
CHARISMA
BLOND
POWER

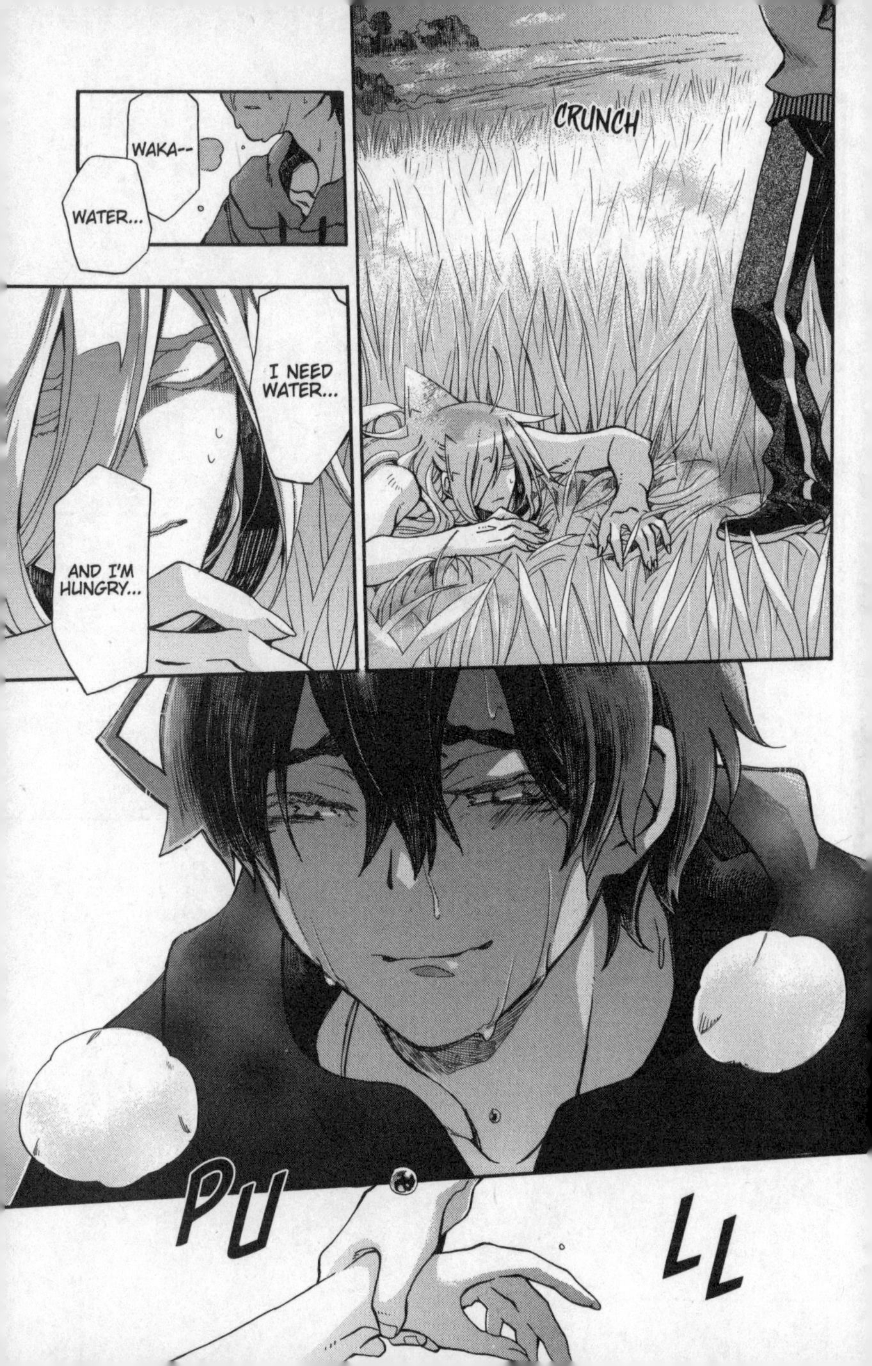
CRUNCH
WAKA--
WATER...
I NEED WATER...
AND I'M HUNGRY...
PU LL

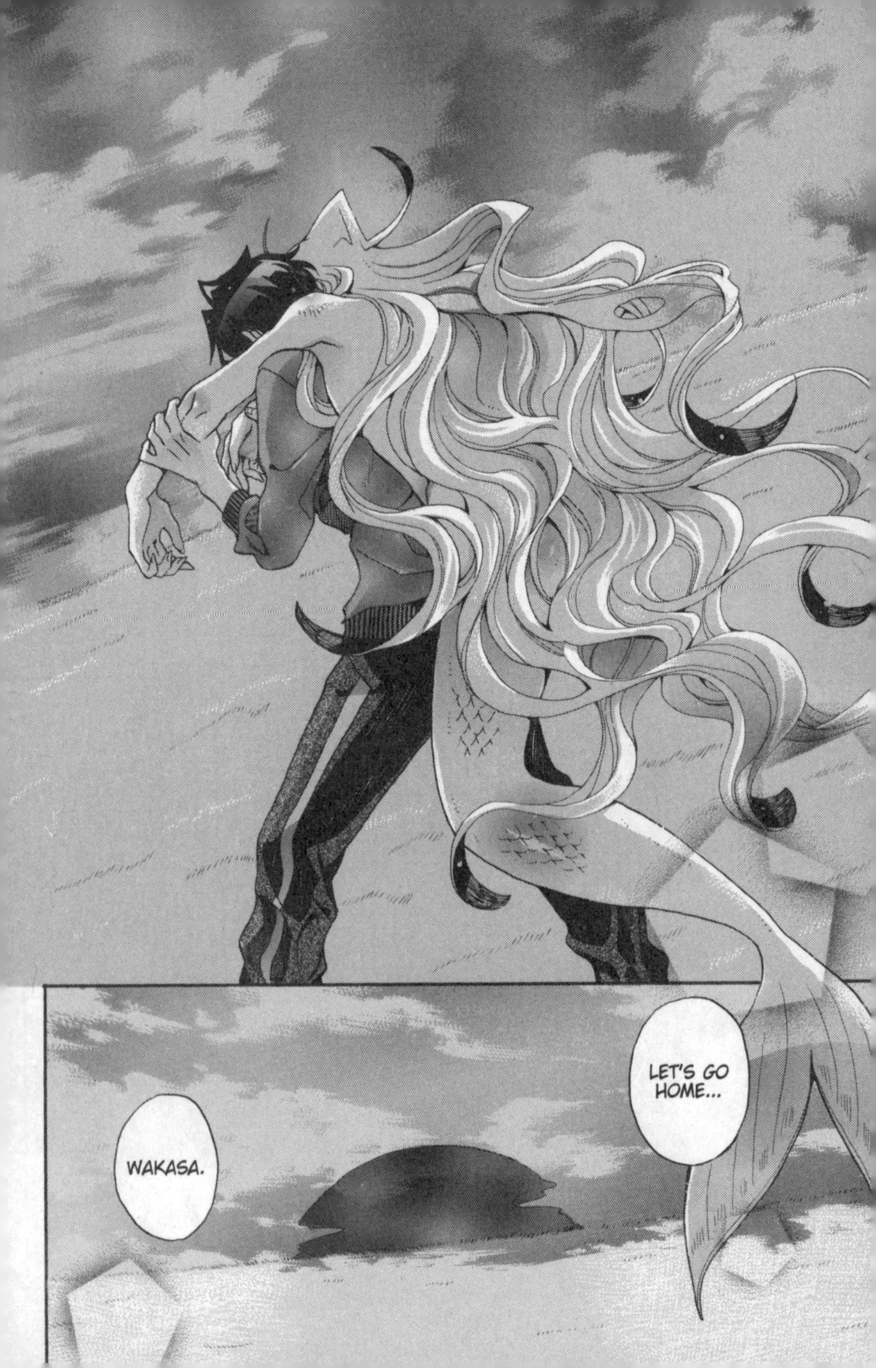
LET'S GO HOME...
WAKASA.

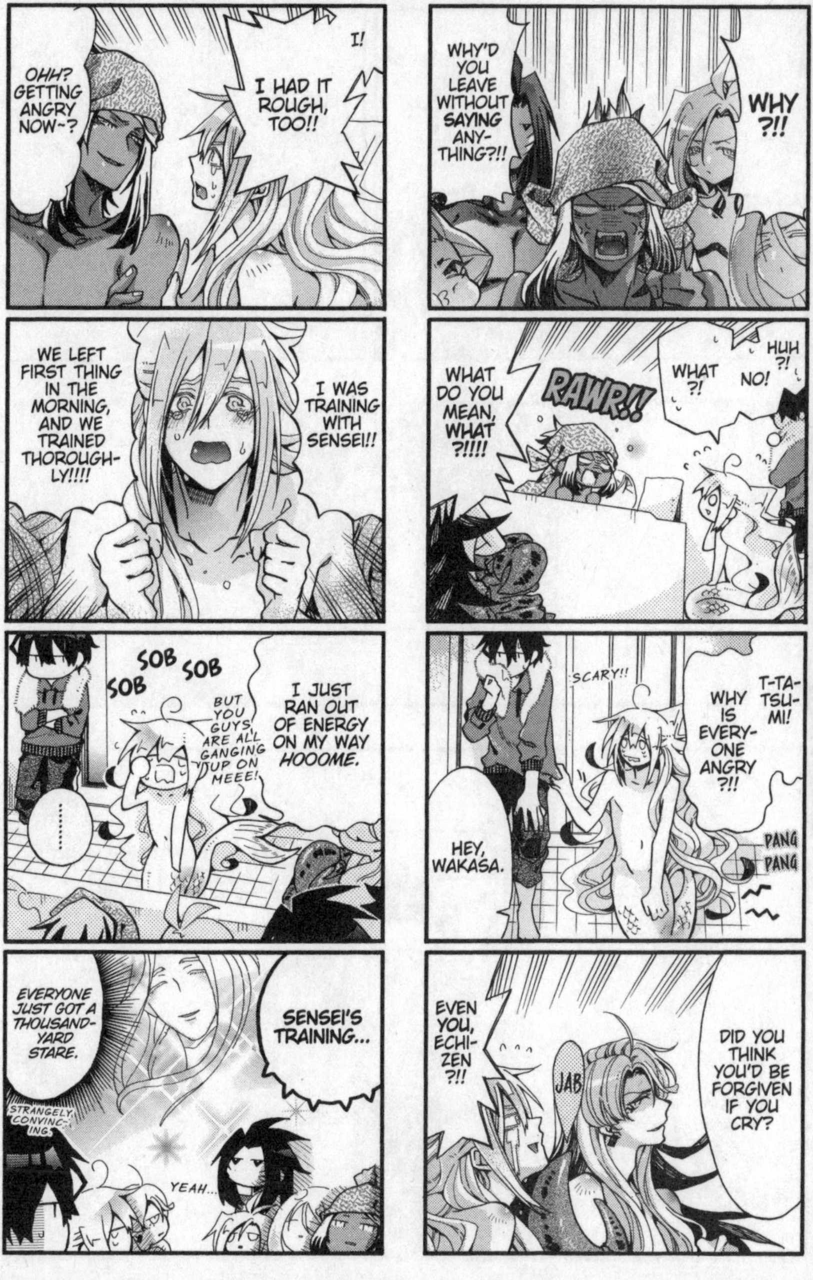
WHY'D YOU LEAVE WITHOUT SAYING ANYTHING?!!
WHY?!!
I!
I HAD IT ROUGH, TOO!!
OHH? GETTING ANGRY NOW~?
HUH?!
NO!
WHAT?!
RAWR!!
WHAT DO YOU MEAN, WHAT?!!!!
I WAS TRAINING WITH SENSEI!!
WE LEFT FIRST THING IN THE MORNING, AND WE TRAINED THOROUGHLY!!!!
T-TA-TSU-MI!
WHY IS EVERYONE ANGRY?!!
SCARY!!
PANG PANG
HEY, WAKASA.
I JUST RAN OUT OF ENERGY ON MY WAY HOOOME.
BUT YOU GUYS ARE ALL GANGING UP ON MEEE!
SOB SOB SOB
......
DID YOU THINK YOU'D BE FORGIVEN IF YOU CRY?
JAB
EVEN YOU, ECHIZEN?!!
SENSEI'S TRAINING...
EVERYONE JUST GOT A THOUSAND-YARD STARE.
STRANGELY CONVINCING.
YEAH...

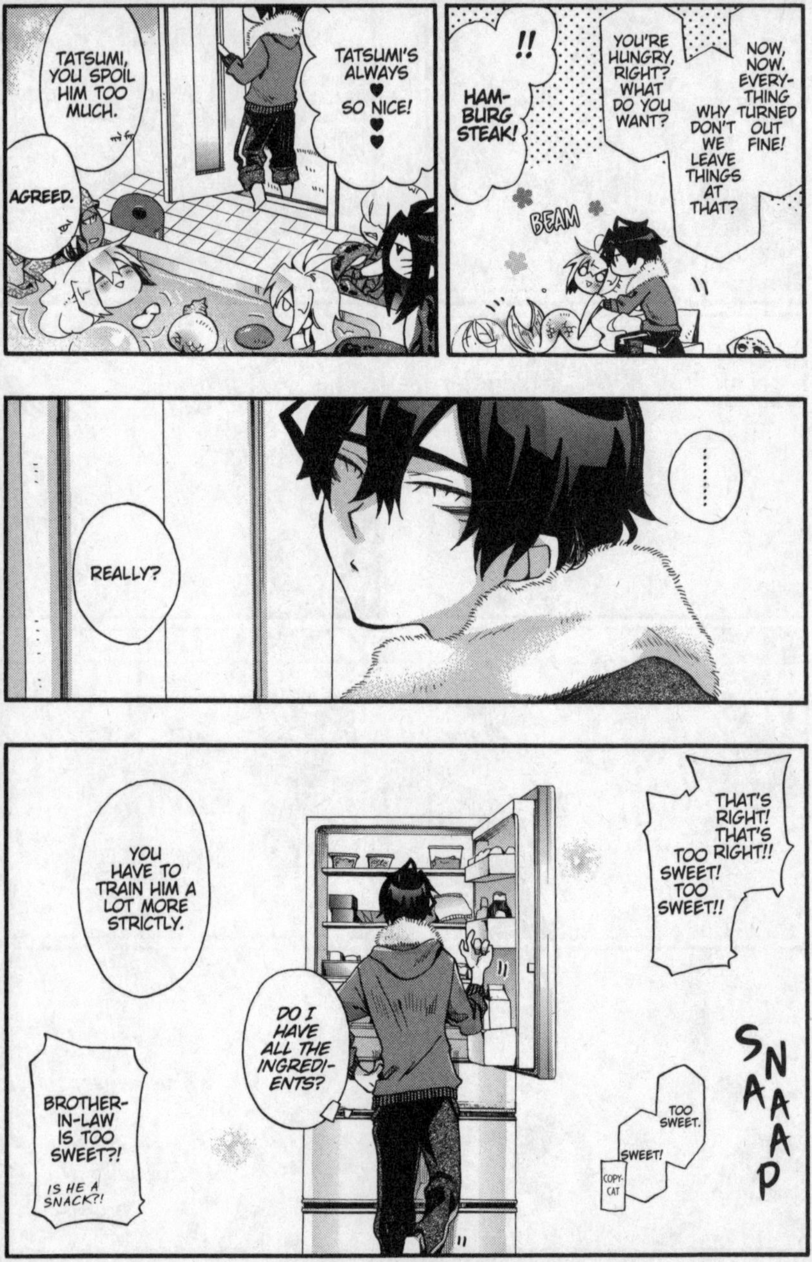
NOW, NOW. EVERYTHING TURNED OUT FINE! WHY DON'T WE LEAVE THINGS AT THAT?
YOU'RE HUNGRY, RIGHT? WHAT DO YOU WANT?
!!
HAMBURG STEAK!
BEAM
TATSUMI'S ALWAYS ♥ SO NICE! ♥ ♥
TATSUMI, YOU SPOIL HIM TOO MUCH.
AGREED.
......
REALLY?
THAT'S RIGHT! THAT'S RIGHT!! TOO SWEET! TOO SWEET!!
SNAAAP
TOO SWEET.
SWEET!
COPY-CAT
YOU HAVE TO TRAIN HIM A LOT MORE STRICTLY.
DO I HAVE ALL THE INGREDIENTS?
BROTHER-IN-LAW IS TOO SWEET?!
IS HE A SNACK?!

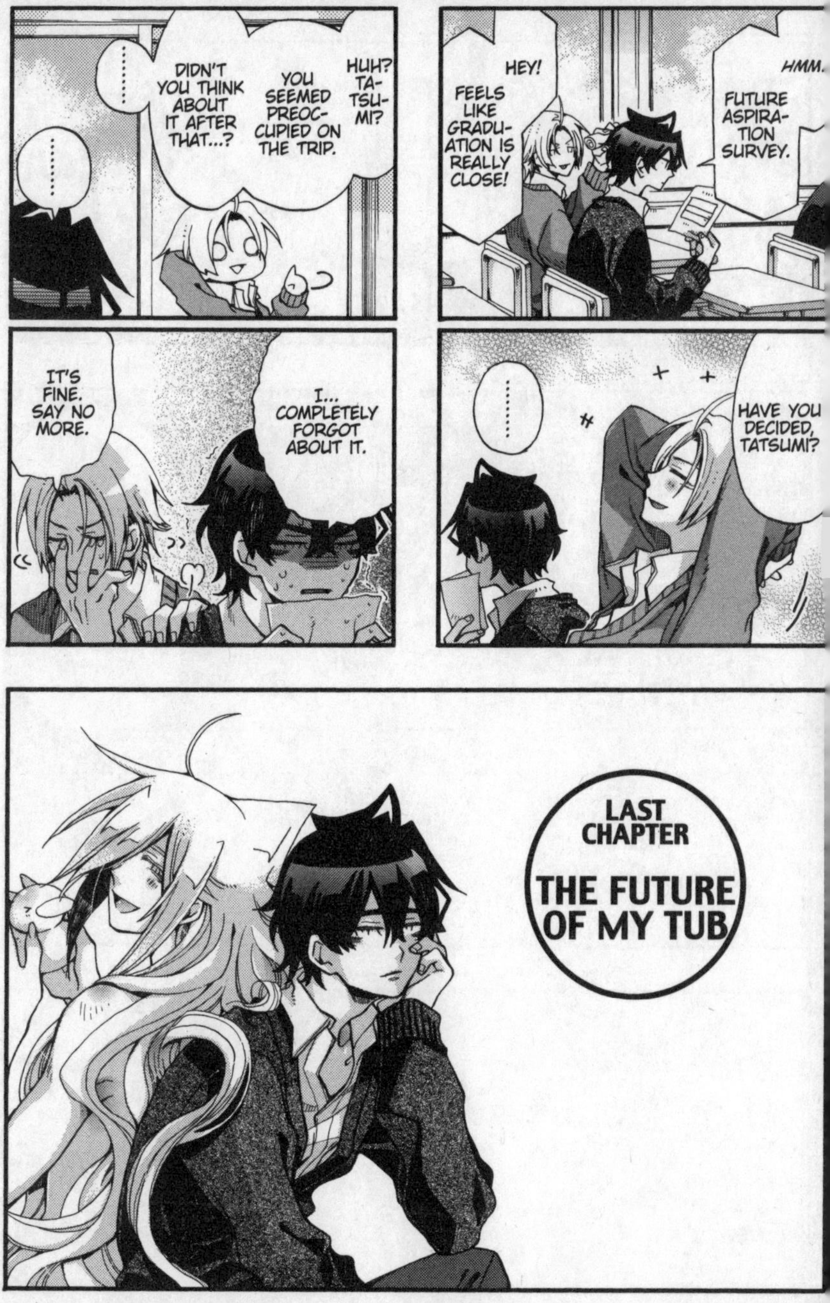
HMM.
FUTURE ASPIRATION SURVEY.
HEY!
FEELS LIKE GRADUATION IS REALLY CLOSE!
HUH? TATSUMI?
YOU SEEMED PREOCCUPIED ON THE TRIP.
DIDN'T YOU THINK ABOUT IT AFTER THAT...?
......
......
HAVE YOU DECIDED, TATSUMI?
......
I... COMPLETELY FORGOT ABOUT IT.
IT'S FINE. SAY NO MORE.
LAST CHAPTER
THE FUTURE OF MY TUB

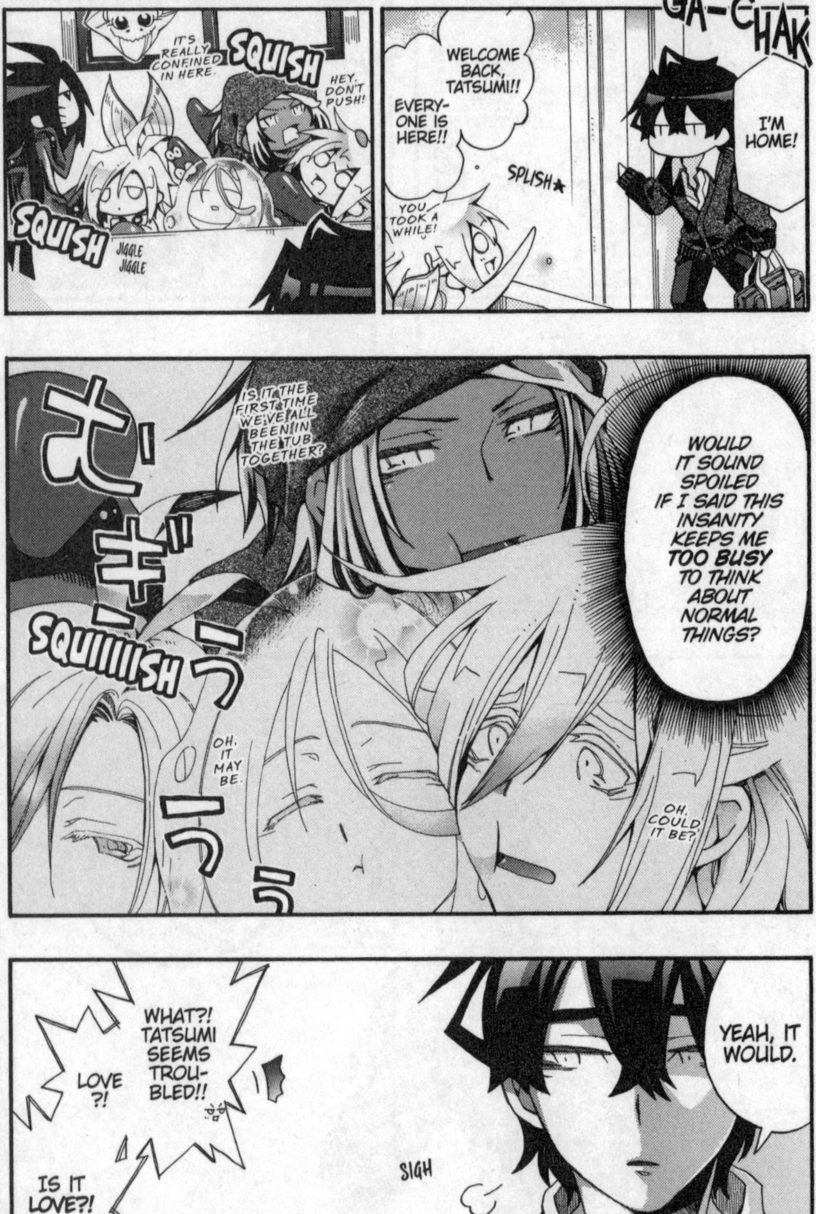
GA-CHAK
I'M HOME!
WELCOME BACK, TATSUMI!!
EVERY-ONE IS HERE!!
SPLISH★
YOU TOOK A WHILE!
HEY, DON'T PUSH!
SQUISH
IT'S REALLY CONFINED IN HERE.
SQUISH
JIGGLE JIGGLE
WOULD IT SOUND SPOILED IF I SAID THIS INSANITY KEEPS ME TOO BUSY TO THINK ABOUT NORMAL THINGS?
IS IT THE FIRST TIME WE'VE ALL BEEN IN THE TUB TOGETHER?
OH, COULD IT BE?
OH, IT MAY BE.
SQUIIIIIISH
YEAH, IT WOULD.
SIGH
WHAT?! TATSUMI SEEMS TROU-BLED!!
LOVE ?!
IS IT LOVE?!

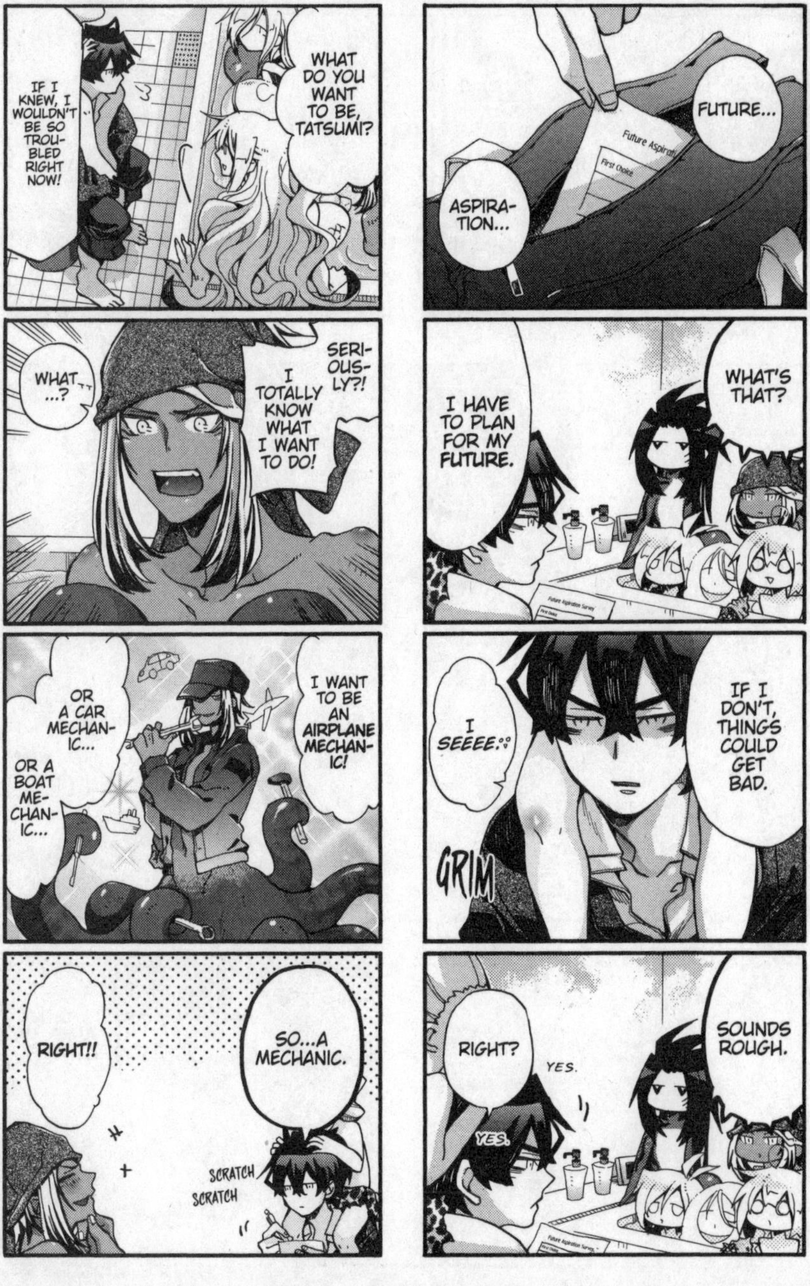
FUTURE...
ASPIRATION...
Future Aspirati
First Choice
WHAT'S THAT?
I HAVE TO PLAN FOR MY FUTURE.
Future Aspiration Survey
IF I DON'T, THINGS COULD GET BAD.
I SEEEE...
GRIM
SOUNDS ROUGH.
RIGHT?
YES.
YES.
WHAT DO YOU WANT TO BE, TATSUMI?
IF I KNEW, I WOULDN'T BE SO TROUBLED RIGHT NOW!
SERIOUSLY?!
I TOTALLY KNOW WHAT I WANT TO DO!
WHAT...?
I WANT TO BE AN AIRPLANE MECHANIC!
OR A CAR MECHANIC...
OR A BOAT MECHANIC...
SO...A MECHANIC.
RIGHT!!
SCRATCH
SCRATCH

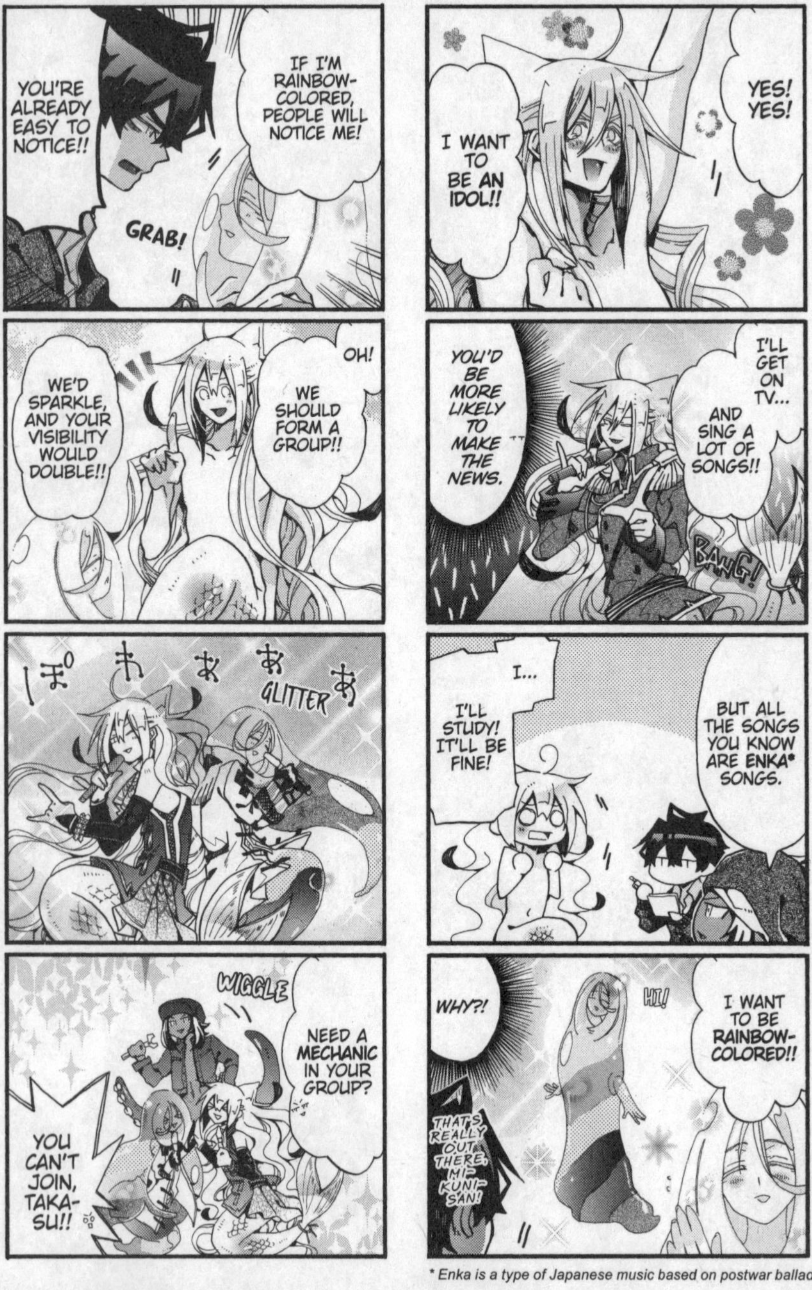
YES! YES!
I WANT TO BE AN IDOL!!
I'LL GET ON TV... AND SING A LOT OF SONGS!!
YOU'D BE MORE LIKELY TO MAKE THE NEWS.
BANG!
BUT ALL THE SONGS YOU KNOW ARE ENKA* SONGS.
I...
I'LL STUDY! IT'LL BE FINE!
I WANT TO BE RAINBOW-COLORED!!
HI!
WHY?!
THAT'S REALLY OUT THERE, MI-KUNI-SAN!
IF I'M RAINBOW-COLORED, PEOPLE WILL NOTICE ME!
YOU'RE ALREADY EASY TO NOTICE!!
GRAB!
OH!
WE SHOULD FORM A GROUP!!
WE'D SPARKLE, AND YOUR VISIBILITY WOULD DOUBLE!!
GLITTER
WIGGLE
NEED A MECHANIC IN YOUR GROUP?
YOU CAN'T JOIN, TAKA-SU!!

* Enka is a type of Japanese music based on postwar ballads.

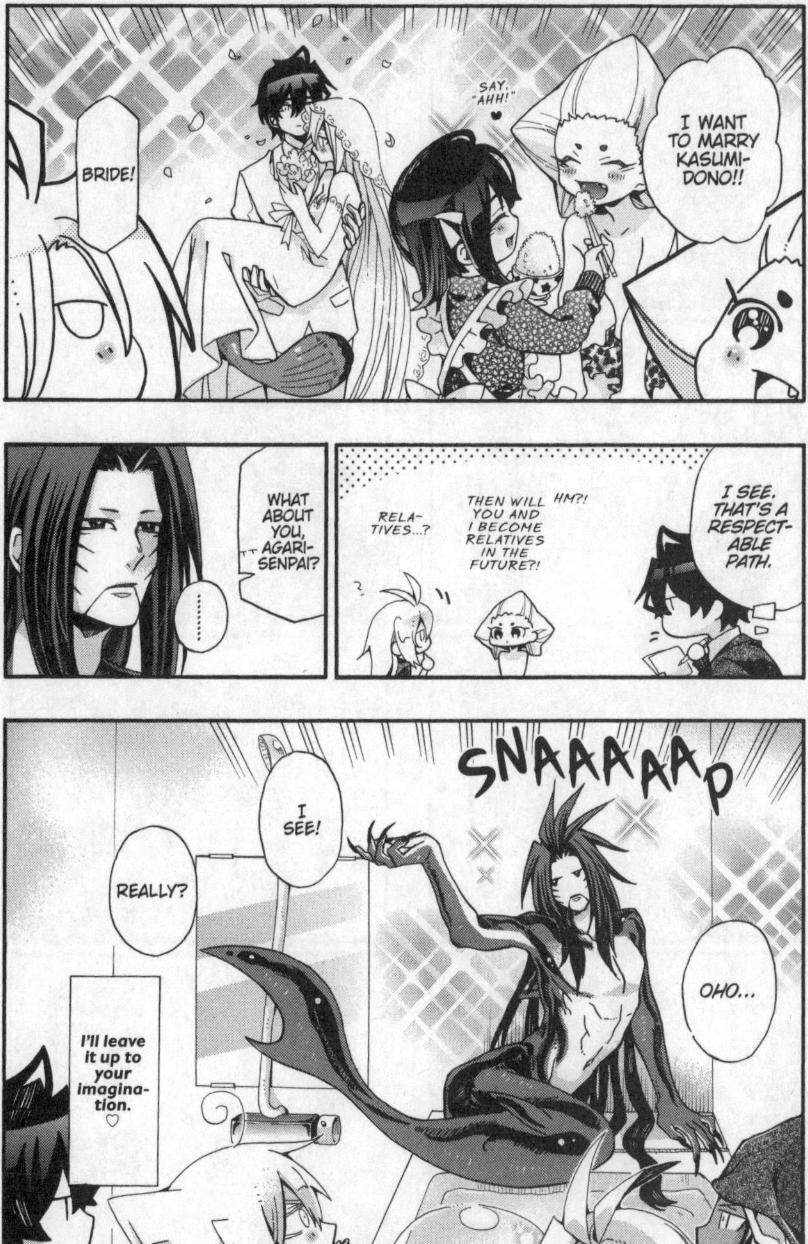
I WANT TO MARRY KASUMI-DONO!!
SAY, "AHH!"
BRIDE!
I SEE. THAT'S A RESPECTABLE PATH.
HM?!
THEN WILL YOU AND I BECOME RELATIVES IN THE FUTURE?!
RELATIVES...?
WHAT ABOUT YOU, AGARI-SENPAI?
......
SNAAAAAP
OHO...
I SEE!
REALLY?
I'll leave it up to your imagination. ♡

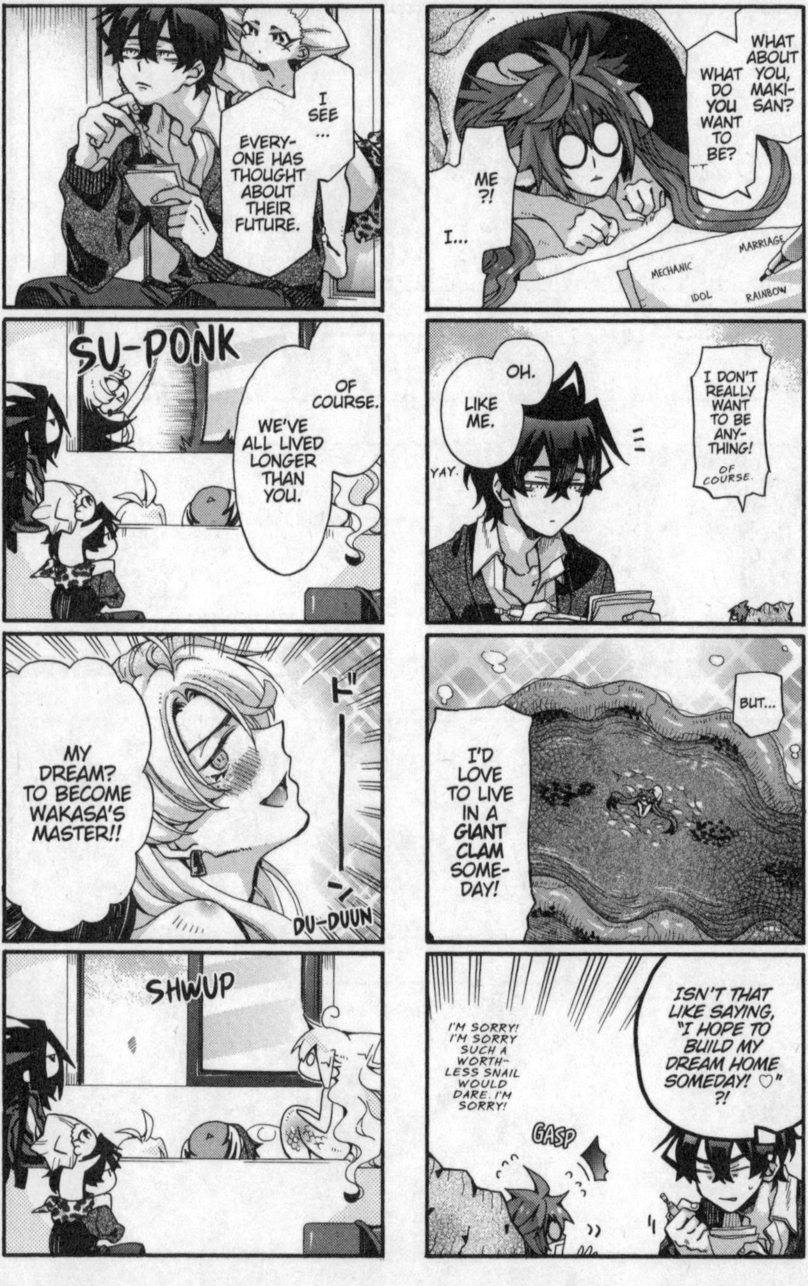
WHAT ABOUT YOU, MAKI-SAN?
WHAT DO YOU WANT TO BE?
ME?!
I...
MARRIAGE
MECHANIC
IDOL
RAINBOW
I SEE...
EVERYONE HAS THOUGHT ABOUT THEIR FUTURE.
I DON'T REALLY WANT TO BE ANYTHING!
OF COURSE.
OH.
LIKE ME.
YAY.
OF COURSE.
WE'VE ALL LIVED LONGER THAN YOU.
SU-PONK
BUT...
I'D LOVE TO LIVE IN A GIANT CLAM SOMEDAY!
MY DREAM? TO BECOME WAKASA'S MASTER!!
DU-DUUN
ISN'T THAT LIKE SAYING, "I HOPE TO BUILD MY DREAM HOME SOMEDAY! ♡"?!
I'M SORRY! I'M SORRY SUCH A WORTHLESS SNAIL WOULD DARE. I'M SORRY!
GASP
SHWUP

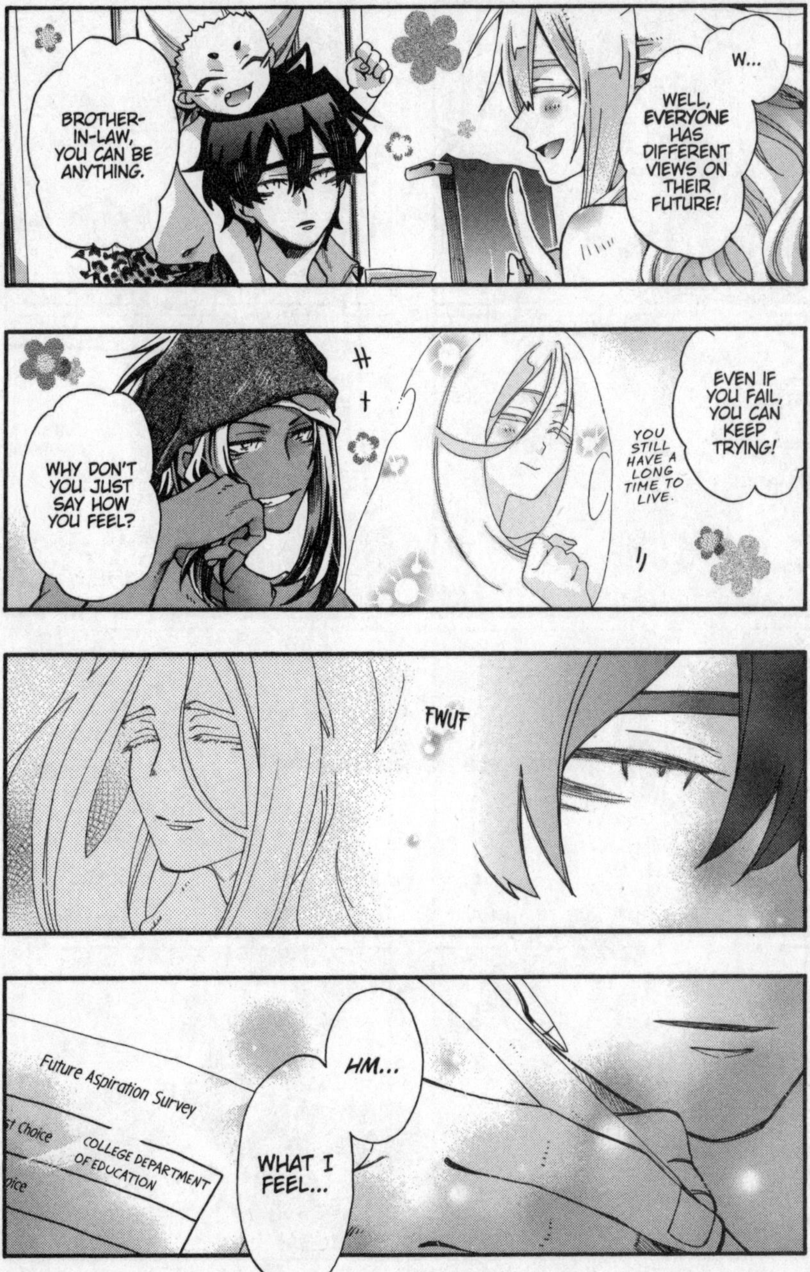
W...
WELL, EVERYONE HAS DIFFERENT VIEWS ON THEIR FUTURE!
BROTHER-IN-LAW, YOU CAN BE ANYTHING.
EVEN IF YOU FAIL, YOU CAN KEEP TRYING!
YOU STILL HAVE A LONG TIME TO LIVE.
WHY DON'T YOU JUST SAY HOW YOU FEEL?
FWUF
HM...
WHAT I FEEL...
Future Aspiration Survey
COLLEGE DEPARTMENT OF EDUCATION

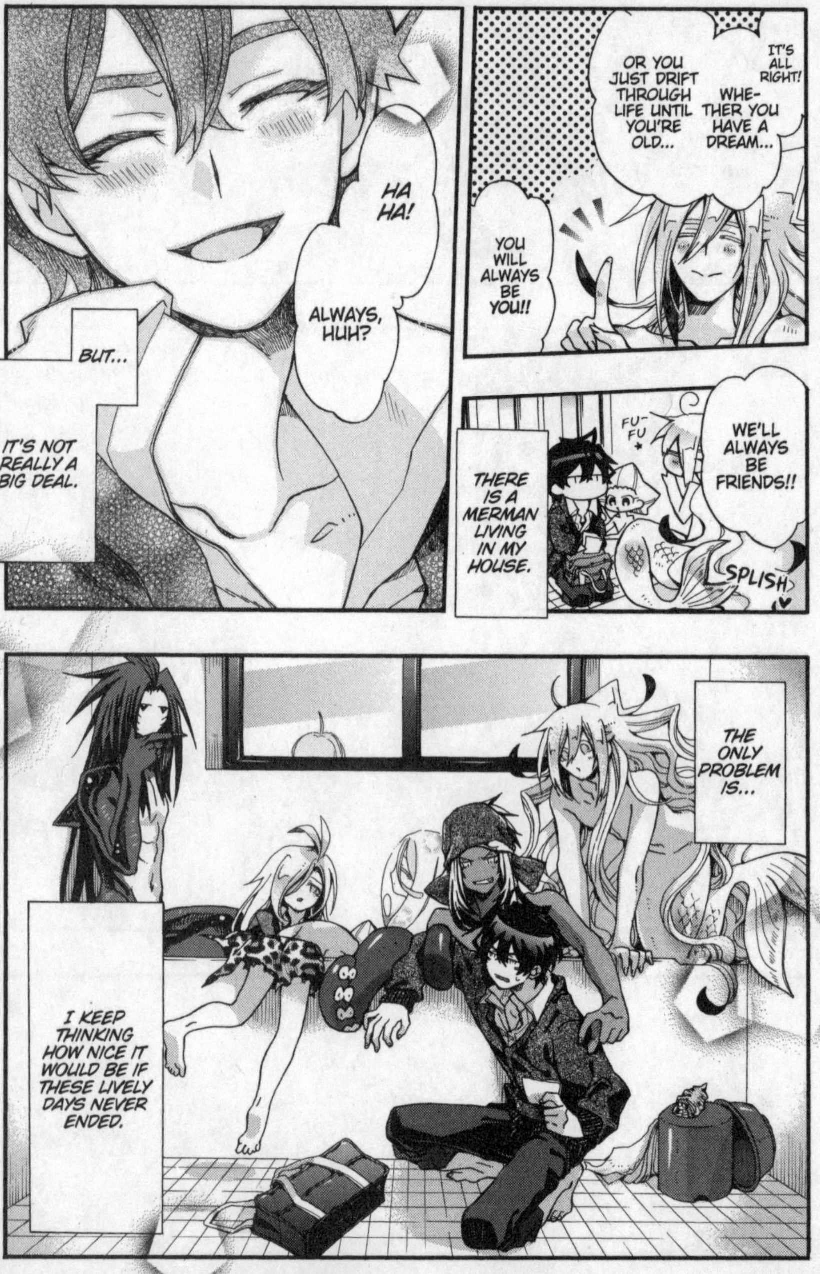
IT'S ALL RIGHT!
WHE-THER YOU HAVE A DREAM...
OR YOU JUST DRIFT THROUGH LIFE UNTIL YOU'RE OLD...
YOU WILL ALWAYS BE YOU!!
WE'LL ALWAYS BE FRIENDS!!
FU-FU
SPLISH
THERE IS A MERMAN LIVING IN MY HOUSE.
HA HA!
ALWAYS, HUH?
BUT...
IT'S NOT REALLY A BIG DEAL.
THE ONLY PROBLEM IS...
I KEEP THINKING HOW NICE IT WOULD BE IF THESE LIVELY DAYS NEVER ENDED.

Merman in My Tub

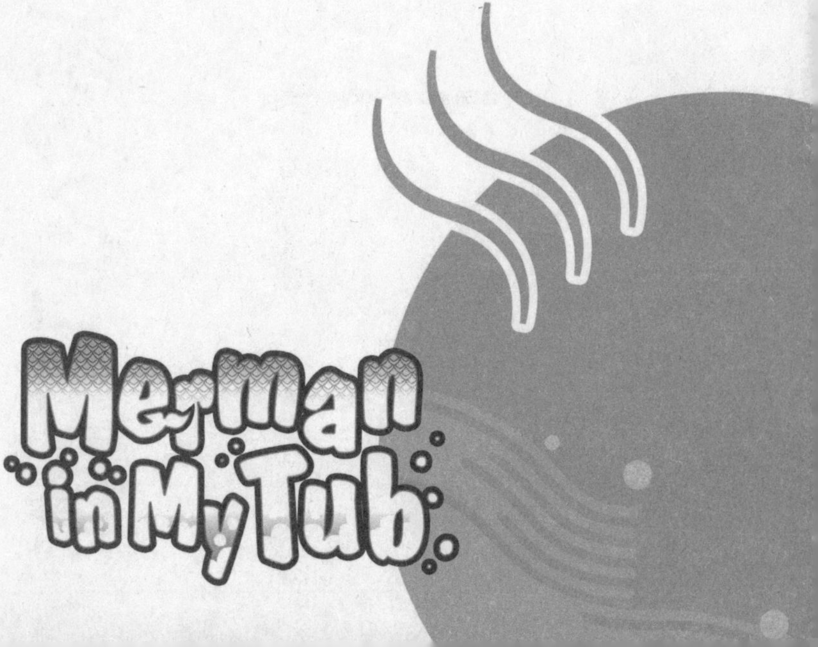

オレん家（ち）のフロ事情

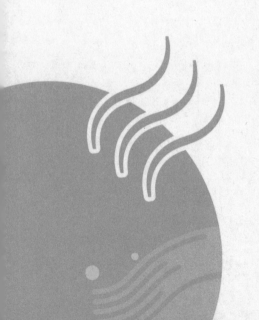

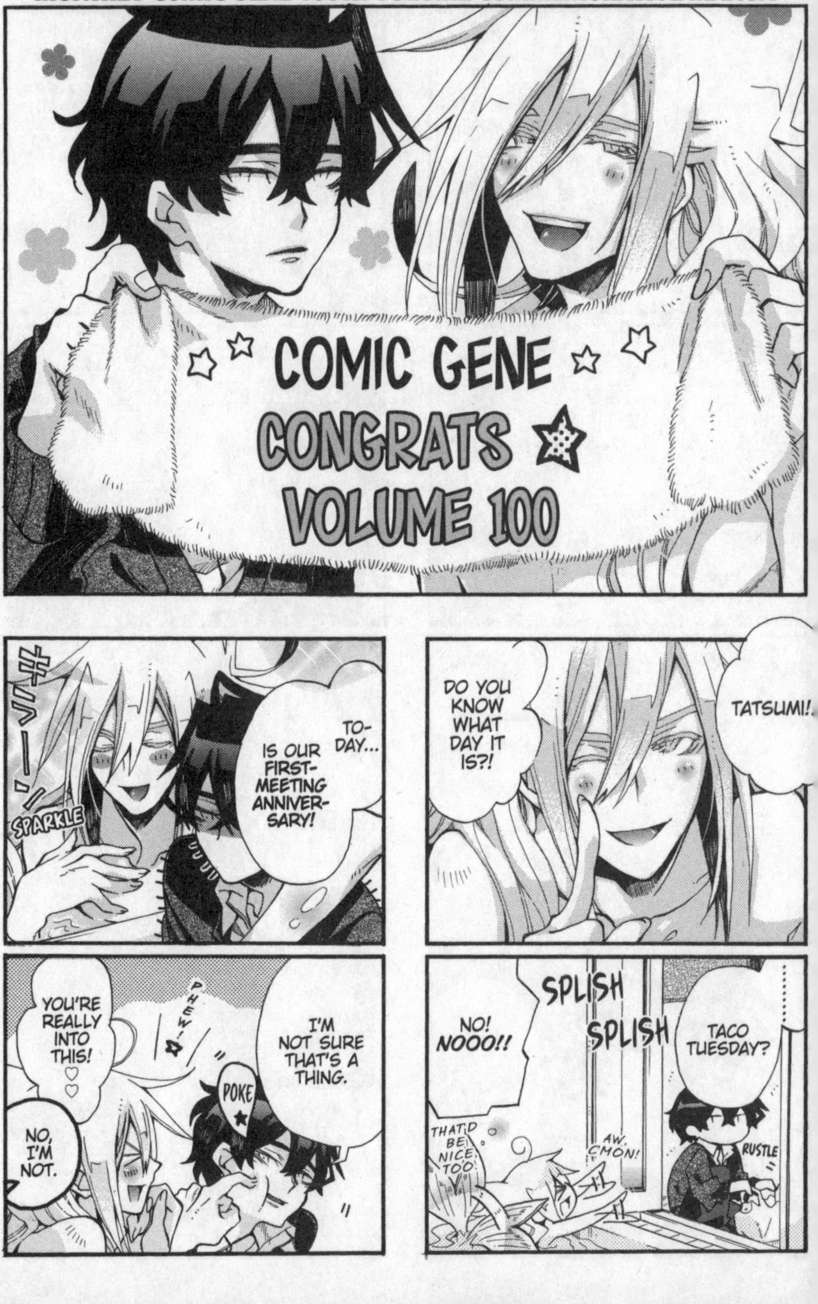
COMIC GENE
CONGRATS
VOLUME 100
TATSUMI!
DO YOU KNOW WHAT DAY IT IS?!
TO-DAY...
IS OUR FIRST-MEETING ANNIVERSARY!
SPARKLE
TACO TUESDAY?
RUSTLE
SPLISH
SPLISH
NO! NOOO!!
AW, C'MON!
THAT'D BE NICE TOO.
I'M NOT SURE THAT'S A THING.
PHEW!
POKE
YOU'RE REALLY INTO THIS!
NO, I'M NOT.

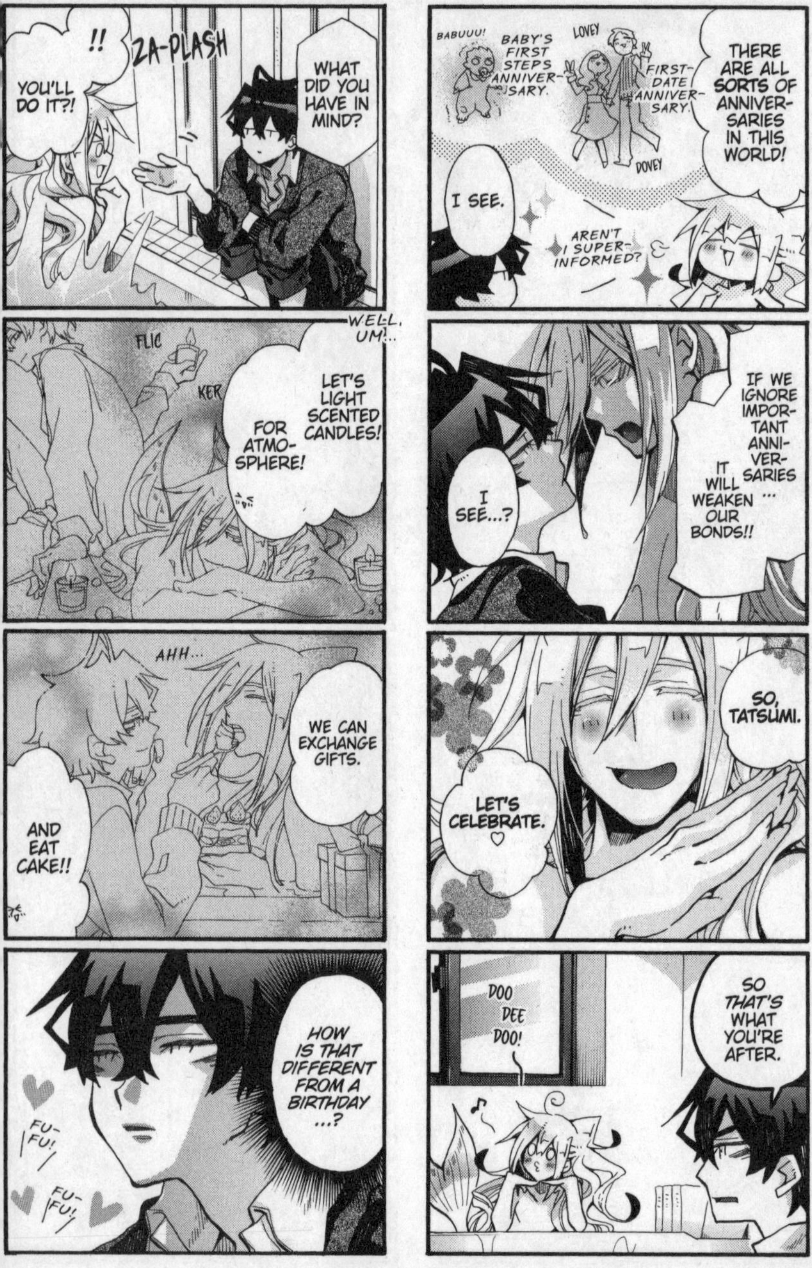
THERE ARE ALL SORTS OF ANNIVERSARIES IN THIS WORLD!
BABUUU!
BABY'S FIRST STEPS ANNIVERSARY.
LOVEY
FIRST-DATE ANNIVERSARY.
DOVEY
I SEE.
AREN'T I SUPER-INFORMED?
IF WE IGNORE IMPORTANT ANNIVERSARIES...
IT WILL WEAKEN OUR BONDS!!
I SEE...?
SO, TATSUMI.
LET'S CELEBRATE. ♡
SO THAT'S WHAT YOU'RE AFTER.
DOO DEE DOO!
WHAT DID YOU HAVE IN MIND?
ZA-PLASH
!!
YOU'LL DO IT?!
WELL, UM...
LET'S LIGHT SCENTED CANDLES!
FOR ATMOSPHERE!
FLIC
KER
AHH...
WE CAN EXCHANGE GIFTS.
AND EAT CAKE!!
HOW IS THAT DIFFERENT FROM A BIRTHDAY...?
FU-FU!
FU-FU!

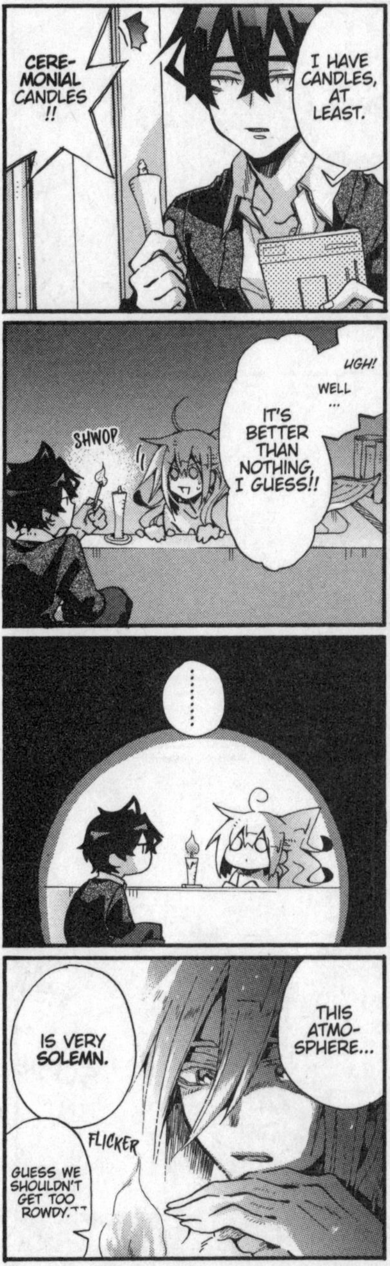
I HAVE CANDLES, AT LEAST.
CERE-MONIAL CANDLES !!
UGH!
WELL ...
IT'S BETTER THAN NOTHING, I GUESS!!
SHWOP
...
THIS ATMOS-PHERE...
IS VERY SOLEMN.
FLICKER
GUESS WE SHOULDN'T GET TOO ROWDY.
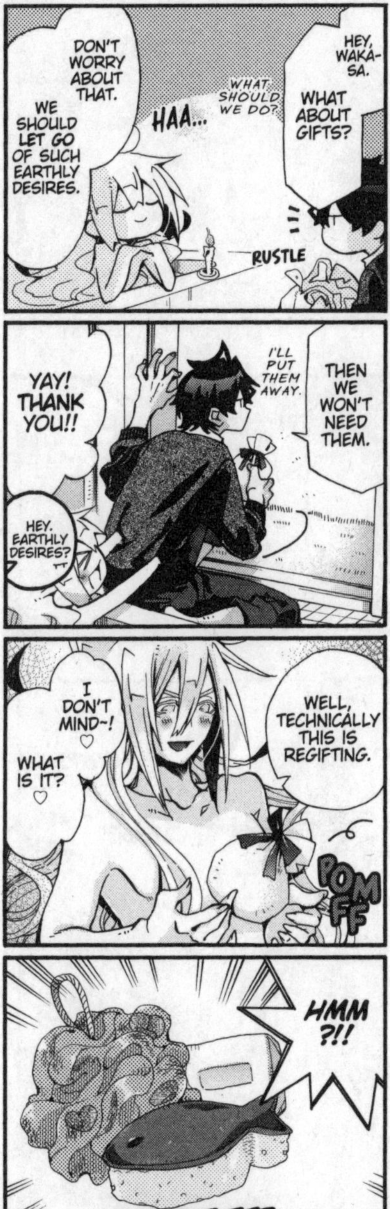
HEY, WAKA-SA.
WHAT ABOUT GIFTS?
WHAT SHOULD WE DO?
HAA...
DON'T WORRY ABOUT THAT.
WE SHOULD LET GO OF SUCH EARTHLY DESIRES.
RUSTLE
THEN WE WON'T NEED THEM.
I'LL PUT THEM AWAY.
YAY! THANK YOU!!
HEY. EARTHLY DESIRES?
WELL, TECHNICALLY THIS IS REGIFTING.
I DON'T MIND~! ♡
WHAT IS IT? ♡
POMFF
HMM ?!!
DA-DAAN

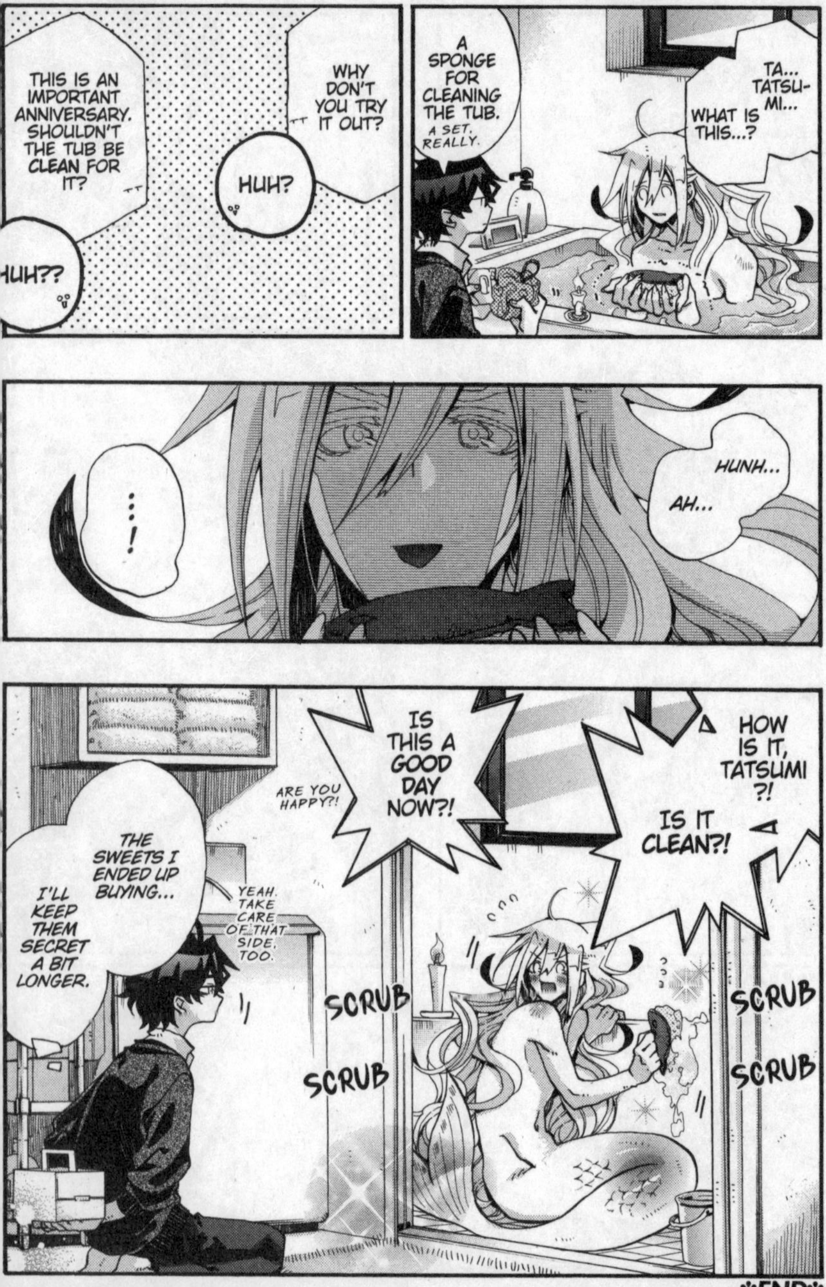
TA... TATSUMI...
WHAT IS THIS...?
A SPONGE FOR CLEANING THE TUB.
A SET, REALLY.
WHY DON'T YOU TRY IT OUT?
HUH?
THIS IS AN IMPORTANT ANNIVERSARY. SHOULDN'T THE TUB BE CLEAN FOR IT?
HUH??
HUNH...
AH...
...!
HOW IS IT, TATSUMI?!
IS IT CLEAN?!
IS THIS A GOOD DAY NOW?!
ARE YOU HAPPY?!
SCRUB
SCRUB
SCRUB
SCRUB
YEAH. TAKE CARE OF THAT SIDE, TOO.
THE SWEETS I ENDED UP BUYING...
I'LL KEEP THEM SECRET A BIT LONGER.

END

Merman in My Tub

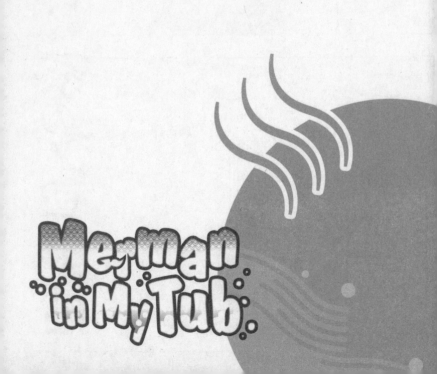

オレん家のフロ事情

SPECIAL EXTRA MANGA: ~IF WAKASA PICKED UP TATSUMI~

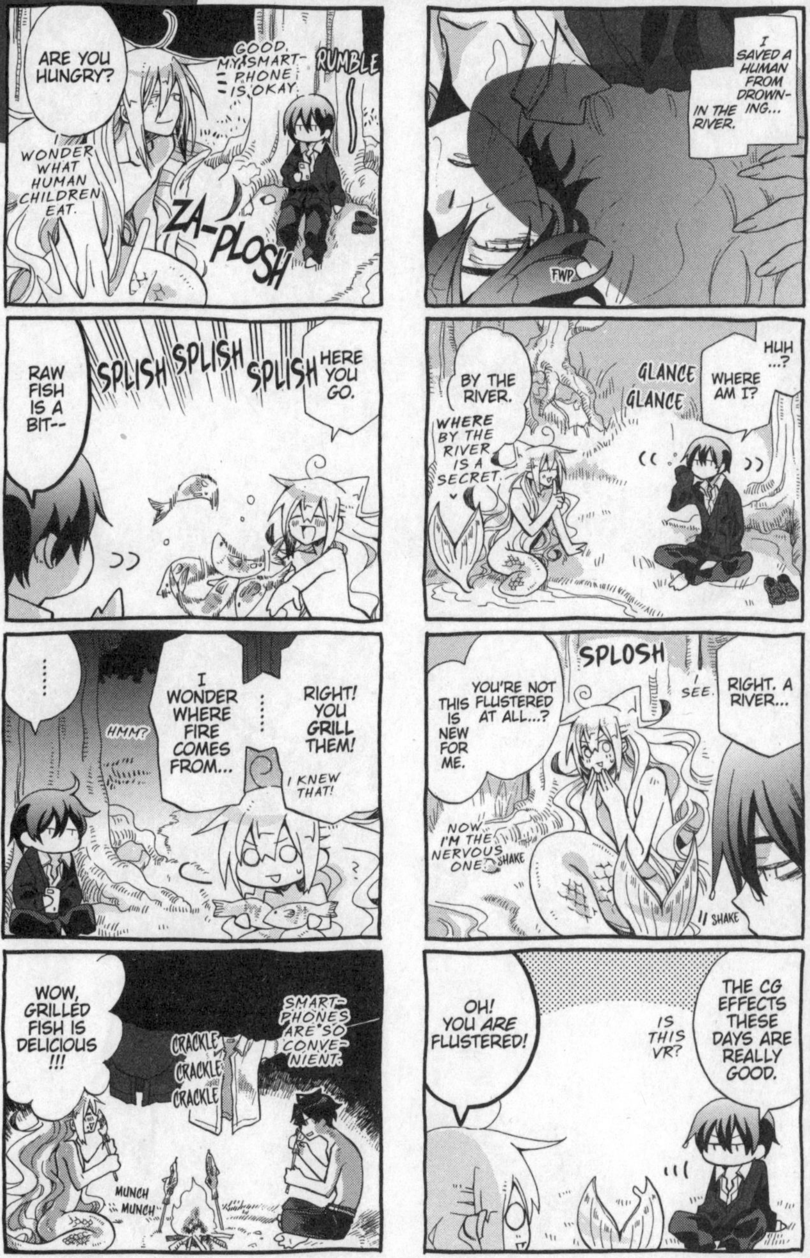
I SAVED A HUMAN FROM DROWNING...
IN THE RIVER.
FWP
RUMBLE
GOOD. MY SMARTPHONE IS OKAY.
ARE YOU HUNGRY?
I WONDER WHAT HUMAN CHILDREN EAT.
ZA-PLOSH
HUH ...?
WHERE AM I?
GLANCE GLANCE
BY THE RIVER.
WHERE BY THE RIVER IS A SECRET.
HERE YOU GO.
SPLISH SPLISH SPLISH
RAW FISH IS A BIT--
RIGHT. A RIVER...
I SEE.
SPLOSH
YOU'RE NOT FLUSTERED AT ALL...?
THIS IS NEW FOR ME.
NOW I'M THE NERVOUS ONE.
SHAKE
SHAKE
RIGHT! YOU GRILL THEM!
I KNEW THAT!
......
I WONDER WHERE FIRE COMES FROM...
HMM?
......
THE CG EFFECTS THESE DAYS ARE REALLY GOOD.
IS THIS VR?
OH! YOU ARE FLUSTERED!
SMARTPHONES ARE SO CONVENIENT.
CRACKLE CRACKLE CRACKLE
WOW, GRILLED FISH IS DELICIOUS!!!
MUNCH MUNCH

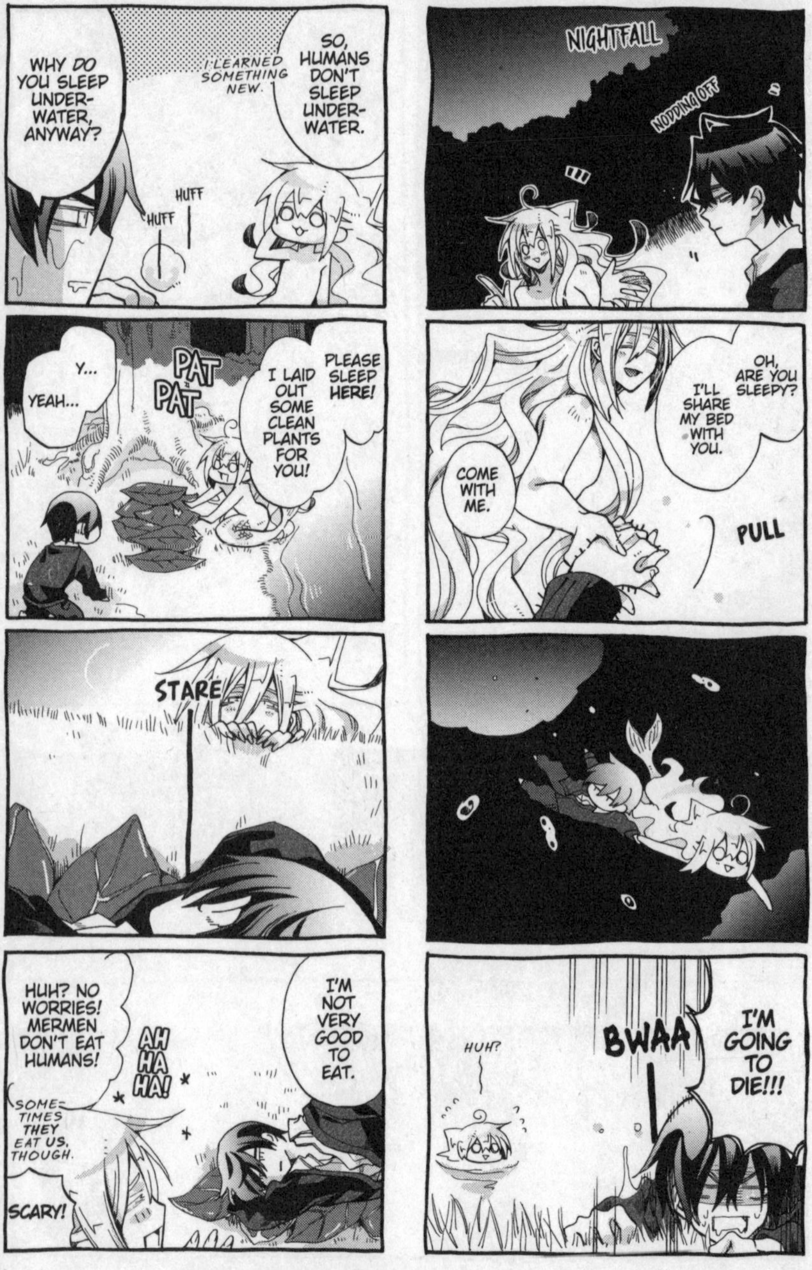
NIGHTFALL
NODDING OFF
OH, ARE YOU SLEEPY?
I'LL SHARE MY BED WITH YOU.
COME WITH ME.
PULL
BWAA
I'M GOING TO DIE!!!
HUH?
SO, HUMANS DON'T SLEEP UNDER-WATER.
I LEARNED SOMETHING NEW.
WHY DO YOU SLEEP UNDER-WATER, ANYWAY?
HUFF
HUFF
PLEASE SLEEP HERE!
I LAID OUT SOME CLEAN PLANTS FOR YOU!
PAT PAT
Y... YEAH...
STARE
I'M NOT VERY GOOD TO EAT.
AH HA HA!
HUH? NO WORRIES! MERMEN DON'T EAT HUMANS!
SOME-TIMES THEY EAT US, THOUGH.
SCARY!

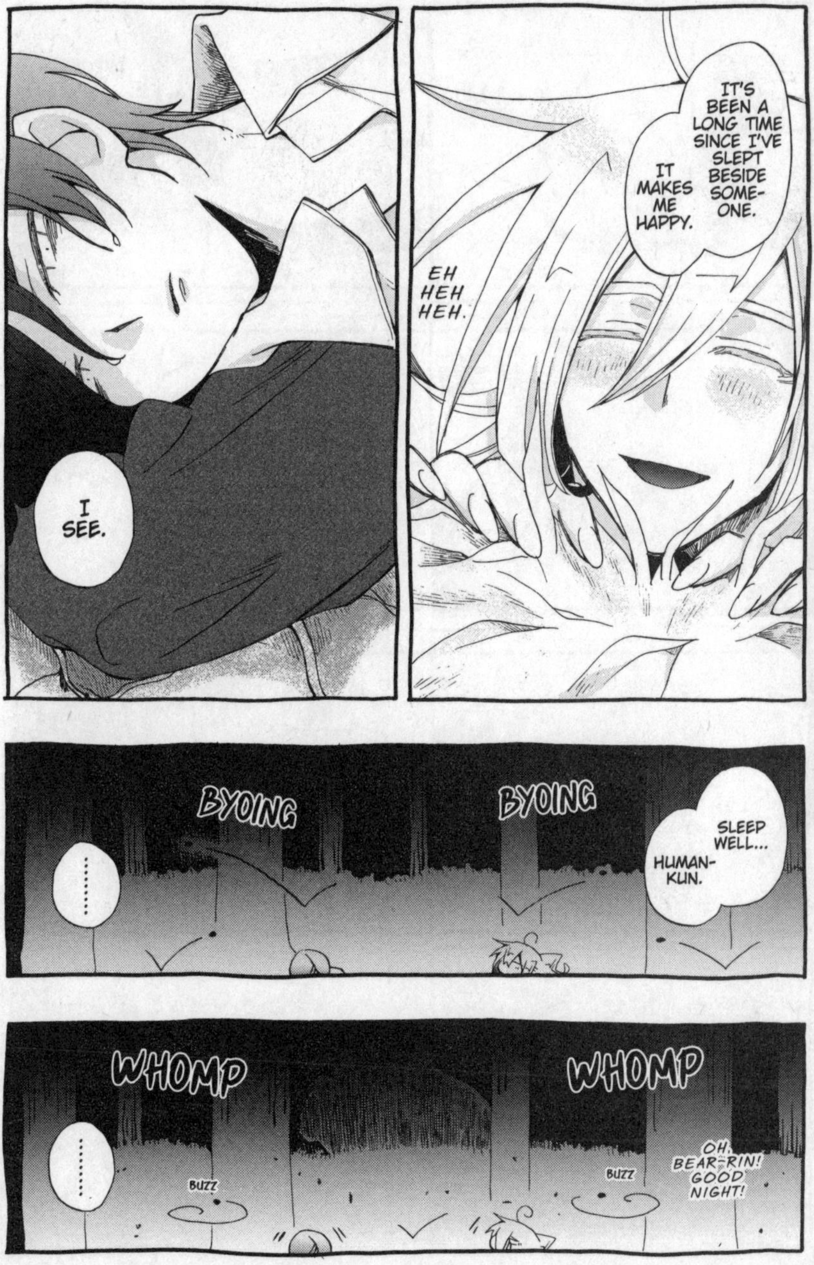
IT'S BEEN A LONG TIME SINCE I'VE SLEPT BESIDE SOME-ONE.
IT MAKES ME HAPPY.
EH HEH HEH.
I SEE.
BYOING
SLEEP WELL... HUMAN-KUN.
BYOING
......
WHOMP
OH, BEAR-RIN! GOOD NIGHT!
BUZZ
WHOMP
BUZZ
......

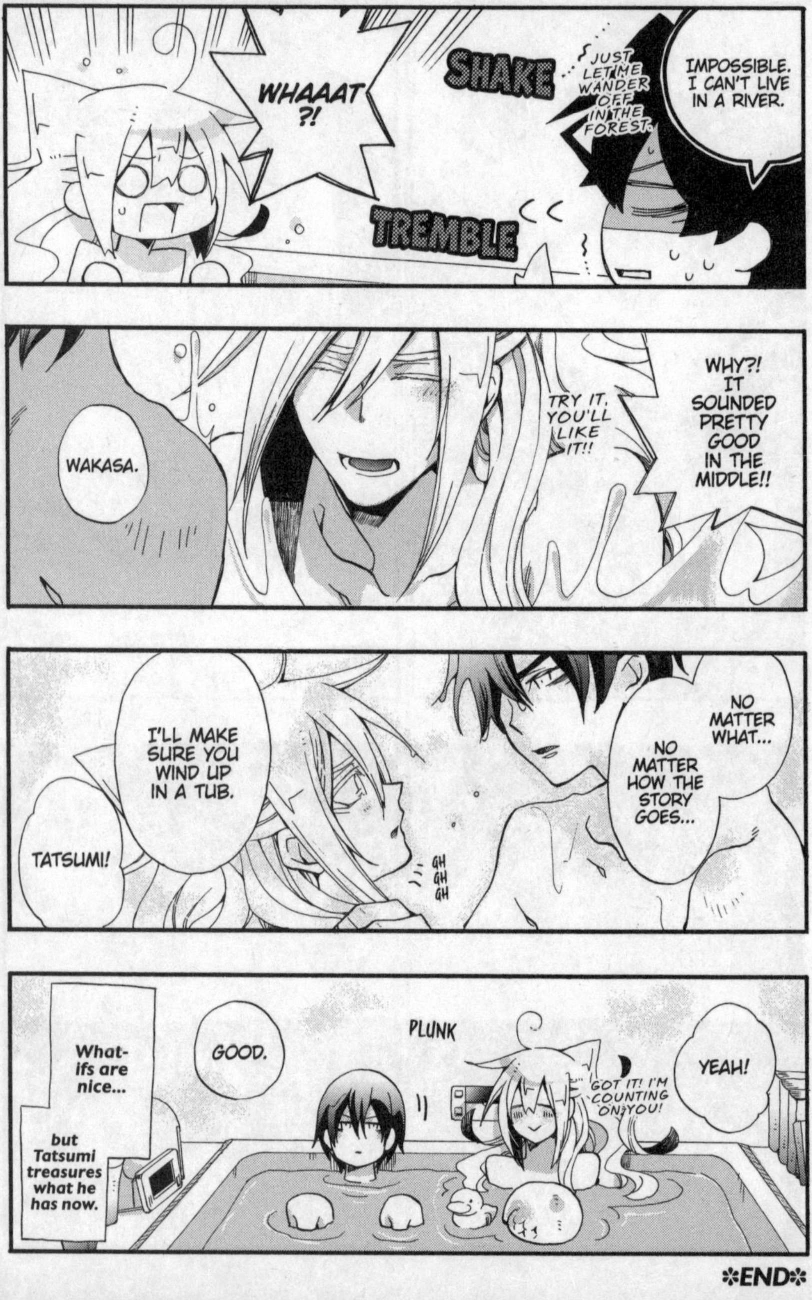
IMPOSSIBLE. I CAN'T LIVE IN A RIVER.
JUST LET ME WANDER OFF IN THE FOREST.
SHAKE
WHAAAT?!
TREMBLE
WHY?! IT SOUNDED PRETTY GOOD IN THE MIDDLE!!
TRY IT. YOU'LL LIKE IT!!
WAKASA.
NO MATTER WHAT...
NO MATTER HOW THE STORY GOES...
I'LL MAKE SURE YOU WIND UP IN A TUB.
GH GH GH
TATSUMI!
YEAH!
GOT IT! I'M COUNTING ON YOU!
PLUNK
GOOD.
What-ifs are nice...
but Tatsumi treasures what he has now.
END

EXTRA: THE BACKGROUND OF MY HOUSE

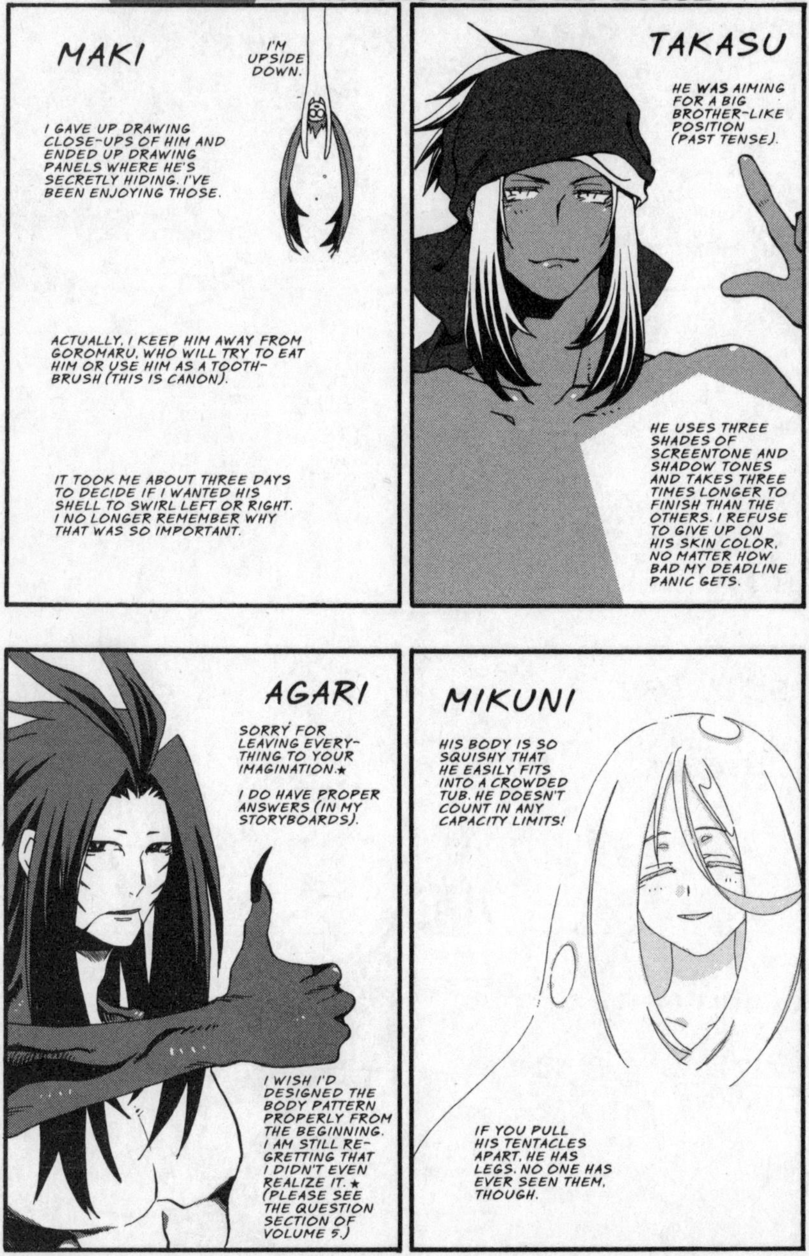

TAKASU
HE WAS AIMING FOR A BIG BROTHER-LIKE POSITION (PAST TENSE).
HE USES THREE SHADES OF SCREENTONE AND SHADOW TONES AND TAKES THREE TIMES LONGER TO FINISH THAN THE OTHERS. I REFUSE TO GIVE UP ON HIS SKIN COLOR, NO MATTER HOW BAD MY DEADLINE PANIC GETS.
MAKI
I'M UPSIDE DOWN.
I GAVE UP DRAWING CLOSE-UPS OF HIM AND ENDED UP DRAWING PANELS WHERE HE'S SECRETLY HIDING. I'VE BEEN ENJOYING THOSE.
ACTUALLY, I KEEP HIM AWAY FROM GOROMARU, WHO WILL TRY TO EAT HIM OR USE HIM AS A TOOTH-BRUSH (THIS IS CANON).
IT TOOK ME ABOUT THREE DAYS TO DECIDE IF I WANTED HIS SHELL TO SWIRL LEFT OR RIGHT. I NO LONGER REMEMBER WHY THAT WAS SO IMPORTANT.
MIKUNI
HIS BODY IS SO SQUISHY THAT HE EASILY FITS INTO A CROWDED TUB. HE DOESN'T COUNT IN ANY CAPACITY LIMITS!
IF YOU PULL HIS TENTACLES APART, HE HAS LEGS. NO ONE HAS EVER SEEN THEM, THOUGH.
AGARI
SORRY FOR LEAVING EVERY-THING TO YOUR IMAGINATION.★
I DO HAVE PROPER ANSWERS (IN MY STORYBOARDS).
I WISH I'D DESIGNED THE BODY PATTERN PROPERLY FROM THE BEGINNING. I AM STILL RE-GRETTING THAT I DIDN'T EVEN REALIZE IT.★ (PLEASE SEE THE QUESTION SECTION OF VOLUME 5.)

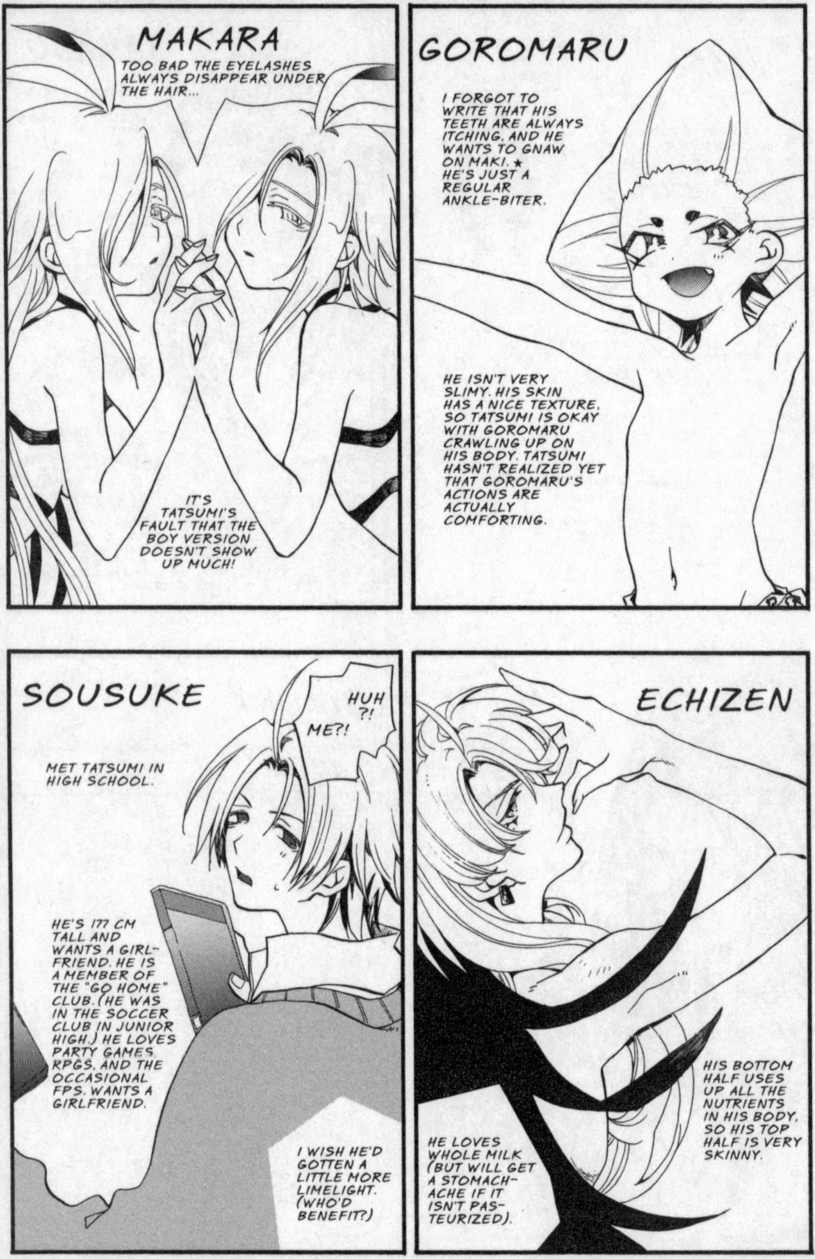
GOROMARU
I FORGOT TO WRITE THAT HIS TEETH ARE ALWAYS ITCHING, AND HE WANTS TO GNAW ON MAKI. ★ HE'S JUST A REGULAR ANKLE-BITER.
HE ISN'T VERY SLIMY. HIS SKIN HAS A NICE TEXTURE, SO TATSUMI IS OKAY WITH GOROMARU CRAWLING UP ON HIS BODY. TATSUMI HASN'T REALIZED YET THAT GOROMARU'S ACTIONS ARE ACTUALLY COMFORTING.
MAKARA
TOO BAD THE EYELASHES ALWAYS DISAPPEAR UNDER THE HAIR...
IT'S TATSUMI'S FAULT THAT THE BOY VERSION DOESN'T SHOW UP MUCH!
ECHIZEN
HIS BOTTOM HALF USES UP ALL THE NUTRIENTS IN HIS BODY, SO HIS TOP HALF IS VERY SKINNY.
HE LOVES WHOLE MILK (BUT WILL GET A STOMACH-ACHE IF IT ISN'T PAS-TEURIZED).
SOUSUKE
HUH ?!
ME?!
MET TATSUMI IN HIGH SCHOOL.
HE'S 177 CM TALL AND WANTS A GIRL-FRIEND. HE IS A MEMBER OF THE "GO HOME" CLUB. (HE WAS IN THE SOCCER CLUB IN JUNIOR HIGH.) HE LOVES PARTY GAMES, RPGS, AND THE OCCASIONAL FPS. WANTS A GIRLFRIEND.
I WISH HE'D GOTTEN A LITTLE MORE LIMELIGHT. (WHO'D BENEFIT?)

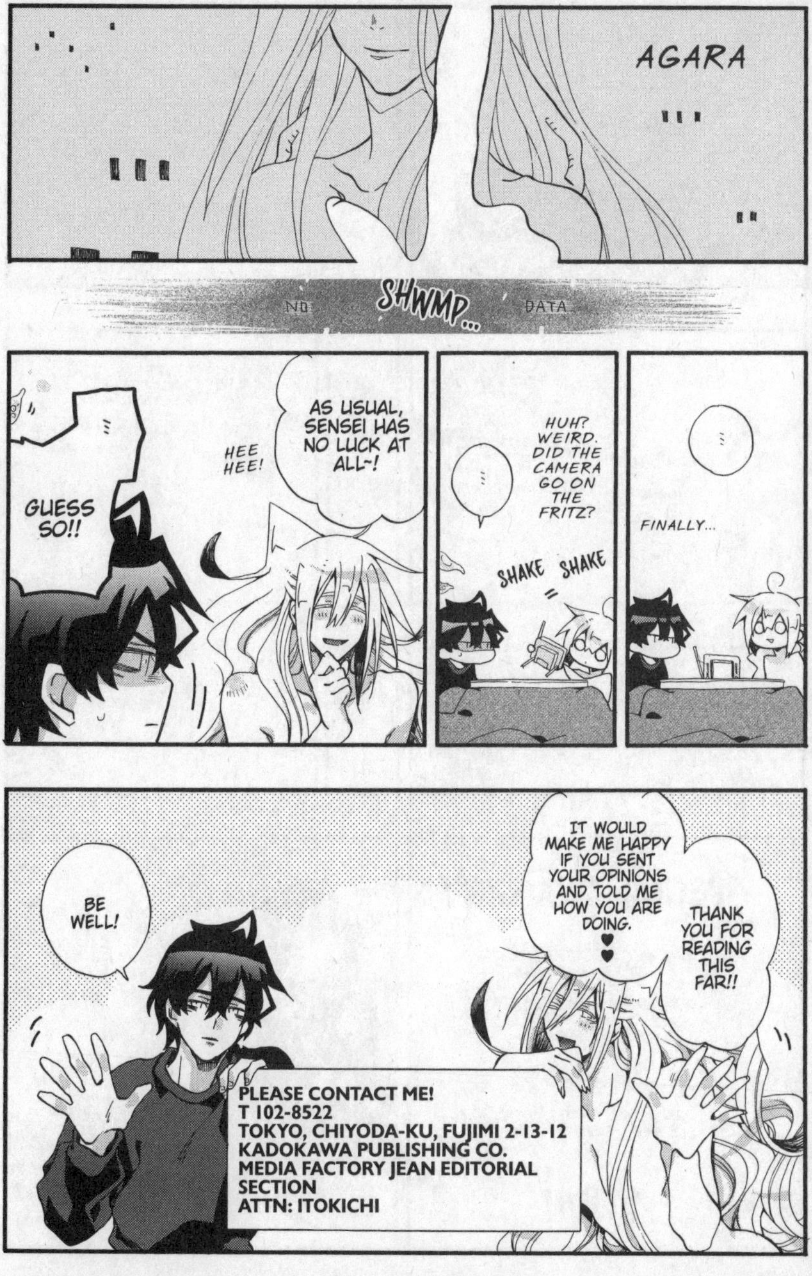
AGARA
SHWMP...
NO DATA
FINALLY...
HUH? WEIRD. DID THE CAMERA GO ON THE FRITZ?
SHAKE SHAKE
AS USUAL, SENSEI HAS NO LUCK AT ALL~!
HEE HEE!
GUESS SO!!
THANK YOU FOR READING THIS FAR!!
IT WOULD MAKE ME HAPPY IF YOU SENT YOUR OPINIONS AND TOLD ME HOW YOU ARE DOING. ♥♥
BE WELL!
PLEASE CONTACT ME!
T 102-8522
TOKYO, CHIYODA-KU, FUJIMI 2-13-12
KADOKAWA PUBLISHING CO.
MEDIA FACTORY JEAN EDITORIAL SECTION
ATTN: ITOKICHI

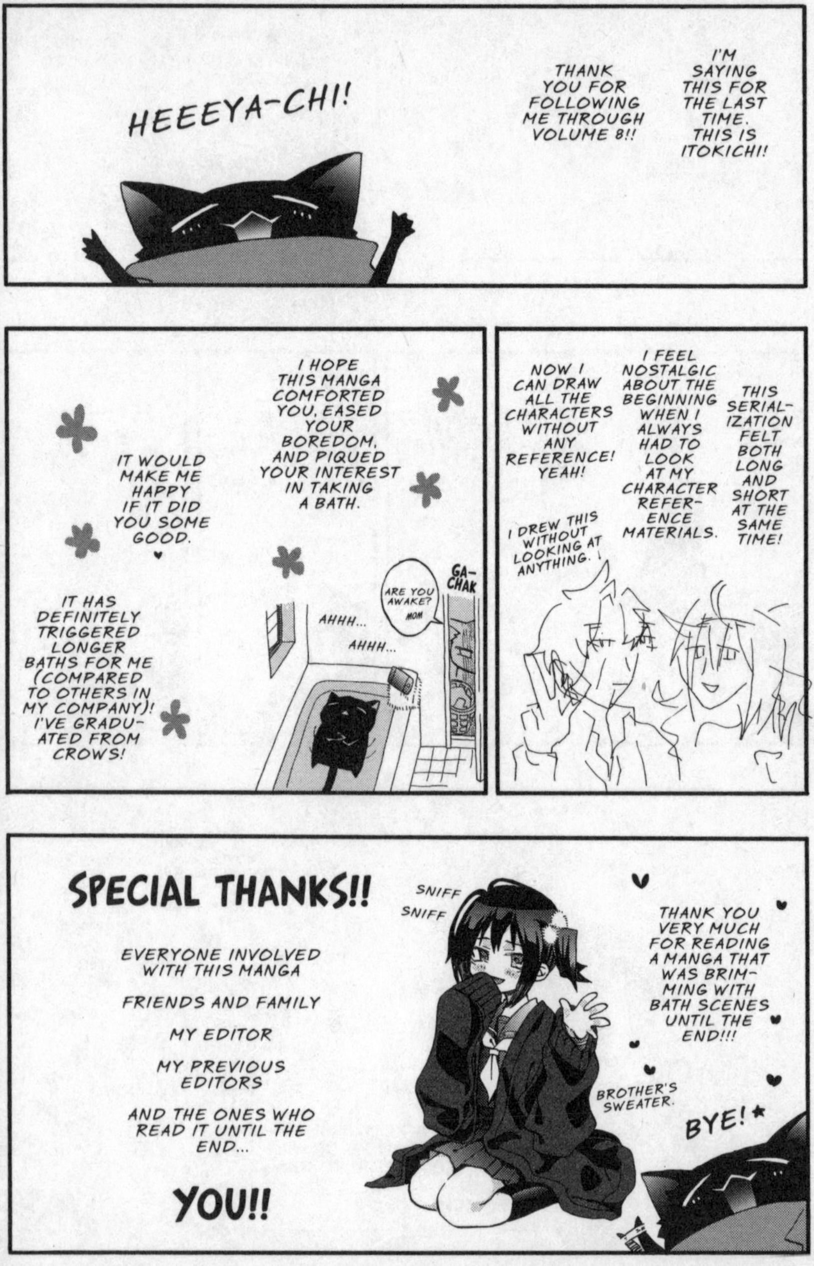
I'M SAYING THIS FOR THE LAST TIME. THIS IS ITOKICHI!
THANK YOU FOR FOLLOWING ME THROUGH VOLUME 8!!
HEEEYA-CHI!
THIS SERIAL-IZATION FELT BOTH LONG AND SHORT AT THE SAME TIME!
I FEEL NOSTALGIC ABOUT THE BEGINNING WHEN I ALWAYS HAD TO LOOK AT MY CHARACTER REFER-ENCE MATERIALS.
NOW I CAN DRAW ALL THE CHARACTERS WITHOUT ANY REFERENCE! YEAH!
I DREW THIS WITHOUT LOOKING AT ANYTHING.
I HOPE THIS MANGA COMFORTED YOU, EASED YOUR BOREDOM, AND PIQUED YOUR INTEREST IN TAKING A BATH.
IT WOULD MAKE ME HAPPY IF IT DID YOU SOME GOOD.
GA-CHAK
ARE YOU AWAKE? MOM
AHHH... AHHH...
IT HAS DEFINITELY TRIGGERED LONGER BATHS FOR ME (COMPARED TO OTHERS IN MY COMPANY)! I'VE GRADU-ATED FROM CROWS!
THANK YOU VERY MUCH FOR READING A MANGA THAT WAS BRIM-MING WITH BATH SCENES UNTIL THE END!!!
BYE!★
BROTHER'S SWEATER.
SNIFF SNIFF
SPECIAL THANKS!!
EVERYONE INVOLVED WITH THIS MANGA
FRIENDS AND FAMILY
MY EDITOR
MY PREVIOUS EDITORS
AND THE ONES WHO READ IT UNTIL THE END...
YOU!!

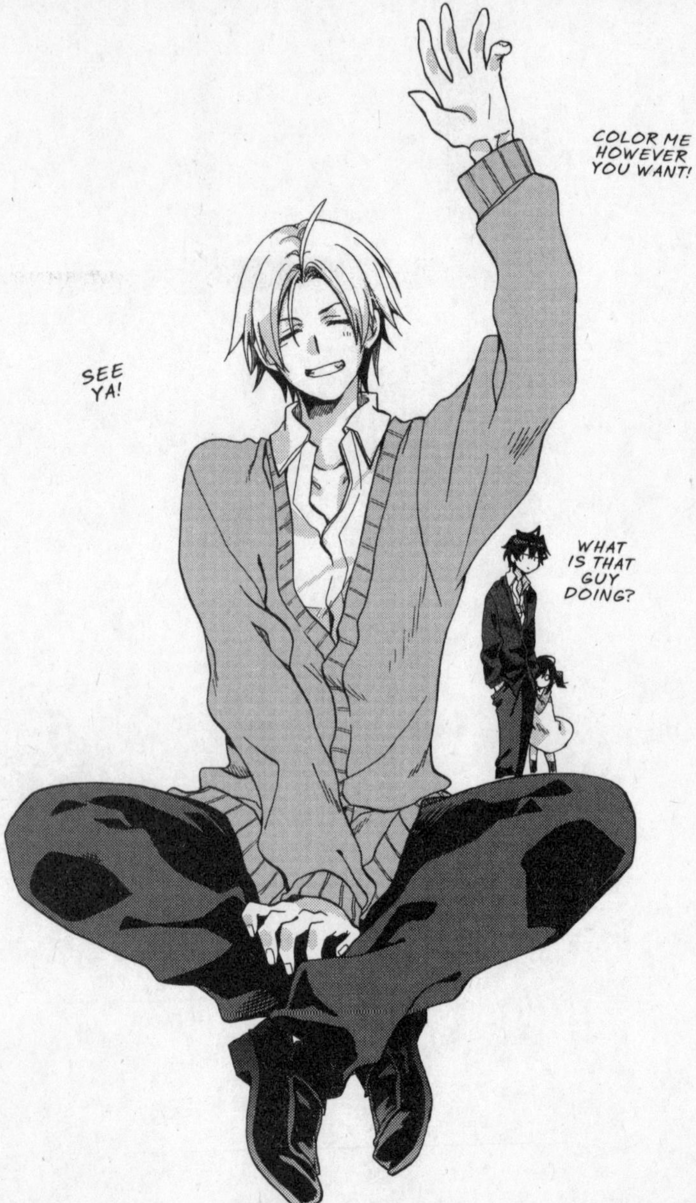
COLOR ME HOWEVER YOU WANT!
SEE YA!
WHAT IS THAT GUY DOING?

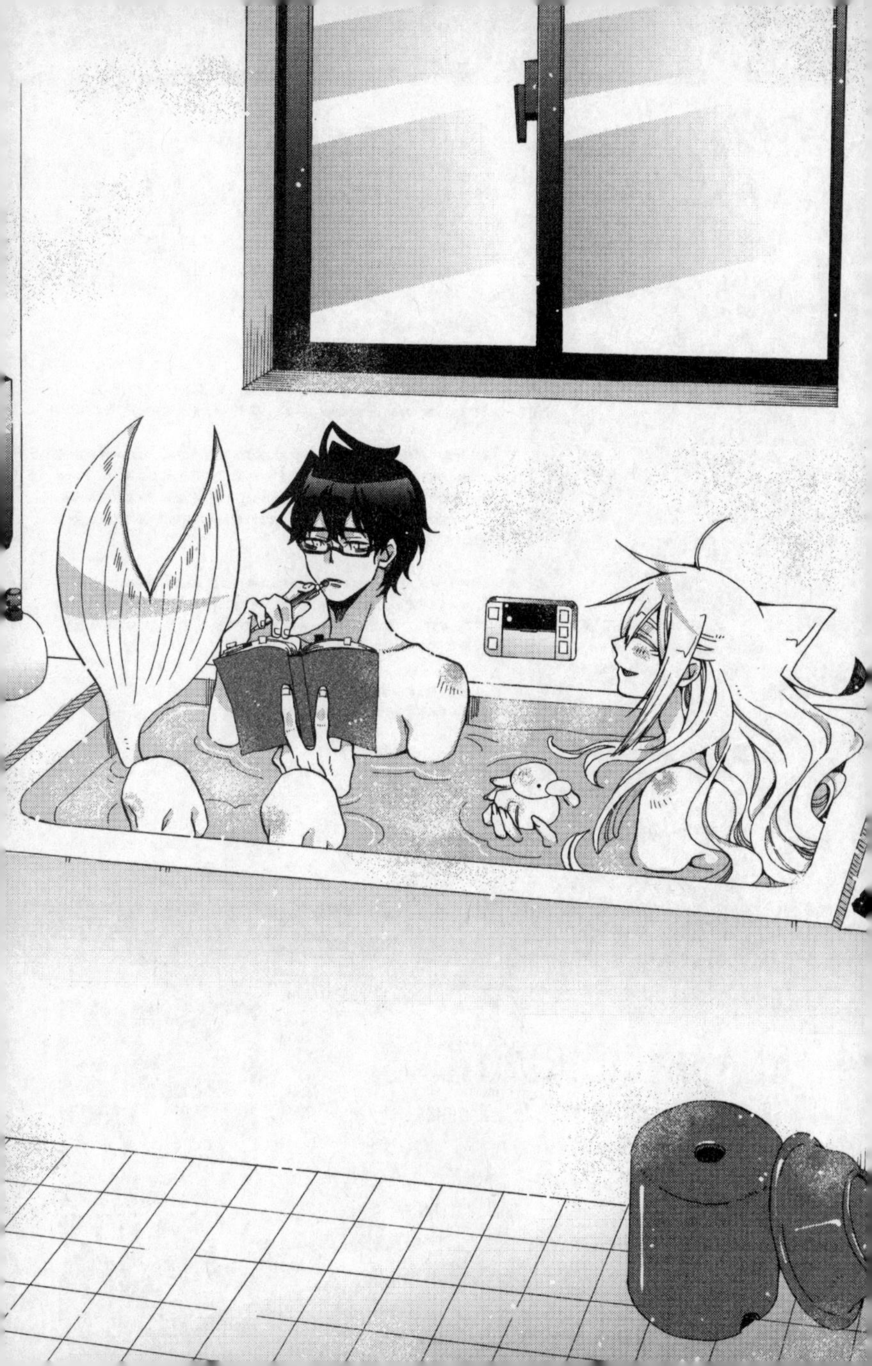

SEVEN SEAS ENTERTAINMENT PRESENTS

Merman in My Tub.

story and art by **ITOKICHI**　　　　　volume 8

TRANSLATION
Angela Liu

ADAPTATION
T Campbell

LETTERING
Chris Burgener

COVER DESIGN
Nicky Lim
(LOGO) **Meaghan Tucker**

PROOFREADER
Kurestin Armada

EDITOR
Shanti Whitesides

PREPRESS TECHNICIAN
Rhiannon Rasmussen-Silverstein

PRODUCTION MANAGER
Lissa Pattillo

MANAGING EDITOR
Julie Davis

ASSOCIATE PUBLISHER
Adam Arnold

PUBLISHER
Jason DeAngelis

MERMAN IN MY TUB VOL. 8
ORENCHI NO FURO JIJO VOL.8
© Itokichi 2020
First published in Japan in 2020 by KADOKAWA CORPORATION, Tokyo.
English translation rights arranged with KADOKAWA CORPORATION, Tokyo.

Seven Seas press and purchase enquiries can be sent to Marketing Manager
Lianne Sentar at press@gomanga.com. Information regarding the distribution
and purchase of digital editions is available from Digital Manager CK Russell
at digital@gomanga.com.

Seven Seas and the Seven Seas logo are trademarks of
Seven Seas Entertainment. All rights reserved.

ISBN: 978-1-626925-79-3

Printed in Canada

First Printing: June 2021

10 9 8 7 6 5 4 3 2 1

FOLLOW US ONLINE: *www.sevenseasentertainment.com*

READING DIRECTIONS

This book reads from *right to left*, Japanese style.
If this is your first time reading manga, you start
reading from the top right panel on each page and
take it from there. If you get lost, just follow the
numbered diagram here. It may seem backwards at
first, but you'll get the hang of it! Have fun!!

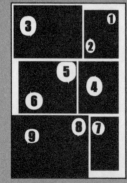